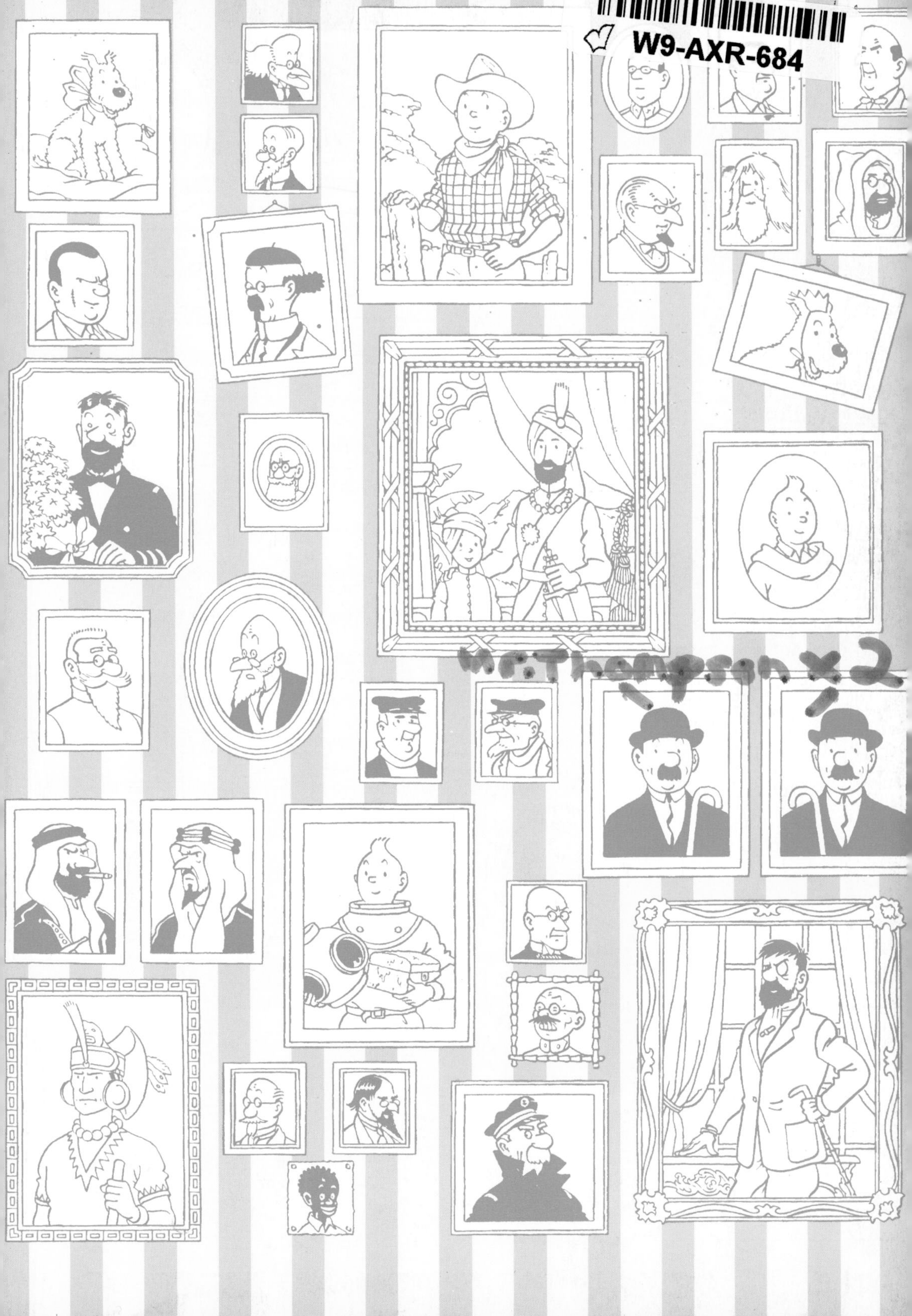
Mr. Thompson x 2

HERGÉ
THE ADVENTURES OF TINTIN

THE BROKEN EAR

EGMONT

This edition first published in 1990
by Methuen Children's Books,
Reprinted in 2003 by Egmont Books Limited,
239 Kensington High Street, London W8 6SA

10 9 8

ISBN 0 416 14872 7

Tintin and the Broken Ear
Artwork © 1945 by Editions Casterman
Text copyright © 1975 by Egmont Books Limited

Printed in Spain

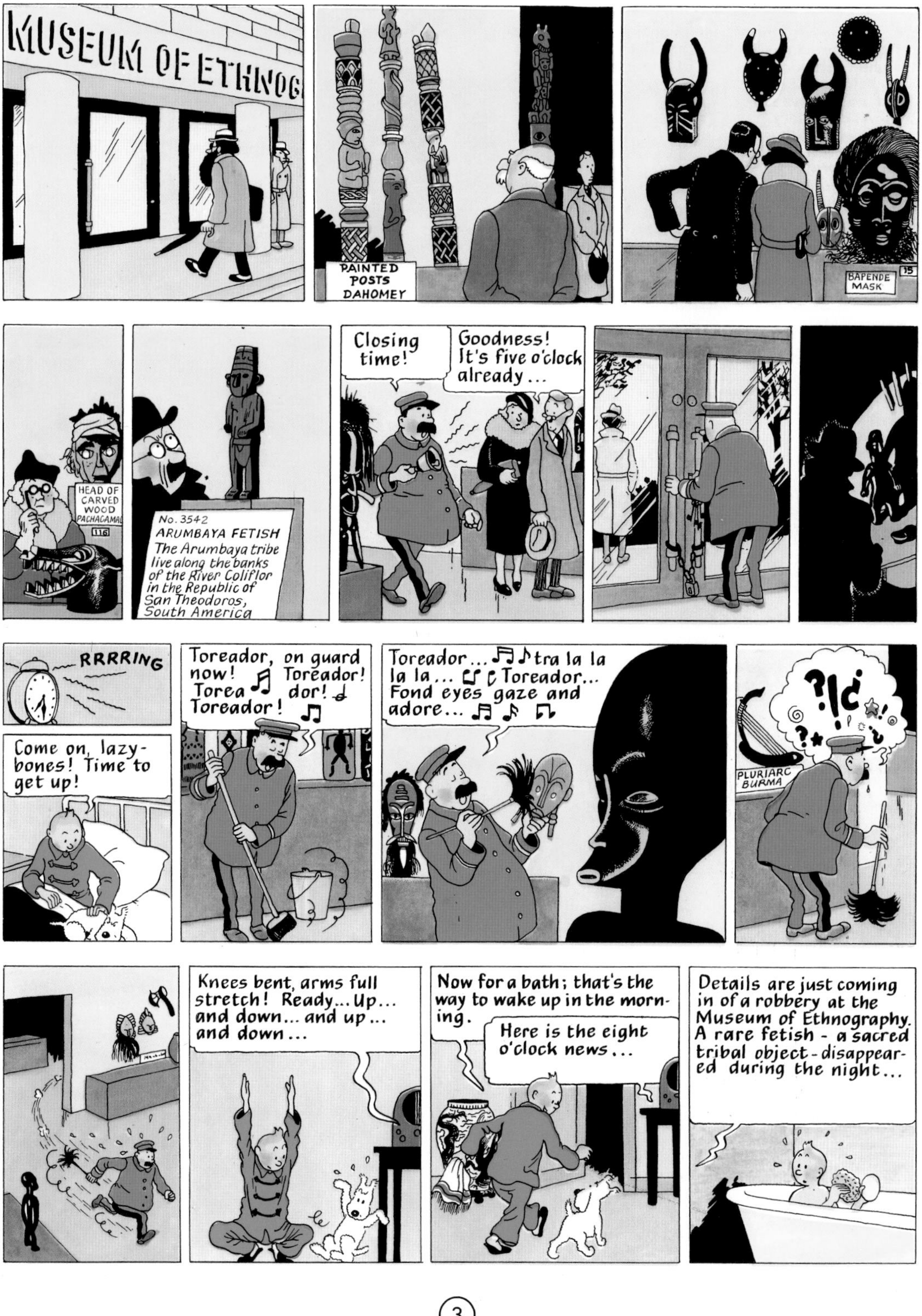

MUSEUM OF ETHNOG
PAINTED POSTS DAHOMEY
BAPENDE MASK
15
HEAD OF CARVED WOOD PACHACAMAC
116
No. 3542
ARUMBAYA FETISH
The Arumbaya tribe live along the banks of the River Coliflor in the Republic of San Theodoros, South America
Closing time!
Goodness! It's five o'clock already ...
RRRRING
Come on, lazy-bones! Time to get up!
Toreador, on guard now! Toreador! Torea dor! Toreador!
Toreador... tra la la la la... Toreador... Fond eyes gaze and adore...
PLURIARC BURMA
Knees bent, arms full stretch! Ready... Up... and down... and up... and down...
Now for a bath; that's the way to wake up in the morning.
Here is the eight o'clock news...
Details are just coming in of a robbery at the Museum of Ethnography. A rare fetish - a sacred tribal object - disappeared during the night...

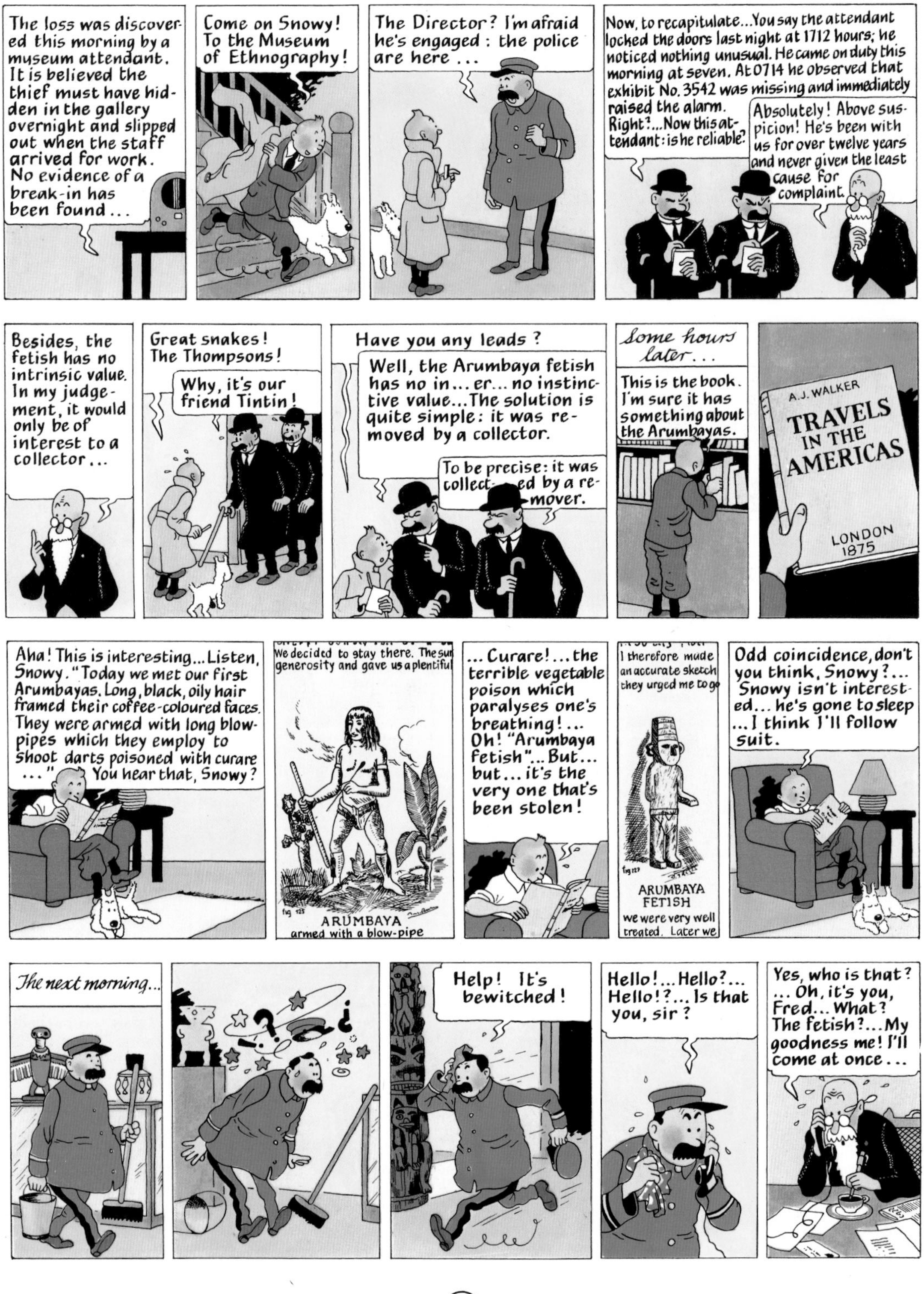
The loss was discovered this morning by a museum attendant. It is believed the thief must have hidden in the gallery overnight and slipped out when the staff arrived for work. No evidence of a break-in has been found ...
Come on Snowy! To the Museum of Ethnography!
The Director? I'm afraid he's engaged : the police are here ...
Now, to recapitulate... You say the attendant locked the doors last night at 1712 hours; he noticed nothing unusual. He came on duty this morning at seven. At 0714 he observed that exhibit No. 3542 was missing and immediately raised the alarm. Right?... Now this attendant: is he reliable?
Absolutely! Above suspicion! He's been with us for over twelve years and never given the least cause for complaint.
Besides, the fetish has no intrinsic value. In my judgement, it would only be of interest to a collector...
Great snakes! The Thompsons!
Why, it's our friend Tintin!
Have you any leads?
Well, the Arumbaya fetish has no in... er... no instinctive value... The solution is quite simple: it was removed by a collector.
To be precise: it was collect-ed by a re-mover.
Some hours later...
This is the book. I'm sure it has something about the Arumbayas.
A. J. WALKER
TRAVELS IN THE AMERICAS
LONDON 1875
Aha! This is interesting... Listen, Snowy. "Today we met our first Arumbayas. Long, black, oily hair framed their coffee-coloured faces. They were armed with long blowpipes which they employ to shoot darts poisoned with curare ..." You hear that, Snowy?
We decided to stay there. The su
generosity and gave us a plentiful
fig 123
ARUMBAYA
armed with a blow-pipe
... Curare!... the terrible vegetable poison which paralyses one's breathing!... Oh! "Arumbaya fetish"... But... but... it's the very one that's been stolen!
I therefore made
an accurate sketch
they urged me to go
ARUMBAYA
FETISH
we were very well
treated. Later we
Odd coincidence, don't you think, Snowy?... Snowy isn't interested... he's gone to sleep ... I think I'll follow suit.
The next morning...
Help! It's bewitched!
Hello!... Hello?... Hello!?... Is that you, sir?
Yes, who is that? ... Oh, it's you, Fred... What? The fetish?... My goodness me! I'll come at once...

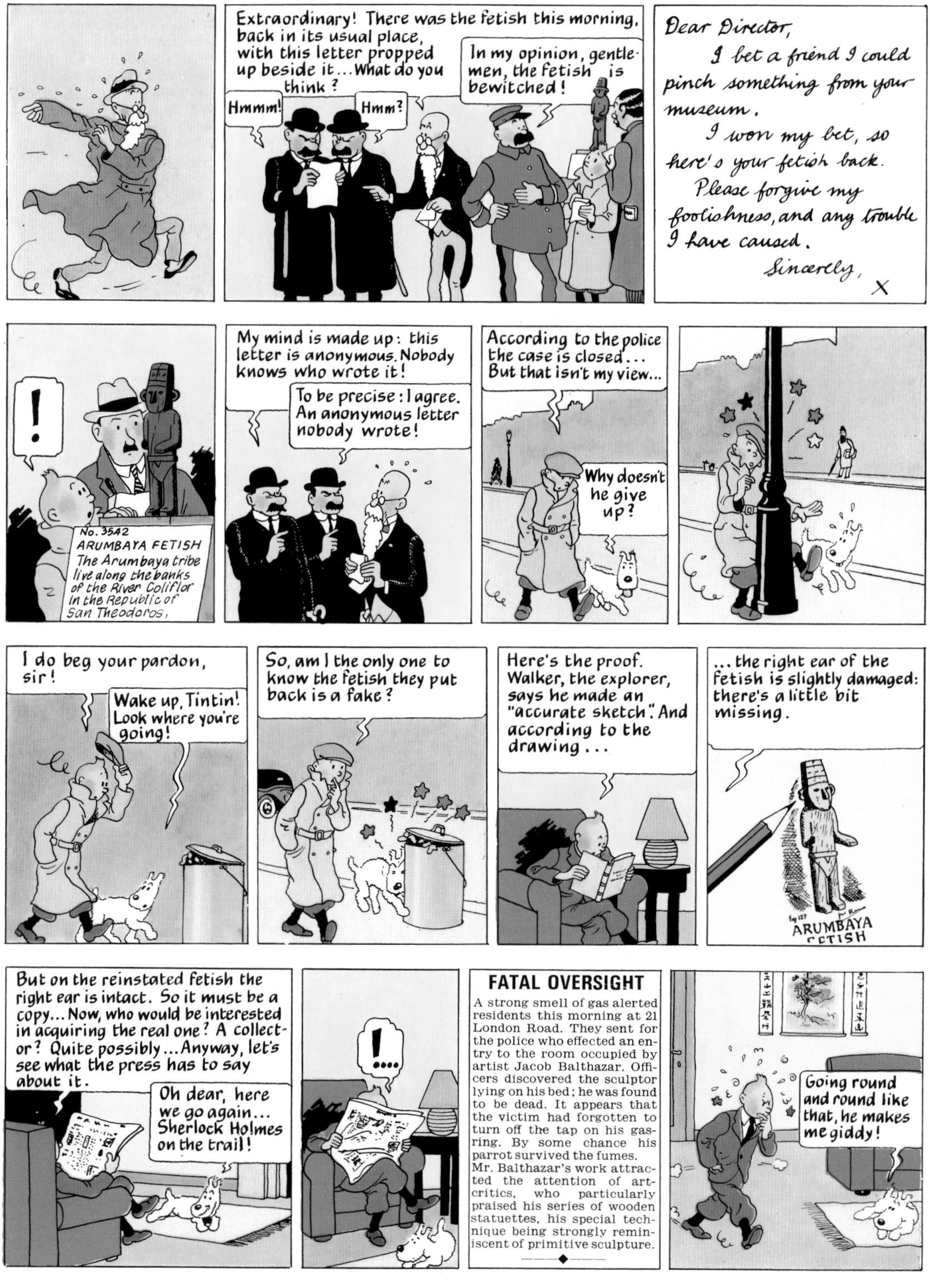
Extraordinary! There was the fetish this morning, back in its usual place, with this letter propped up beside it...What do you think?
Hmmm!
Hmm?
In my opinion, gentlemen, the fetish is bewitched!
Dear Director,
I bet a friend I could pinch something from your museum.
I won my bet, so here's your fetish back.
Please forgive my foolishness, and any trouble I have caused.
Sincerely, X
!
No. 3542
ARUMBAYA FETISH
The Arumbaya tribe live along the banks of the River Coliflor in the Republic of San Theodoros,
My mind is made up: this letter is anonymous. Nobody knows who wrote it!
To be precise: I agree. An anonymous letter nobody wrote!
According to the police the case is closed... But that isn't my view...
Why doesn't he give up?
I do beg your pardon, sir!
Wake up, Tintin! Look where you're going!
So, am I the only one to know the fetish they put back is a fake?
Here's the proof. Walker, the explorer, says he made an "accurate sketch". And according to the drawing...
...the right ear of the fetish is slightly damaged: there's a little bit missing.
ARUMBAYA FETISH
But on the reinstated fetish the right ear is intact. So it must be a copy... Now, who would be interested in acquiring the real one? A collector? Quite possibly... Anyway, let's see what the press has to say about it.
Oh dear, here we go again... Sherlock Holmes on the trail!
!....
FATAL OVERSIGHT
A strong smell of gas alerted residents this morning at 21 London Road. They sent for the police who effected an entry to the room occupied by artist Jacob Balthazar. Officers discovered the sculptor lying on his bed; he was found to be dead. It appears that the victim had forgotten to turn off the tap on his gas-ring. By some chance his parrot survived the fumes.
Mr. Balthazar's work attracted the attention of art-critics, who particularly praised his series of wooden statuettes, his special technique being strongly reminiscent of primitive sculpture.
Going round and round like that, he makes me giddy!

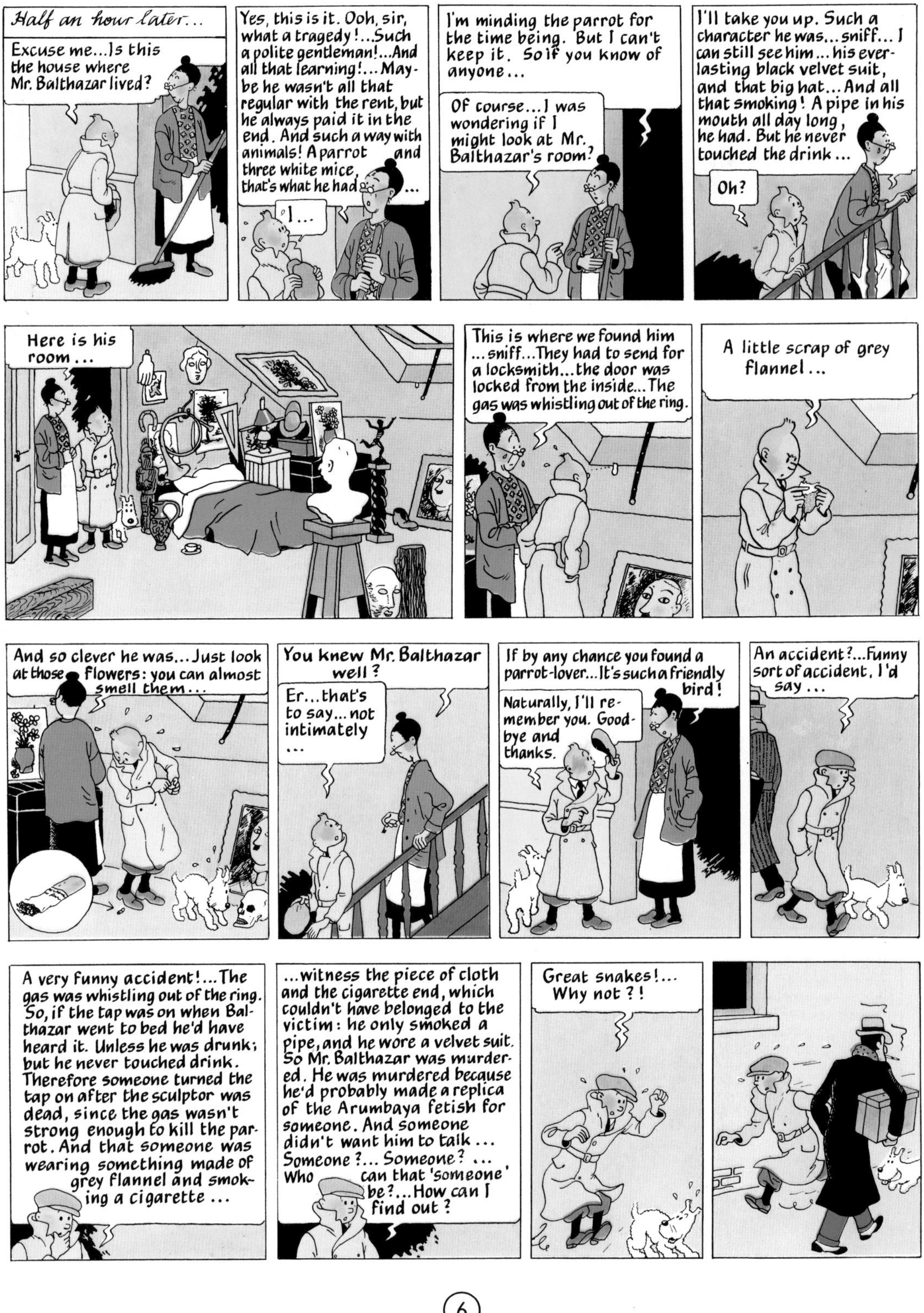
Half an hour later...
Excuse me...Is this the house where Mr. Balthazar lived?
Yes, this is it. Ooh, sir, what a tragedy!...Such a polite gentleman!...And all that learning!... May-be he wasn't all that regular with the rent, but he always paid it in the end. And such a way with animals! A parrot and three white mice, that's what he had ...
I...
I'm minding the parrot for the time being. But I can't keep it. So if you know of anyone...
Of course...I was wondering if I might look at Mr. Balthazar's room?
I'll take you up. Such a character he was... sniff... I can still see him... his ever-lasting black velvet suit, and that big hat... And all that smoking! A pipe in his mouth all day long, he had. But he never touched the drink...
Oh?
Here is his room...
This is where we found him ...sniff...They had to send for a locksmith...the door was locked from the inside...The gas was whistling out of the ring.
A little scrap of grey flannel...
And so clever he was...Just look at those flowers: you can almost smell them...
You knew Mr. Balthazar well?
Er...that's to say...not intimately ...
If by any chance you found a parrot-lover...It's such a friendly bird!
Naturally, I'll re-member you. Good-bye and thanks.
An accident?...Funny sort of accident, I'd say...
A very funny accident!...The gas was whistling out of the ring. So, if the tap was on when Bal-thazar went to bed he'd have heard it. Unless he was drunk; but he never touched drink. Therefore someone turned the tap on after the sculptor was dead, since the gas wasn't strong enough to kill the par-rot. And that someone was wearing something made of grey flannel and smok-ing a cigarette ...
...witness the piece of cloth and the cigarette end, which couldn't have belonged to the victim: he only smoked a pipe, and he wore a velvet suit. So Mr. Balthazar was murder-ed. He was murdered because he'd probably made a replica of the Arumbaya fetish for someone. And someone didn't want him to talk ... Someone?... Someone? ... Who can that 'someone' be?...How can I find out?
Great snakes!... Why not?!

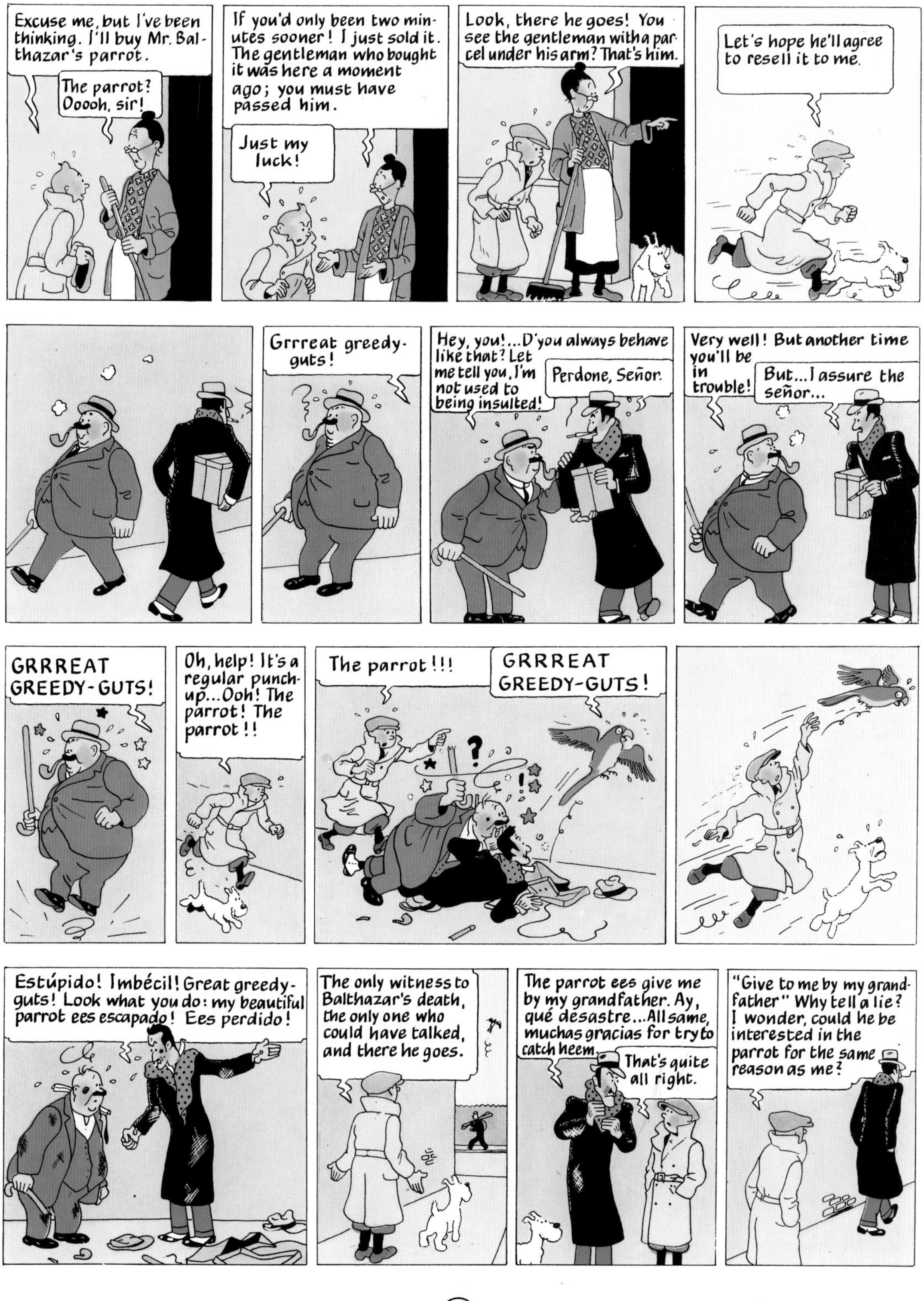

Excuse me, but I've been thinking. I'll buy Mr. Balthazar's parrot.
The parrot? Ooooh, sir!
If you'd only been two minutes sooner! I just sold it. The gentleman who bought it was here a moment ago; you must have passed him.
Just my luck!
Look, there he goes! You see the gentleman with a parcel under his arm? That's him.
Let's hope he'll agree to resell it to me.
Grrreat greedy-guts!
Hey, you!...D'you always behave like that? Let me tell you, I'm not used to being insulted!
Perdone, Señor.
Very well! But another time you'll be in trouble!
But...I assure the señor...
GRRREAT GREEDY-GUTS!
Oh, help! It's a regular punch-up...Ooh! The parrot! The parrot!!
The parrot!!!
GRRREAT GREEDY-GUTS!
Estúpido! Imbécil! Great greedy-guts! Look what you do: my beautiful parrot ees escapado! Ees perdido!
The only witness to Balthazar's death, the only one who could have talked, and there he goes.
The parrot ees give me by my grandfather. Ay, qué desastre...All same, muchas gracias for try to catch heem.
That's quite all right.
"Give to me by my grandfather" Why tell a lie? I wonder, could he be interested in the parrot for the same reason as me?

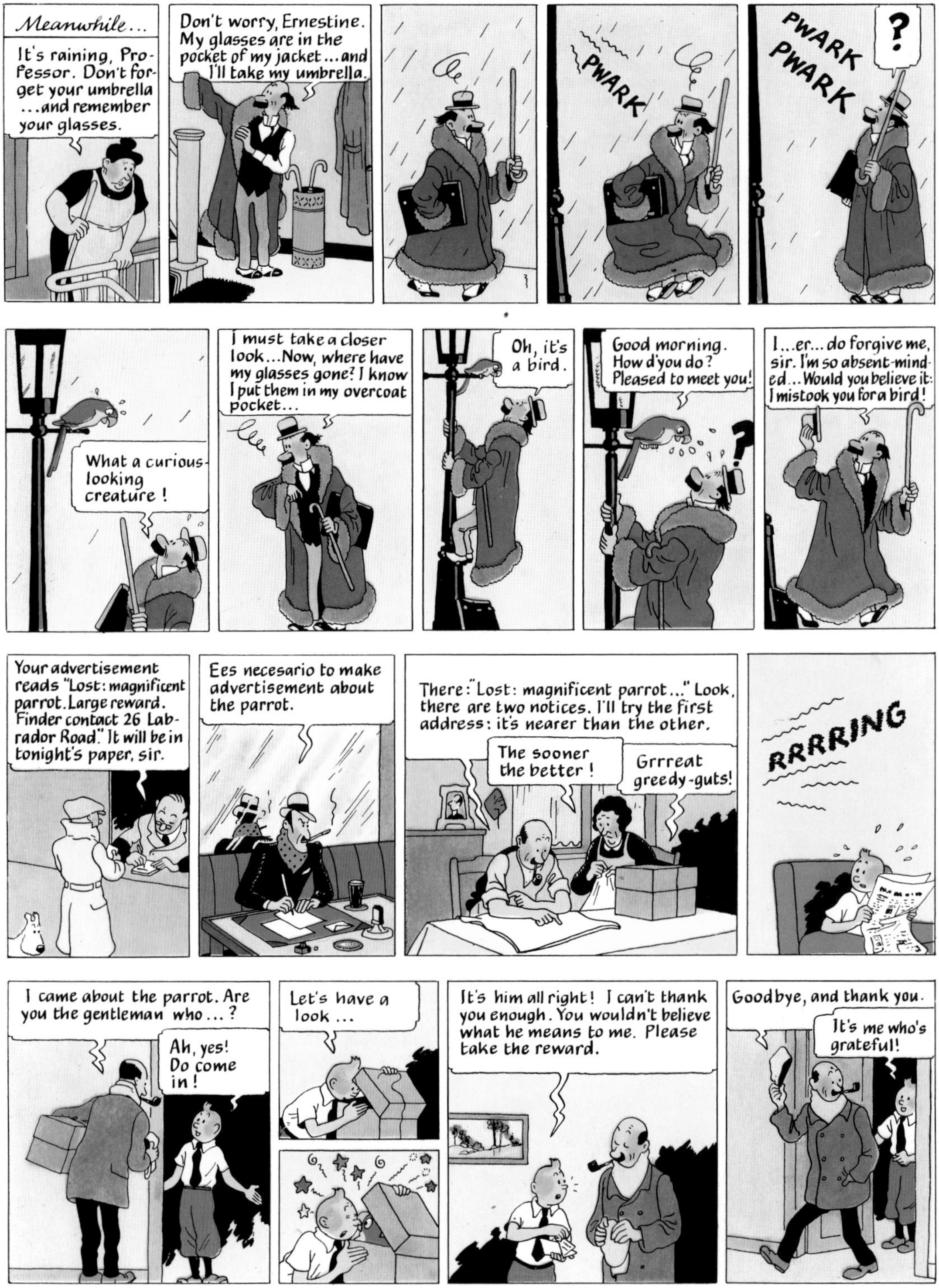

Meanwhile...
It's raining, Professor. Don't forget your umbrella ...and remember your glasses.
Don't worry, Ernestine. My glasses are in the pocket of my jacket ... and I'll take my umbrella.
PWARK
PWARK PWARK
?
What a curious-looking creature!
I must take a closer look...Now, where have my glasses gone? I know I put them in my overcoat pocket...
Oh, it's a bird.
Good morning. How d'you do? Pleased to meet you!
?
I...er...do forgive me, sir. I'm so absent-minded...Would you believe it: I mistook you for a bird!
Your advertisement reads "Lost: magnificent parrot. Large reward. Finder contact 26 Labrador Road." It will be in tonight's paper, sir.
Ees necesario to make advertisement about the parrot.
There: "Lost: magnificent parrot..." Look, there are two notices. I'll try the first address: it's nearer than the other.
The sooner the better!
Grrreat greedy-guts!
RRRRING
I came about the parrot. Are you the gentleman who...?
Ah, yes! Do come in!
Let's have a look ...
It's him all right! I can't thank you enough. You wouldn't believe what he means to me. Please take the reward.
Goodbye, and thank you.
It's me who's grateful!

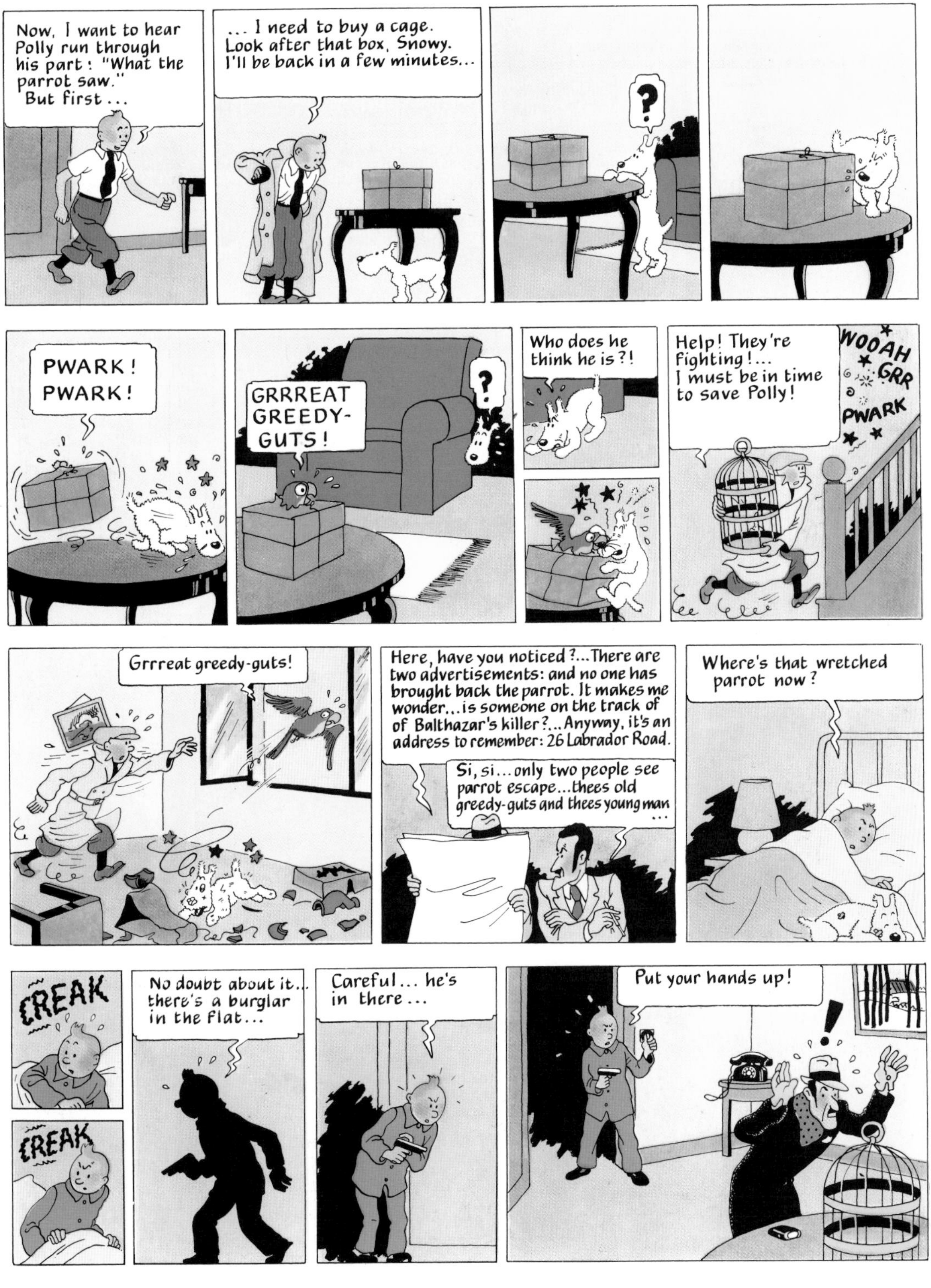
Now, I want to hear Polly run through his part: "What the parrot saw." But first...
... I need to buy a cage. Look after that box, Snowy. I'll be back in a few minutes...
?
PWARK! PWARK!
GRRREAT GREEDY-GUTS!
?
Who does he think he is?!
Help! They're fighting!... I must be in time to save Polly!
WOOAH
GRR
PWARK
Grrreat greedy-guts!
Here, have you noticed?... There are two advertisements: and no one has brought back the parrot. It makes me wonder... is someone on the track of of Balthazar's killer?... Anyway, it's an address to remember: 26 Labrador Road.
Si, si... only two people see parrot escape... thees old greedy-guts and thees young man...
Where's that wretched parrot now?
CREAK
CREAK
No doubt about it... there's a burglar in the flat...
Careful... he's in there...
Put your hands up!
!

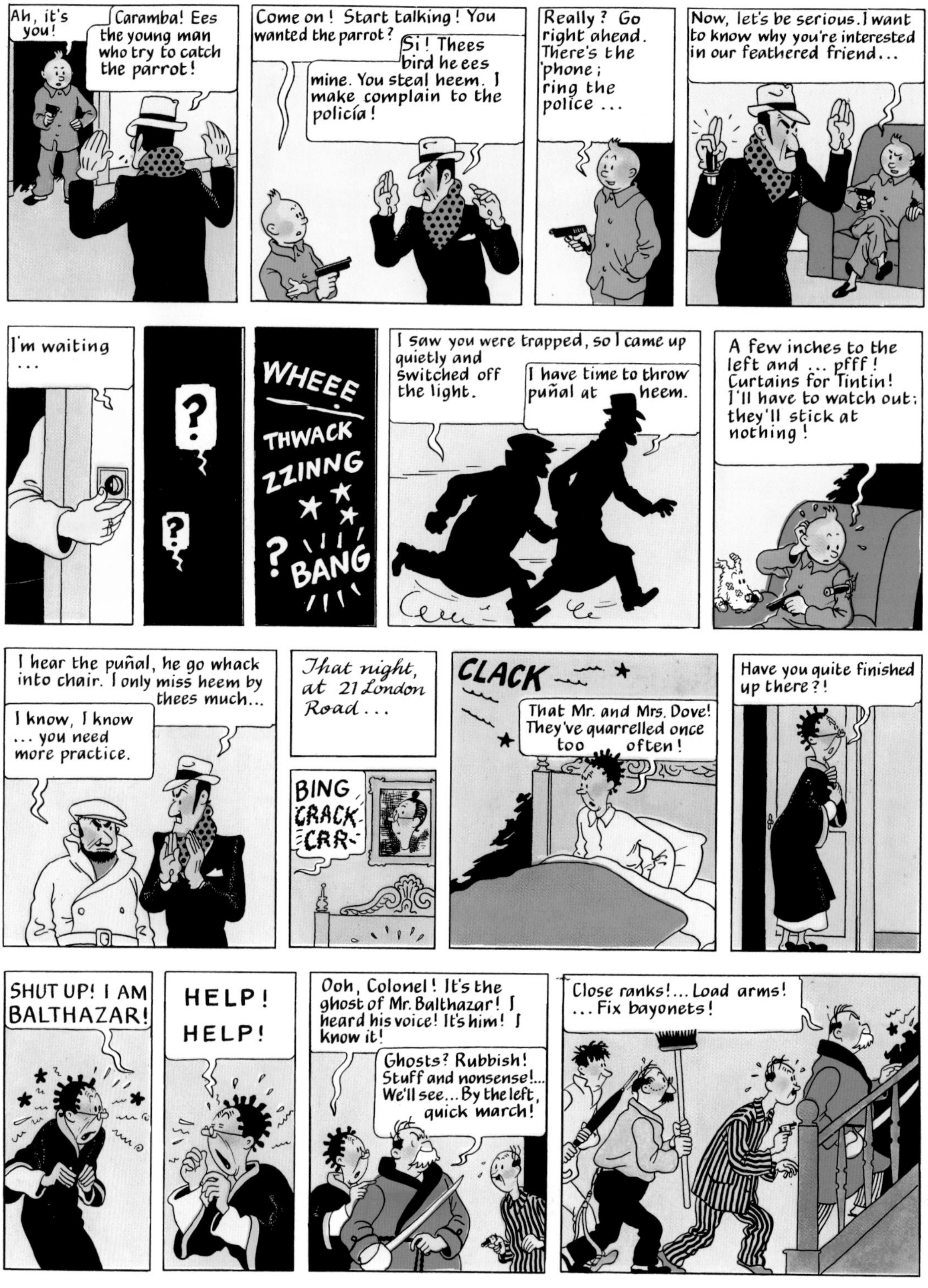

Ah, it's you!
Caramba! Ees the young man who try to catch the parrot!
Come on! Start talking! You wanted the parrot?
Si! Thees bird he ees mine. You steal heem. I make complain to the policía!
Really? Go right ahead. There's the 'phone; ring the police ...
Now, let's be serious. I want to know why you're interested in our feathered friend...
I'm waiting ...
?
?
WHEEE
THWACK
ZZINNG
?
BANG
I saw you were trapped, so I came up quietly and switched off the light.
I have time to throw puñal at heem.
A few inches to the left and ... pfff! Curtains for Tintin! I'll have to watch out: they'll stick at nothing!
I hear the puñal, he go whack into chair. I only miss heem by thees much...
I know, I know ... you need more practice.
That night, at 21 London Road...
BING
CRACK
CRR
CLACK
That Mr. and Mrs. Dove! They've quarrelled once too often!
Have you quite finished up there?!
SHUT UP! I AM BALTHAZAR!
HELP! HELP!
Ooh, Colonel! It's the ghost of Mr. Balthazar! I heard his voice! It's him! I know it!
Ghosts? Rubbish! Stuff and nonsense!... We'll see... By the left, quick march!
Close ranks!... Load arms! ... Fix bayonets!

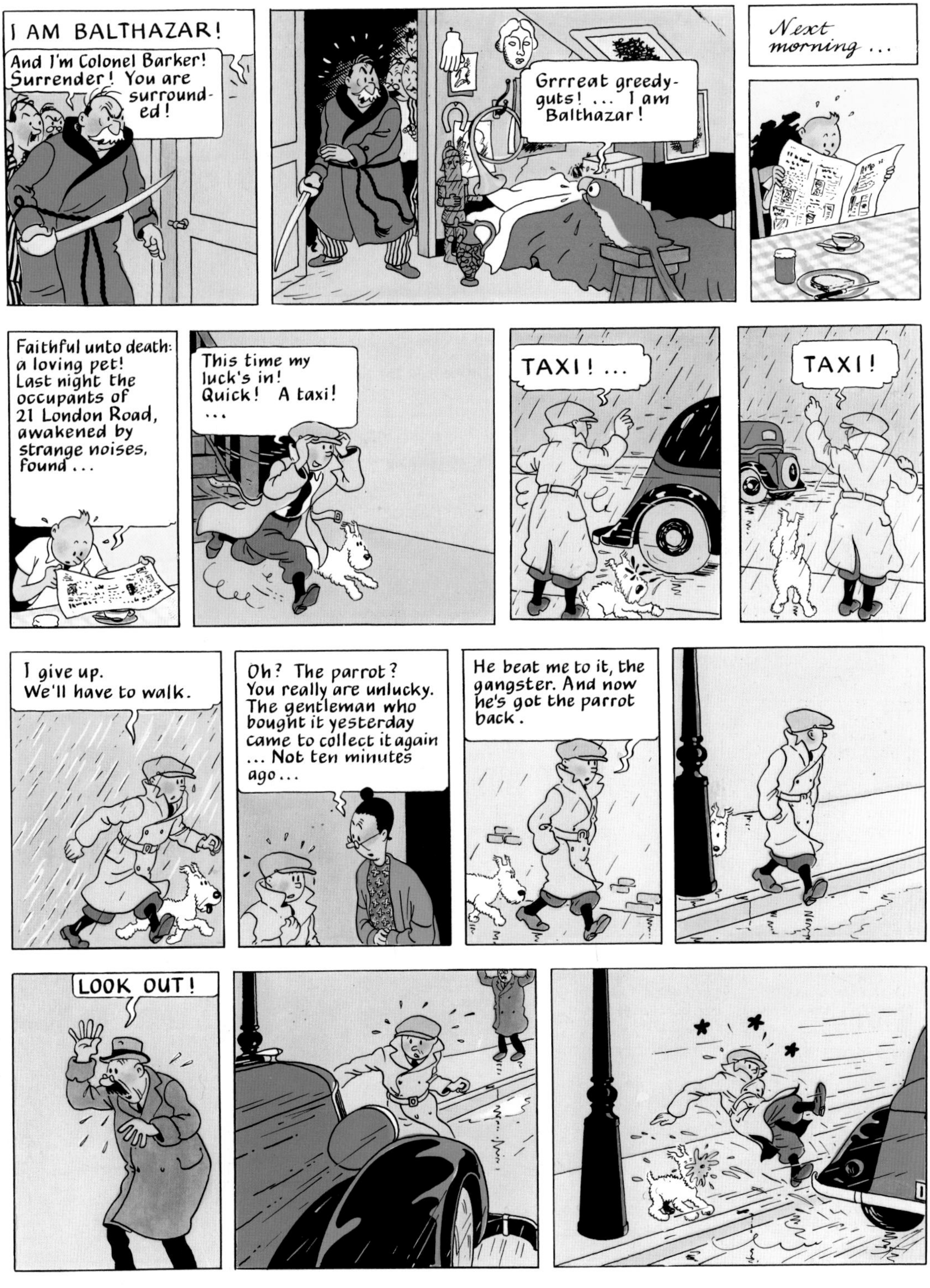
I AM BALTHAZAR!
And I'm Colonel Barker! Surrender! You are surrounded!
Grrreat greedy-guts! ... I am Balthazar!
Next morning ...
Faithful unto death: a loving pet! Last night the occupants of 21 London Road, awakened by strange noises, found ...
This time my luck's in! Quick! A taxi! ...
TAXI! ...
TAXI!
I give up. We'll have to walk.
Oh? The parrot? You really are unlucky. The gentleman who bought it yesterday came to collect it again ... Not ten minutes ago ...
He beat me to it, the gangster. And now he's got the parrot back.
LOOK OUT!

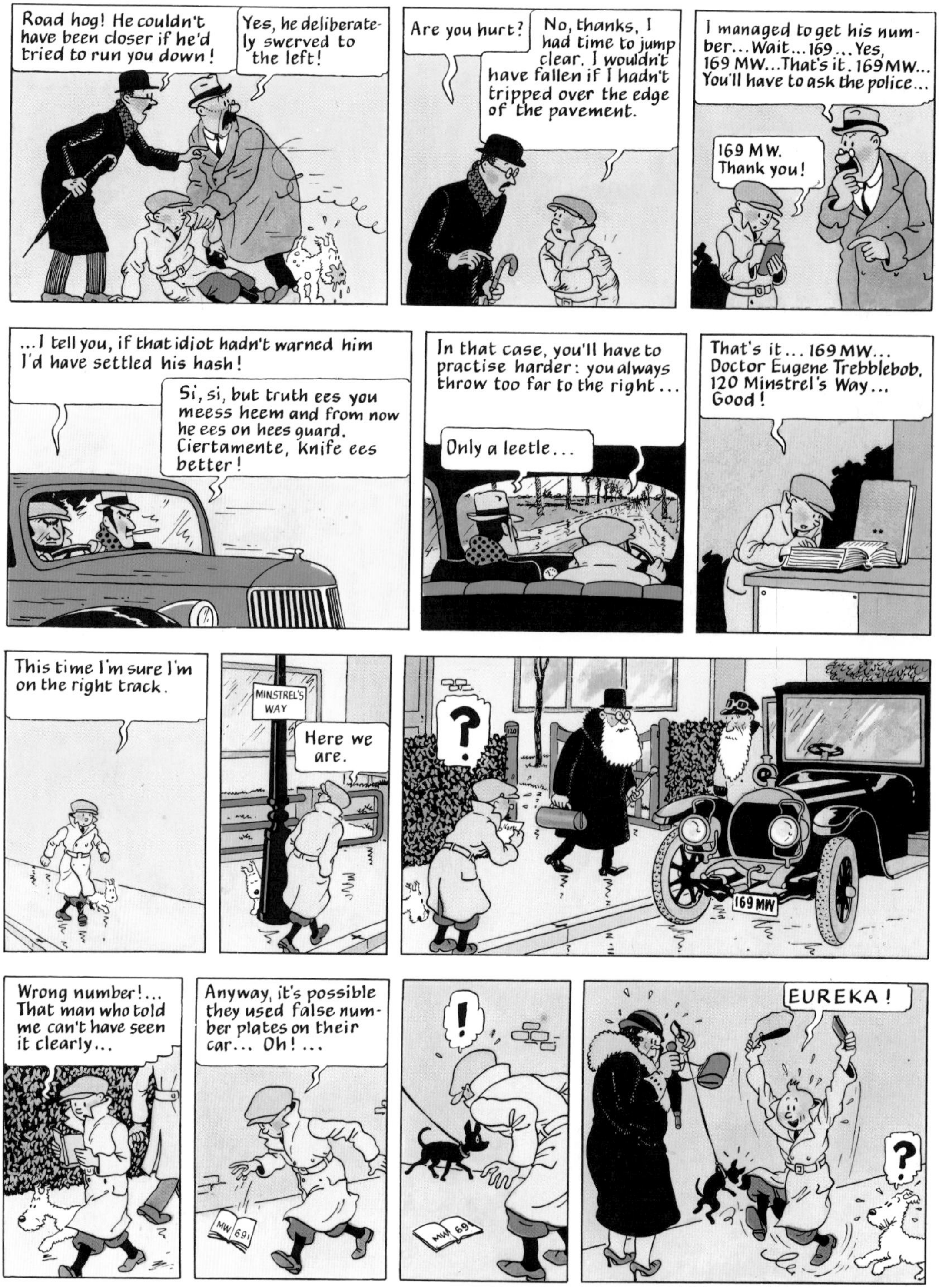

Road hog! He couldn't have been closer if he'd tried to run you down!
Yes, he deliberately swerved to the left!
Are you hurt?
No, thanks, I had time to jump clear. I wouldn't have fallen if I hadn't tripped over the edge of the pavement.
I managed to get his number... Wait... 169... Yes, 169 MW... That's it. 169 MW... You'll have to ask the police...
169 MW. Thank you!
...I tell you, if that idiot hadn't warned him I'd have settled his hash!
Si, si, but truth ees you meess heem and from now he ees on hees guard. Ciertamente, knife ees better!
In that case, you'll have to practise harder: you always throw too far to the right...
Only a leetle...
That's it... 169 MW... Doctor Eugene Trebblebob, 120 Minstrel's Way... Good!
This time I'm sure I'm on the right track.
MINSTREL'S WAY
Here we are.
?
120
169 MW
Wrong number!... That man who told me can't have seen it clearly...
Anyway, it's possible they used false number plates on their car... Oh!...
MW 691
!
MW 69
EUREKA!
?

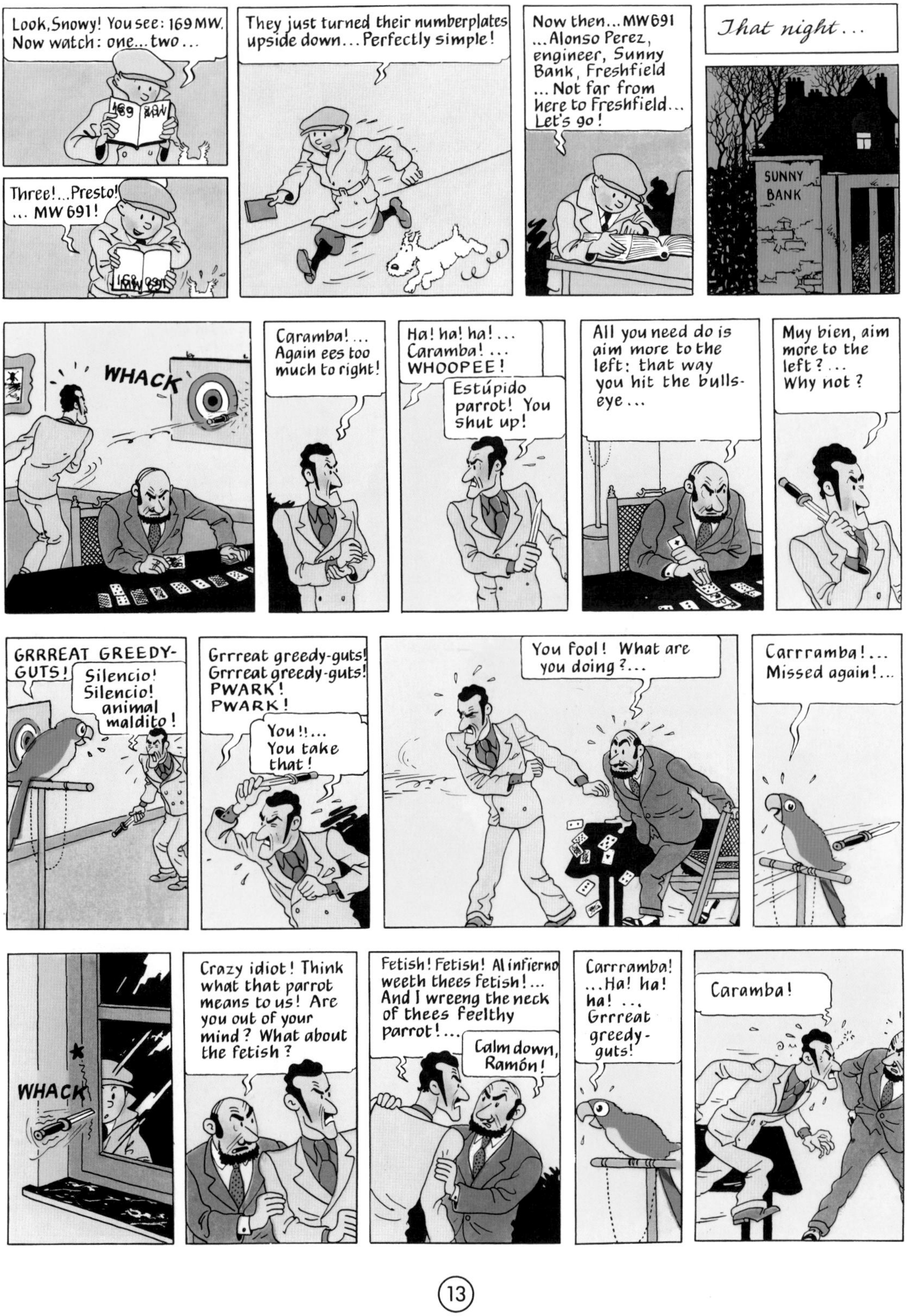
Look, Snowy! You see: 169 MW. Now watch: one... two...
Three!... Presto! ... MW 691!
They just turned their numberplates upside down... Perfectly simple!
Now then... MW 691 ... Alonso Perez, engineer, Sunny Bank, Freshfield ... Not far from here to Freshfield... Let's go!
That night...
SUNNY BANK
WHACK
Caramba!... Again ees too much to right!
Ha! ha! ha!... Caramba!... WHOOPEE!
Estúpido parrot! You shut up!
All you need do is aim more to the left: that way you hit the bulls-eye...
Muy bien, aim more to the left?... Why not?
GRRREAT GREEDY-GUTS!
Silencio! Silencio! animal maldito!
Grrreat greedy-guts! Grrreat greedy-guts! PWARK! PWARK!
You!!... You take that!
You fool! What are you doing?...
Carrramba!... Missed again!...
WHACK
Crazy idiot! Think what that parrot means to us! Are you out of your mind? What about the fetish?
Fetish! Fetish! Al infierno weeth thees fetish!... And I wreeng the neck of thees feelthy parrot!...
Calm down, Ramón!
Carrramba! ...Ha! ha! ha! ... Grrreat greedy-guts!
Caramba!

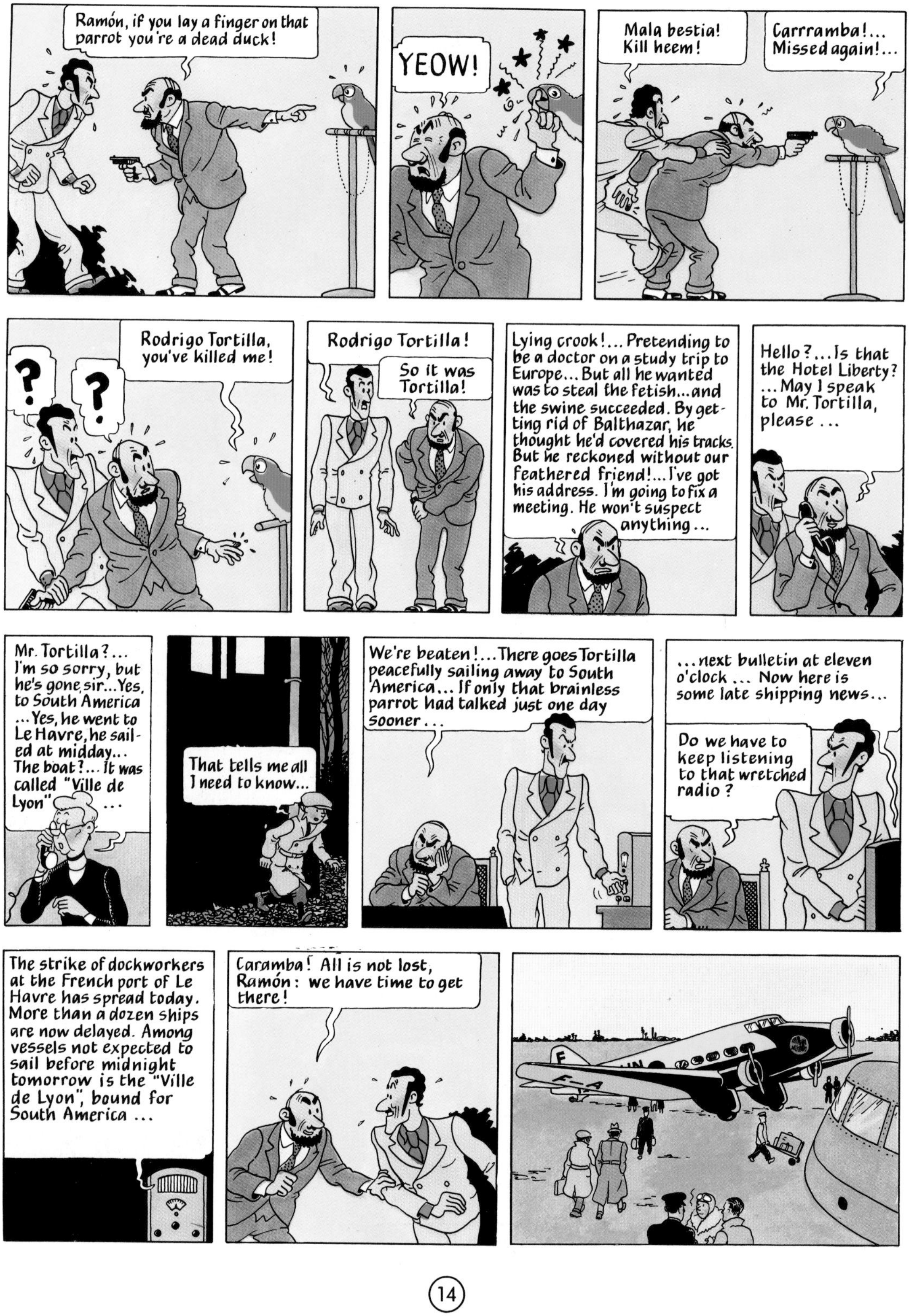

Ramón, if you lay a finger on that parrot you're a dead duck!
YEOW!
Mala bestia! Kill heem!
Carrramba!... Missed again!...
Rodrigo Tortilla, you've killed me!
?
?
Rodrigo Tortilla!
So it was Tortilla!
Lying crook!... Pretending to be a doctor on a study trip to Europe... But all he wanted was to steal the fetish...and the swine succeeded. By getting rid of Balthazar, he thought he'd covered his tracks. But he reckoned without our feathered friend!... I've got his address. I'm going to fix a meeting. He won't suspect anything...
Hello?... Is that the Hotel Liberty? ... May I speak to Mr. Tortilla, please...
Mr. Tortilla?... I'm so sorry, but he's gone, sir... Yes, to South America ... Yes, he went to Le Havre, he sailed at midday... The boat?... It was called "Ville de Lyon" ...
That tells me all I need to know...
We're beaten!... There goes Tortilla peacefully sailing away to South America... If only that brainless parrot had talked just one day sooner...
...next bulletin at eleven o'clock ... Now here is some late shipping news...
Do we have to keep listening to that wretched radio?
The strike of dockworkers at the French port of Le Havre has spread today. More than a dozen ships are now delayed. Among vessels not expected to sail before midnight tomorrow is the "Ville de Lyon", bound for South America ...
Caramba! All is not lost, Ramón: we have time to get there!

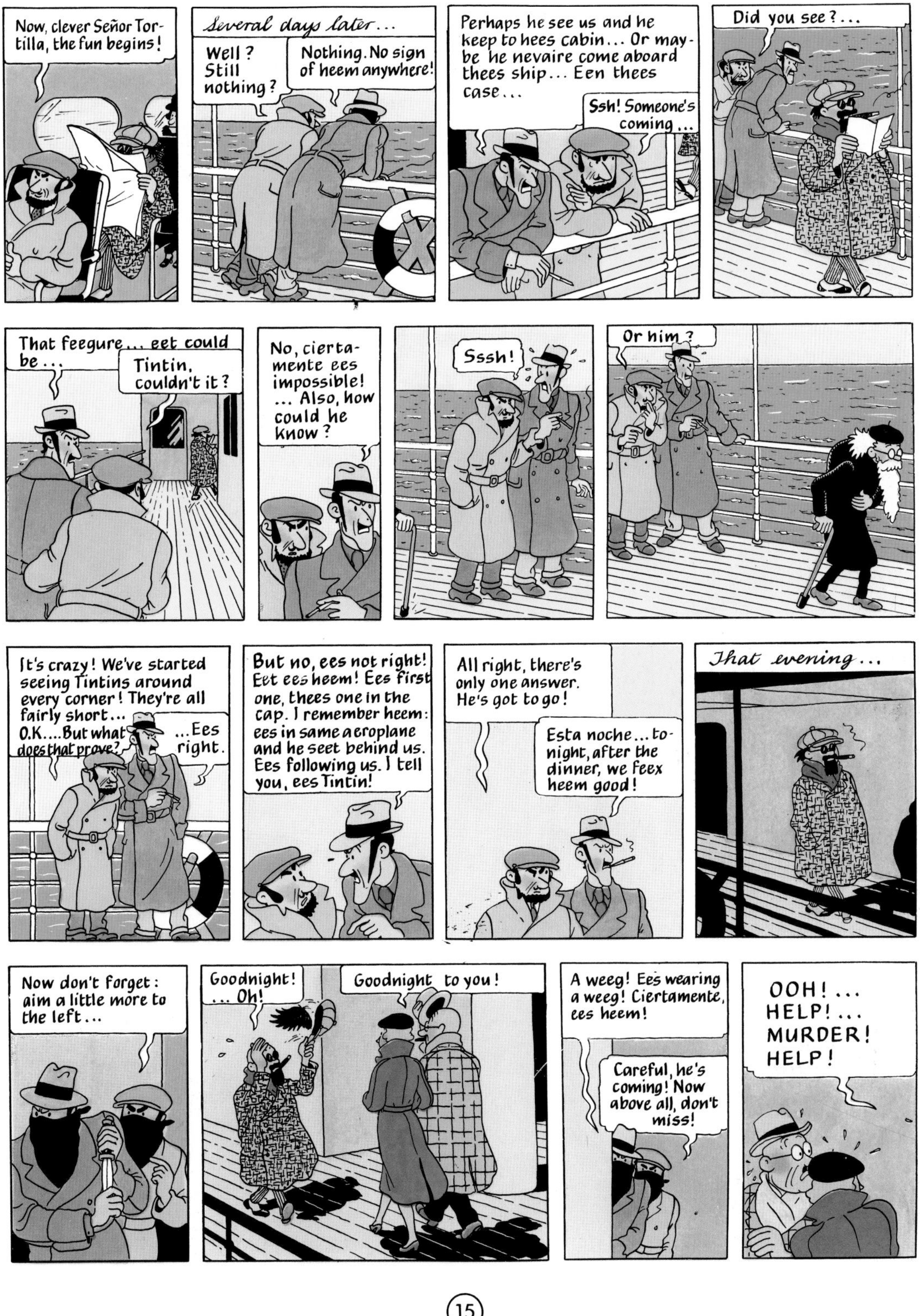
Now, clever Señor Tortilla, the fun begins!
Several days later...
Well? Still nothing?
Nothing. No sign of heem anywhere!
Perhaps he see us and he keep to hees cabin... Or maybe he nevaire come aboard thees ship... Een thees case...
Ssh! Someone's coming...
Did you see?...
That feegure... eet could be...
Tintin, couldn't it?
No, ciertamente ees impossible! ... Also, how could he know?
Sssh!
Or him?
It's crazy! We've started seeing Tintins around every corner! They're all fairly short... O.K.... But what does that prove?
...Ees right.
But no, ees not right! Eet ees heem! Ees first one, thees one in the cap. I remember heem: ees in same aeroplane and he seet behind us. Ees following us. I tell you, ees Tintin!
All right, there's only one answer. He's got to go!
Esta noche... tonight, after the dinner, we feex heem good!
That evening...
Now don't forget: aim a little more to the left...
Goodnight! ... Oh!
Goodnight to you!
A weeg! Ees wearing a weeg! Ciertamente, ees heem!
Careful, he's coming! Now above all, don't miss!
OOH!... HELP!... MURDER! HELP!

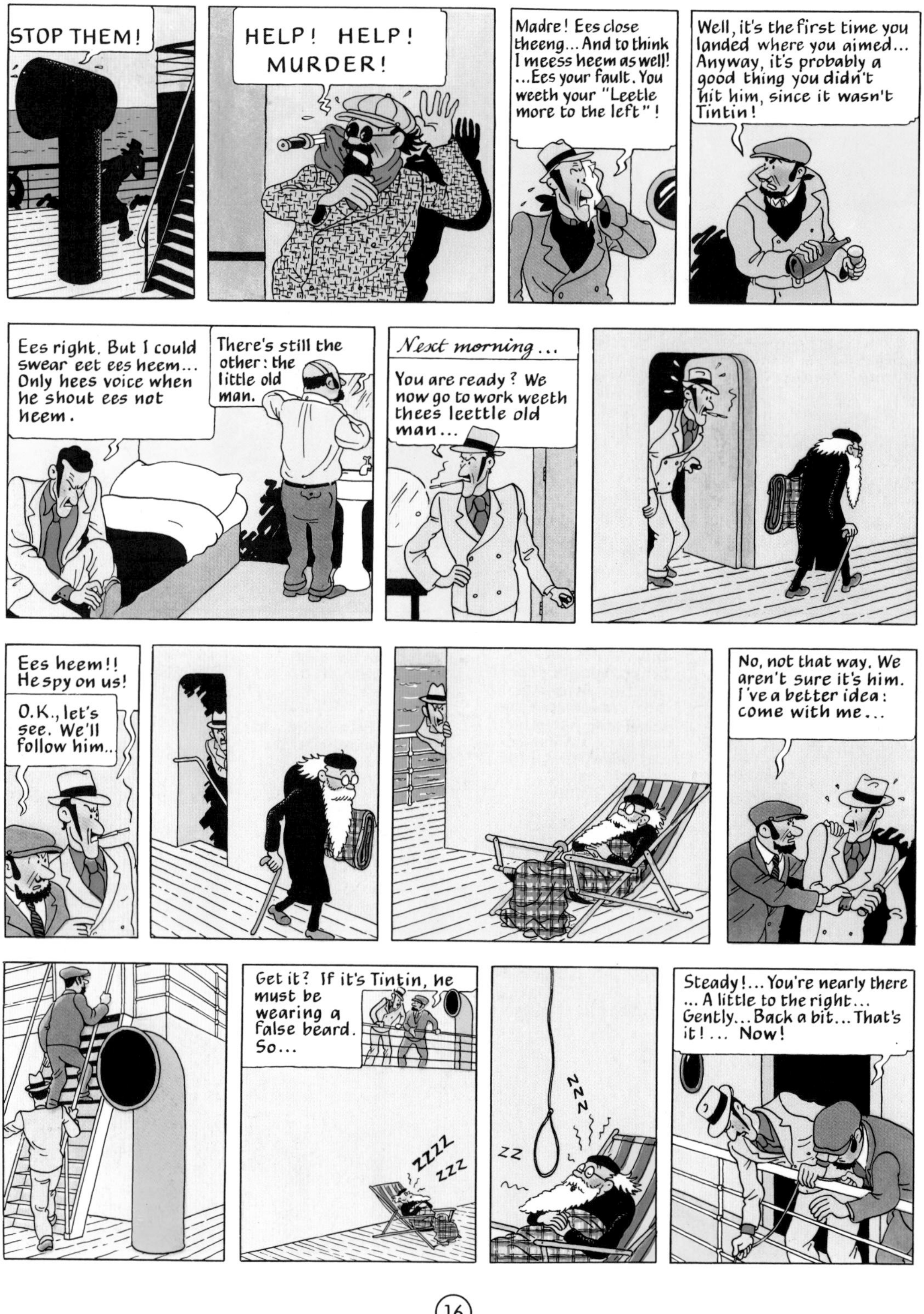
STOP THEM!
HELP! HELP! MURDER!
Madre! Ees close theeng... And to think I meess heem as well! ...Ees your fault. You weeth your "Leetle more to the left"!
Well, it's the first time you landed where you aimed... Anyway, it's probably a good thing you didn't hit him, since it wasn't Tintin!
Ees right. But I could swear eet ees heem... Only hees voice when he shout ees not heem.
There's still the other: the little old man.
Next morning...
You are ready? We now go to work weeth thees leettle old man...
Ees heem!! He spy on us!
O.K., let's see. We'll follow him..
No, not that way. We aren't sure it's him. I've a better idea: come with me...
Get it? If it's Tintin, he must be wearing a false beard. So...
ZZZZ
ZZZ
ZZ
ZZ
Steady!... You're nearly there ... A little to the right... Gently... Back a bit... That's it!... Now!

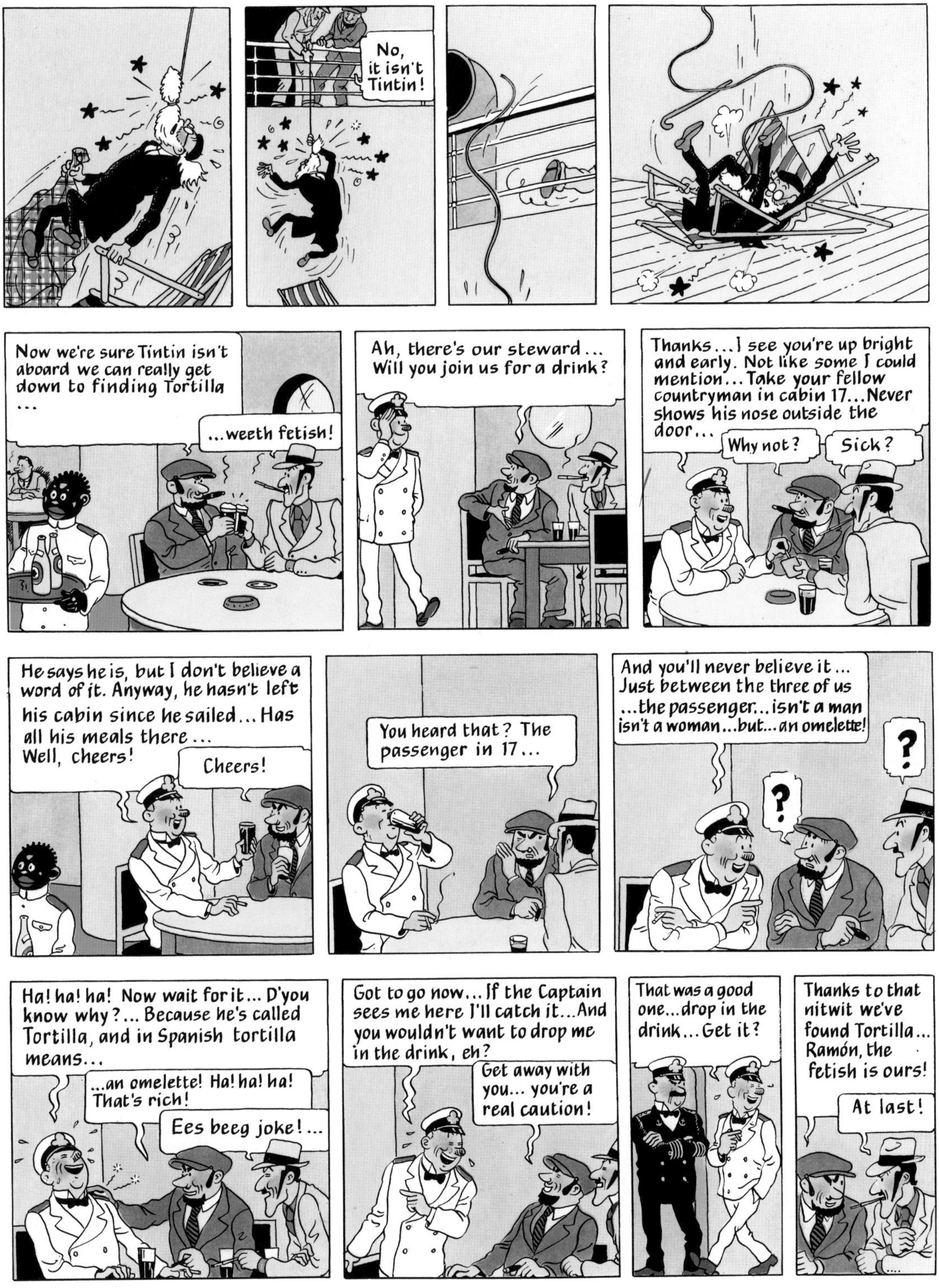
No, it isn't Tintin!
Now we're sure Tintin isn't aboard we can really get down to finding Tortilla ...
...weeth fetish!
Ah, there's our steward ... Will you join us for a drink?
Thanks ... I see you're up bright and early. Not like some I could mention... Take your fellow countryman in cabin 17... Never shows his nose outside the door...
Why not?
Sick?
He says he is, but I don't believe a word of it. Anyway, he hasn't left his cabin since he sailed... Has all his meals there ... Well, cheers!
Cheers!
You heard that? The passenger in 17...
And you'll never believe it ... Just between the three of us ...the passenger... isn't a man isn't a woman...but... an omelette!
?
?
Ha! ha! ha! Now wait for it... D'you know why?... Because he's called Tortilla, and in Spanish tortilla means...
...an omelette! Ha! ha! ha! That's rich!
Ees beeg joke!...
Got to go now... If the Captain sees me here I'll catch it... And you wouldn't want to drop me in the drink, eh?
Get away with you... you're a real caution!
That was a good one... drop in the drink... Get it?
Thanks to that nitwit we've found Tortilla... Ramón, the fetish is ours!
At last!

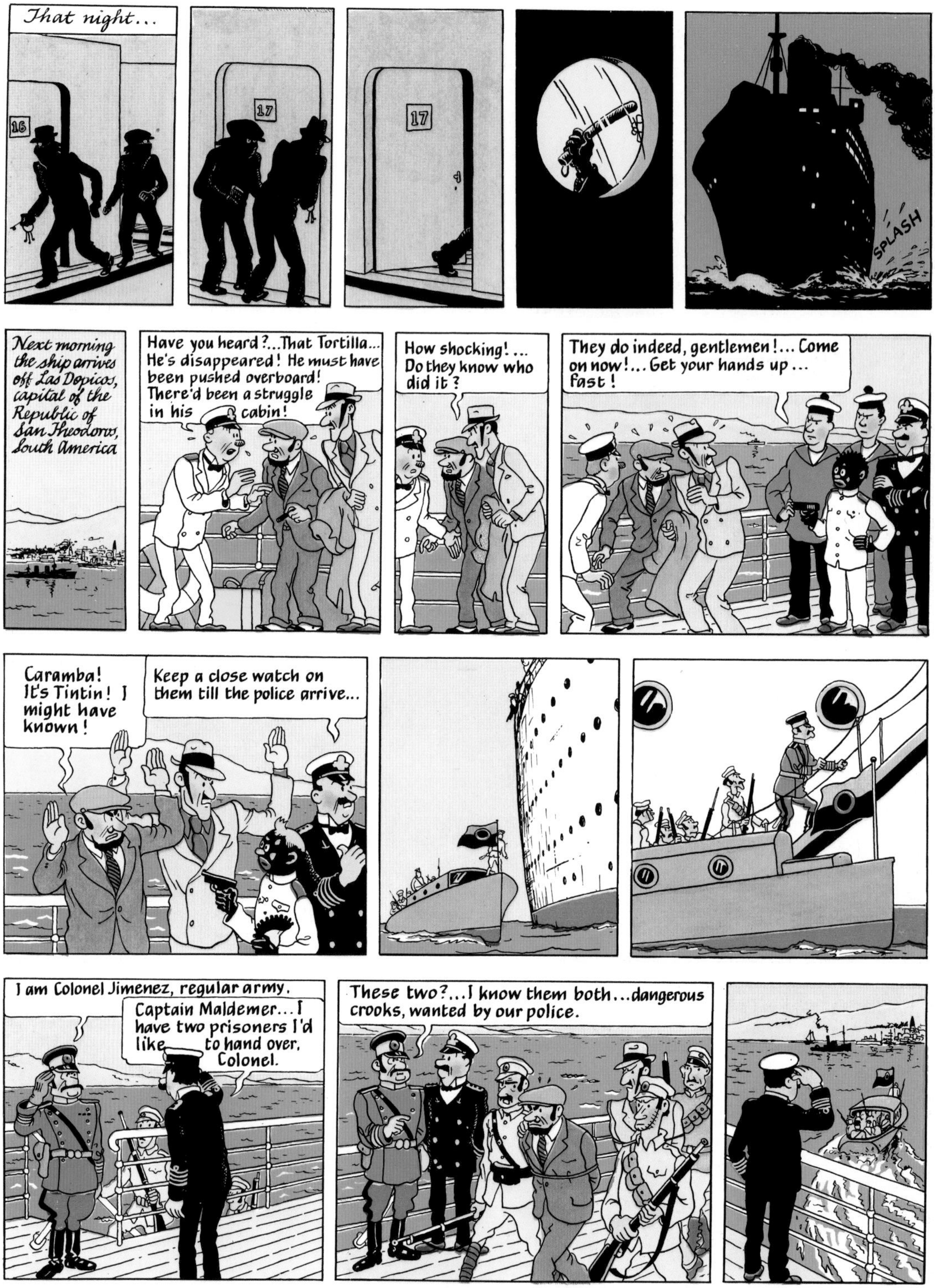
That night...
SPLASH
Next morning the ship arrives off Las Dopicos, capital of the Republic of San Theodoros, South America
Have you heard?...That Tortilla... He's disappeared! He must have been pushed overboard! There'd been a struggle in his cabin!
How shocking!... Do they know who did it?
They do indeed, gentlemen!... Come on now!... Get your hands up... fast!
Caramba! It's Tintin! I might have known!
Keep a close watch on them till the police arrive...
I am Colonel Jimenez, regular army.
Captain Maldemer... I have two prisoners I'd like to hand over, Colonel.
These two?...I know them both...dangerous crooks, wanted by our police.

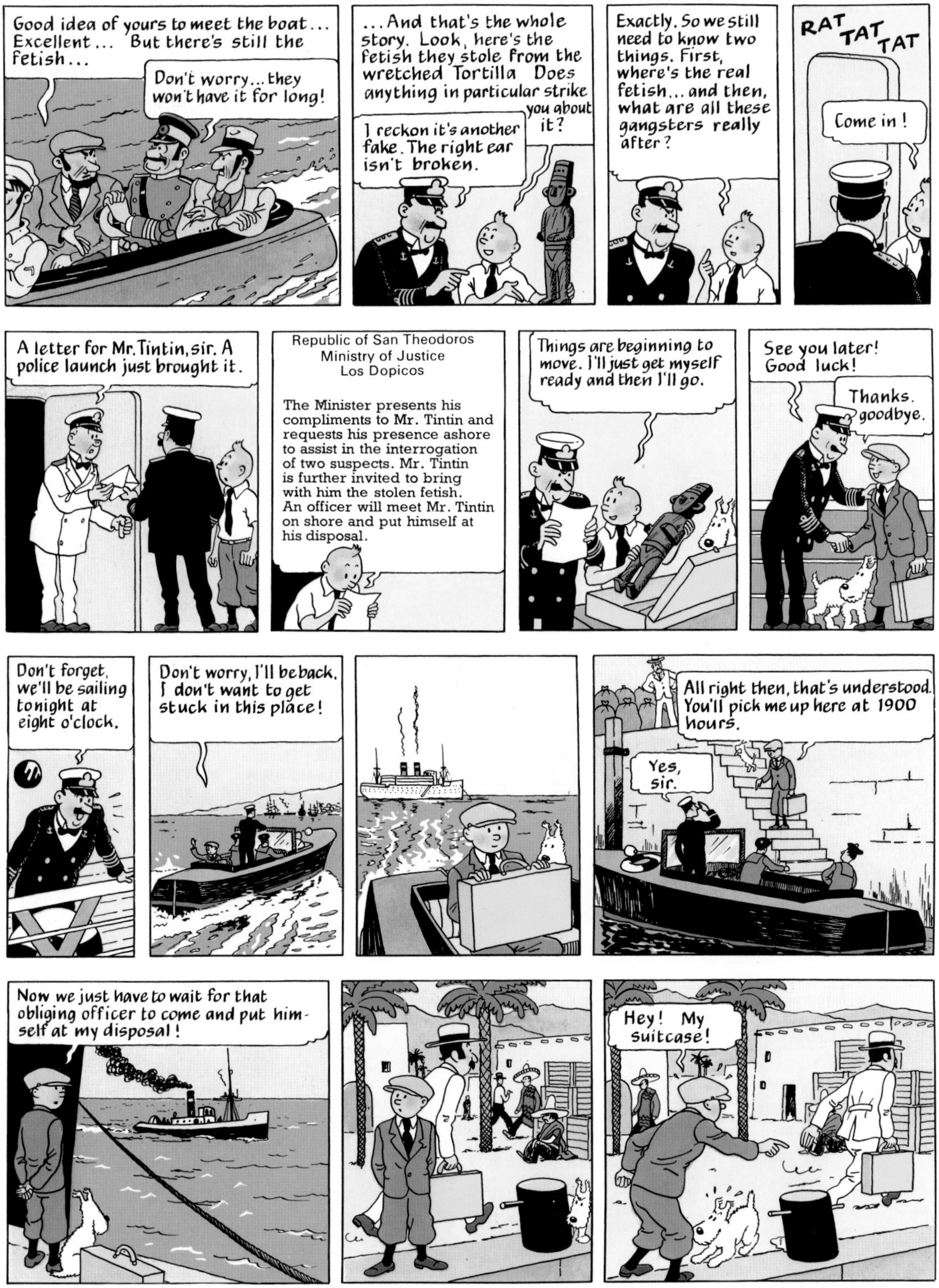
Good idea of yours to meet the boat... Excellent... But there's still the fetish...
Don't worry... they won't have it for long!
...And that's the whole story. Look, here's the fetish they stole from the wretched Tortilla Does anything in particular strike you about it?
I reckon it's another fake. The right ear isn't broken.
Exactly. So we still need to know two things. First, where's the real fetish... and then, what are all these gangsters really after?
RAT TAT TAT
Come in!
A letter for Mr. Tintin, sir. A police launch just brought it.
Republic of San Theodoros
Ministry of Justice
Los Dopicos
The Minister presents his compliments to Mr. Tintin and requests his presence ashore to assist in the interrogation of two suspects. Mr. Tintin is further invited to bring with him the stolen fetish. An officer will meet Mr. Tintin on shore and put himself at his disposal.
Things are beginning to move. I'll just get myself ready and then I'll go.
See you later! Good luck!
Thanks. goodbye.
Don't forget, we'll be sailing tonight at eight o'clock.
Don't worry, I'll be back. I don't want to get stuck in this place!
All right then, that's understood. You'll pick me up here at 1900 hours.
Yes, sir.
Now we just have to wait for that obliging officer to come and put himself at my disposal!
Hey! My suitcase!

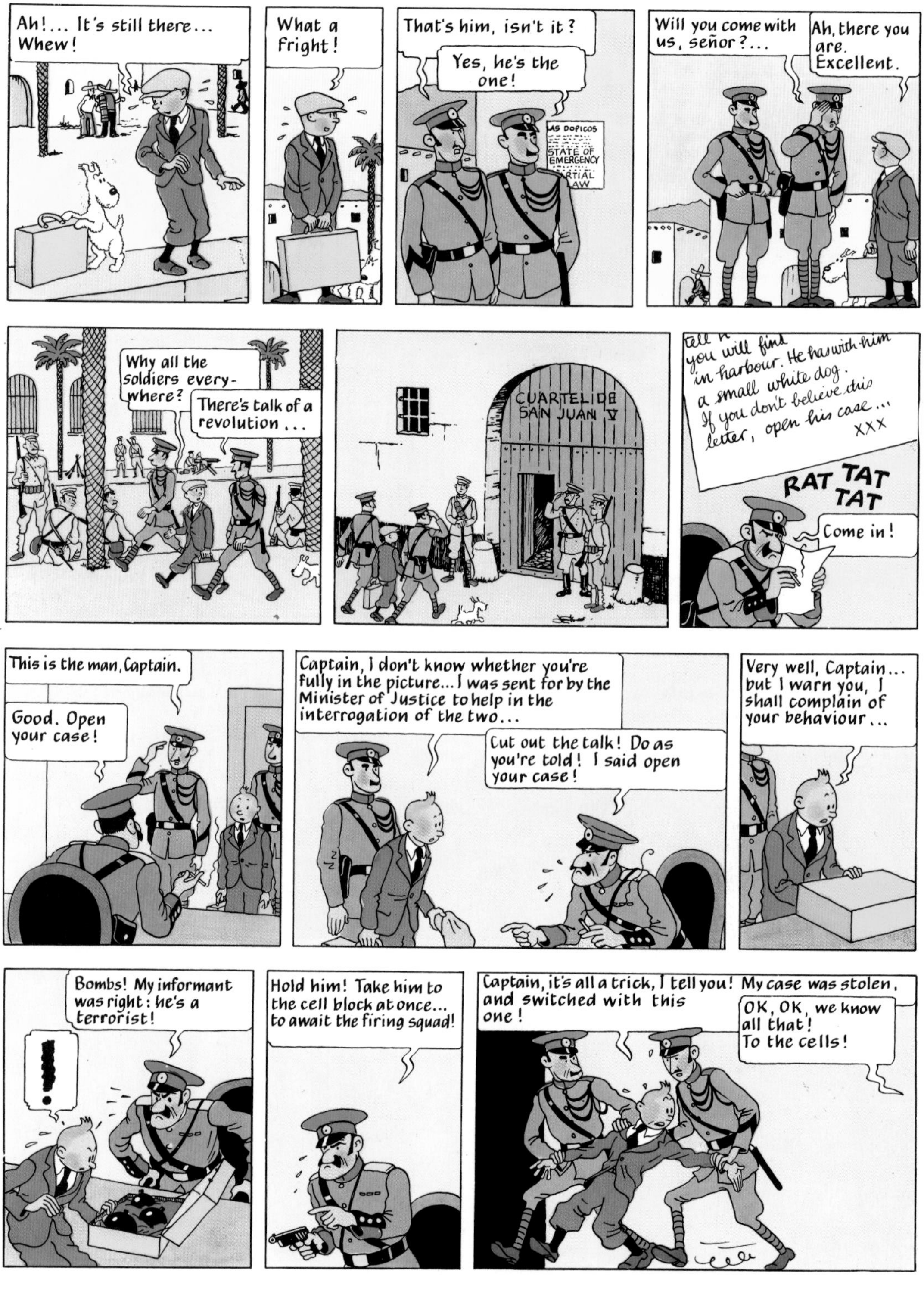

Ah!... It's still there... Whew!
What a fright!
That's him, isn't it?
Yes, he's the one!
LAS DOPICOS
STATE OF EMERGENCY
Will you come with us, señor?...
Ah, there you are. Excellent.
Why all the soldiers every-where?
There's talk of a revolution...
CUARTEL DE SAN JUAN V
you will find
in harbour. He has with him
a small white dog.
If you don't believe this
letter, open his case...
XXX
RAT TAT TAT
Come in!
This is the man, Captain.
Good. Open your case!
Captain, I don't know whether you're fully in the picture... I was sent for by the Minister of Justice to help in the interrogation of the two...
Cut out the talk! Do as you're told! I said open your case!
Very well, Captain... but I warn you, I shall complain of your behaviour...
Bombs! My informant was right: he's a terrorist!
Hold him! Take him to the cell block at once... to await the firing squad!
Captain, it's all a trick, I tell you! My case was stolen, and switched with this one!
OK, OK, we know all that! To the cells!

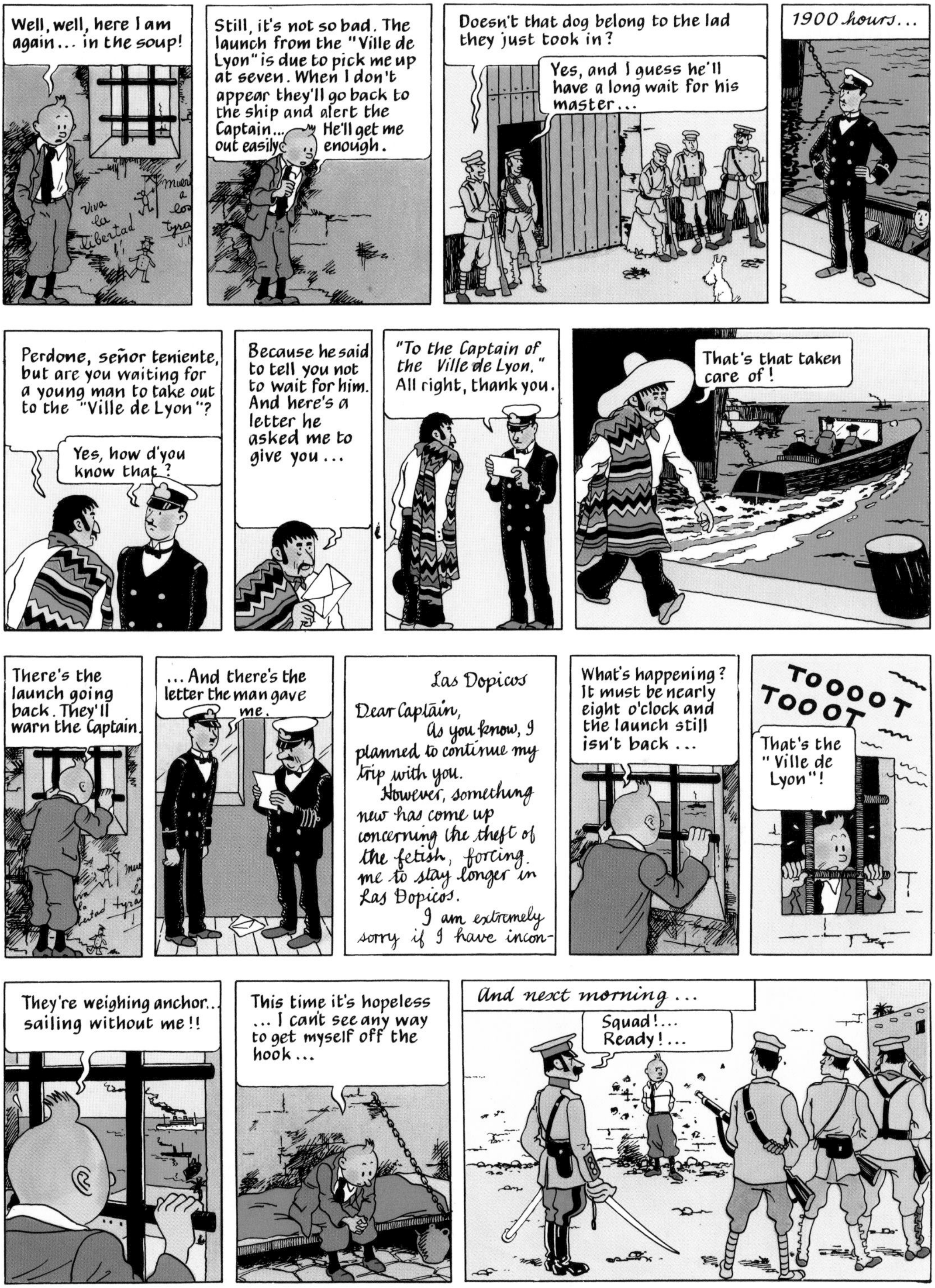

Well, well, here I am again... in the soup!
Still, it's not so bad. The launch from the "Ville de Lyon" is due to pick me up at seven. When I don't appear they'll go back to the ship and alert the Captain... He'll get me out easily enough.
Doesn't that dog belong to the lad they just took in?
Yes, and I guess he'll have a long wait for his master...
1900 hours...
Perdone, señor teniente, but are you waiting for a young man to take out to the "Ville de Lyon"?
Yes, how d'you know that?
Because he said to tell you not to wait for him. And here's a letter he asked me to give you...
"To the Captain of the Ville de Lyon." All right, thank you.
That's that taken care of!
There's the launch going back. They'll warn the Captain.
...And there's the letter the man gave me.
Las Dopicos
Dear Captain,
As you know, I planned to continue my trip with you.
However, something new has come up concerning the theft of the fetish, forcing me to stay longer in Las Dopicos.
I am extremely sorry if I have incon-
What's happening? It must be nearly eight o'clock and the launch still isn't back...
TOOOOT TOOOT
That's the "Ville de Lyon"!
They're weighing anchor.. sailing without me!!
This time it's hopeless ... I can't see any way to get myself off the hook...
And next morning...
Squad!... Ready!...

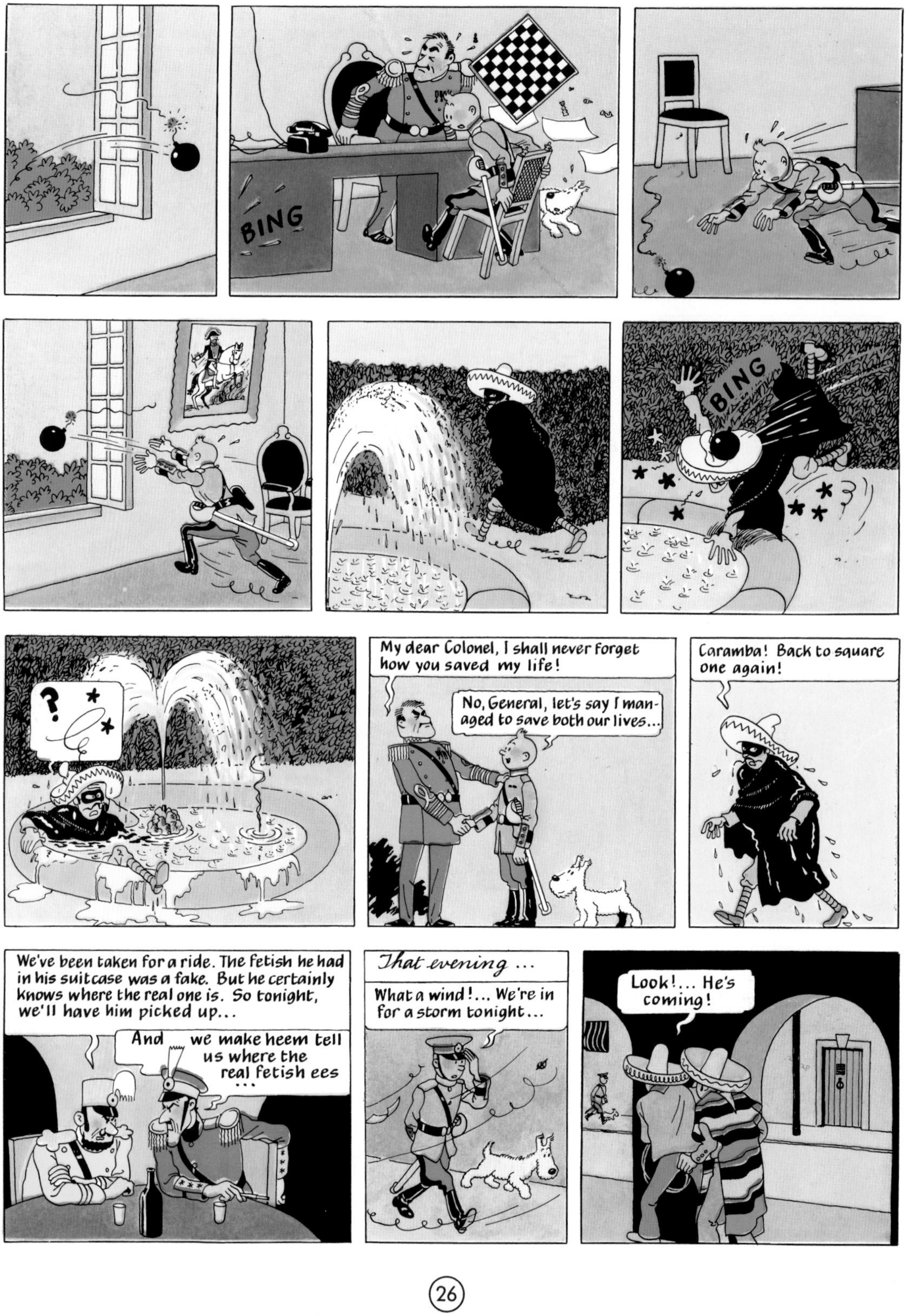
BING
BING
My dear Colonel, I shall never forget how you saved my life!
No, General, let's say I managed to save both our lives...
Caramba! Back to square one again!
We've been taken for a ride. The fetish he had in his suitcase was a fake. But he certainly knows where the real one is. So tonight, we'll have him picked up...
And we make heem tell us where the real fetish ees ...
That evening ...
What a wind!... We're in for a storm tonight...
Look!... He's coming!

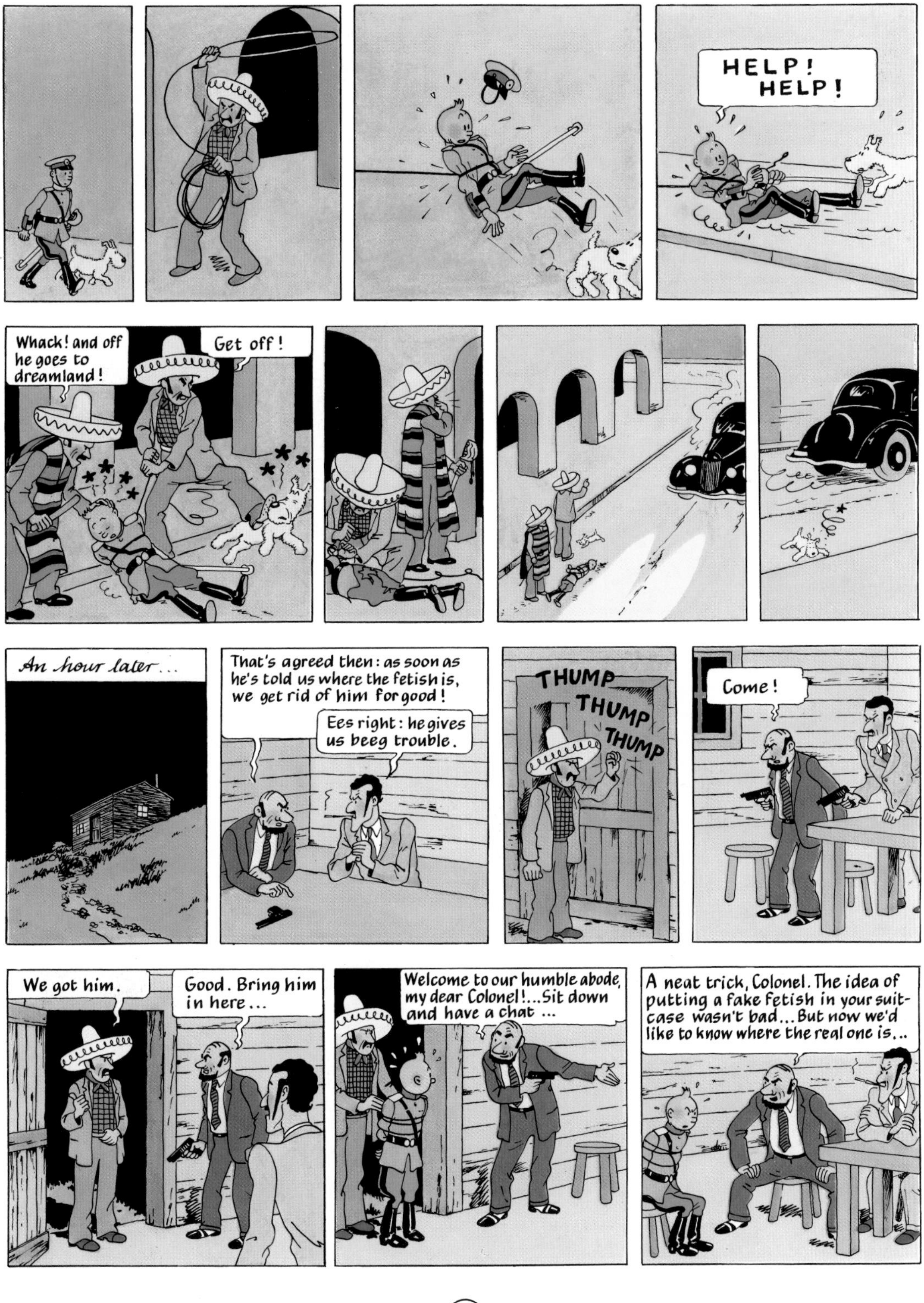

HELP! HELP!
Whack! and off he goes to dreamland!
Get off!
An hour later...
That's agreed then: as soon as he's told us where the fetish is, we get rid of him for good!
Ees right: he gives us beeg trouble.
THUMP THUMP THUMP
Come!
We got him.
Good. Bring him in here...
Welcome to our humble abode, my dear Colonel!... Sit down and have a chat ...
A neat trick, Colonel. The idea of putting a fake fetish in your suitcase wasn't bad... But now we'd like to know where the real one is...

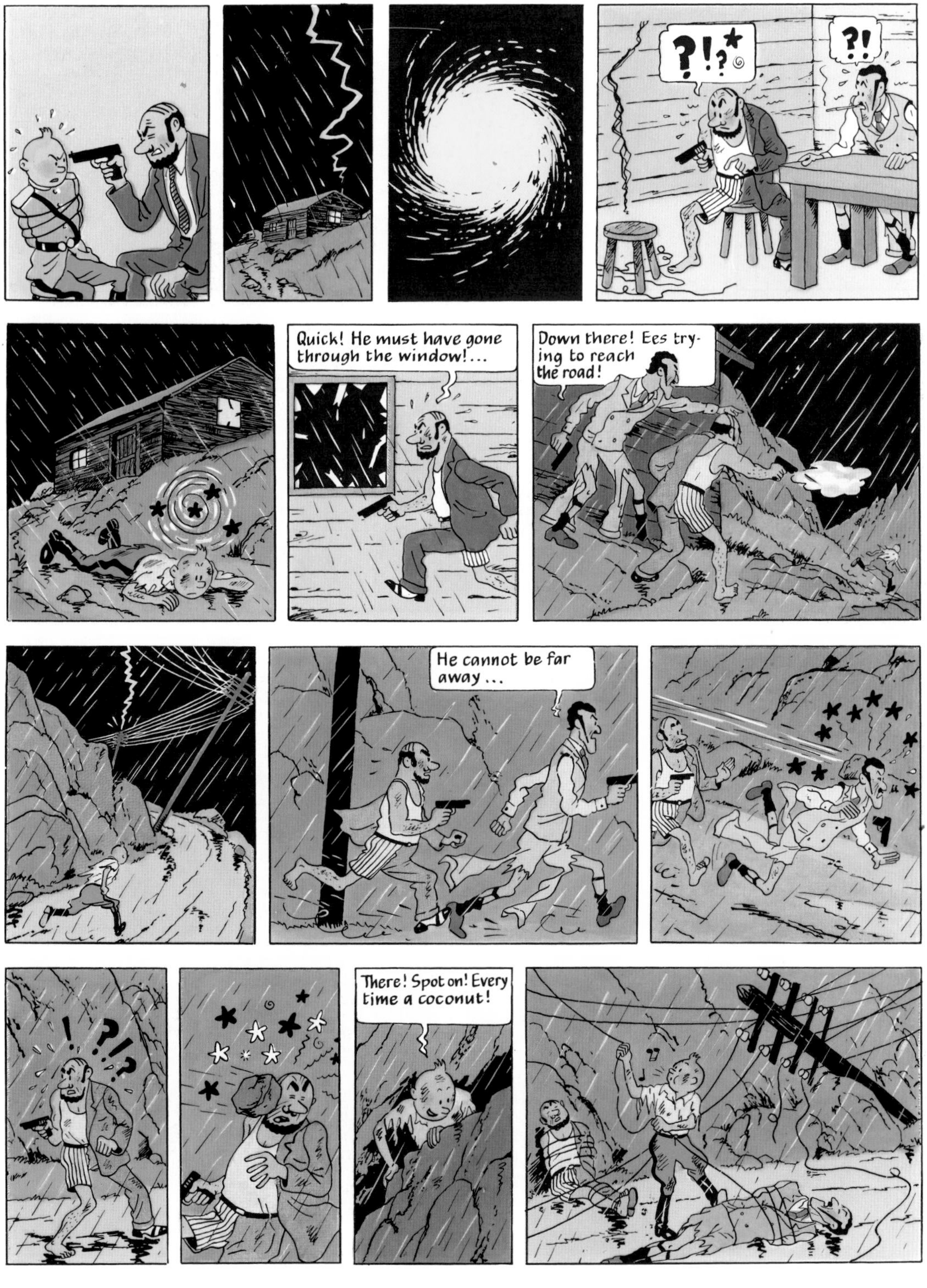
?!?★
?!
Quick! He must have gone through the window!...
Down there! Ees trying to reach the road!
He cannot be far away...
!?!?
There! Spot on! Every time a coconut!

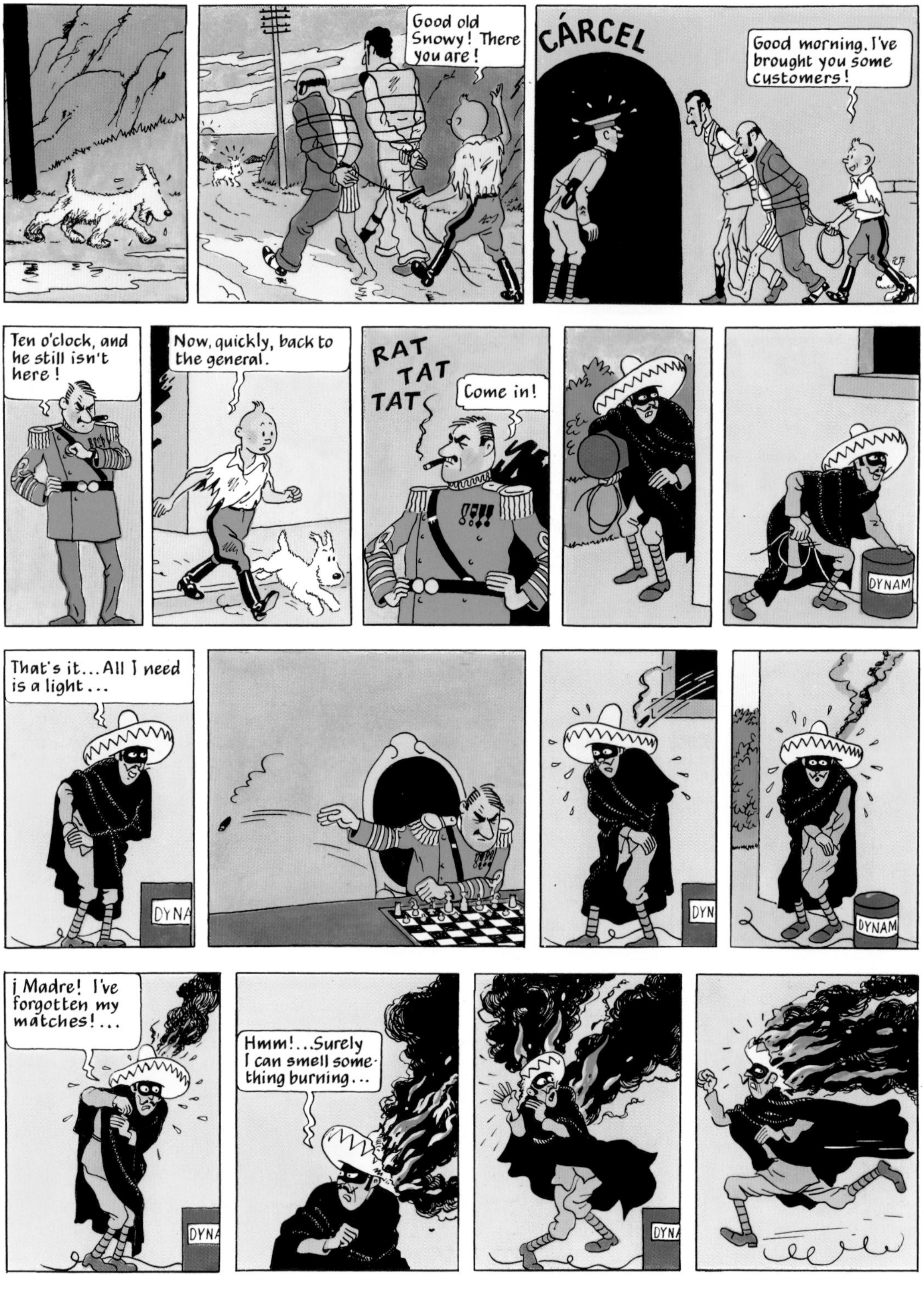
Good old Snowy! There you are!
CÁRCEL
Good morning. I've brought you some customers!
Ten o'clock, and he still isn't here!
Now, quickly, back to the general.
RAT TAT TAT
Come in!
DYNAM
That's it... All I need is a light...
DYNA
DYN
DYNAM
¡Madre! I've forgotten my matches!...
DYNA
Hmm!...Surely I can smell something burning...
DYNA

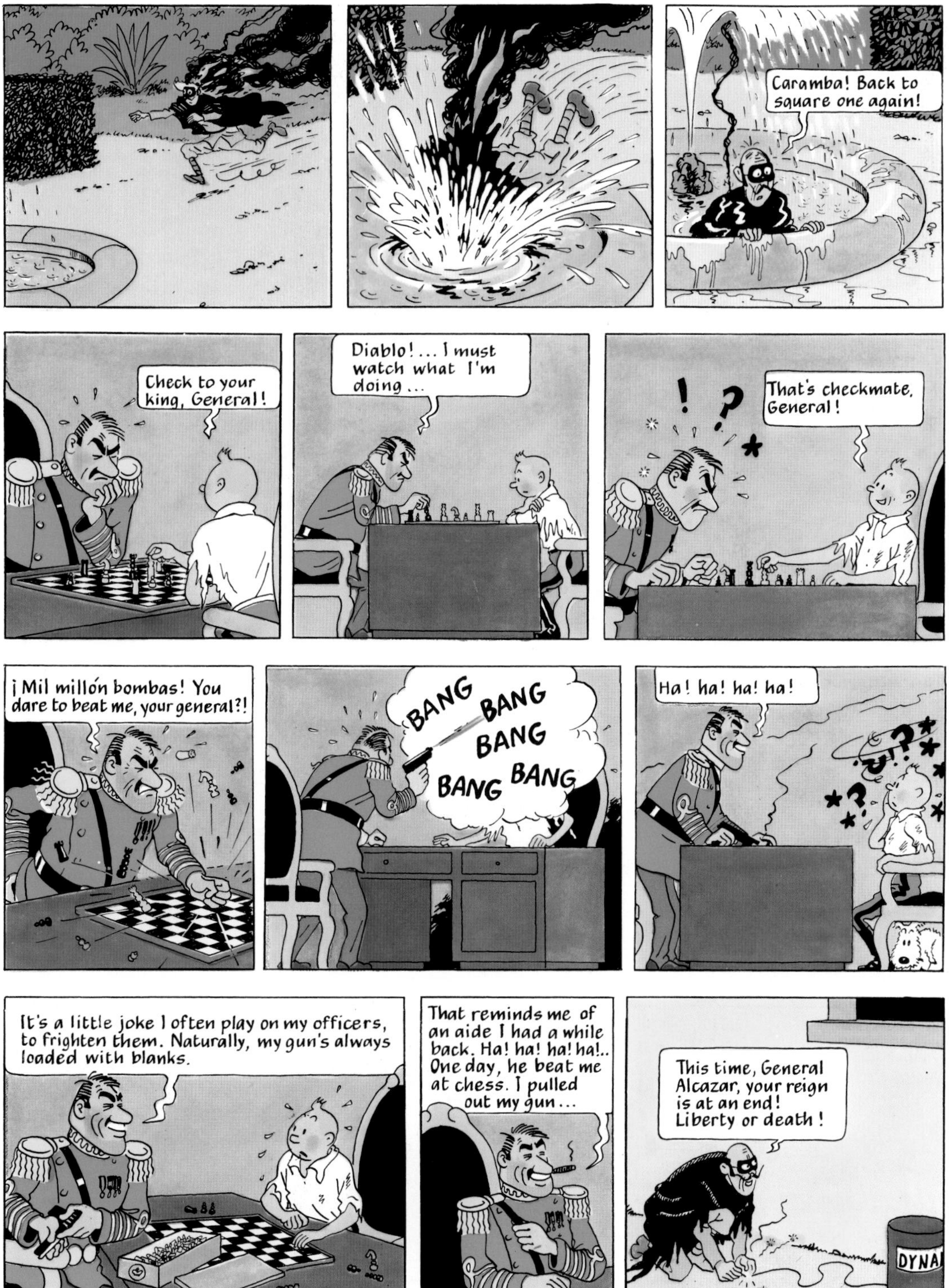
Caramba! Back to square one again!
Check to your king, General!
Diablo!... I must watch what I'm doing...
That's checkmate, General!
¡ Mil millón bombas! You dare to beat me, your general?!
BANG BANG BANG BANG BANG
Ha! ha! ha! ha!
It's a little joke I often play on my officers, to frighten them. Naturally, my gun's always loaded with blanks.
That reminds me of an aide I had a while back. Ha! ha! ha! ha!.. One day, he beat me at chess. I pulled out my gun...
This time, General Alcazar, your reign is at an end! Liberty or death!
DYNA

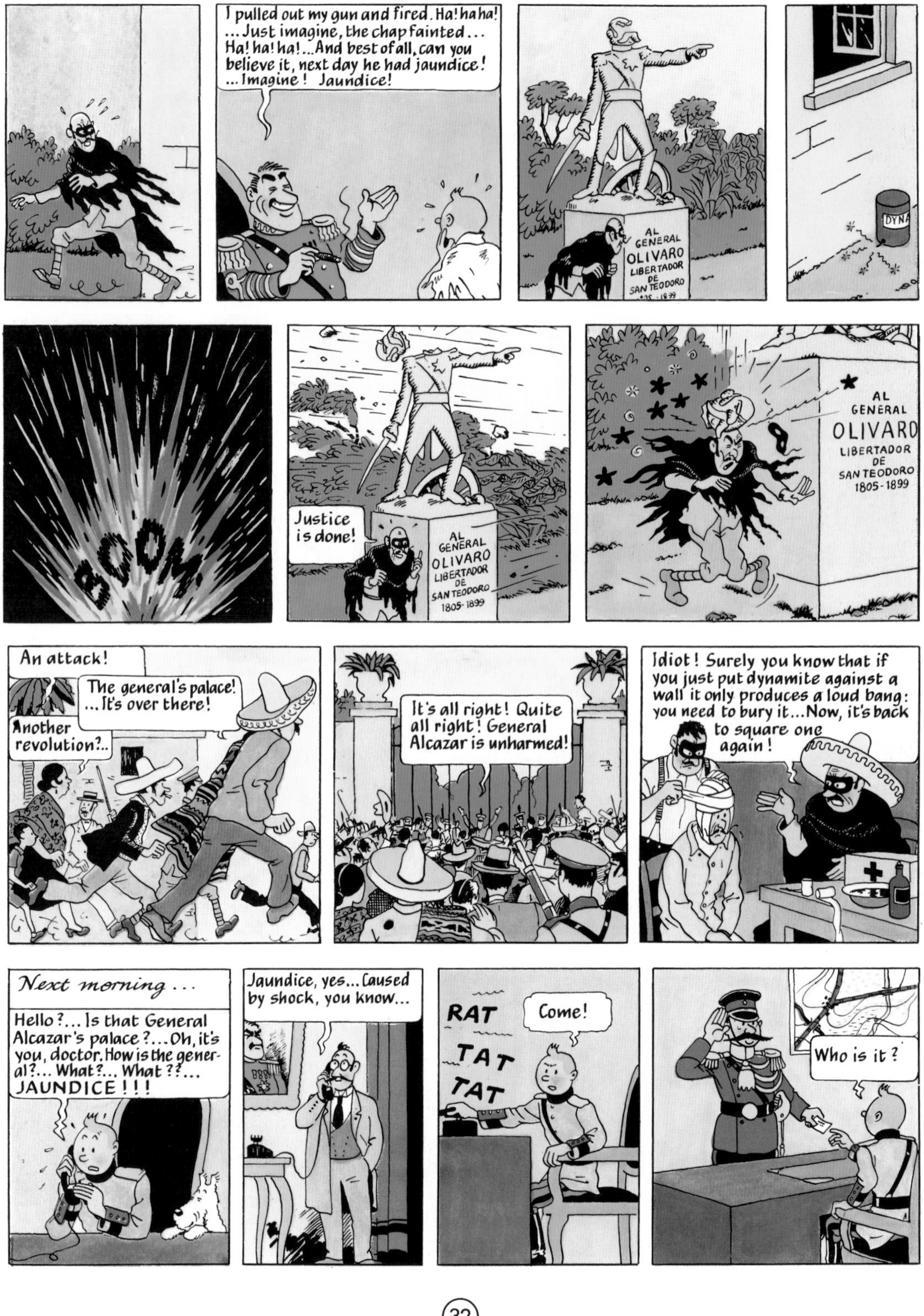
I pulled out my gun and fired. Ha! ha ha! ... Just imagine, the chap fainted ... Ha! ha! ha! ... And best of all, can you believe it, next day he had jaundice! ... Imagine! Jaundice!
AL GENERAL OLIVARO LIBERTADOR DE SAN TEODORO
DYNA
BOOM
Justice is done!
AL GENERAL OLIVARO LIBERTADOR DE SAN TEODORO 1805-1899
AL GENERAL OLIVARO LIBERTADOR DE SAN TEODORO 1805-1899
An attack!
The general's palace! ... It's over there!
Another revolution?..
It's all right! Quite all right! General Alcazar is unharmed!
Idiot! Surely you know that if you just put dynamite against a wall it only produces a loud bang: you need to bury it ... Now, it's back to square one again!
Next morning ...
Hello? ... Is that General Alcazar's palace? ... Oh, it's you, doctor. How is the general? ... What? ... What?? ... JAUNDICE!!!
Jaundice, yes ... Caused by shock, you know ...
RAT TAT TAT
Come!
Who is it?

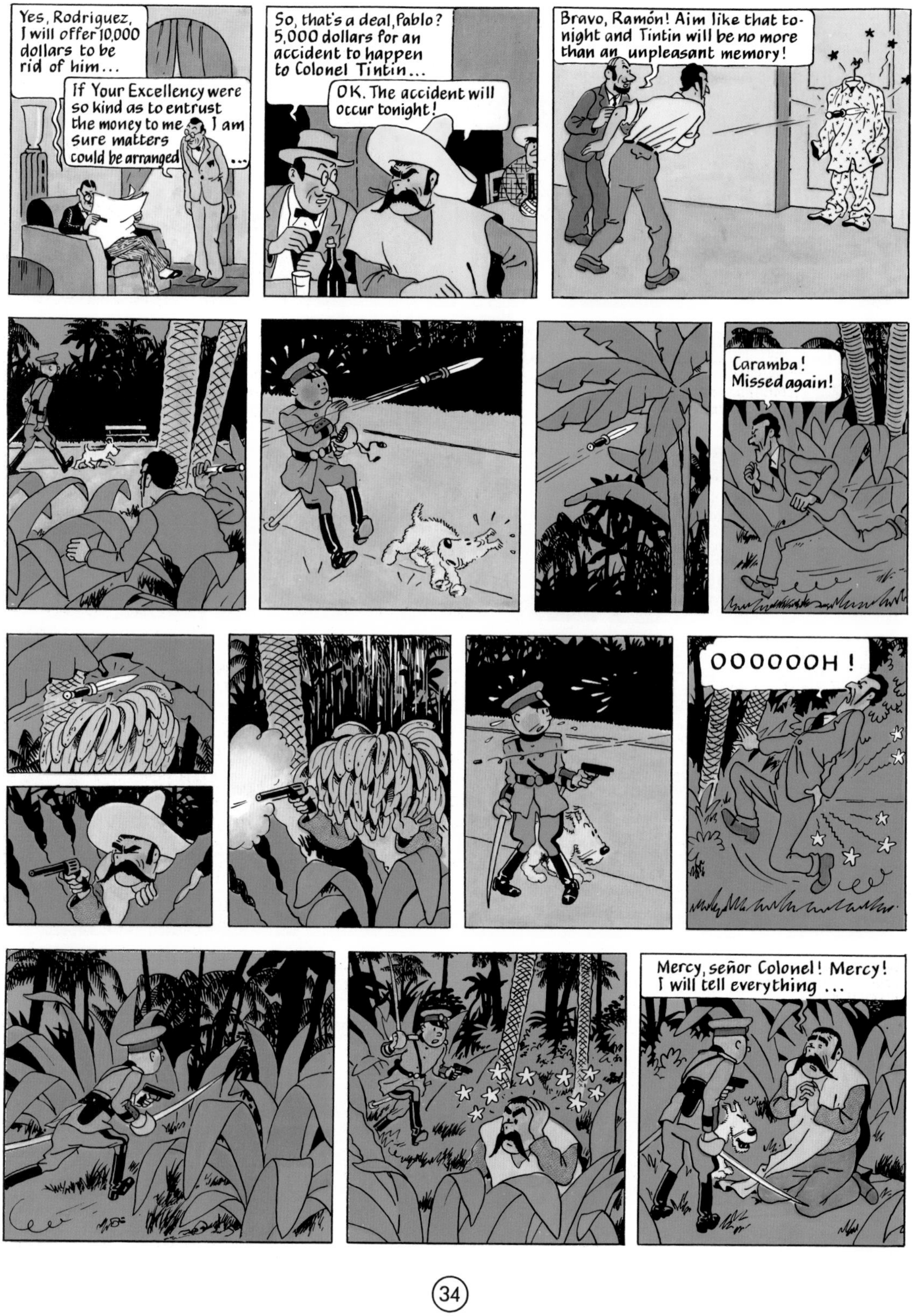
Yes, Rodriguez, I will offer 10,000 dollars to be rid of him...
If Your Excellency were so kind as to entrust the money to me I am sure matters could be arranged ...
So, that's a deal, Pablo? 5,000 dollars for an accident to happen to Colonel Tintin...
OK. The accident will occur tonight!
Bravo, Ramón! Aim like that to-night and Tintin will be no more than an unpleasant memory!
Caramba! Missed again!
OOOOOOH!
Mercy, señor Colonel! Mercy! I will tell everything ...

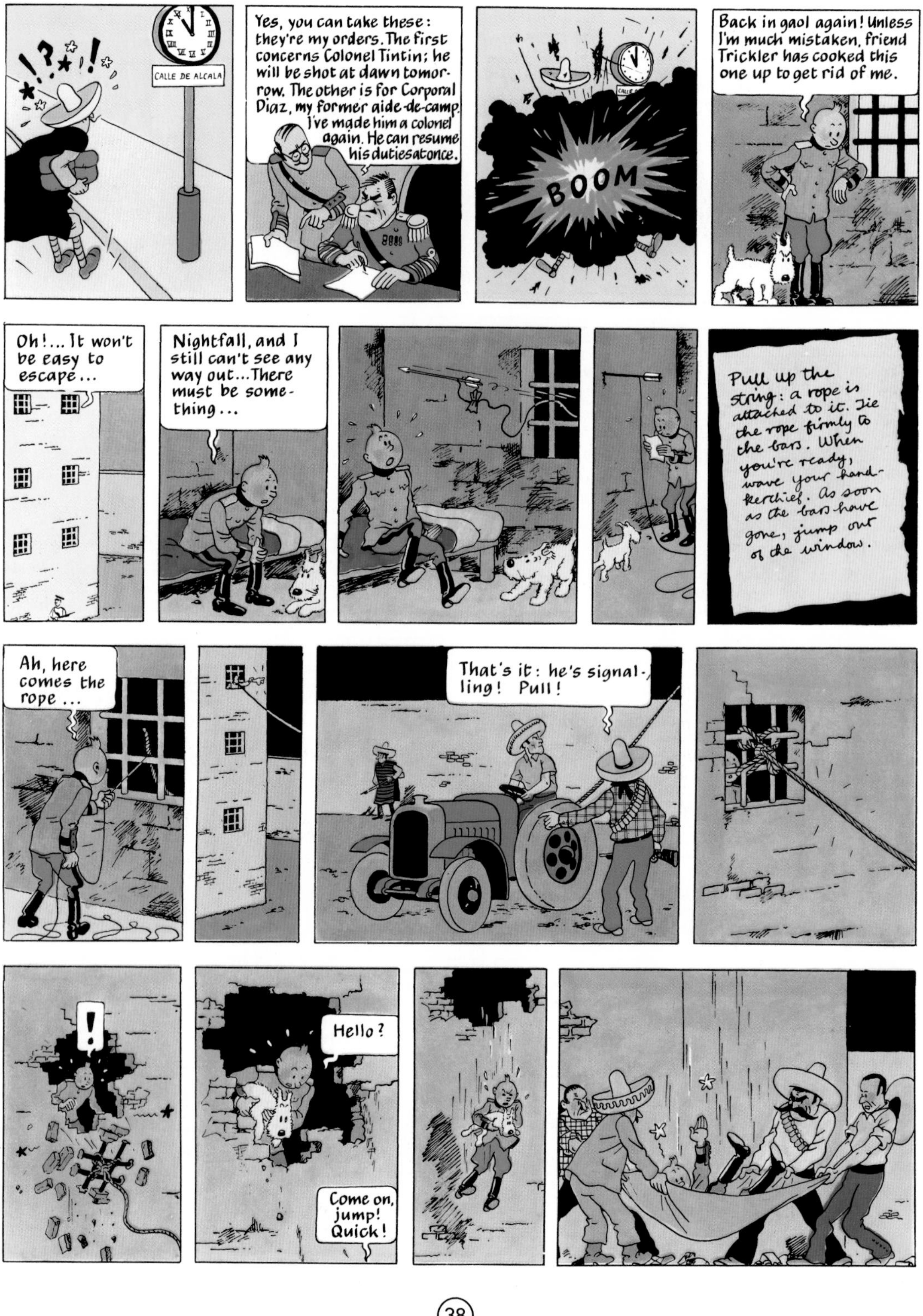

!?!
CALLE DE ALCALA
Yes, you can take these: they're my orders. The first concerns Colonel Tintin; he will be shot at dawn tomorrow. The other is for Corporal Diaz, my former aide-de-camp. I've made him a colonel again. He can resume his duties at once.
BOOM
Back in gaol again! Unless I'm much mistaken, friend Trickler has cooked this one up to get rid of me.
Oh!... It won't be easy to escape...
Nightfall, and I still can't see any way out... There must be something...
Pull up the string: a rope is attached to it. Tie the rope firmly to the bars. When you're ready, wave your handkerchief. As soon as the bars have gone, jump out of the window.
Ah, here comes the rope...
That's it: he's signalling! Pull!
!
Hello?
Come on, jump! Quick!

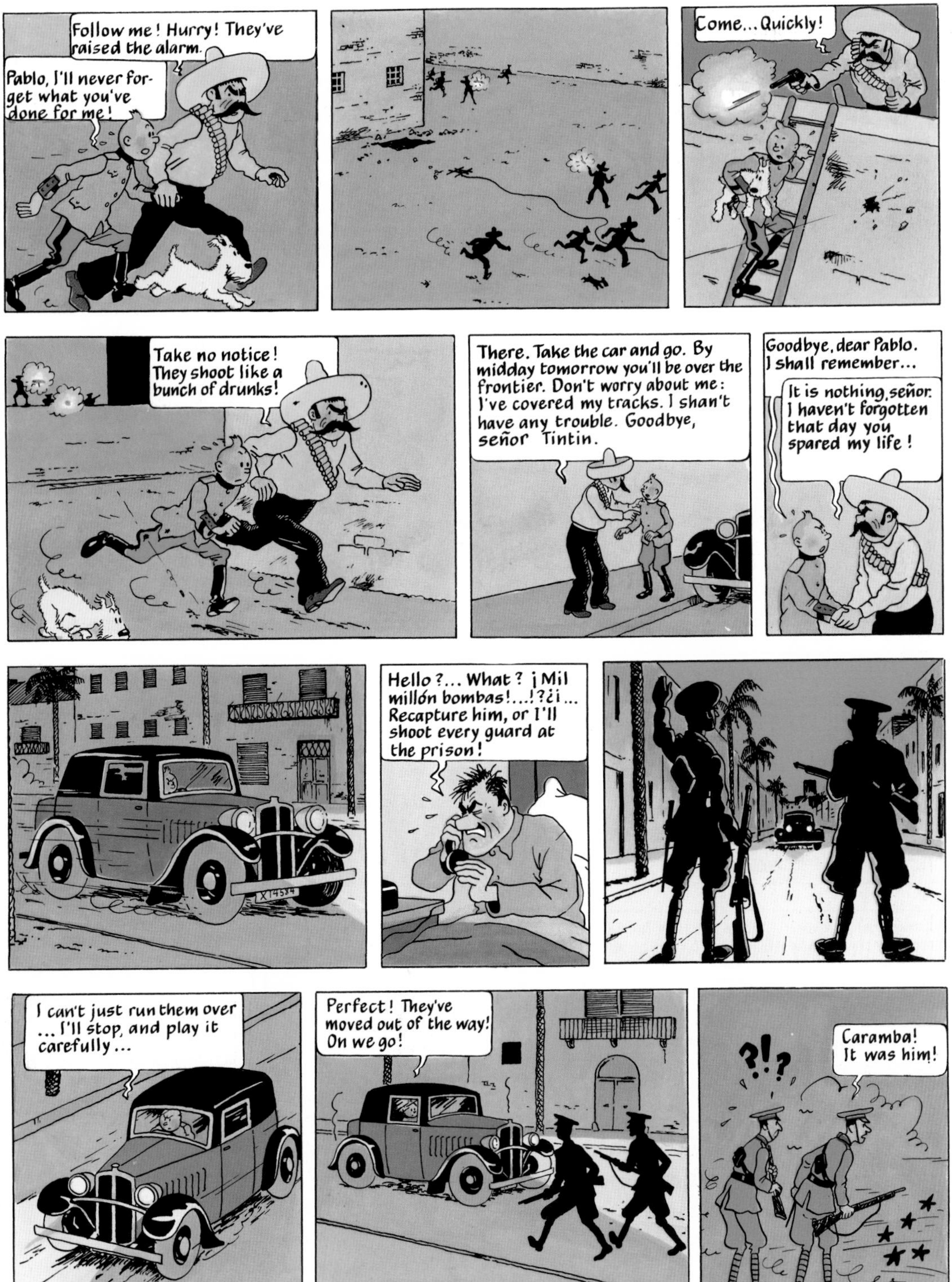
Follow me! Hurry! They've raised the alarm.
Pablo, I'll never forget what you've done for me!
Come... Quickly!
Take no notice! They shoot like a bunch of drunks!
There. Take the car and go. By midday tomorrow you'll be over the frontier. Don't worry about me: I've covered my tracks. I shan't have any trouble. Goodbye, señor Tintin.
Goodbye, dear Pablo. I shall remember...
It is nothing, señor. I haven't forgotten that day you spared my life!
Hello?... What? ¡Mil millón bombas!...!?¿i... Recapture him, or I'll shoot every guard at the prison!
I can't just run them over ... I'll stop, and play it carefully...
Perfect! They've moved out of the way! On we go!
?!?
Caramba! It was him!

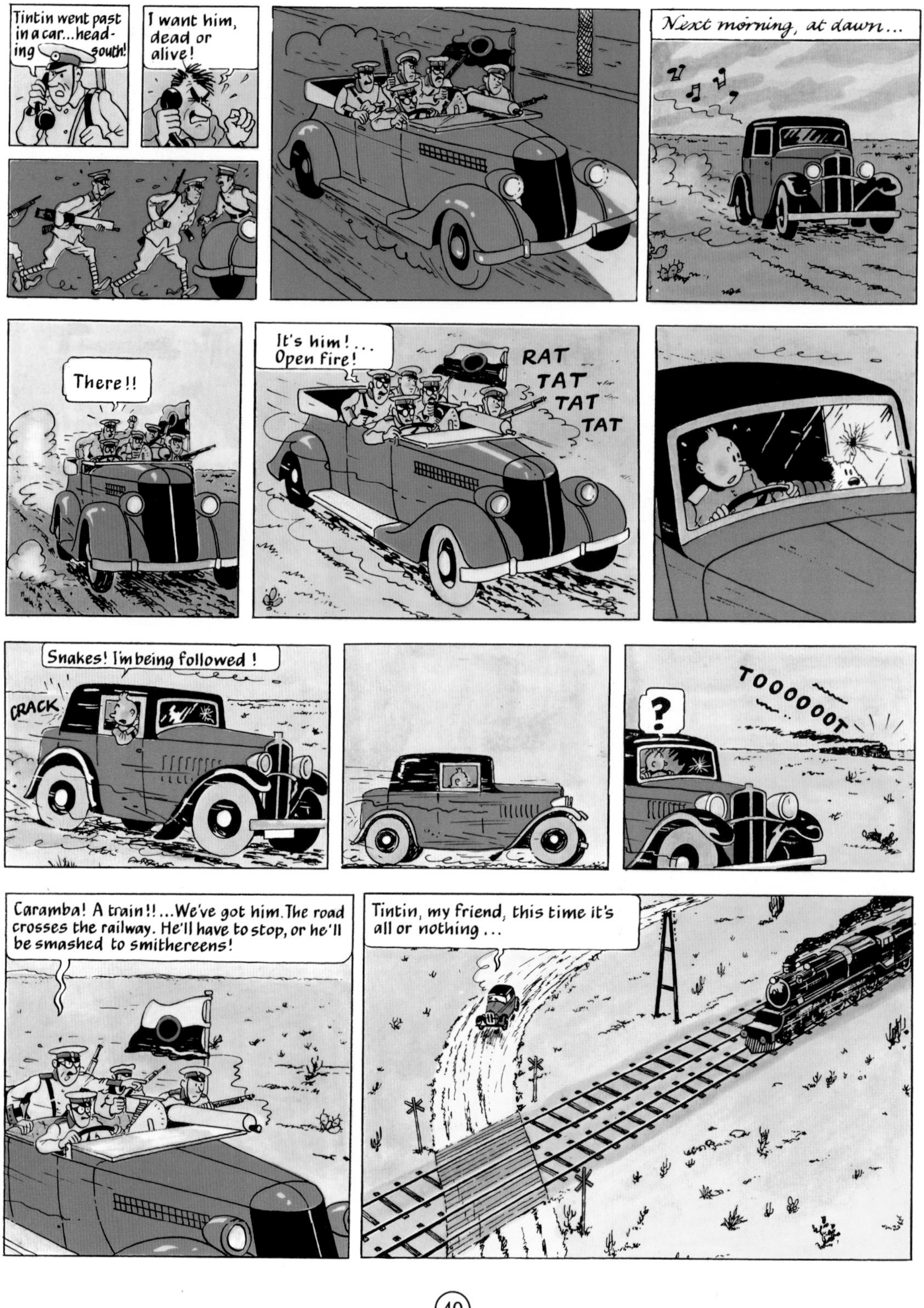

Tintin went past in a car... heading south!
I want him, dead or alive!
Next morning, at dawn...
There!!
It's him!... Open fire!
RAT TAT TAT TAT
Snakes! I'm being followed!
CRACK
?
TOOOOOOT
Caramba! A train!! ...We've got him. The road crosses the railway. He'll have to stop, or he'll be smashed to smithereens!
Tintin, my friend, this time it's all or nothing...

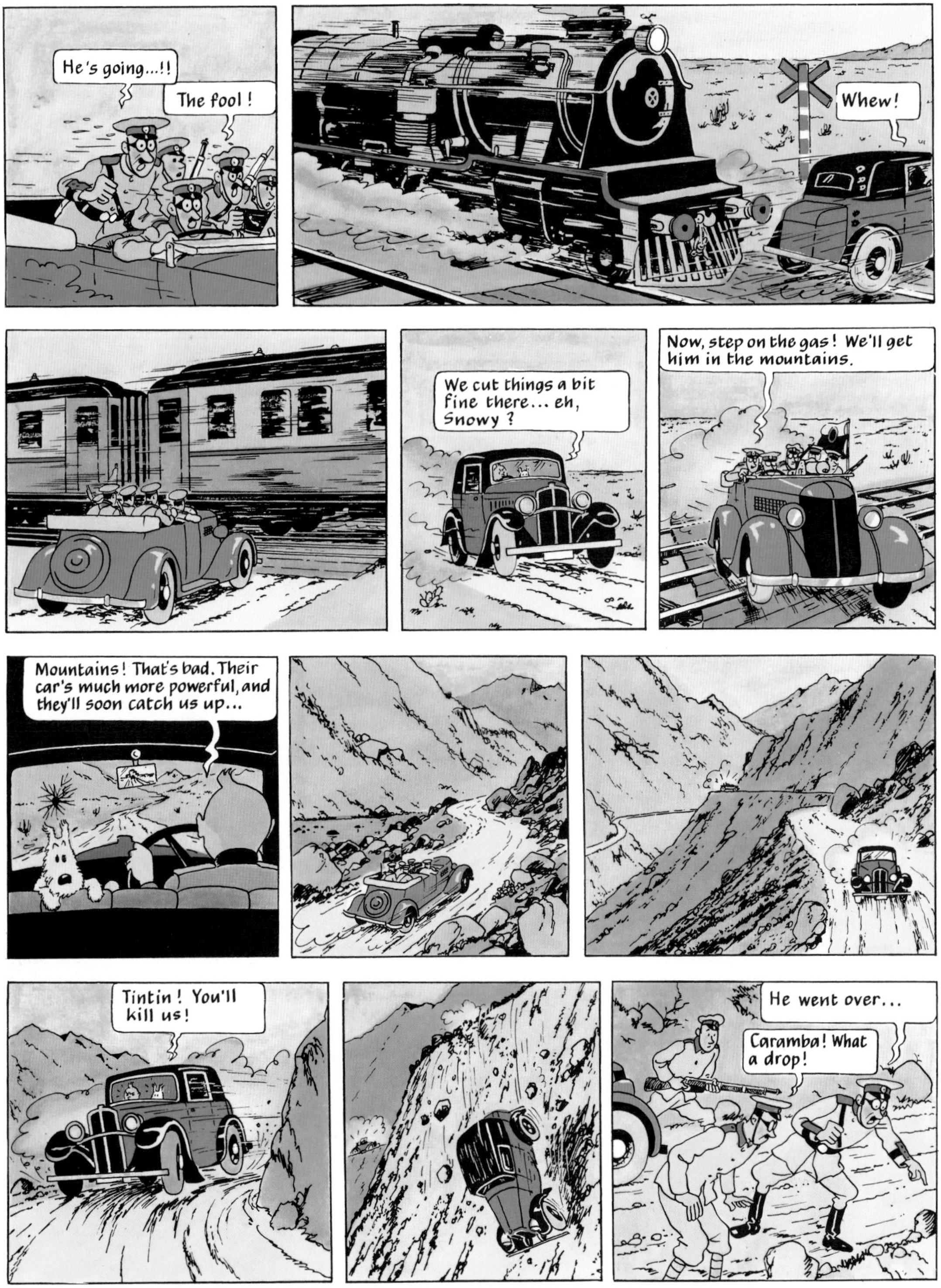
He's going...!!
The fool !
Whew!
We cut things a bit fine there... eh, Snowy ?
Now, step on the gas! We'll get him in the mountains.
Mountains! That's bad. Their car's much more powerful, and they'll soon catch us up...
Tintin! You'll kill us!
He went over...
Caramba! What a drop!

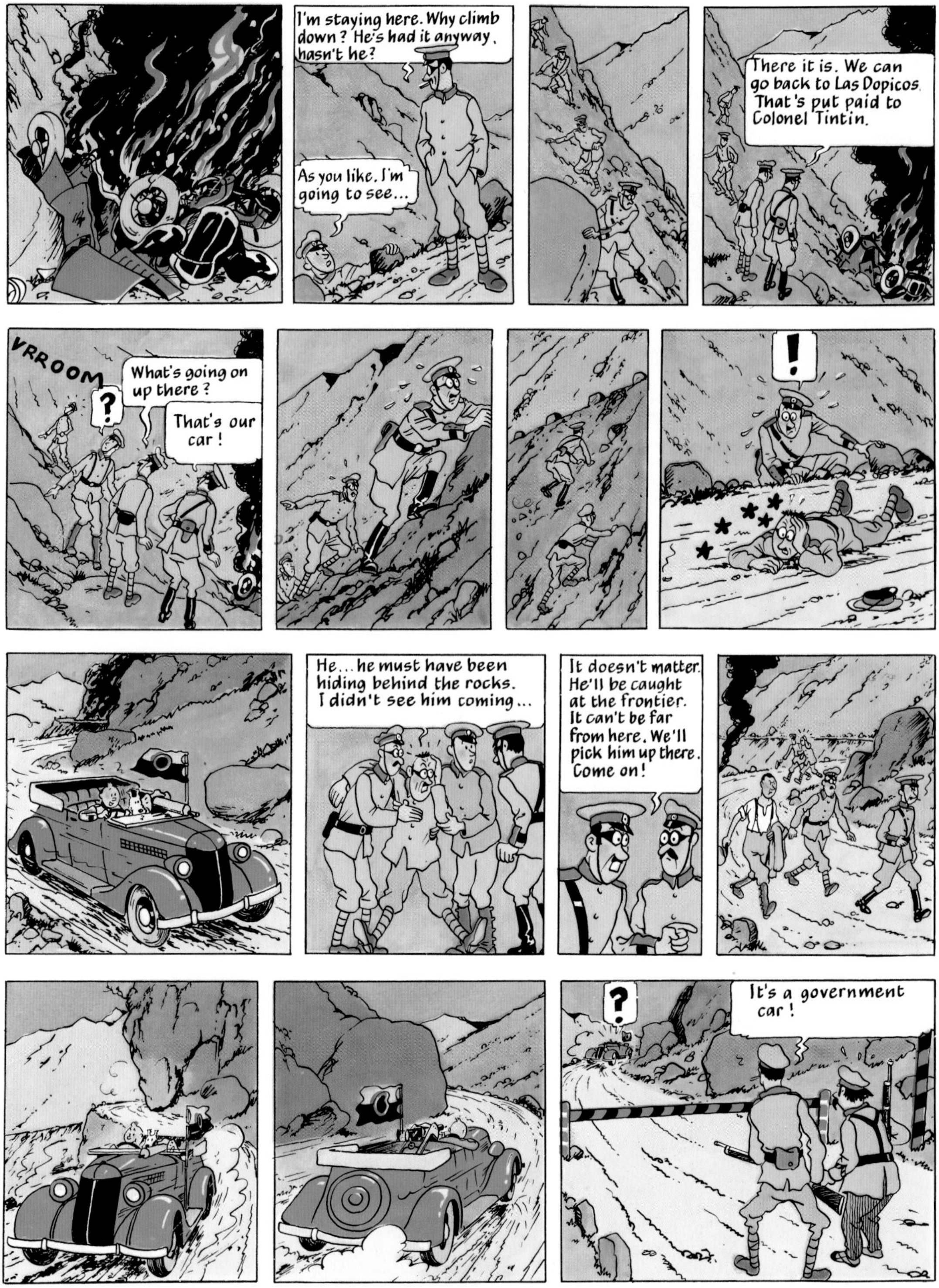

I'm staying here. Why climb down? He's had it anyway, hasn't he?
As you like. I'm going to see...
There it is. We can go back to Las Dopicos. That's put paid to Colonel Tintin.
VRROOM
What's going on up there?
That's our car!
!
He... he must have been hiding behind the rocks. I didn't see him coming...
It doesn't matter. He'll be caught at the frontier. It can't be far from here. We'll pick him up there. Come on!
?
It's a government car!

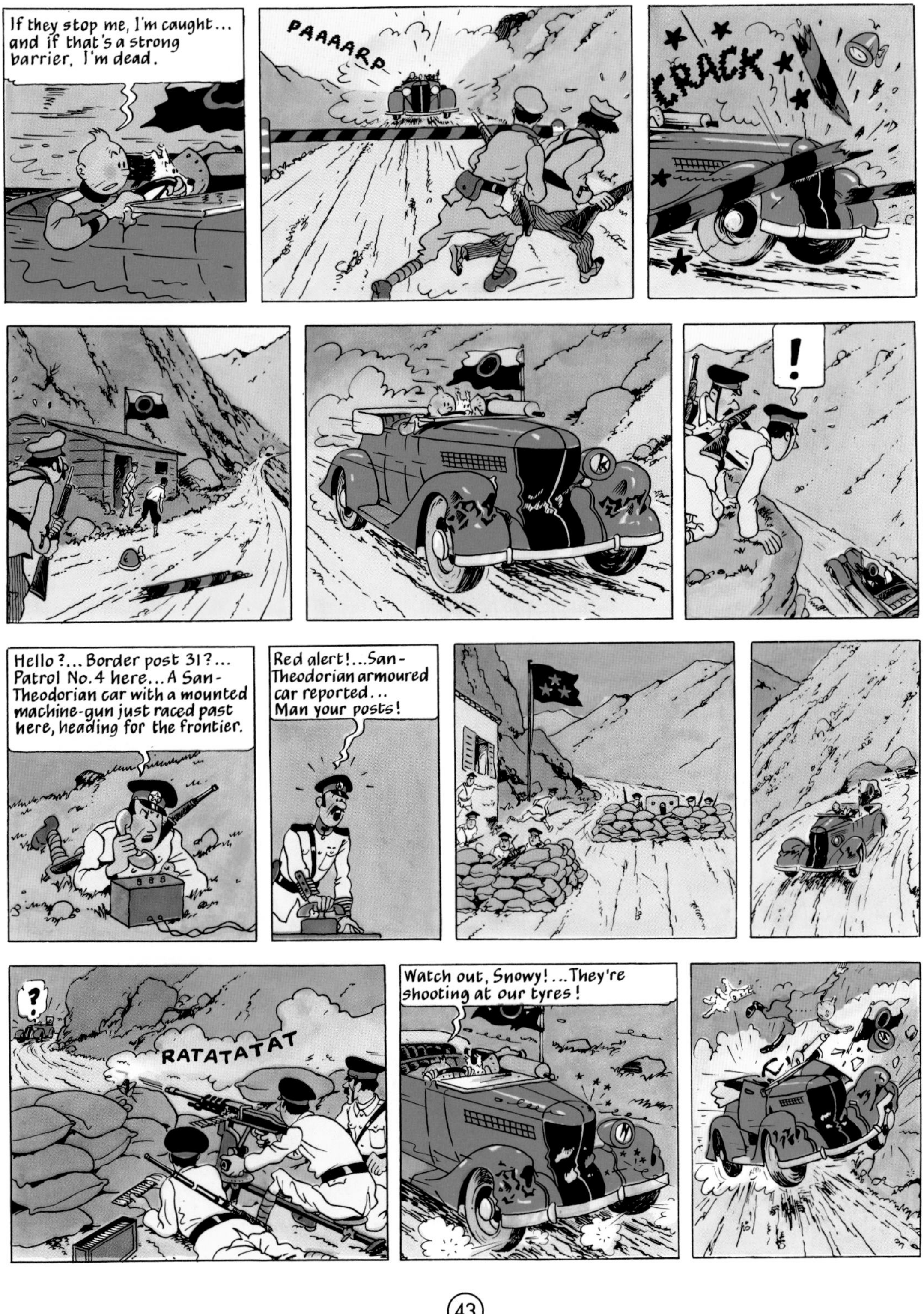
If they stop me, I'm caught... and if that's a strong barrier, I'm dead.
PAAAARP
CRACK
!
Hello?... Border post 31?... Patrol No.4 here... A San-Theodorian car with a mounted machine-gun just raced past here, heading for the frontier.
Red alert!...San-Theodorian armoured car reported... Man your posts!
?
RATATATAT
Watch out, Snowy!...They're shooting at our tyres!

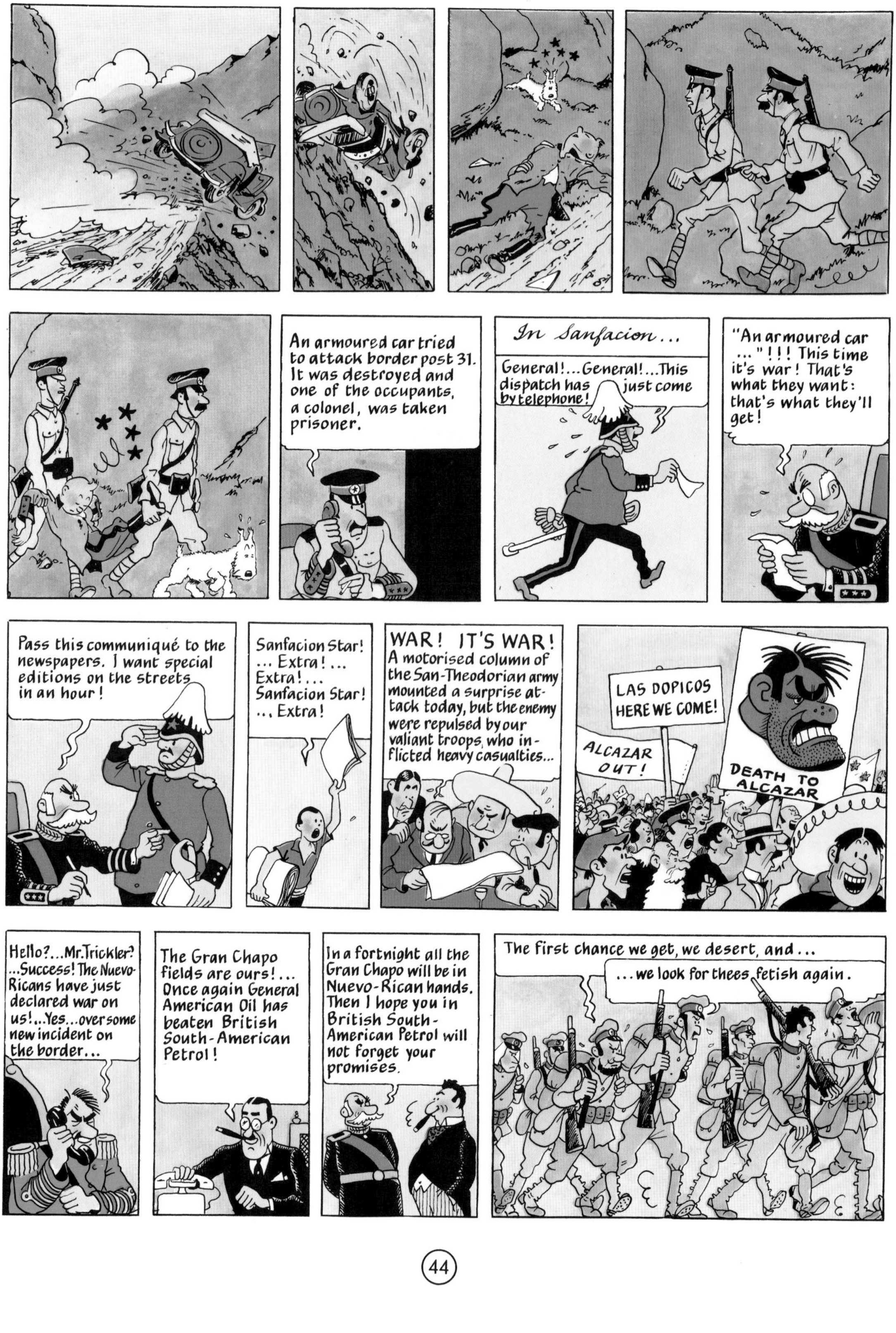
An armoured car tried to attack border post 31. It was destroyed and one of the occupants, a colonel, was taken prisoner.
In Sanfacion ...
General!...General!...This dispatch has just come by telephone!
"An armoured car ..."!!! This time it's war! That's what they want: that's what they'll get!
Pass this communiqué to the newspapers. I want special editions on the streets in an hour!
Sanfacion Star! ... Extra! ... Extra! ... Sanfacion Star! ... Extra!
WAR! IT'S WAR! A motorised column of the San-Theodorian army mounted a surprise attack today, but the enemy were repulsed by our valiant troops, who inflicted heavy casualties...
LAS DOPICOS HERE WE COME!
ALCAZAR OUT!
DEATH TO ALCAZAR
Hello?...Mr.Trickler? ...Success! The Nuevo-Ricans have just declared war on us!...Yes...over some new incident on the border...
The Gran Chapo fields are ours!... Once again General American Oil has beaten British South-American Petrol!
In a fortnight all the Gran Chapo will be in Nuevo-Rican hands. Then I hope you in British South-American Petrol will not forget your promises.
The first chance we get, we desert, and ...
... we look for thees fetish again.

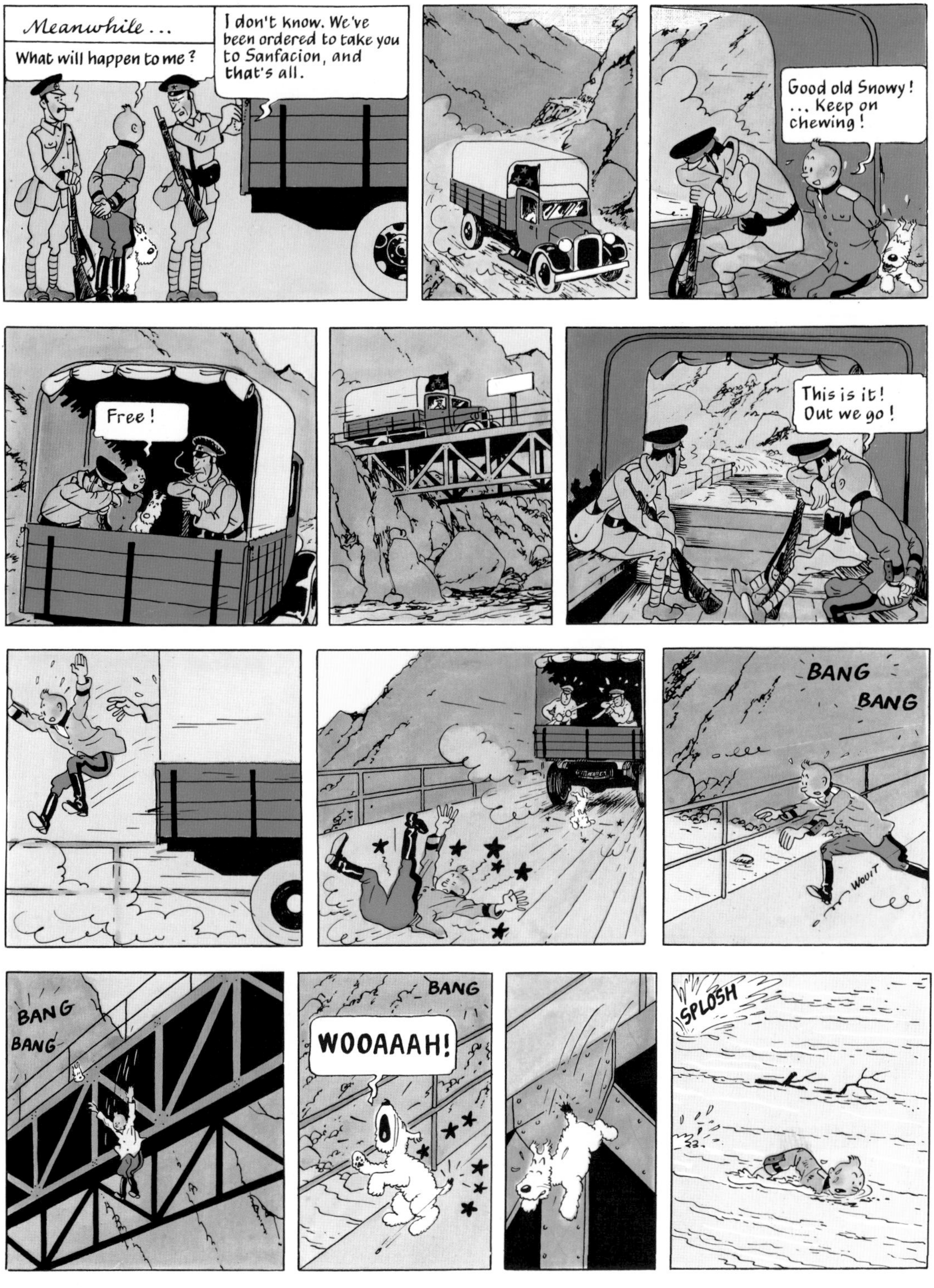
Meanwhile ...
What will happen to me?
I don't know. We've been ordered to take you to Sanfacion, and that's all.
Good old Snowy! ... Keep on chewing!
Free!
This is it! Out we go!
BANG
BANG
WOUIT
BANG
BANG
BANG
WOOAAAH!
SPLOSH

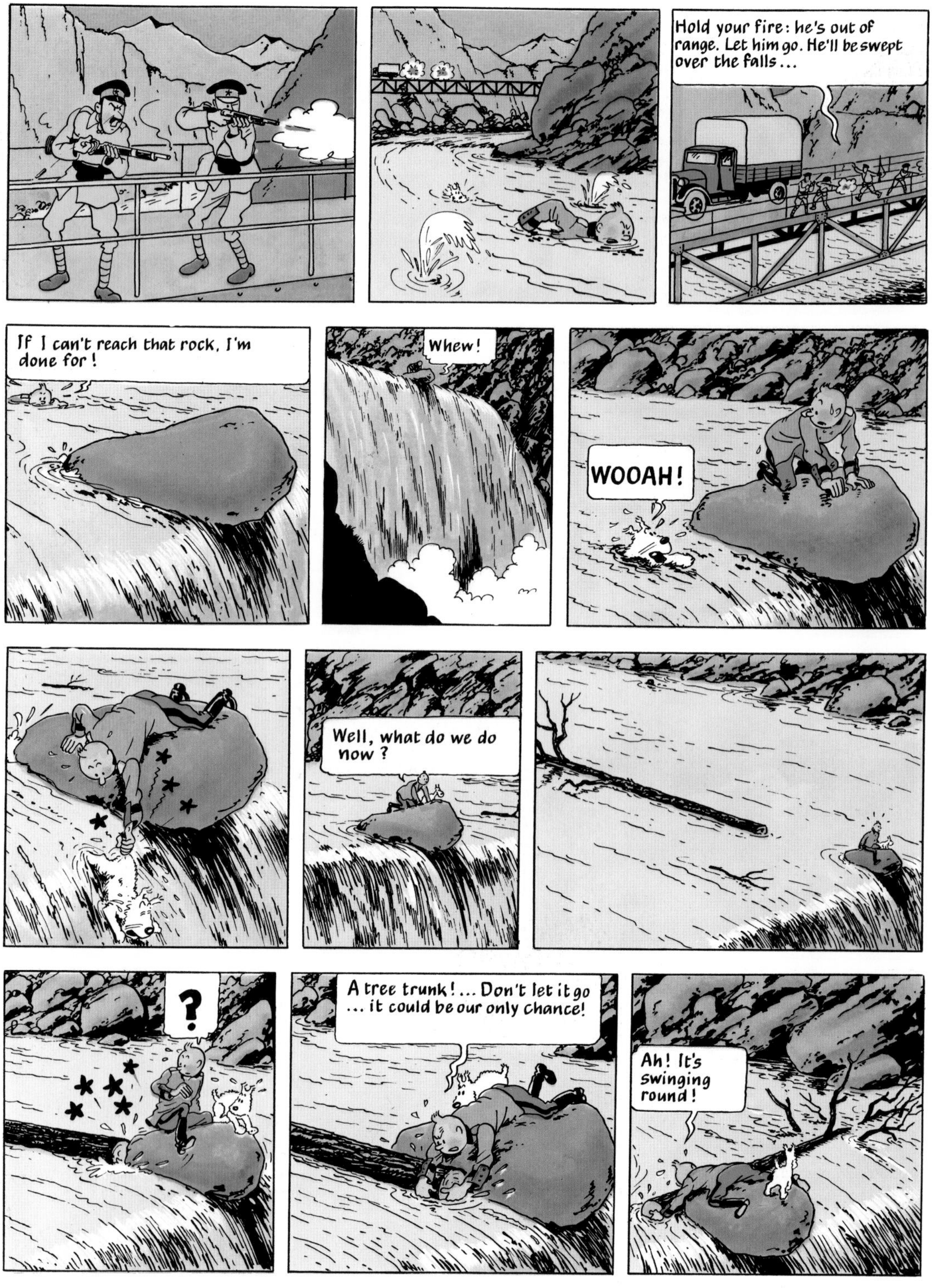
Hold your fire: he's out of range. Let him go. He'll be swept over the falls ...
If I can't reach that rock, I'm done for!
Whew!
WOOAH!
Well, what do we do now?
?
A tree trunk! ... Don't let it go ... it could be our only chance!
Ah! It's swinging round!

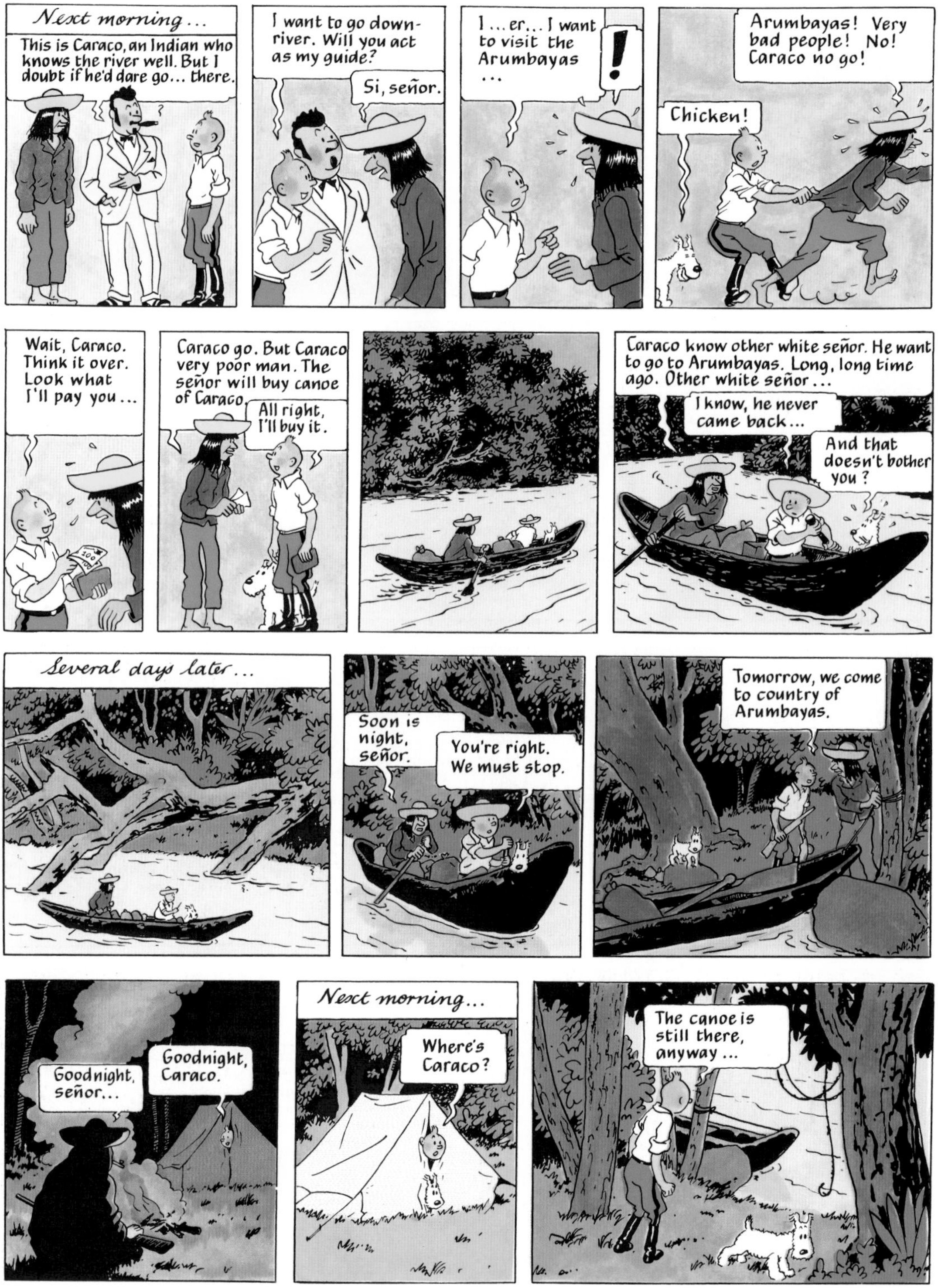

Next morning ...
This is Caraco, an Indian who knows the river well. But I doubt if he'd dare go ... there.
I want to go down-river. Will you act as my guide?
Si, señor.
I ... er ... I want to visit the Arumbayas ...
!
Arumbayas! Very bad people! No! Caraco no go!
Chicken!
Wait, Caraco. Think it over. Look what I'll pay you ...
100
Caraco go. But Caraco very poor man. The señor will buy canoe of Caraco.
All right, I'll buy it.
Caraco know other white señor. He want to go to Arumbayas. Long, long time ago. Other white señor ...
I know, he never came back ...
And that doesn't bother you?
Several days later ...
Soon is night, señor.
You're right. We must stop.
Tomorrow, we come to country of Arumbayas.
Goodnight, señor ...
Goodnight, Caraco.
Next morning ...
Where's Caraco?
The canoe is still there, anyway ...

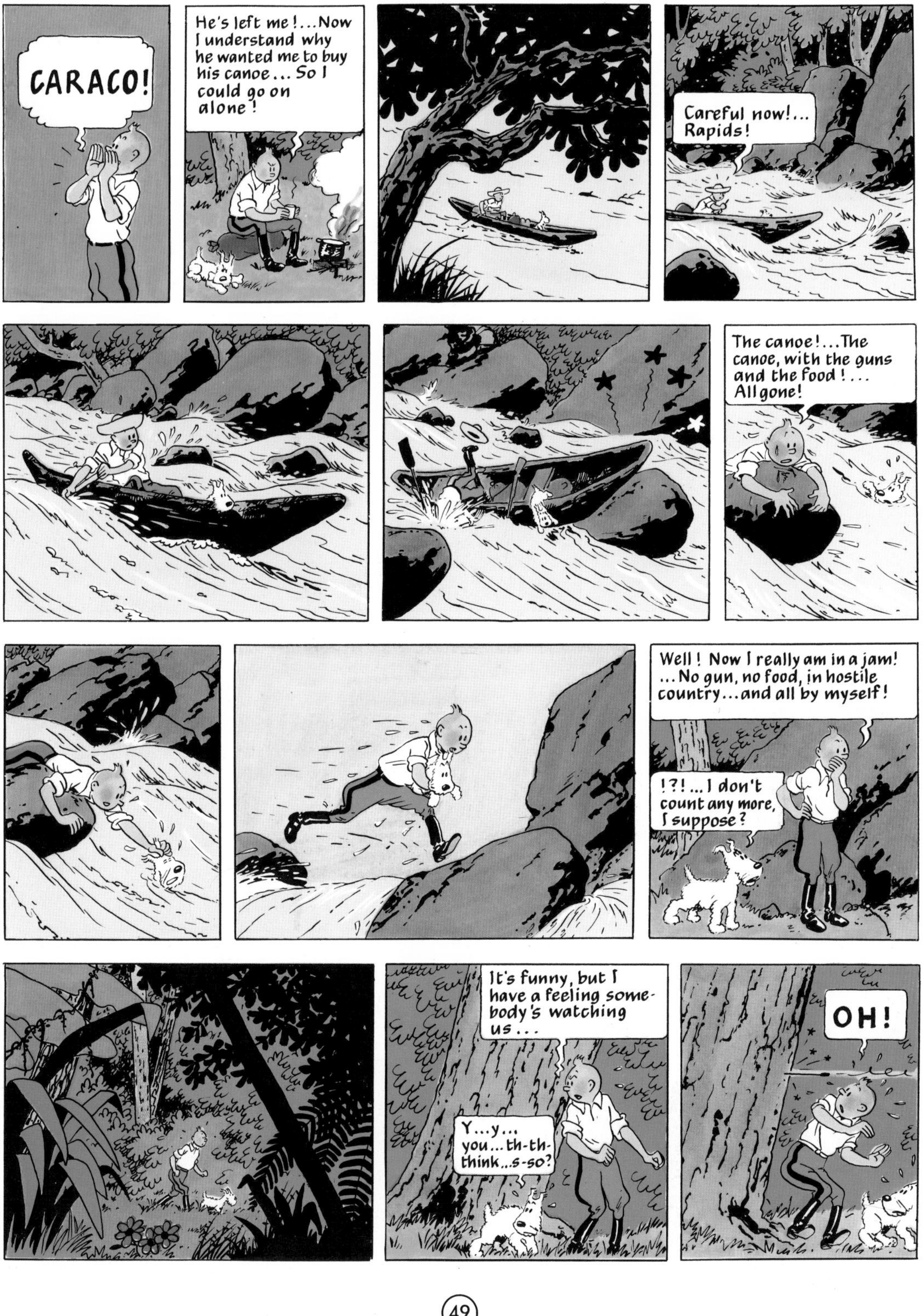
CARACO!
He's left me!...Now I understand why he wanted me to buy his canoe... So I could go on alone!
Careful now!... Rapids!
The canoe!...The canoe, with the guns and the food!... All gone!
Well! Now I really am in a jam! ...No gun, no food, in hostile country...and all by myself!
!?!...I don't count any more, I suppose?
It's funny, but I have a feeling somebody's watching us...
Y...y... you...th-th-think...s-so?
OH!

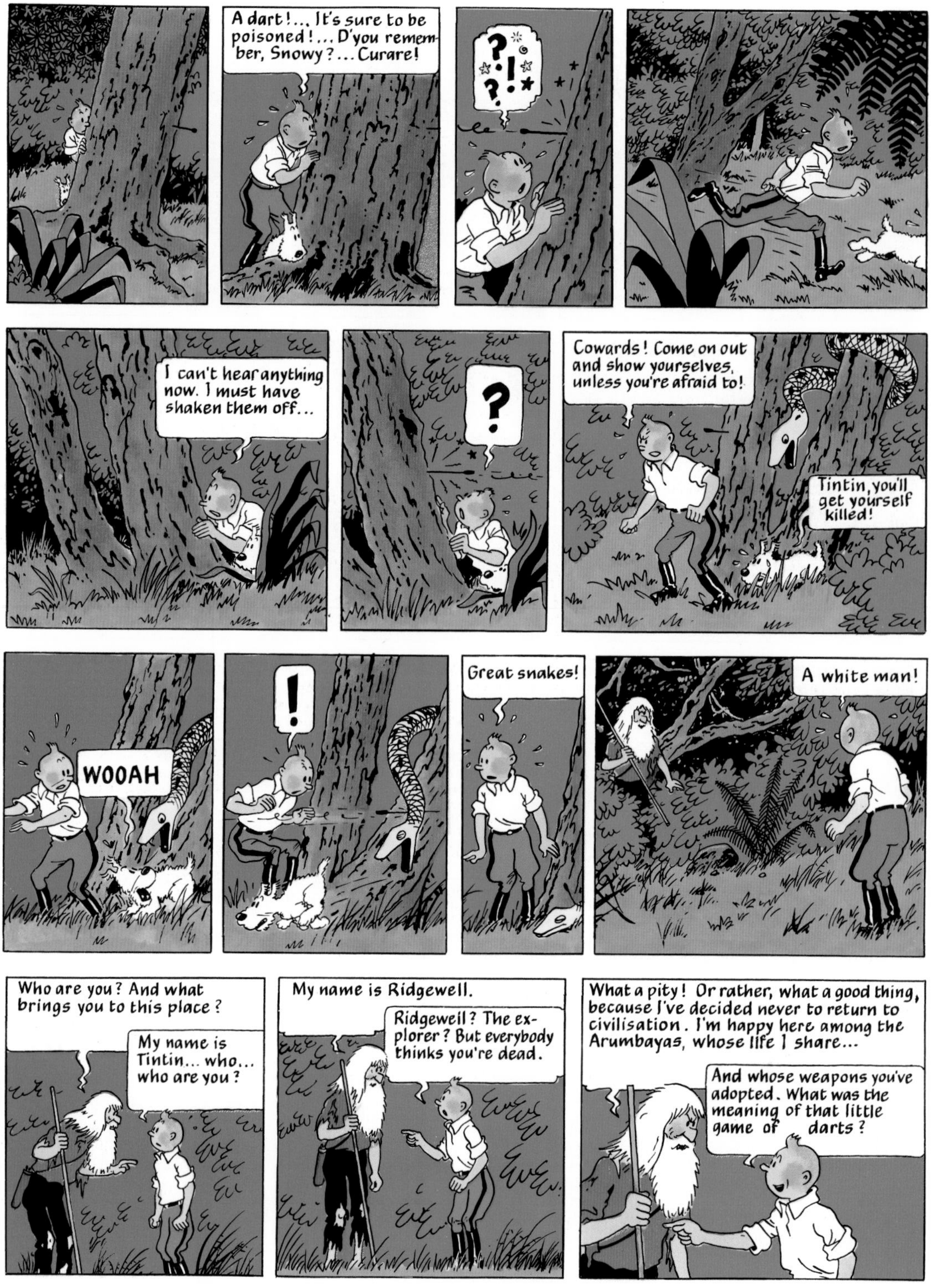
A dart!... It's sure to be poisoned!... D'you remember, Snowy?... Curare!
?!?
I can't hear anything now. I must have shaken them off...
?
Cowards! Come on out and show yourselves, unless you're afraid to!
Tintin, you'll get yourself killed!
WOOAH
!
Great snakes!
A white man!
Who are you? And what brings you to this place?
My name is Tintin... who... who are you?
My name is Ridgewell.
Ridgewell? The explorer? But everybody thinks you're dead.
What a pity! Or rather, what a good thing, because I've decided never to return to civilisation. I'm happy here among the Arumbayas, whose life I share...
And whose weapons you've adopted. What was the meaning of that little game of darts?

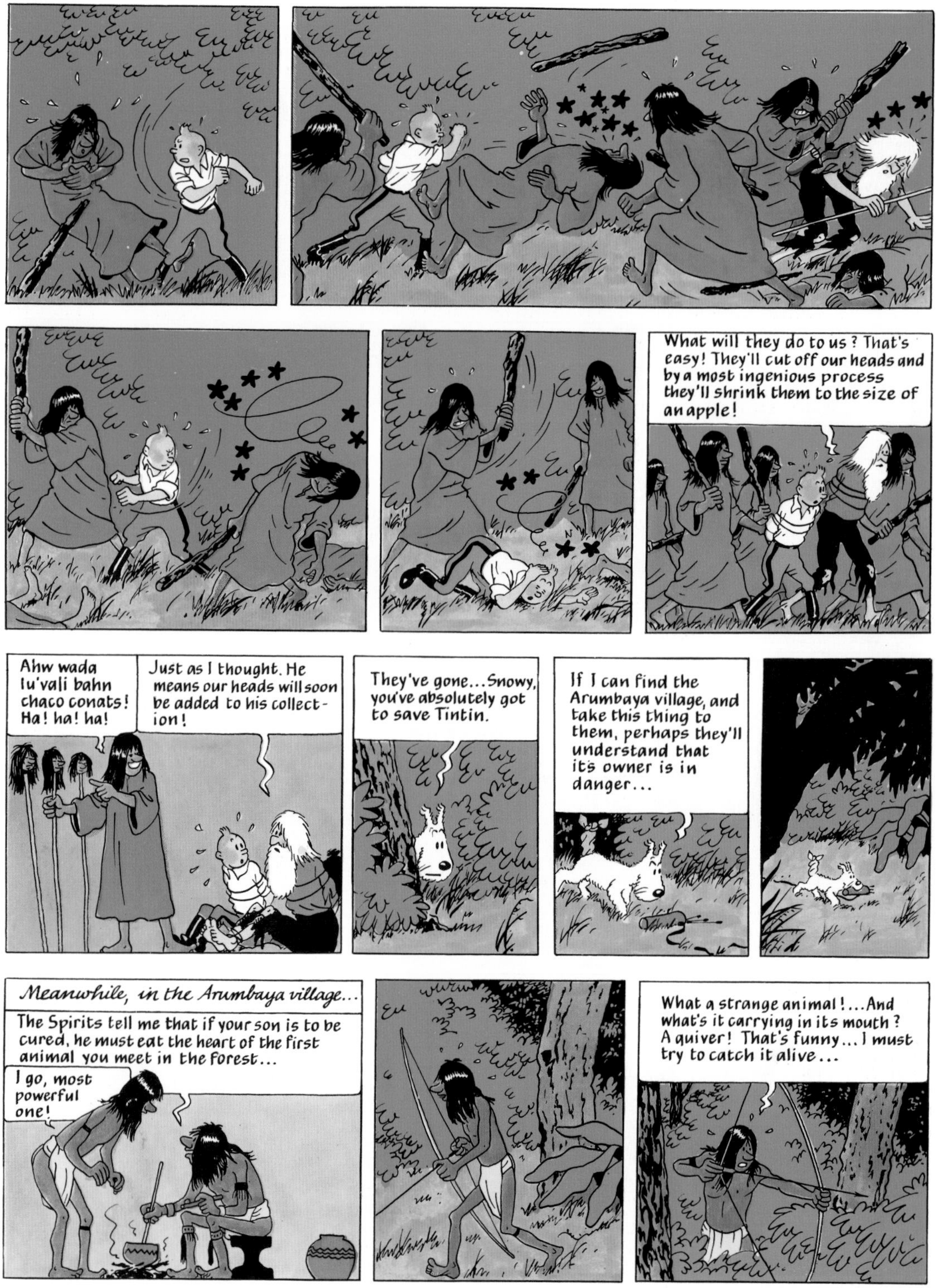
What will they do to us ? That's easy! They'll cut off our heads and by a most ingenious process they'll shrink them to the size of an apple!
Ahw wada lu'vali bahn chaco conats! Ha! ha! ha!
Just as I thought. He means our heads will soon be added to his collection!
They've gone... Snowy, you've absolutely got to save Tintin.
If I can find the Arumbaya village, and take this thing to them, perhaps they'll understand that its owner is in danger...
Meanwhile, in the Arumbaya village...
The Spirits tell me that if your son is to be cured, he must eat the heart of the first animal you meet in the forest...
I go, most powerful one!
What a strange animal!... And what's it carrying in its mouth ? A quiver! That's funny... I must try to catch it alive...

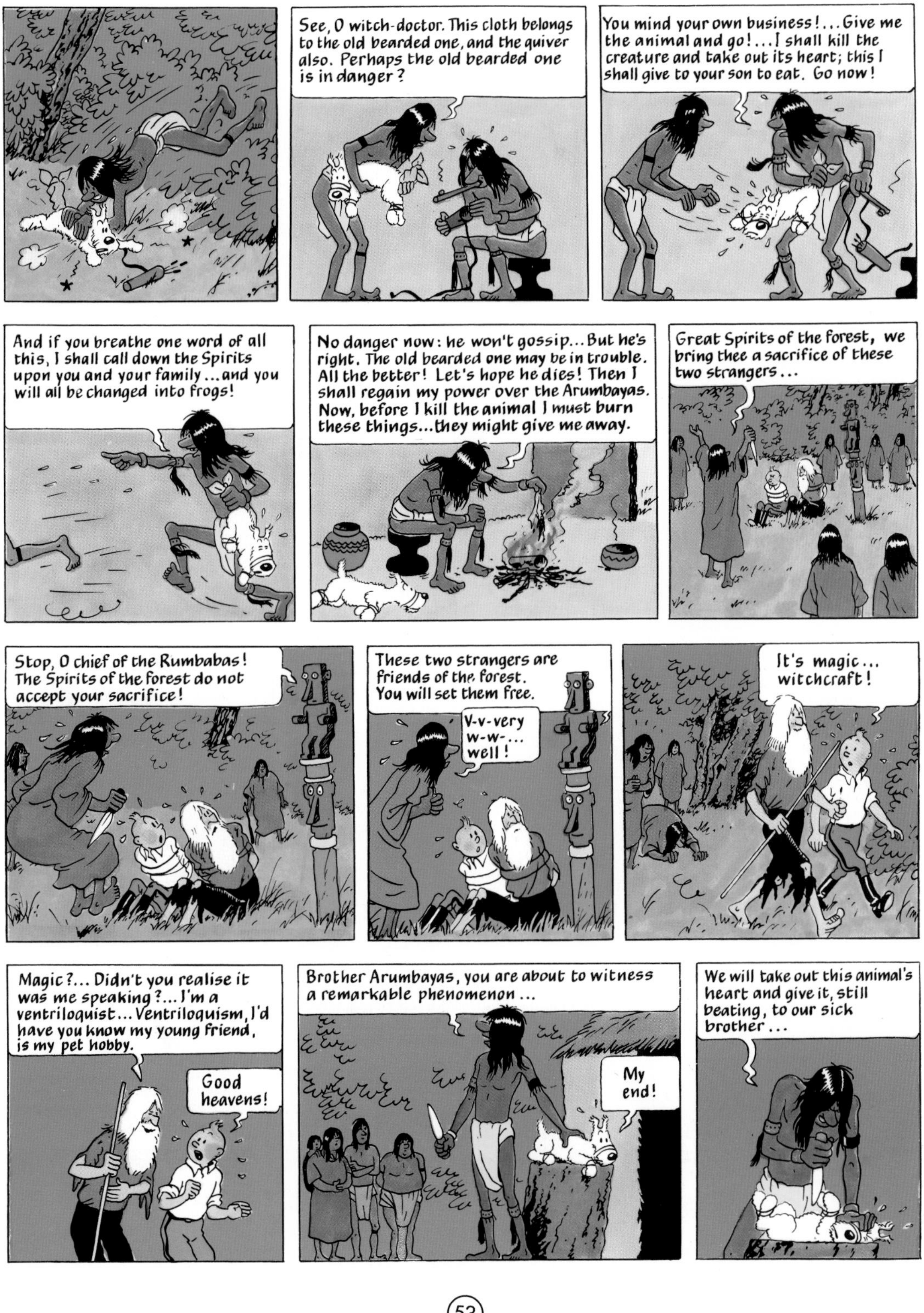
See, O witch-doctor. This cloth belongs to the old bearded one, and the quiver also. Perhaps the old bearded one is in danger?
You mind your own business!... Give me the animal and go!... I shall kill the creature and take out its heart; this I shall give to your son to eat. Go now!
And if you breathe one word of all this, I shall call down the Spirits upon you and your family... and you will all be changed into frogs!
No danger now: he won't gossip... But he's right. The old bearded one may be in trouble. All the better! Let's hope he dies! Then I shall regain my power over the Arumbayas. Now, before I kill the animal I must burn these things... they might give me away.
Great Spirits of the forest, we bring thee a sacrifice of these two strangers...
Stop, O chief of the Rumbabas! The Spirits of the forest do not accept your sacrifice!
These two strangers are friends of the forest. You will set them free.
V-v-very w-w-... well!
It's magic... witchcraft!
Magic?... Didn't you realise it was me speaking?... I'm a ventriloquist... Ventriloquism, I'd have you know my young friend, is my pet hobby.
Good heavens!
Brother Arumbayas, you are about to witness a remarkable phenomenon...
My end!
We will take out this animal's heart and give it, still beating, to our sick brother...

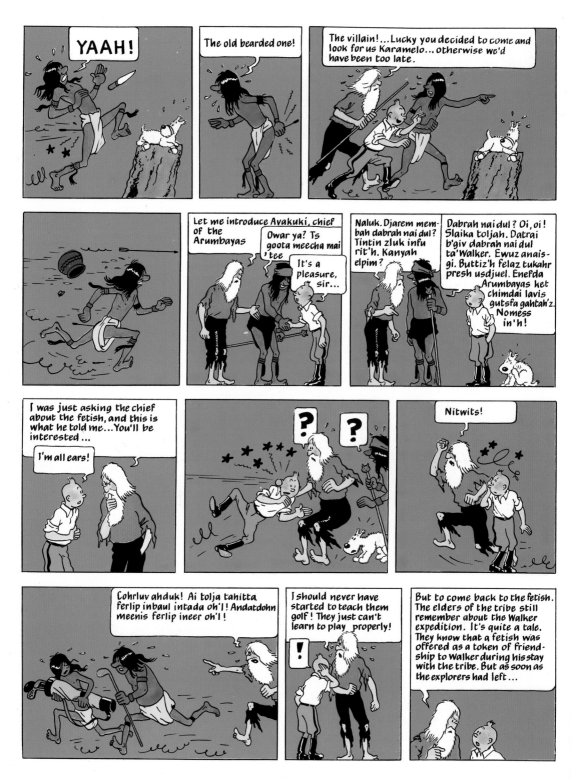

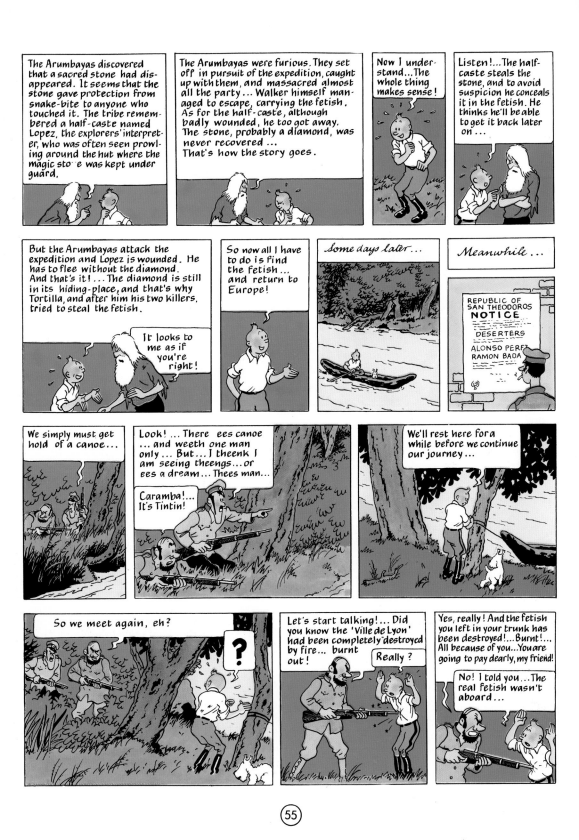

The Arumbayas discovered that a sacred stone had disappeared. It seems that the stone gave protection from snake-bite to anyone who touched it. The tribe remembered a half-caste named Lopez, the explorers' interpreter, who was often seen prowling around the hut where the magic stone was kept under guard.

The Arumbayas were furious. They set off in pursuit of the expedition, caught up with them, and massacred almost all the party... Walker himself managed to escape, carrying the fetish. As for the half-caste, although badly wounded, he too got away. The stone, probably a diamond, was never recovered... That's how the story goes.

Now I understand... The whole thing makes sense!

Listen!...The half-caste steals the stone, and to avoid suspicion he conceals it in the fetish. He thinks he'll be able to get it back later on...

But the Arumbayas attack the expedition and Lopez is wounded. He has to flee without the diamond. And that's it!... The diamond is still in its hiding-place, and that's why Tortilla, and after him his two killers, tried to steal the fetish.

It looks to me as if you're right!

So now all I have to do is find the fetish... and return to Europe!

Some days later...

Meanwhile...

REPUBLIC OF
SAN THEODOROS
NOTICE

DESERTERS

ALONSO PEREZ
RAMON BADA

We simply must get hold of a canoe...

Look!... There ees canoe... and weeth one man only... But... I theenk I am seeing theengs...or ees a dream... Thees man...

Caramba!... It's Tintin!

We'll rest here for a while before we continue our journey...

So we meet again, eh?

?

Let's start talking!... Did you know the 'Ville de Lyon' had been completely destroyed by fire... burnt out!

Really?

Yes, really! And the fetish you left in your trunk has been completely destroyed!...Burnt!... All because of you...You are going to pay dearly, my friend!

No! I told you...The real fetish wasn't aboard...

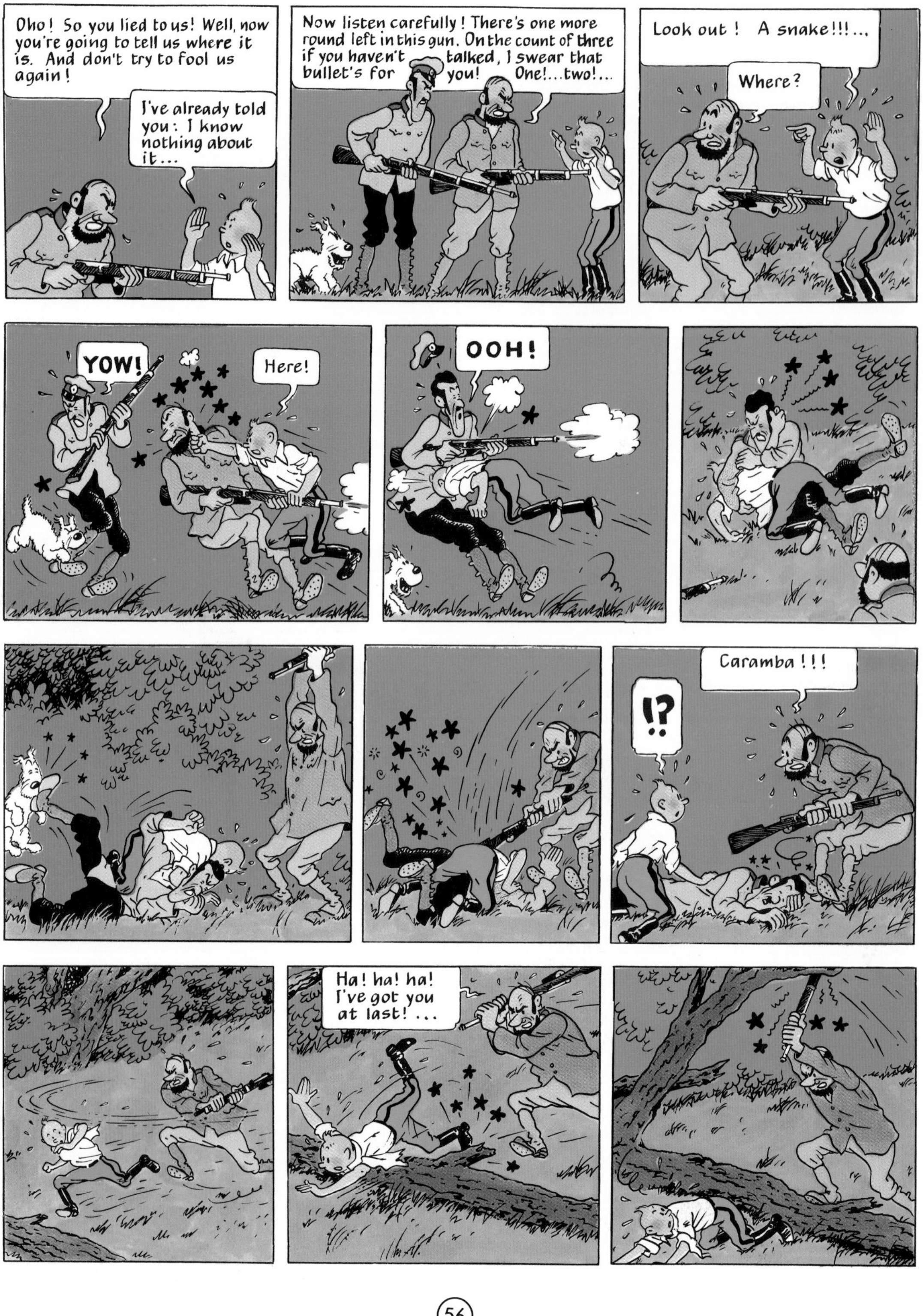
Oho! So you lied to us! Well, now you're going to tell us where it is. And don't try to fool us again!
I've already told you: I know nothing about it...
Now listen carefully! There's one more round left in this gun. On the count of three if you haven't talked, I swear that bullet's for you! One!...two!...
Look out! A snake!!!...
Where?
YOW!
Here!
OOH!
Caramba!!!
!?
Ha! ha! ha! I've got you at last!...

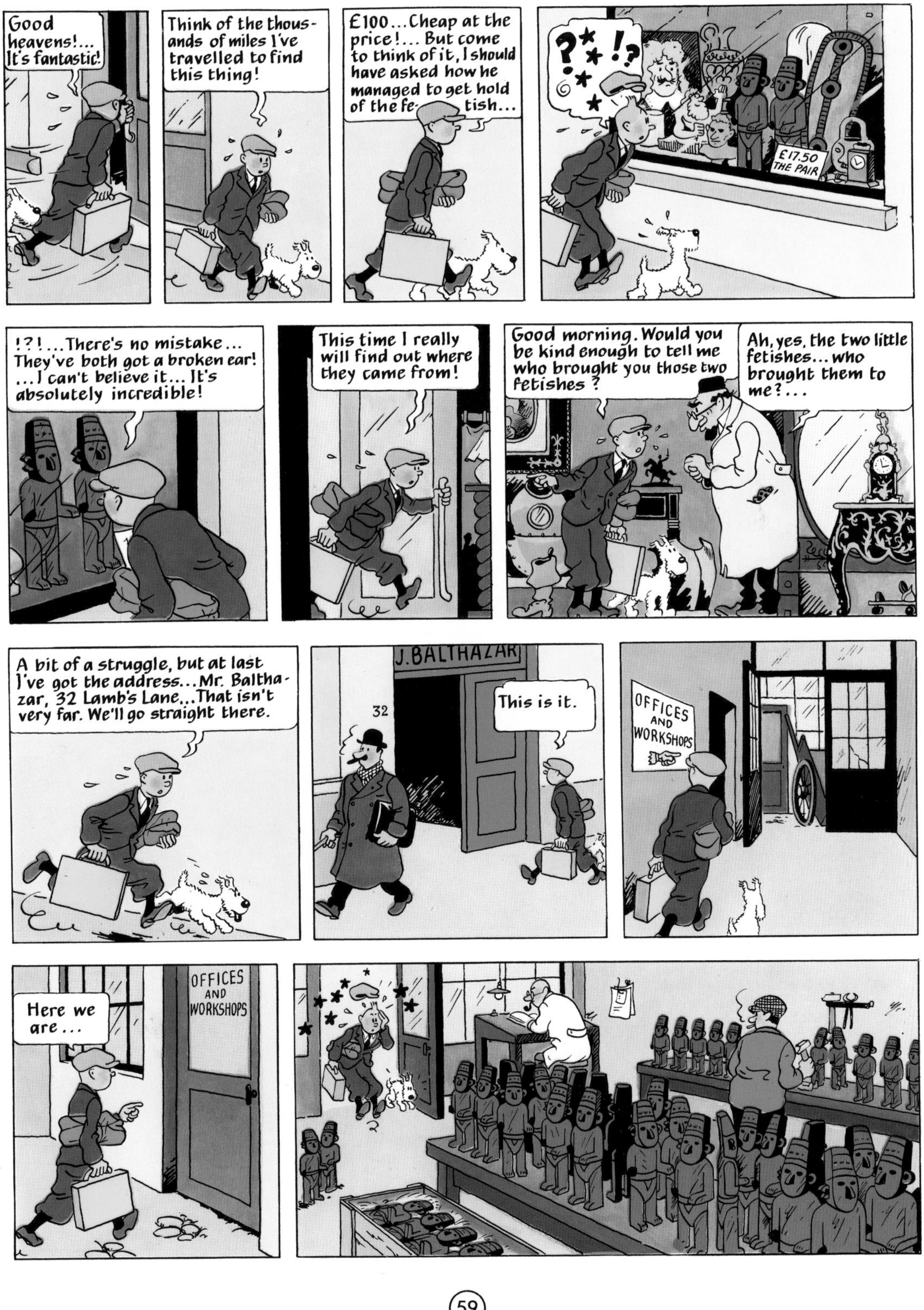
Good heavens!... It's fantastic!
Think of the thous-ands of miles I've travelled to find this thing!
£100... Cheap at the price!... But come to think of it, I should have asked how he managed to get hold of the fe- tish...
?*!?
£17.50 THE PAIR
!?!... There's no mistake... They've both got a broken ear! ...I can't believe it... It's absolutely incredible!
This time I really will find out where they came from!
Good morning. Would you be kind enough to tell me who brought you those two fetishes?
Ah, yes, the two little fetishes... who brought them to me?...
A bit of a struggle, but at last I've got the address... Mr. Balthazar, 32 Lamb's Lane... That isn't very far. We'll go straight there.
J. BALTHAZAR
32
This is it.
OFFICES AND WORKSHOPS
Here we are...
OFFICES AND WORKSHOPS

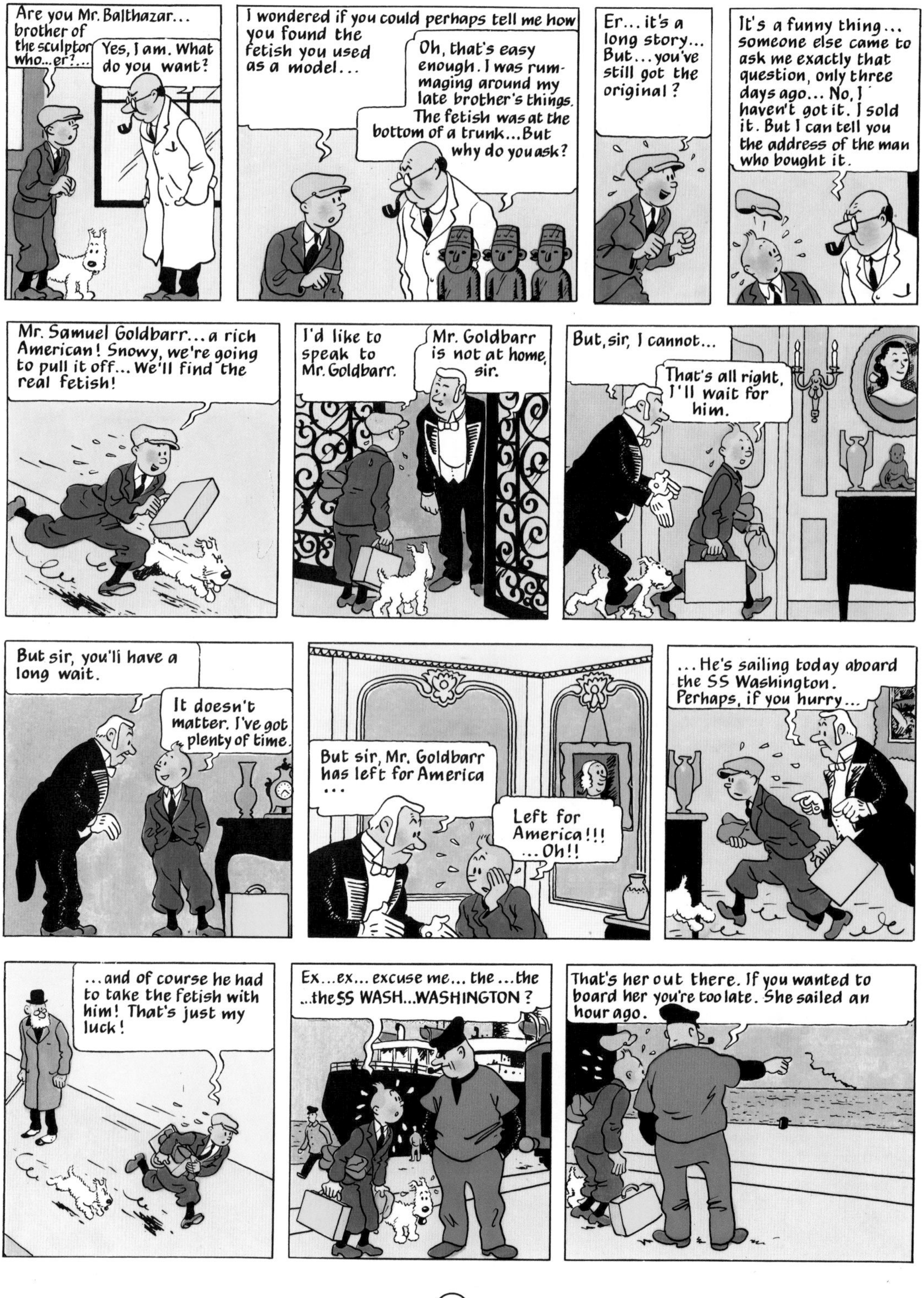
Are you Mr. Balthazar... brother of the sculptor who...er?...
Yes, I am. What do you want?
I wondered if you could perhaps tell me how you found the fetish you used as a model...
Oh, that's easy enough. I was rummaging around my late brother's things. The fetish was at the bottom of a trunk... But why do you ask?
Er... it's a long story... But... you've still got the original?
It's a funny thing... someone else came to ask me exactly that question, only three days ago... No, I haven't got it. I sold it. But I can tell you the address of the man who bought it.
Mr. Samuel Goldbarr... a rich American! Snowy, we're going to pull it off... We'll find the real fetish!
I'd like to speak to Mr. Goldbarr.
Mr. Goldbarr is not at home, sir.
But, sir, I cannot...
That's all right, I'll wait for him.
But sir, you'll have a long wait.
It doesn't matter. I've got plenty of time.
But sir, Mr. Goldbarr has left for America...
Left for America!!! ...Oh!!
... He's sailing today aboard the SS Washington. Perhaps, if you hurry...
...and of course he had to take the fetish with him! That's just my luck!
Ex...ex... excuse me... the ...the ...the SS WASH...WASHINGTON?
That's her out there. If you wanted to board her you're too late. She sailed an hour ago.

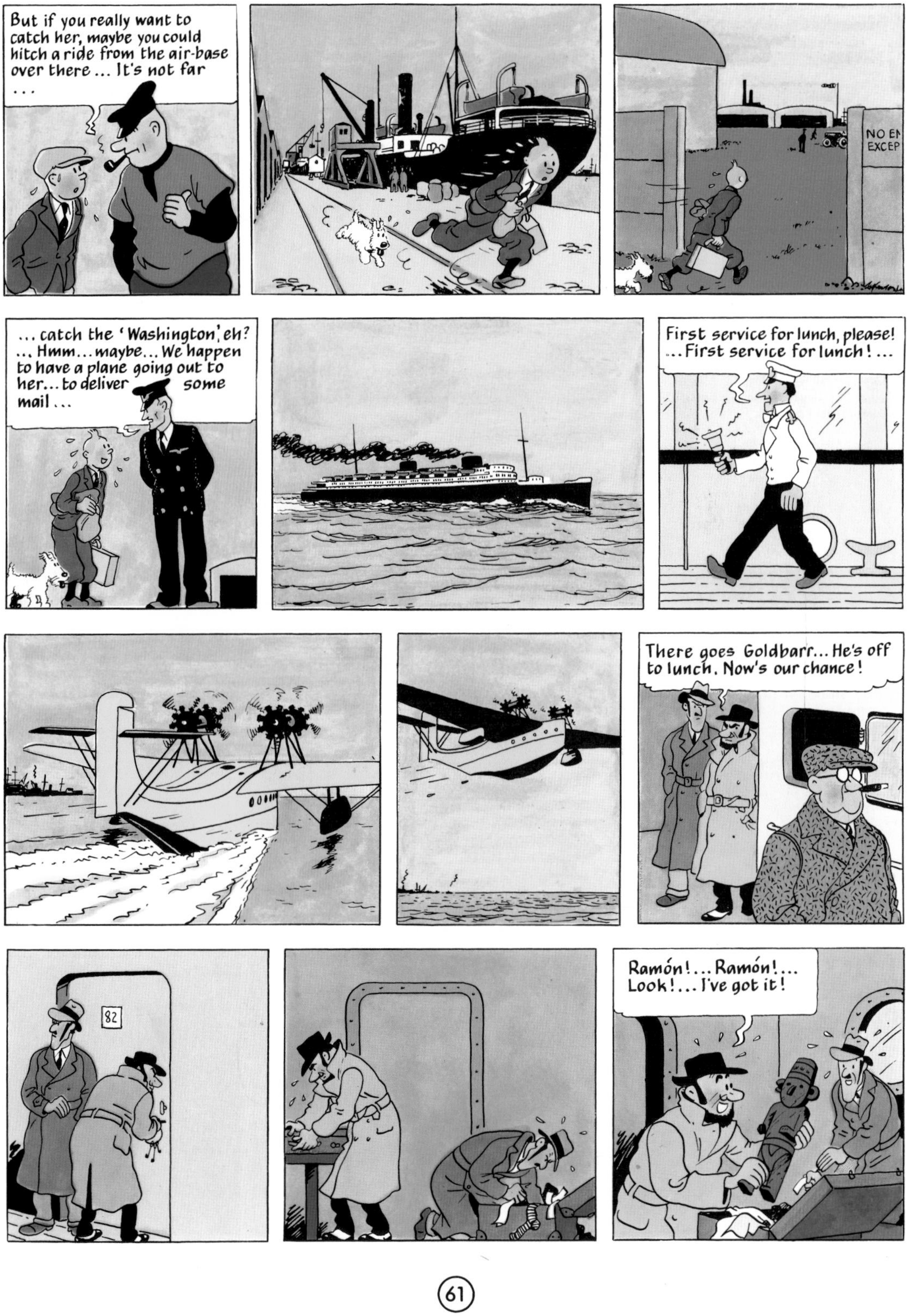
But if you really want to catch her, maybe you could hitch a ride from the air-base over there ... It's not far ...
NO EN
EXCEP
... catch the 'Washington', eh? ... Hmm ... maybe ... We happen to have a plane going out to her ... to deliver some mail ...
First service for lunch, please! ... First service for lunch! ...
There goes Goldbarr ... He's off to lunch. Now's our chance!
82
Ramón! ... Ramón! ... Look! ... I've got it!

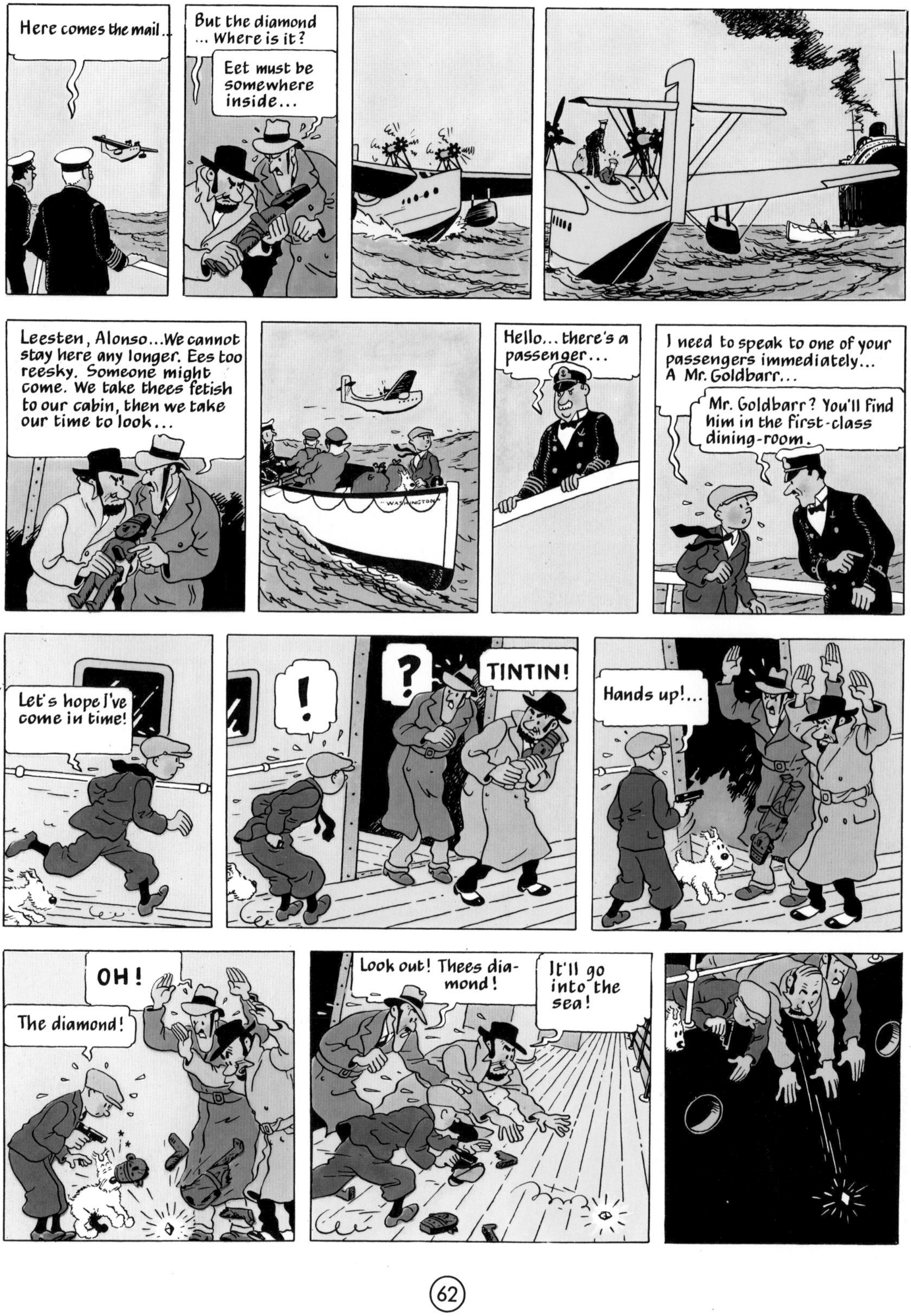

Here comes the mail...
But the diamond ... Where is it?
Eet must be somewhere inside...
Leesten, Alonso...We cannot stay here any longer. Ees too reesky. Someone might come. We take thees fetish to our cabin, then we take our time to look...
"WASHINGTON"
Hello... there's a passenger...
I need to speak to one of your passengers immediately... A Mr. Goldbarr...
Mr. Goldbarr? You'll find him in the first-class dining-room.
Let's hope I've come in time!
!
?
TINTIN!
Hands up!...
OH!
The diamond!
Look out! Thees diamond!
It'll go into the sea!

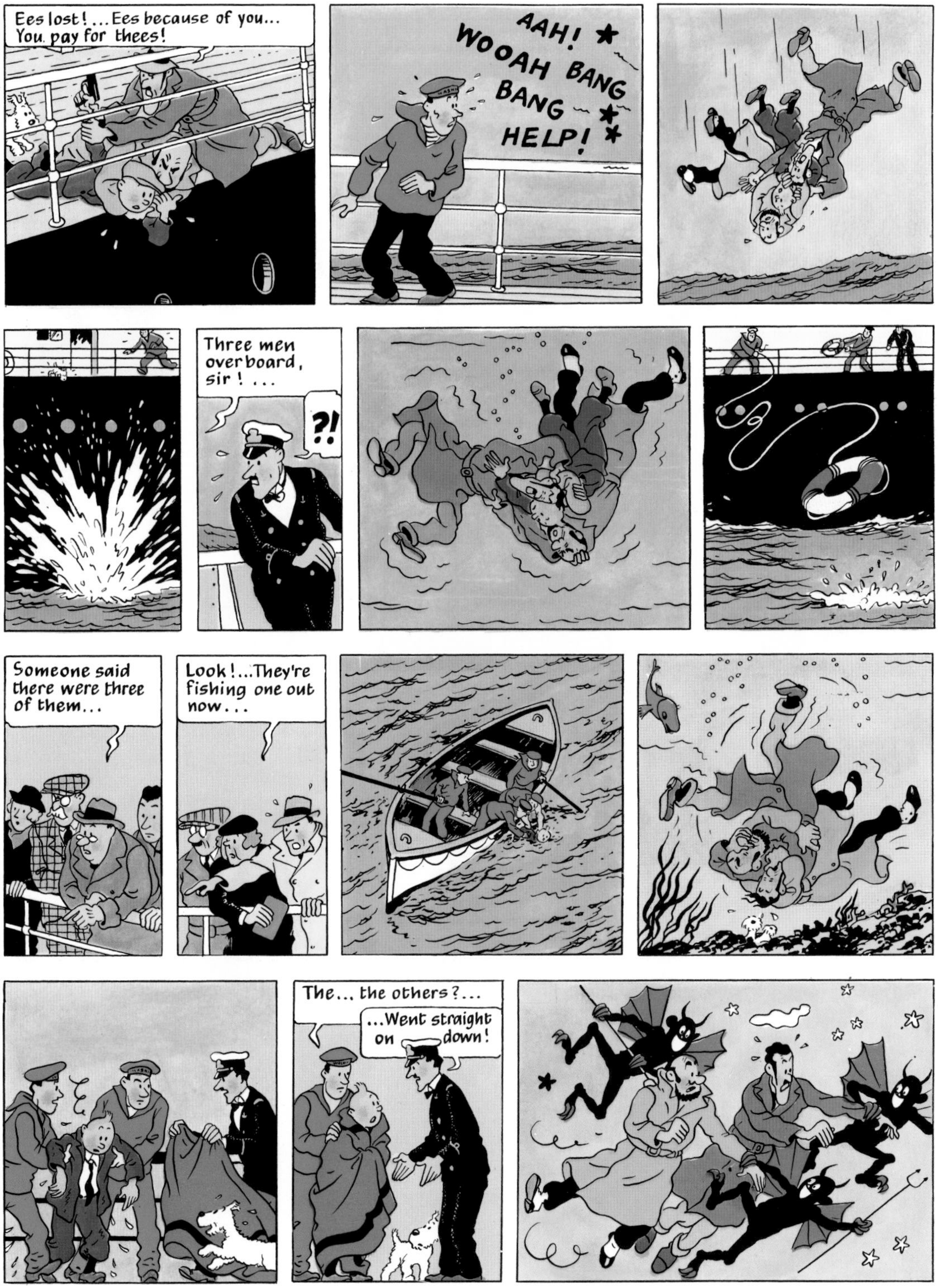
Ees lost! ... Ees because of you... You pay for thees!
AAH! WOOAH BANG BANG HELP!
Three men overboard, sir! ...
?!
Someone said there were three of them...
Look! ... They're fishing one out now...
The... the others? ...
...Went straight on down!

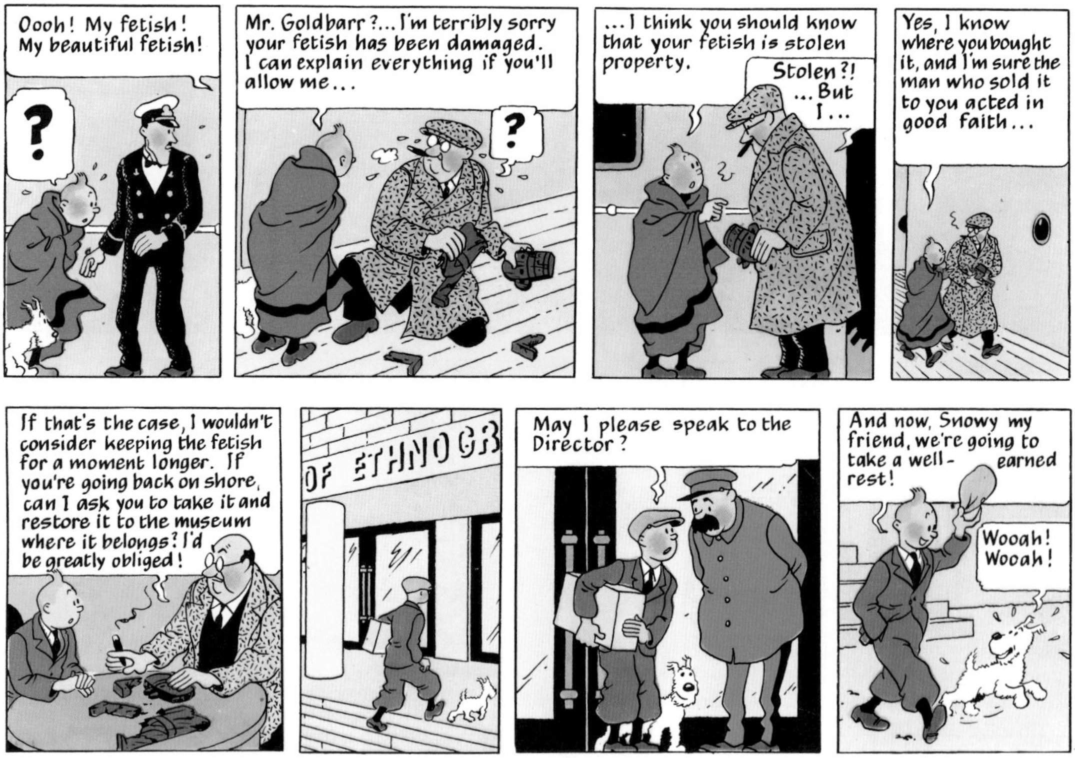
Oooh! My fetish! My beautiful fetish!
?
Mr. Goldbarr?... I'm terribly sorry your fetish has been damaged. I can explain everything if you'll allow me...
?
... I think you should know that your fetish is stolen property.
Stolen?! ... But I...
Yes, I know where you bought it, and I'm sure the man who sold it to you acted in good faith...
If that's the case, I wouldn't consider keeping the fetish for a moment longer. If you're going back on shore, can I ask you to take it and restore it to the museum where it belongs? I'd be greatly obliged!
OF ETHNOGR
May I please speak to the Director?
And now, Snowy my friend, we're going to take a well-earned rest!
Wooah! Wooah!

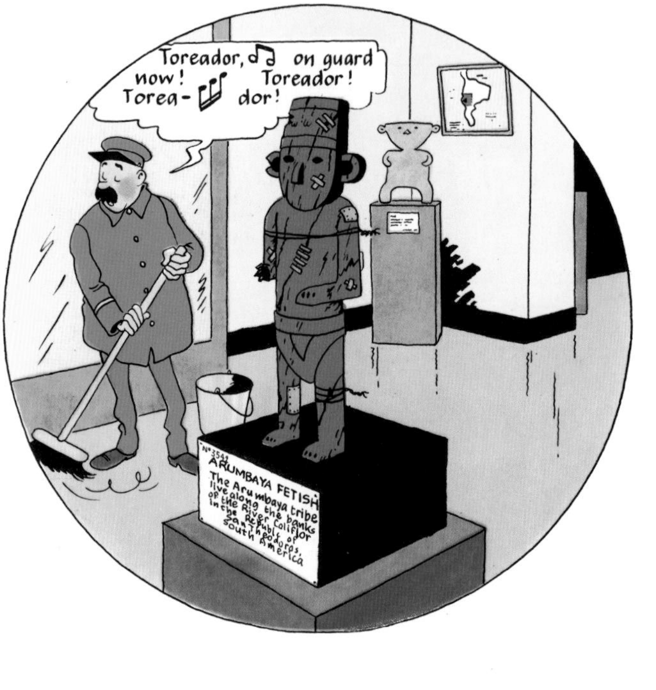
Toreador, on guard now! Toreador! Torea- dor!
Nº 3549
ARUMBAYA FETISH
The Arumbaya tribe live along the banks of the River Coliflor in the Republic of San Theodoros, South America

HERGÉ

THE ADVENTURES OF TINTIN

THE BLACK ISLAND

THE BLACK ISLAND

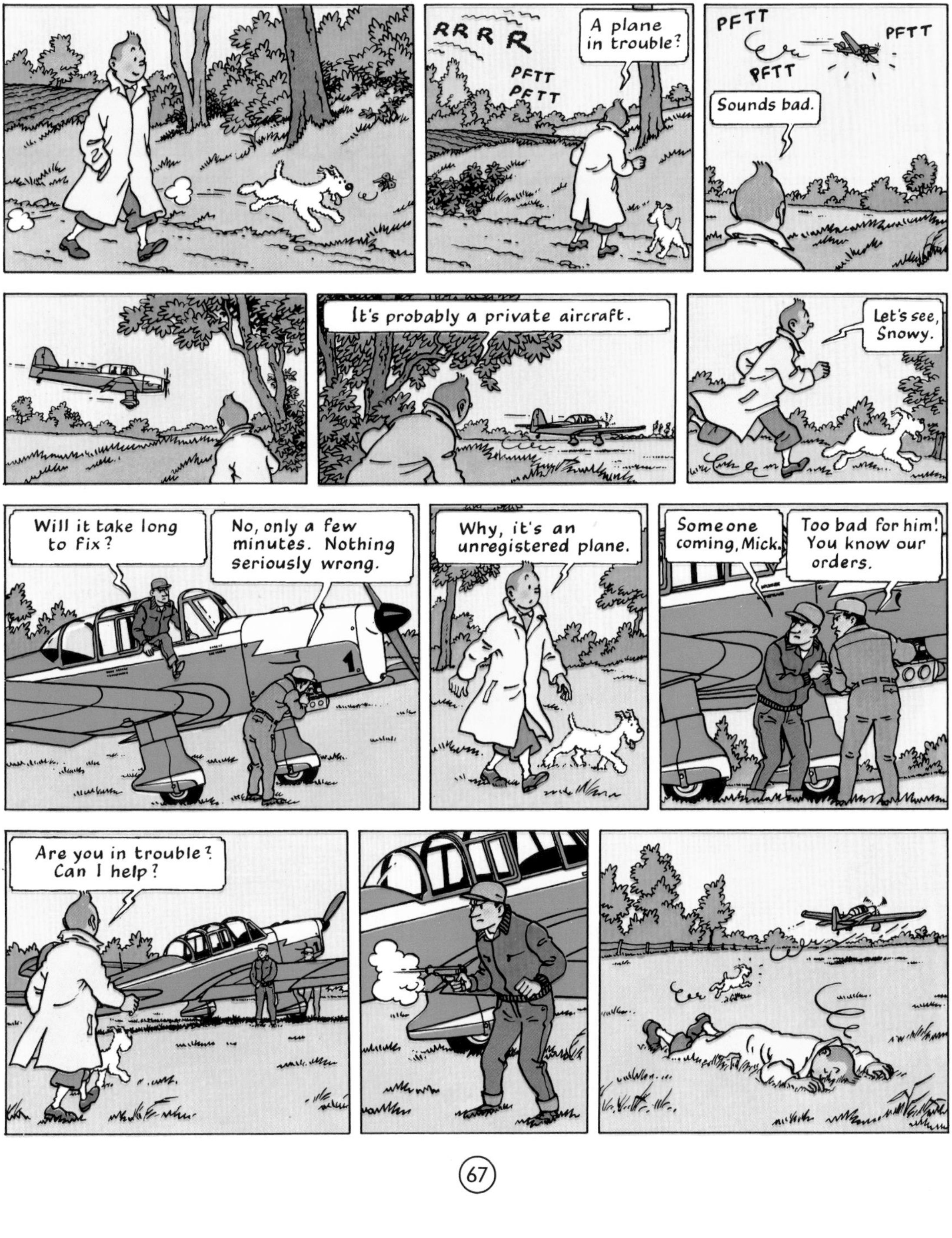

RRRR
PFTT
PFTT
A plane in trouble?
PFTT
PFTT
PFTT
Sounds bad.
It's probably a private aircraft.
Let's see, Snowy.
Will it take long to fix?
No, only a few minutes. Nothing seriously wrong.
Why, it's an unregistered plane.
Someone coming, Mick.
Too bad for him! You know our orders.
Are you in trouble? Can I help?

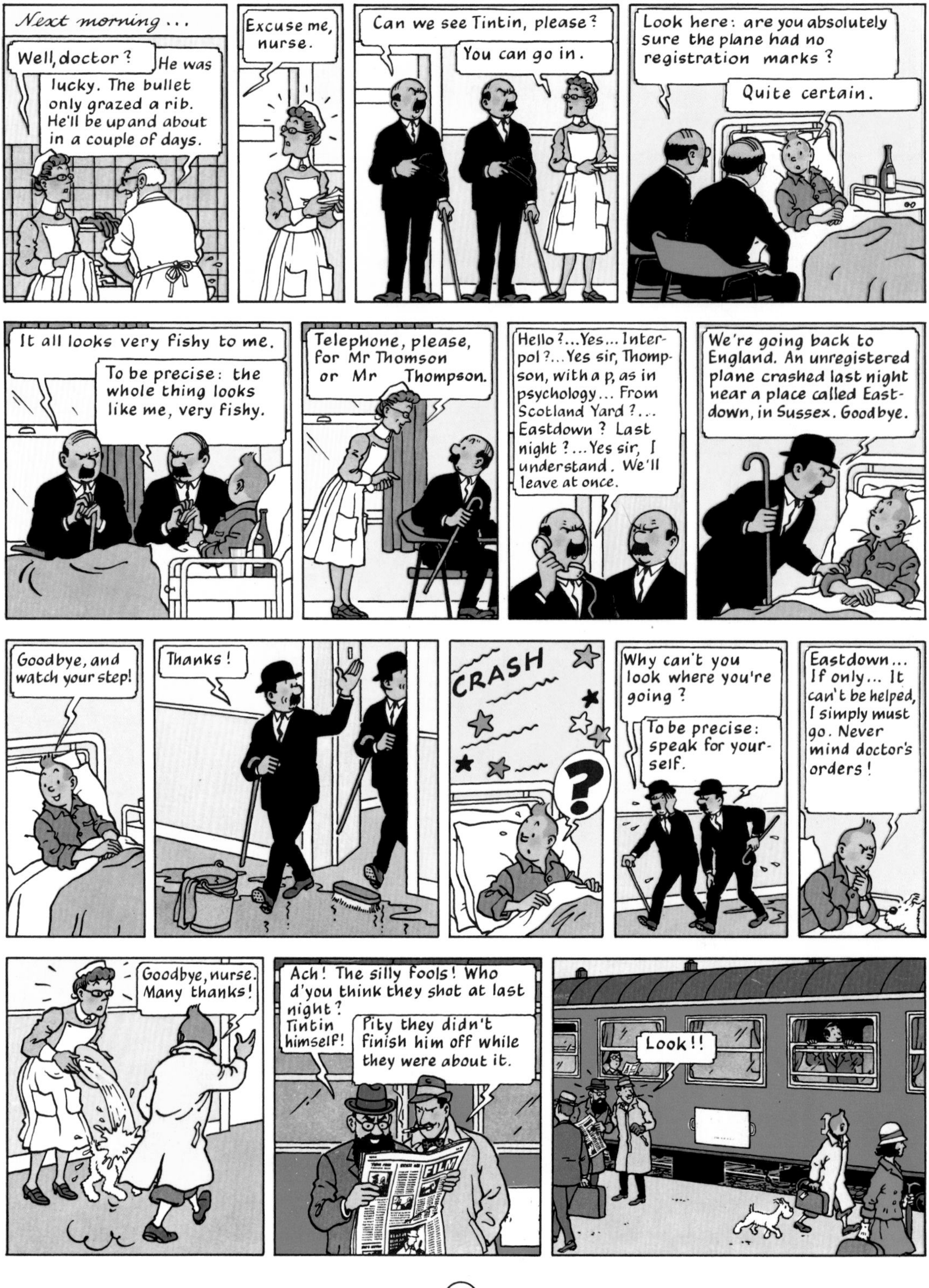
Next morning...
Well, doctor?
He was lucky. The bullet only grazed a rib. He'll be up and about in a couple of days.
Excuse me, nurse.
Can we see Tintin, please?
You can go in.
Look here: are you absolutely sure the plane had no registration marks?
Quite certain.
It all looks very fishy to me.
To be precise: the whole thing looks like me, very fishy.
Telephone, please, for Mr Thomson or Mr Thompson.
Hello?... Yes... Interpol?... Yes sir, Thompson, with a p, as in psychology... From Scotland Yard?... Eastdown? Last night?... Yes sir, I understand. We'll leave at once.
We're going back to England. An unregistered plane crashed last night near a place called Eastdown, in Sussex. Goodbye.
Goodbye, and watch your step!
Thanks!
CRASH
?
Why can't you look where you're going?
To be precise: speak for yourself.
Eastdown... If only... It can't be helped, I simply must go. Never mind doctor's orders!
Goodbye, nurse. Many thanks!
Ach! The silly fools! Who d'you think they shot at last night? Tintin himself!
Pity they didn't finish him off while they were about it.
FILM
Look!!

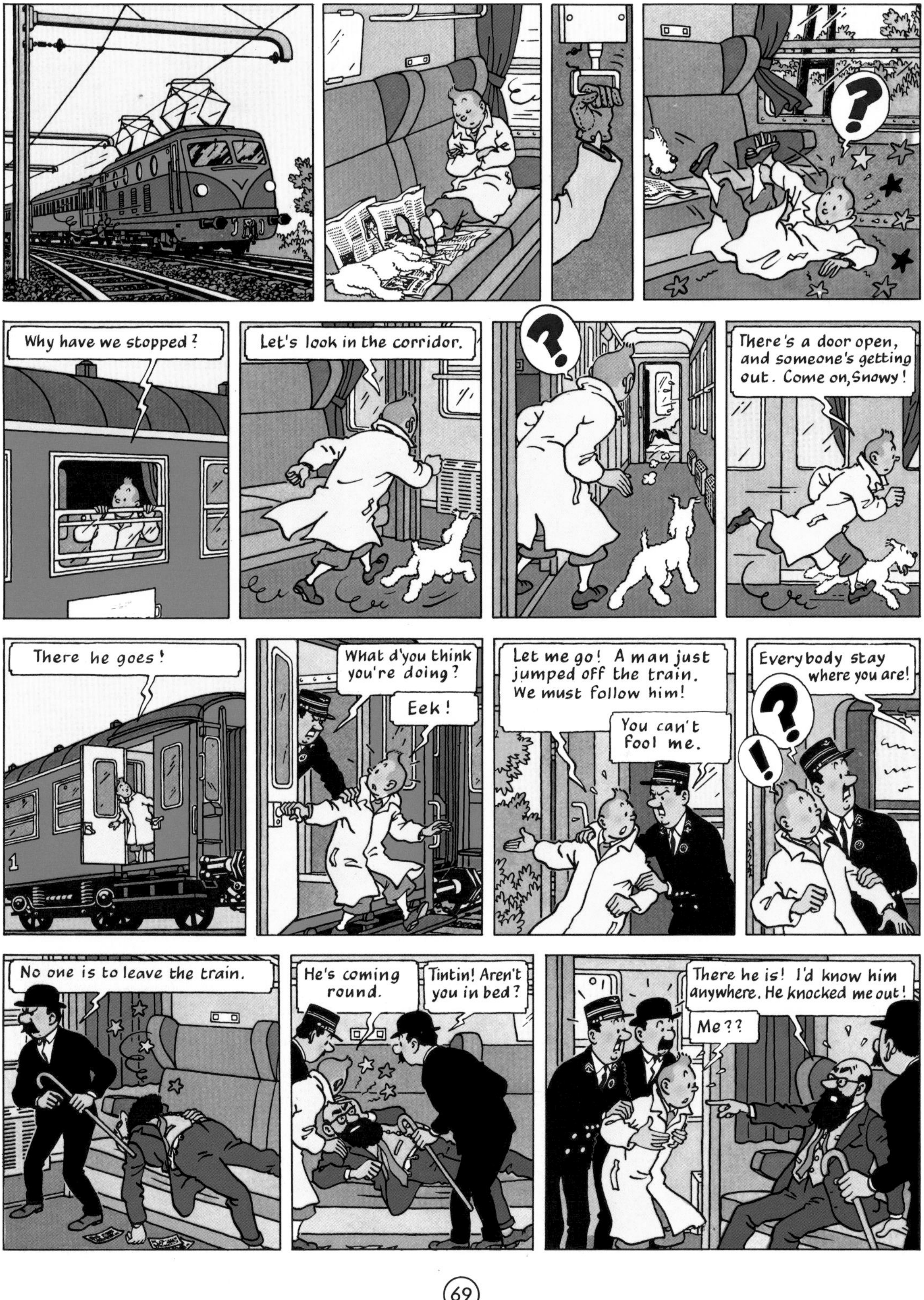
Why have we stopped?
Let's look in the corridor.
There's a door open, and someone's getting out. Come on, Snowy!
There he goes!
What d'you think you're doing?
Eek!
Let me go! A man just jumped off the train. We must follow him!
You can't fool me.
Everybody stay where you are!
No one is to leave the train.
He's coming round.
Tintin! Aren't you in bed?
There he is! I'd know him anywhere. He knocked me out!
Me??

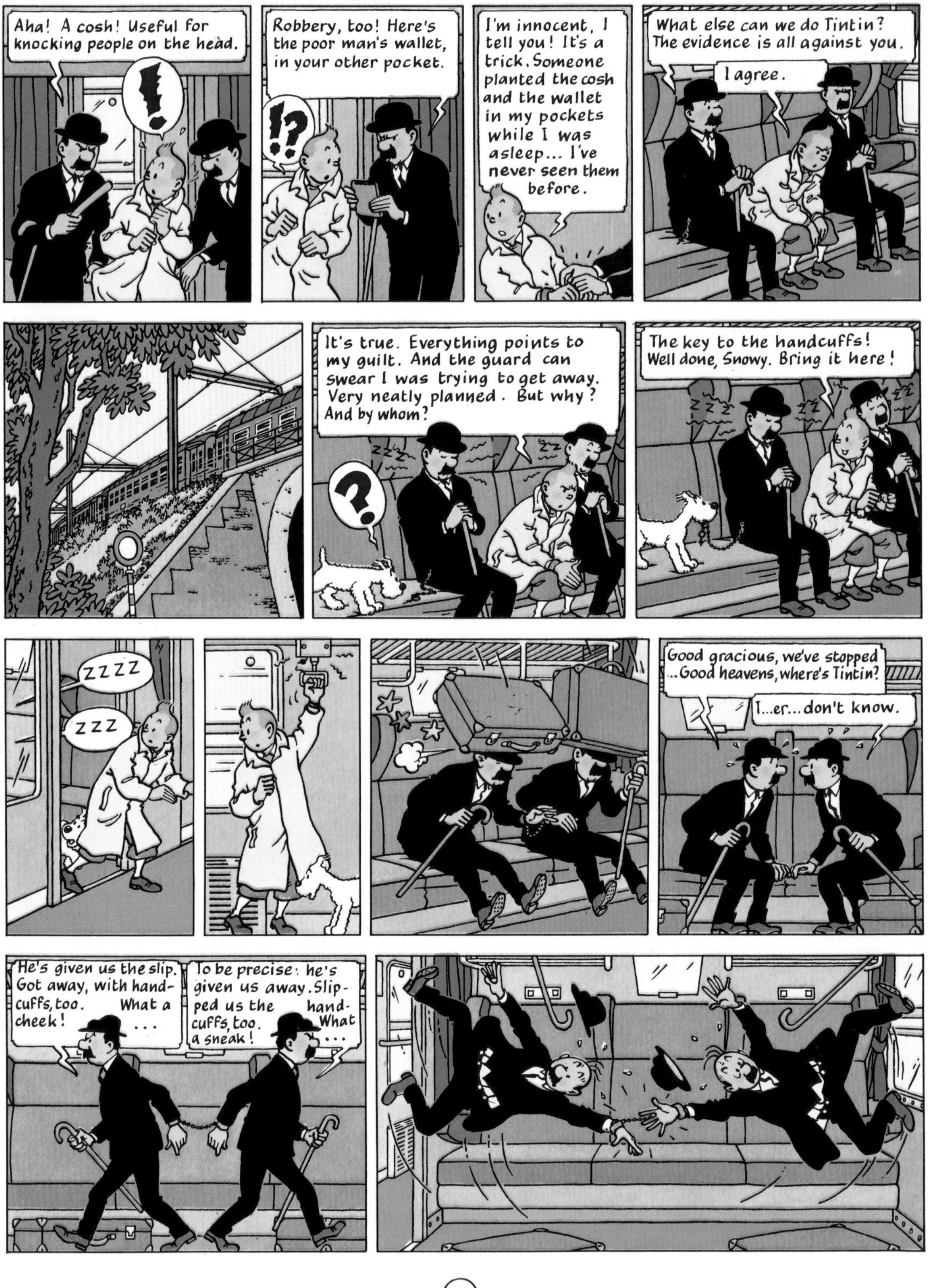
Aha! A cosh! Useful for knocking people on the head.
!
Robbery, too! Here's the poor man's wallet, in your other pocket.
!?
I'm innocent, I tell you! It's a trick. Someone planted the cosh and the wallet in my pockets while I was asleep... I've never seen them before.
What else can we do Tintin? The evidence is all against you.
I agree.
It's true. Everything points to my guilt. And the guard can swear I was trying to get away. Very neatly planned. But why? And by whom?
?
The key to the handcuffs! Well done, Snowy. Bring it here!
ZZZZ
ZZZ
Good gracious, we've stopped ...Good heavens, where's Tintin?
I...er...don't know.
He's given us the slip. Got away, with handcuffs, too. What a cheek! ...
To be precise: he's given us away. Slipped us the handcuffs, too. What a sneak! ...

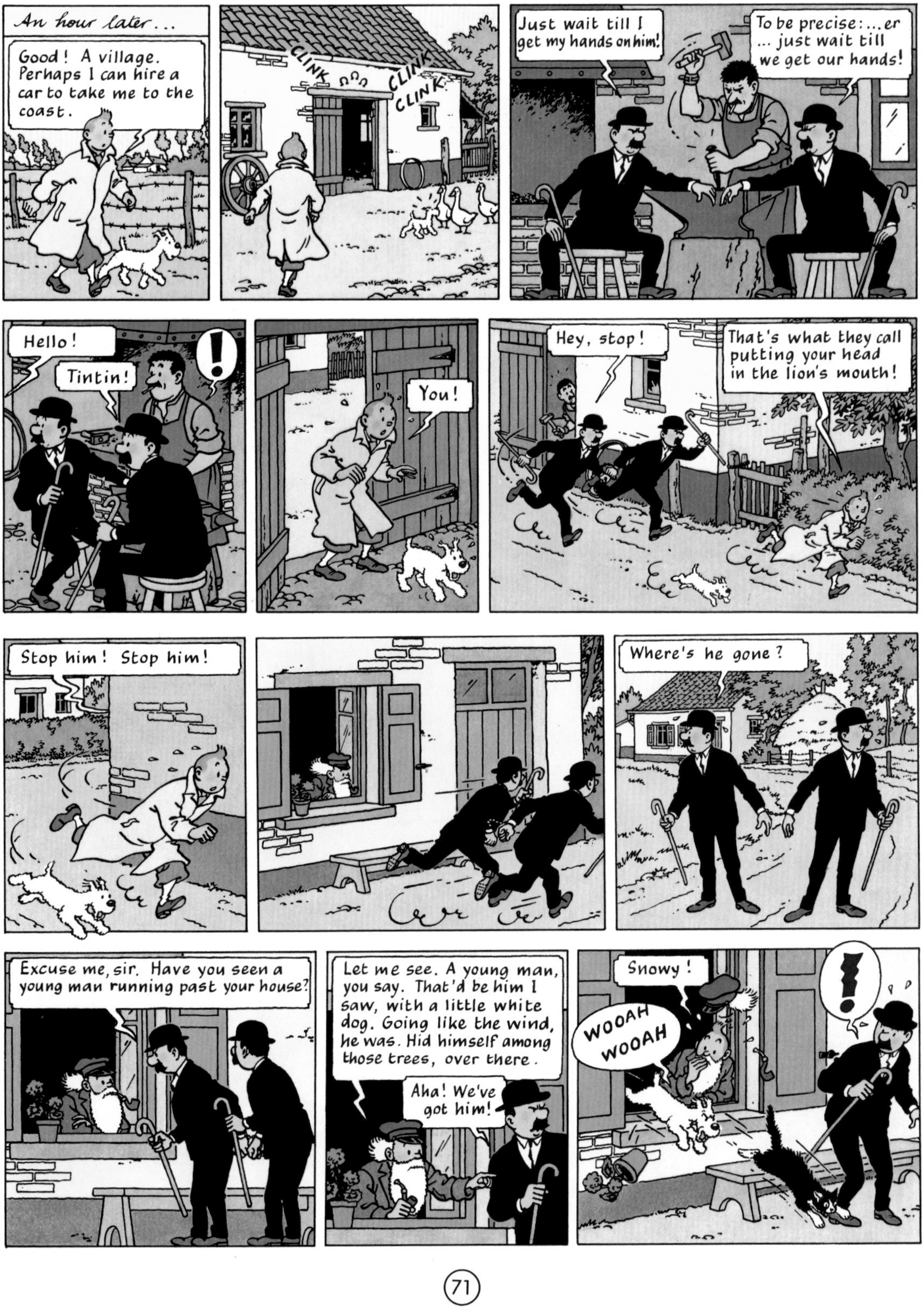
An hour later...
Good! A village. Perhaps I can hire a car to take me to the coast.
CLINK
CLINK
CLINK
Just wait till I get my hands on him!
To be precise:...er ... just wait till we get our hands!
Hello!
Tintin!
!
You!
Hey, stop!
That's what they call putting your head in the lion's mouth!
Stop him! Stop him!
Where's he gone?
Excuse me, sir. Have you seen a young man running past your house?
Let me see. A young man, you say. That'd be him I saw, with a little white dog. Going like the wind, he was. Hid himself among those trees, over there.
Aha! We've got him!
Snowy!
WOOAH WOOAH
!

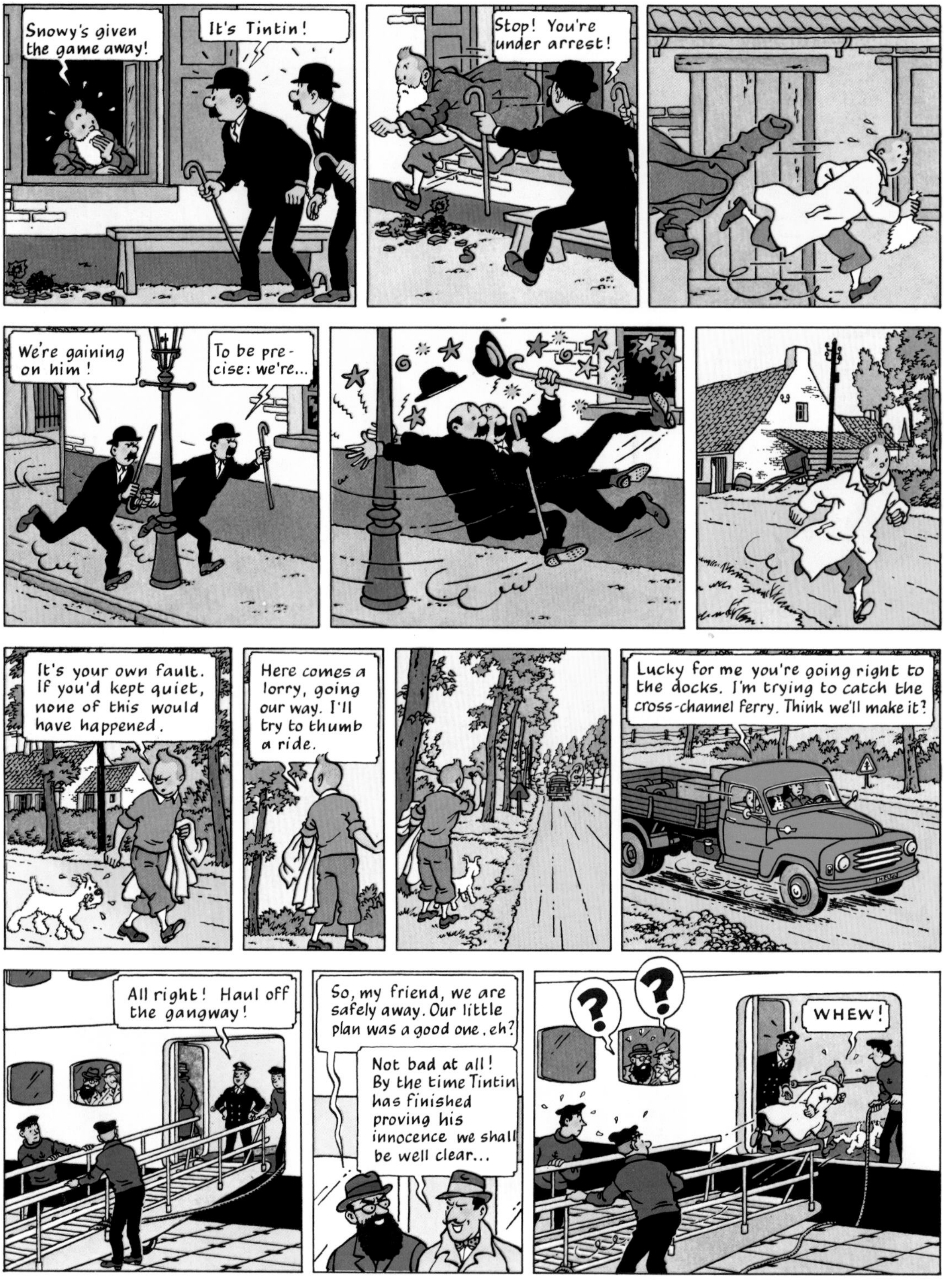
Snowy's given the game away!
It's Tintin!
Stop! You're under arrest!
We're gaining on him!
To be precise: we're...
It's your own fault. If you'd kept quiet, none of this would have happened.
Here comes a lorry, going our way. I'll try to thumb a ride.
Lucky for me you're going right to the docks. I'm trying to catch the cross-channel ferry. Think we'll make it?
All right! Haul off the gangway!
So, my friend, we are safely away. Our little plan was a good one, eh?
Not bad at all! By the time Tintin has finished proving his innocence we shall be well clear...
?
?
WHEW!

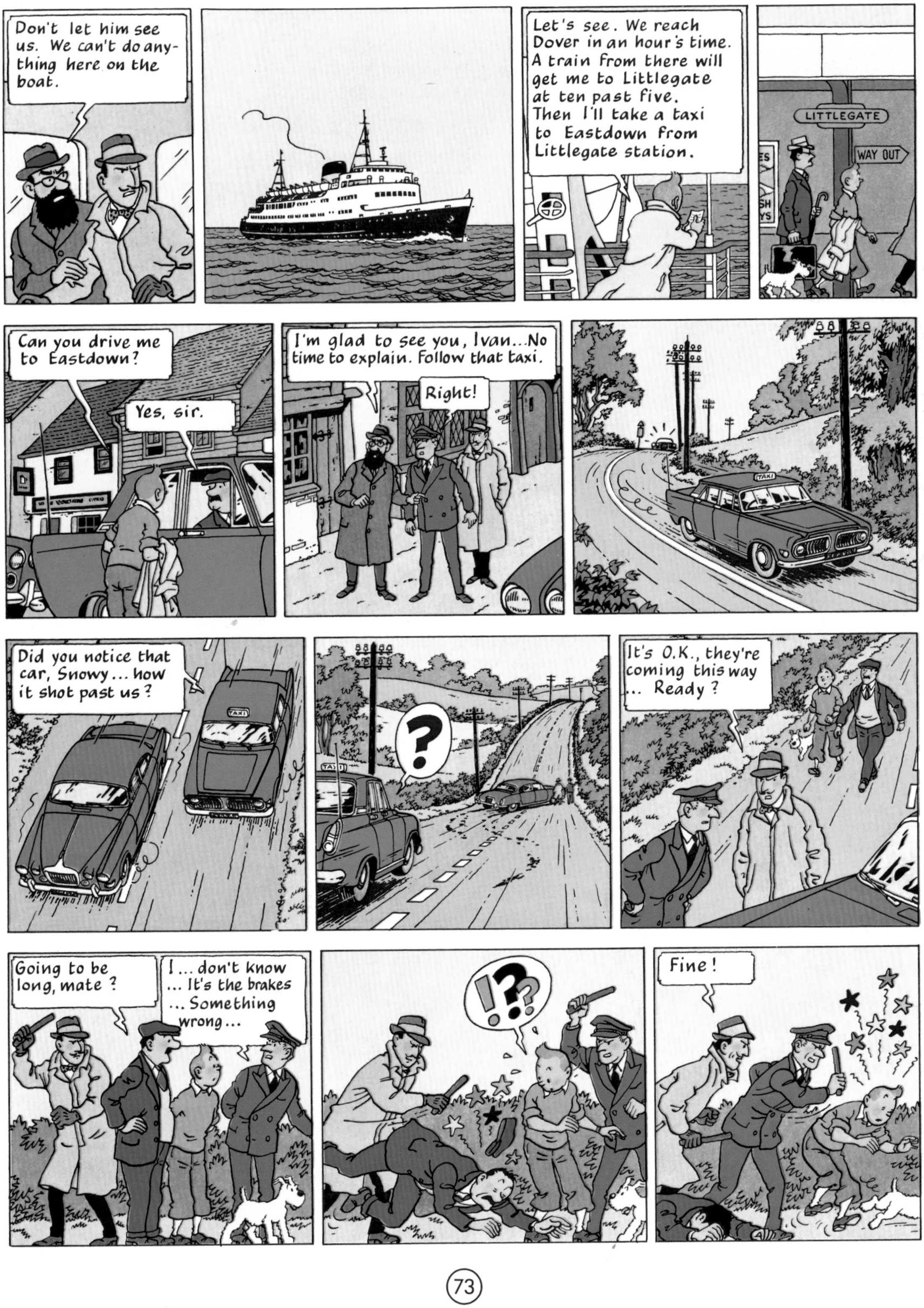
Don't let him see us. We can't do anything here on the boat.
Let's see. We reach Dover in an hour's time. A train from there will get me to Littlegate at ten past five. Then I'll take a taxi to Eastdown from Littlegate station.
LITTLEGATE
WAY OUT
Can you drive me to Eastdown?
Yes, sir.
I'm glad to see you, Ivan... No time to explain. Follow that taxi.
Right!
TAXI
Did you notice that car, Snowy... how it shot past us?
TAXI
?
TAXI
It's O.K., they're coming this way ... Ready?
Going to be long, mate?
I... don't know ... It's the brakes ... Something wrong...
!??
Fine!

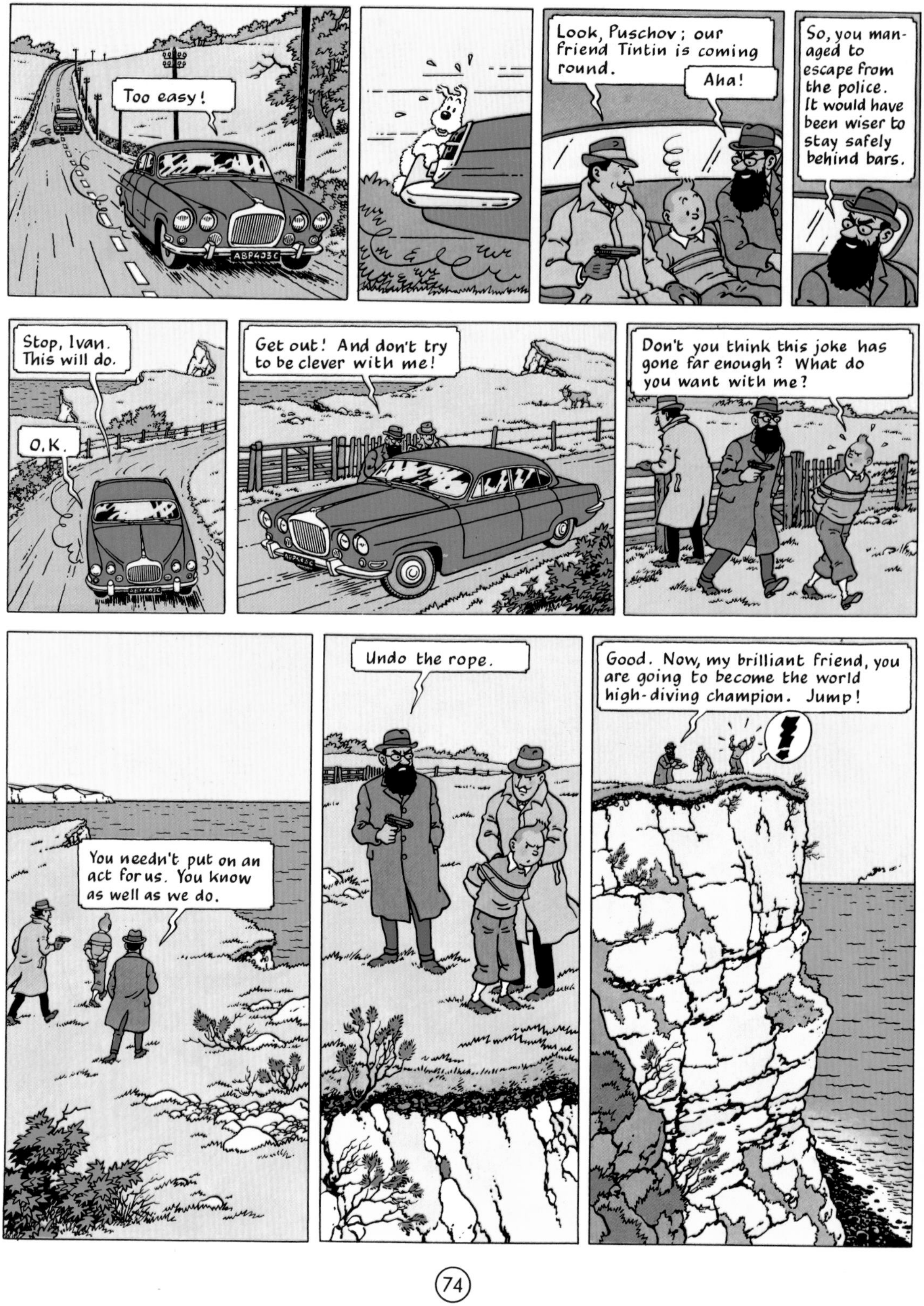

Too easy!
Look, Puschov; our friend Tintin is coming round.
Aha!
So, you managed to escape from the police. It would have been wiser to stay safely behind bars.
Stop, Ivan. This will do.
O.K.
Get out! And don't try to be clever with me!
Don't you think this joke has gone far enough? What do you want with me?
You needn't put on an act for us. You know as well as we do.
Undo the rope.
Good. Now, my brilliant friend, you are going to become the world high-diving champion. Jump!

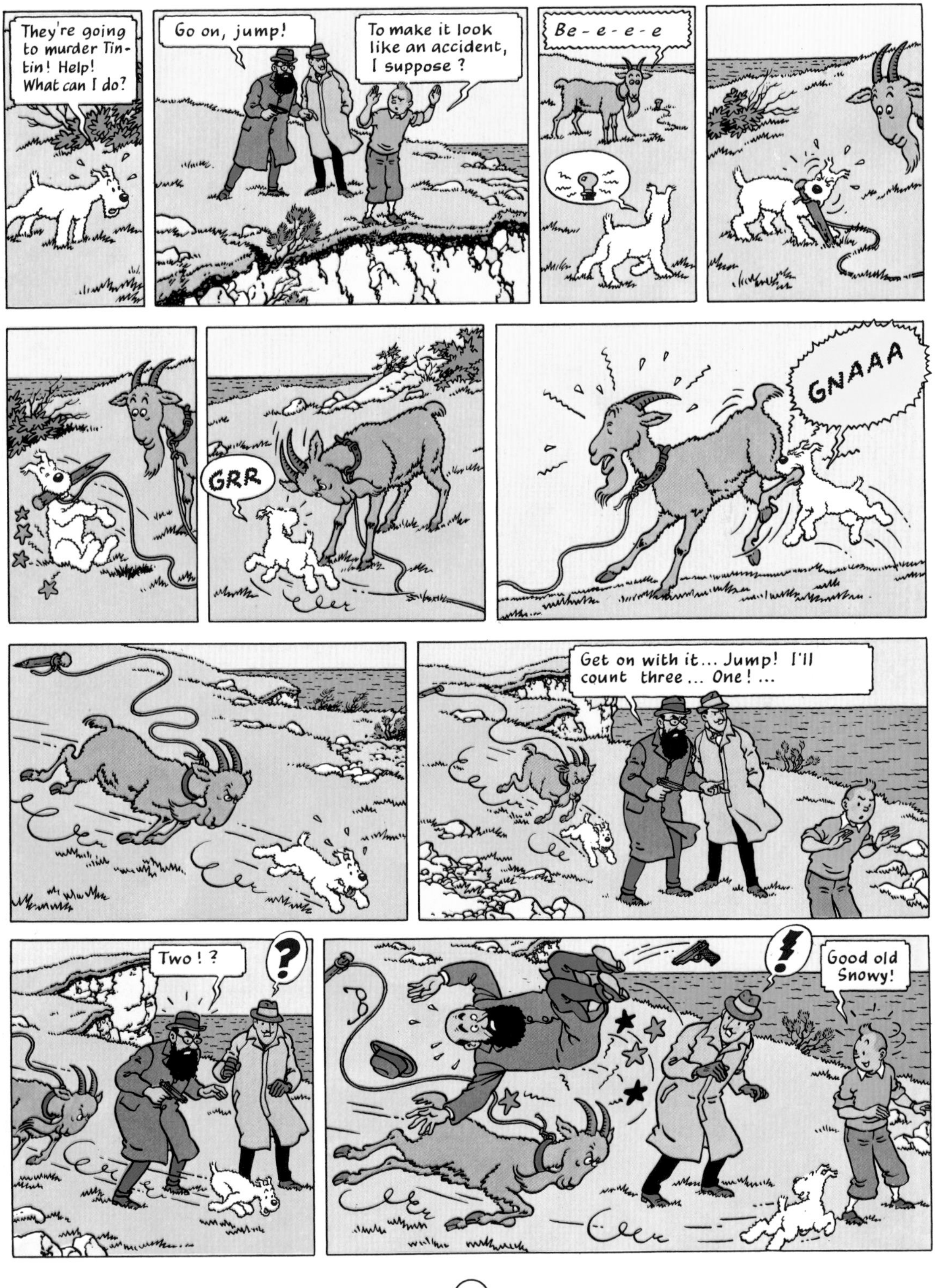
They're going to murder Tintin! Help! What can I do?
Go on, jump!
To make it look like an accident, I suppose?
Be-e-e-e
GRR
GNAAA
Get on with it... Jump! I'll count three... One!...
Two!?
?
!
Good old Snowy!

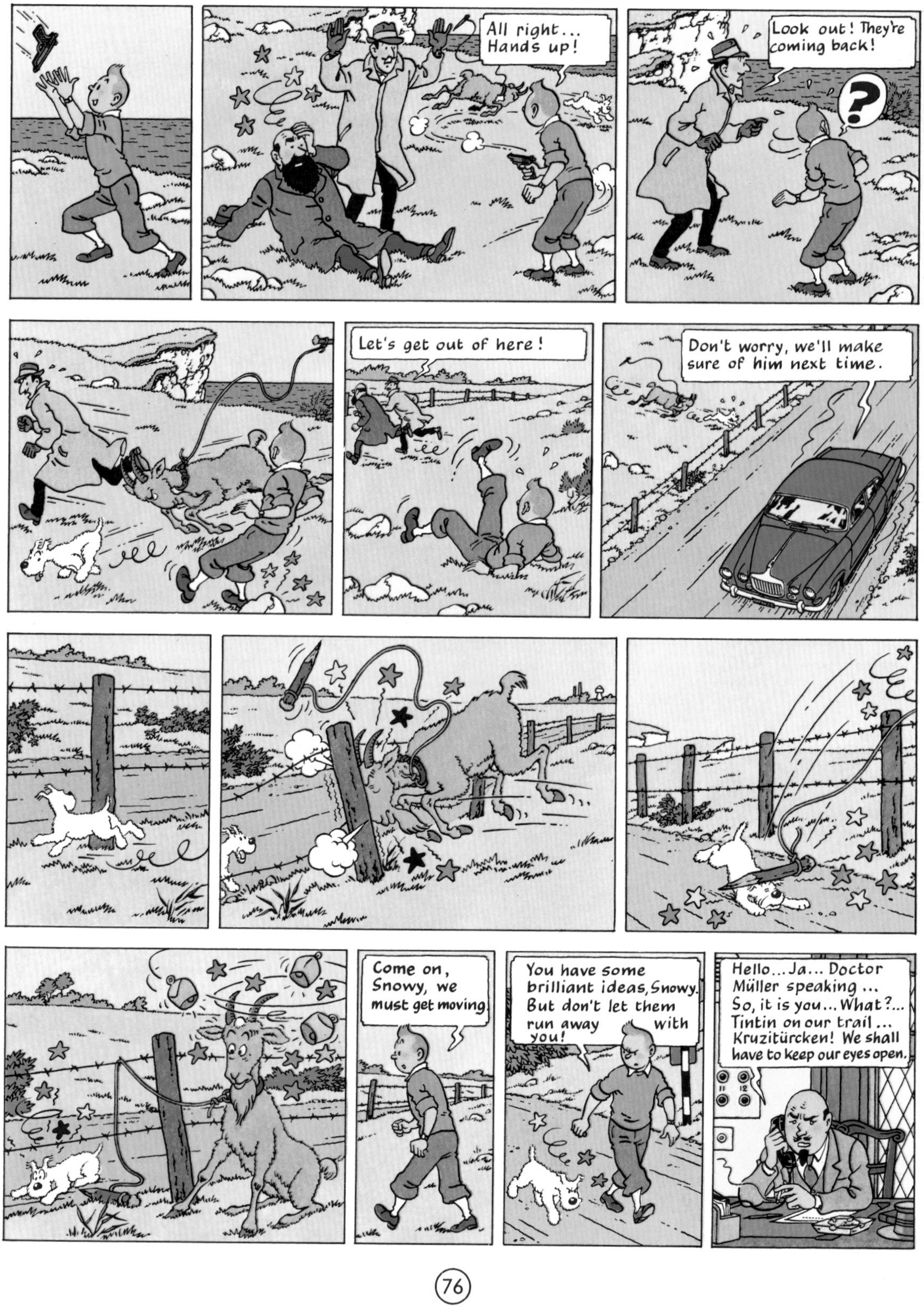
All right... Hands up!
Look out! They're coming back!
?
Let's get out of here!
Don't worry, we'll make sure of him next time.
Come on, Snowy, we must get moving.
You have some brilliant ideas, Snowy. But don't let them run away with you!
Hello... Ja... Doctor Müller speaking... So, it is you... What?... Tintin on our trail... Kruzitürcken! We shall have to keep our eyes open.

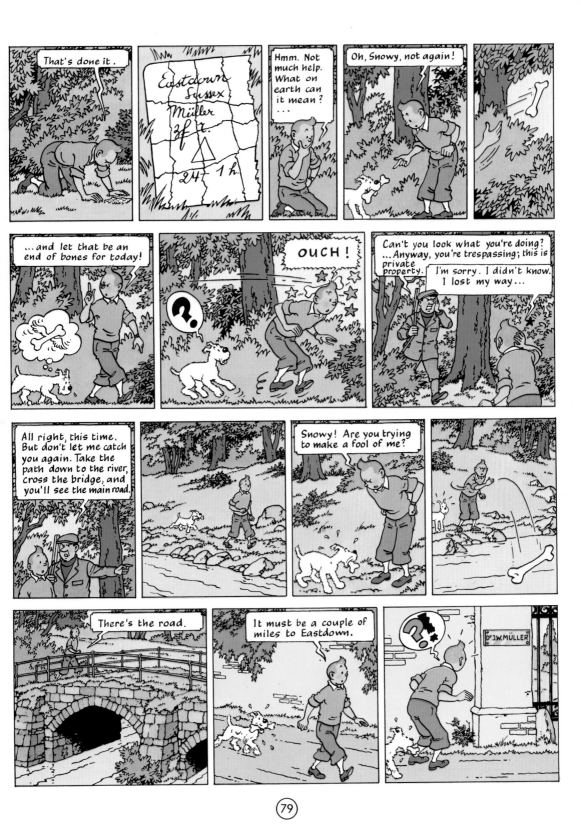

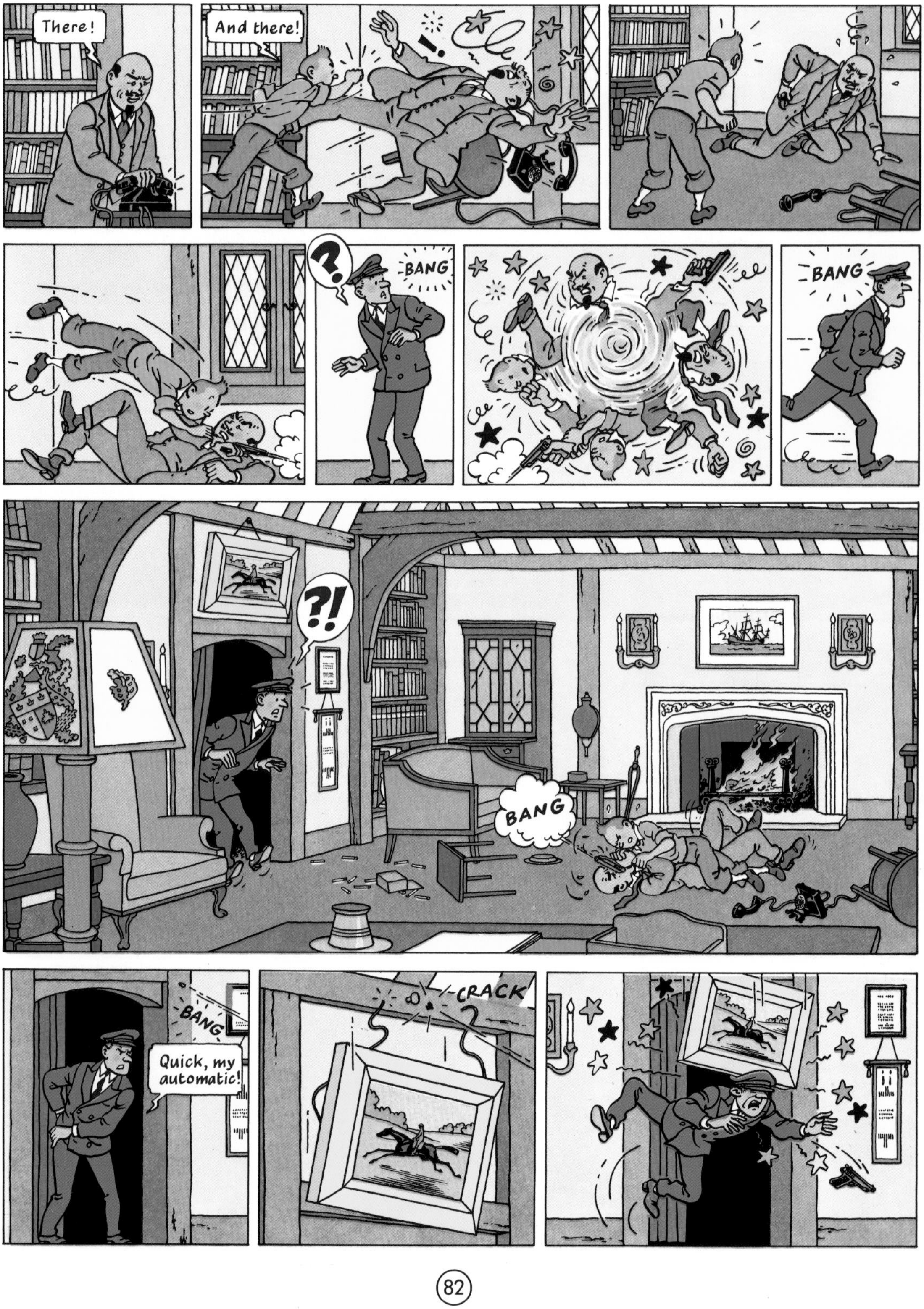
There!
And there!
?
BANG
BANG
?!
BANG
BANG
Quick, my automatic!
CRACK

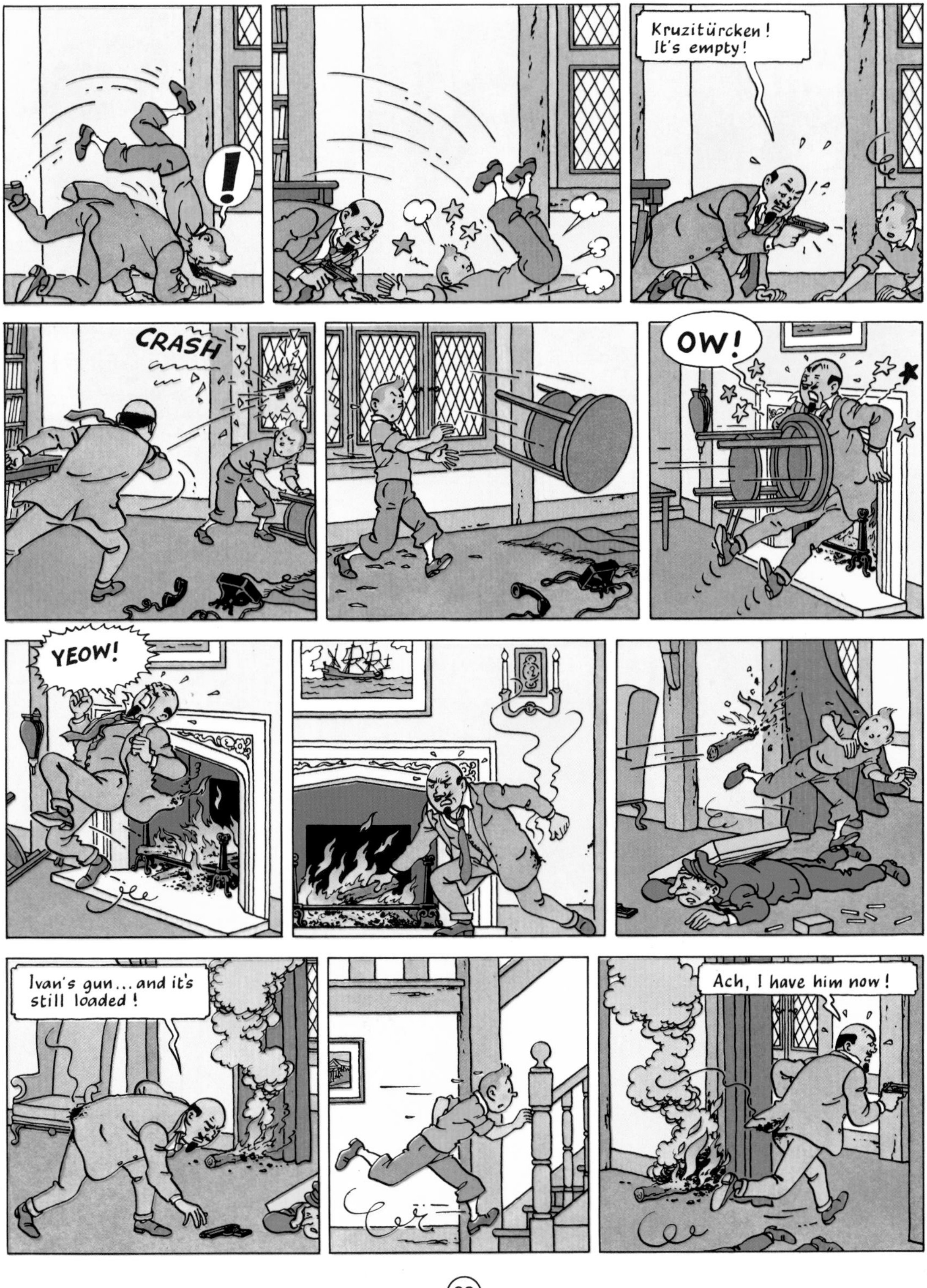
!
Kruzitürcken! It's empty!
CRASH
OW!
YEOW!
Ivan's gun... and it's still loaded!
Ach, I have him now!

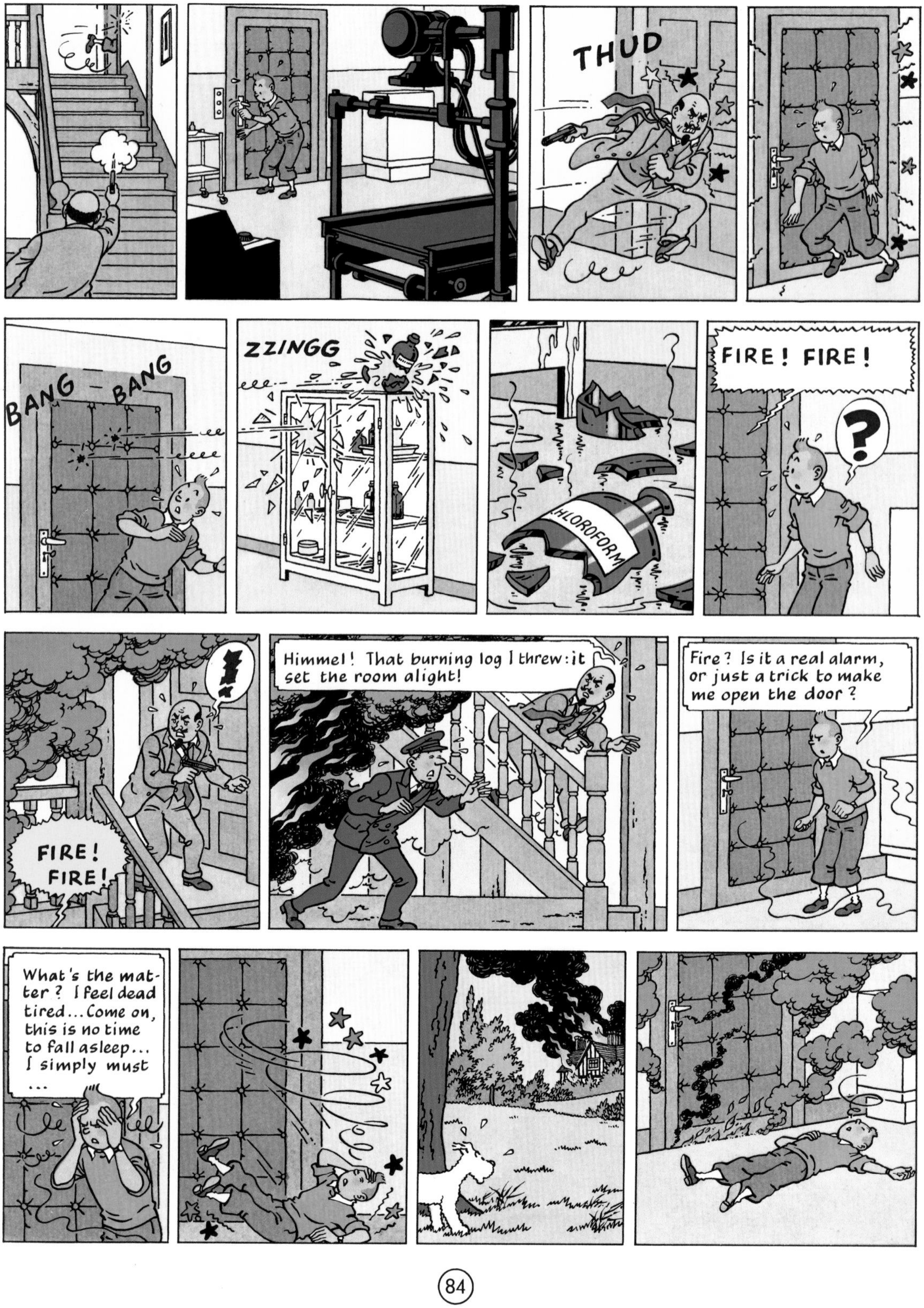
THUD
BANG
BANG
ZZINGG
CHLOROFORM
FIRE! FIRE!
FIRE! FIRE!
Himmel! That burning log I threw: it set the room alight!
Fire? Is it a real alarm, or just a trick to make me open the door?
What's the matter? I feel dead tired... Come on, this is no time to fall asleep... I simply must ...

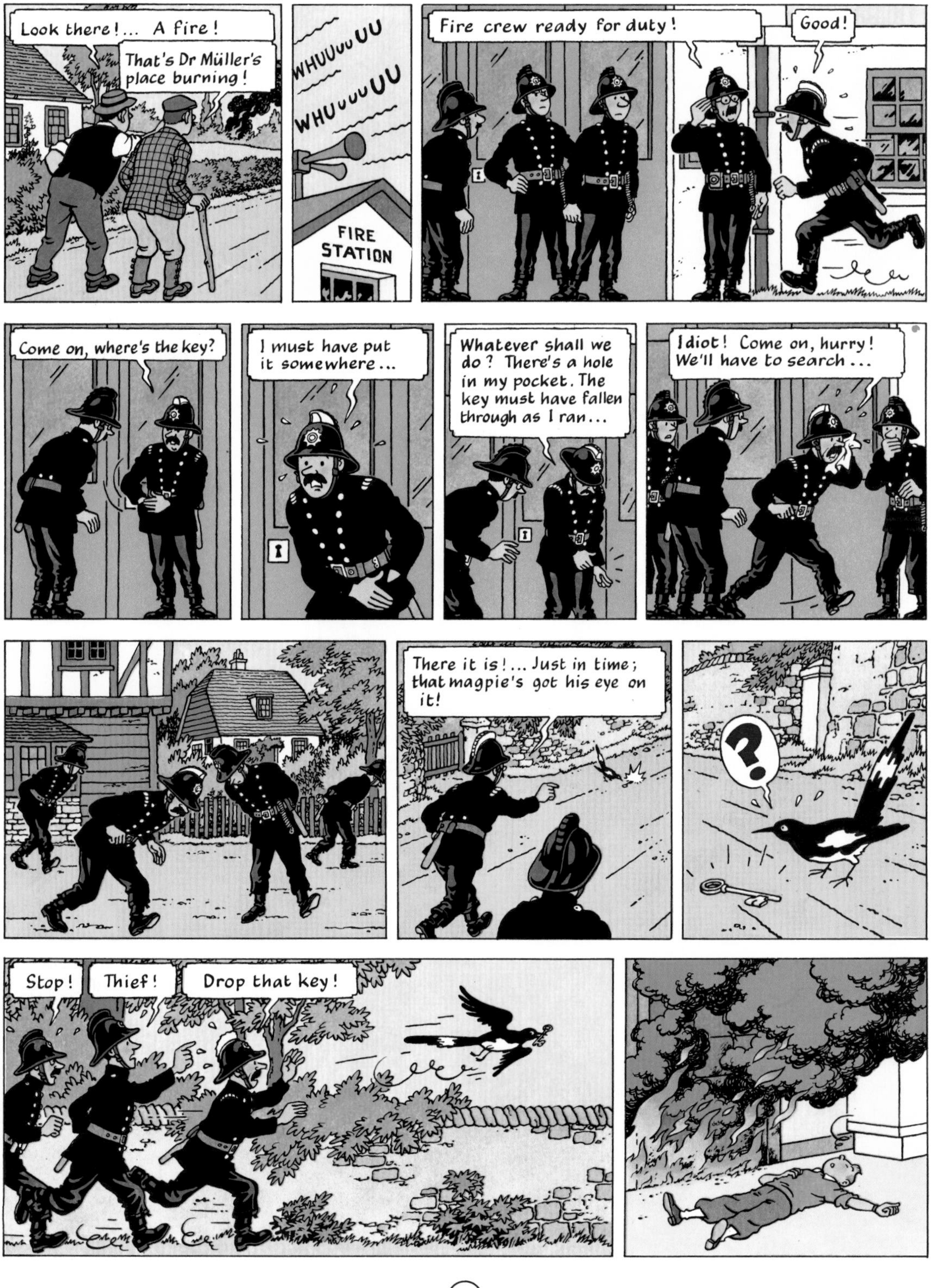

Look there!... A fire!
That's Dr Müller's place burning!
WHUUuuUU
WHUuuuUU
FIRE STATION
Fire crew ready for duty!
Good!
Come on, where's the key?
I must have put it somewhere...
Whatever shall we do? There's a hole in my pocket. The key must have fallen through as I ran...
Idiot! Come on, hurry! We'll have to search...
There it is!... Just in time; that magpie's got his eye on it!
?
Stop!
Thief!
Drop that key!

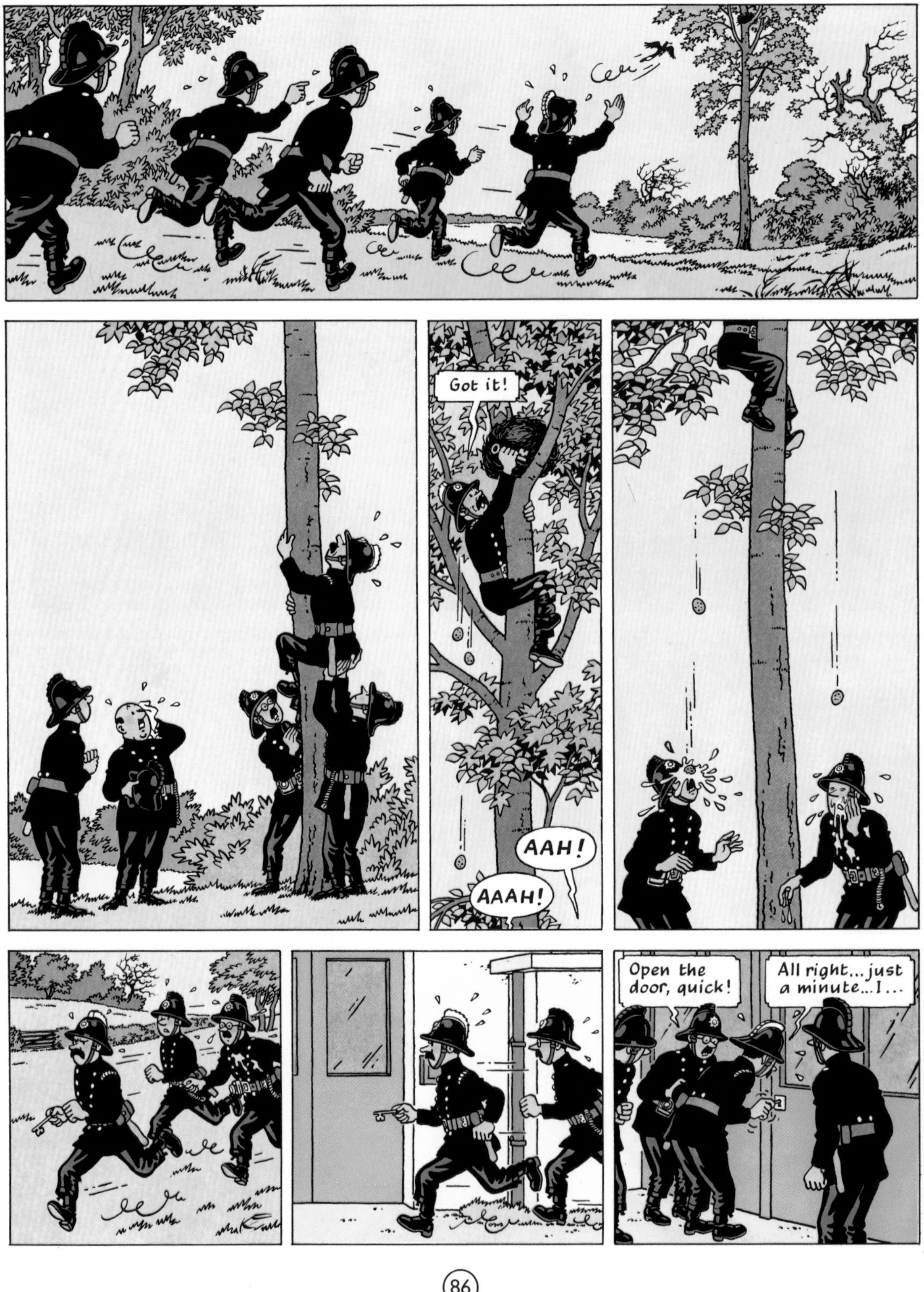
Got it!
AAH!
AAAH!
Open the door, quick!
All right... just a minute... I...

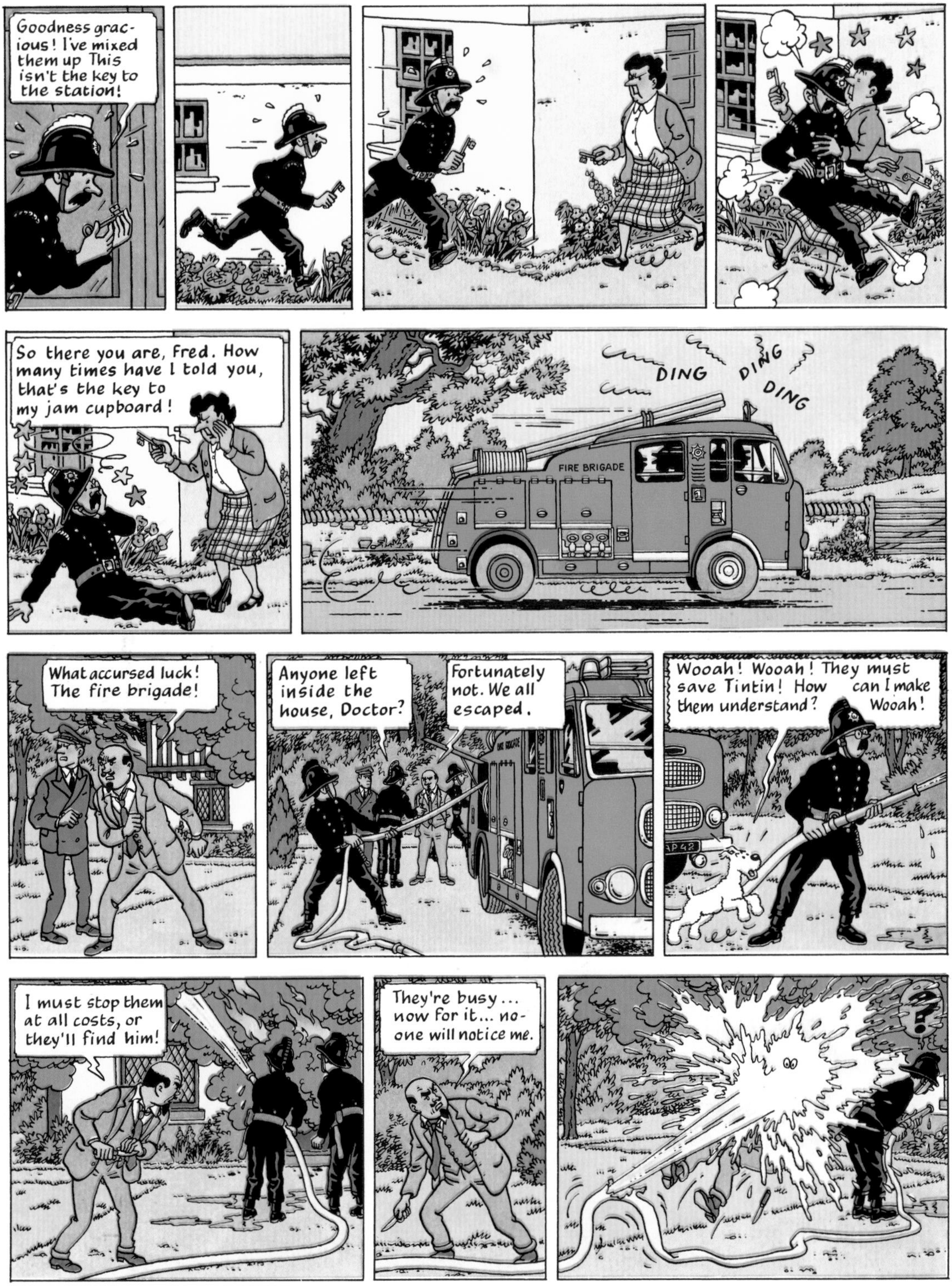

Goodness gracious! I've mixed them up This isn't the key to the station!
So there you are, Fred. How many times have I told you, that's the key to my jam cupboard!
DING
DING
DING
FIRE BRIGADE
What accursed luck! The fire brigade!
Anyone left inside the house, Doctor?
Fortunately not. We all escaped.
Wooah! Wooah! They must save Tintin! How can I make them understand? Wooah!
I must stop them at all costs, or they'll find him!
They're busy... now for it... no-one will notice me.

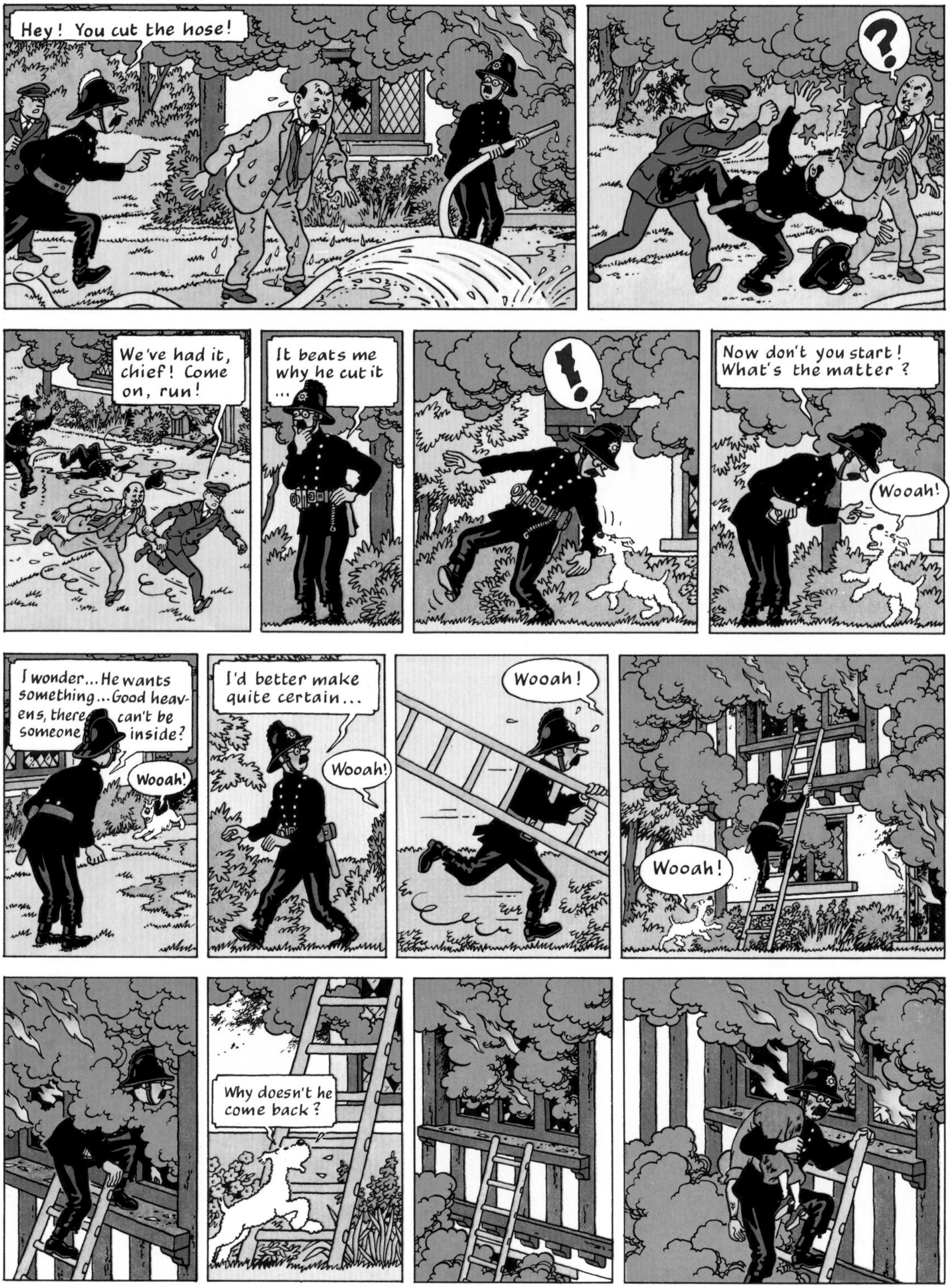
Hey! You cut the hose!
?
We've had it, chief! Come on, run!
It beats me why he cut it ...
!
Now don't you start! What's the matter?
Wooah!
I wonder... He wants something... Good heavens, there can't be someone inside?
Wooah!
I'd better make quite certain...
Wooah!
Wooah!
Wooah!
Why doesn't he come back?

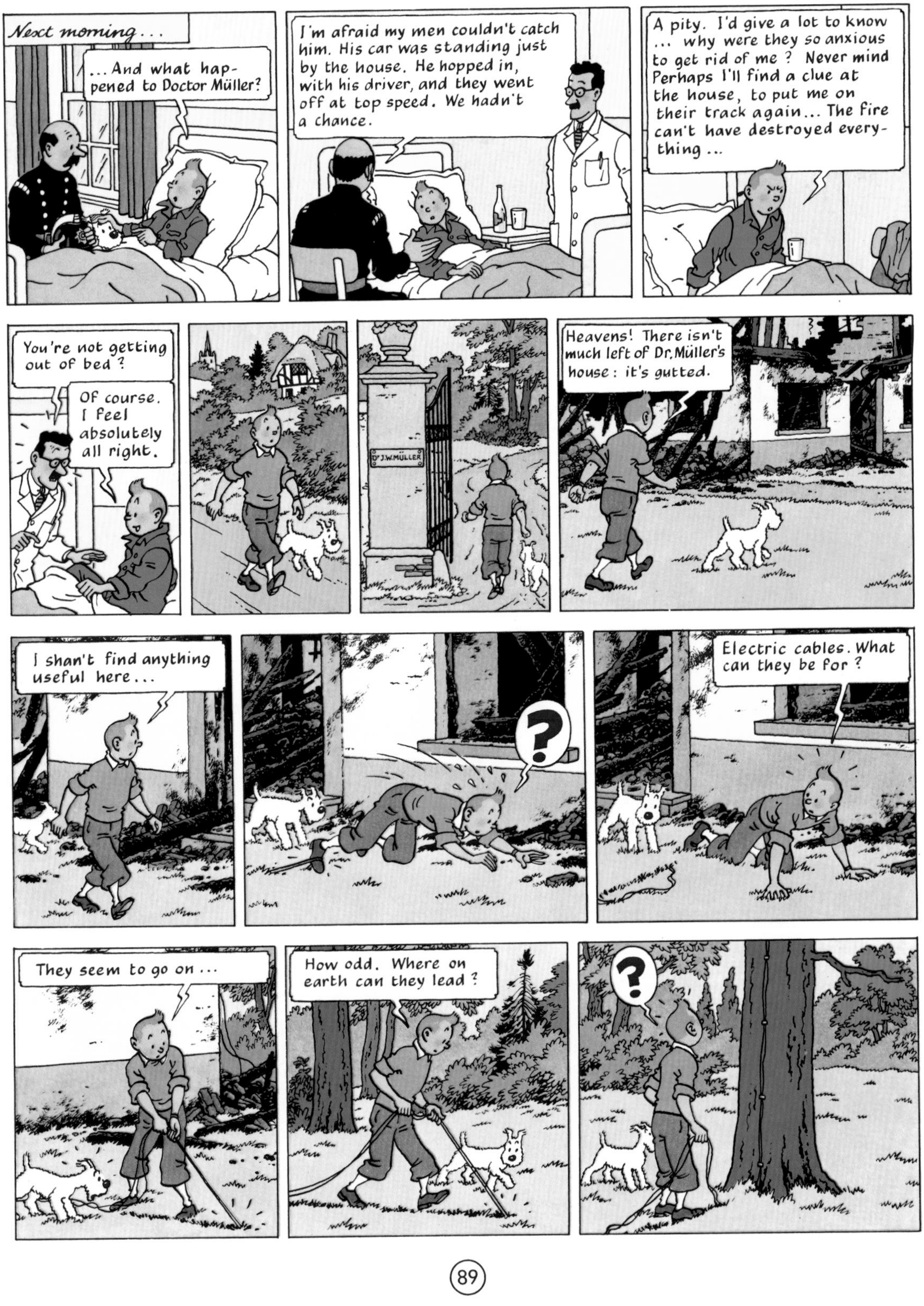

Next morning . . .
. . . And what happened to Doctor Müller?
I'm afraid my men couldn't catch him. His car was standing just by the house. He hopped in, with his driver, and they went off at top speed. We hadn't a chance.
A pity. I'd give a lot to know . . . why were they so anxious to get rid of me? Never mind Perhaps I'll find a clue at the house, to put me on their track again . . . The fire can't have destroyed everything . . .
You're not getting out of bed?
Of course. I feel absolutely all right.
Dr J.W. MÜLLER
Heavens! There isn't much left of Dr. Müller's house: it's gutted.
I shan't find anything useful here . . .
?
Electric cables. What can they be for?
They seem to go on . . .
How odd. Where on earth can they lead?
?

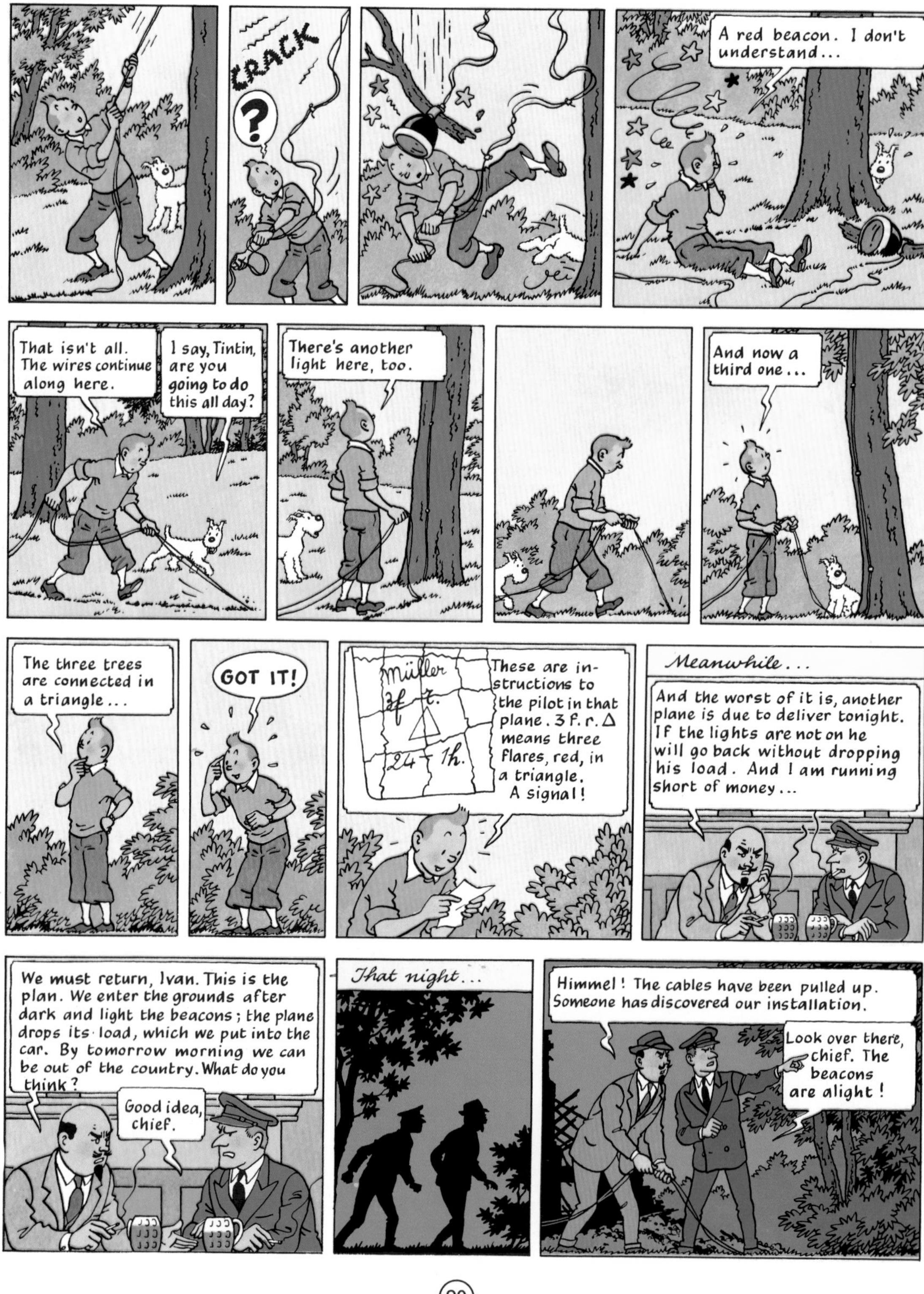
CRACK
?
A red beacon. I don't understand...
That isn't all. The wires continue along here.
I say, Tintin, are you going to do this all day?
There's another light here, too.
And now a third one...
The three trees are connected in a triangle...
GOT IT!
Müller
3f r.
24 1h.
These are instructions to the pilot in that plane. 3 f. r. Δ means three flares, red, in a triangle. A signal!
Meanwhile...
And the worst of it is, another plane is due to deliver tonight. If the lights are not on he will go back without dropping his load. And I am running short of money...
We must return, Ivan. This is the plan. We enter the grounds after dark and light the beacons; the plane drops its load, which we put into the car. By tomorrow morning we can be out of the country. What do you think?
Good idea, chief.
That night...
Himmel! The cables have been pulled up. Someone has discovered our installation.
Look over there, chief. The beacons are alight!

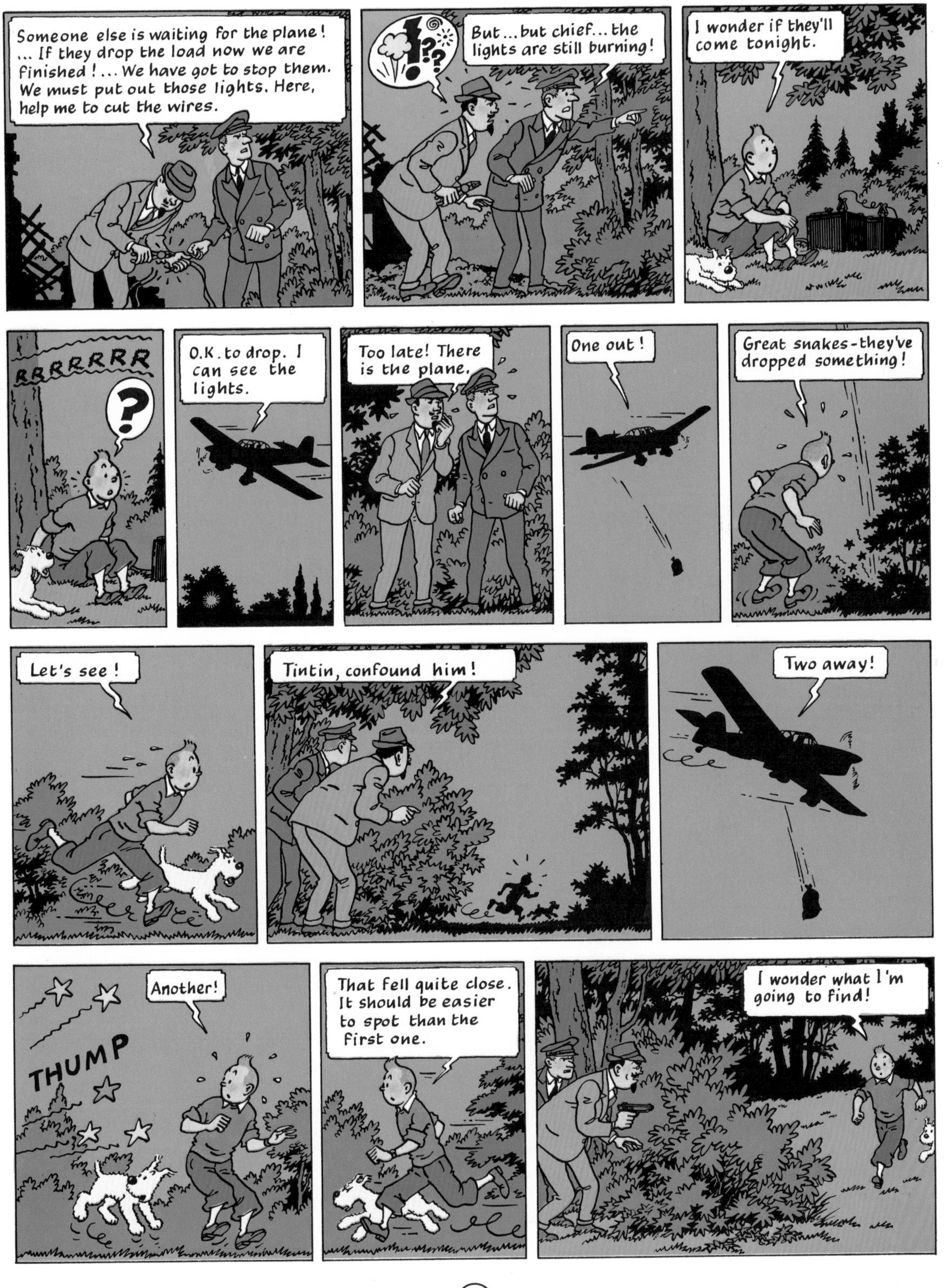
Someone else is waiting for the plane! ... If they drop the load now we are finished! ... We have got to stop them. We must put out those lights. Here, help me to cut the wires.
!??
But ... but chief ... the lights are still burning!
I wonder if they'll come tonight.
RRRRRRR
?
O.K. to drop. I can see the lights.
Too late! There is the plane.
One out!
Great snakes - they've dropped something!
Let's see!
Tintin, confound him!
Two away!
Another!
THUMP
That fell quite close. It should be easier to spot than the first one.
I wonder what I'm going to find!

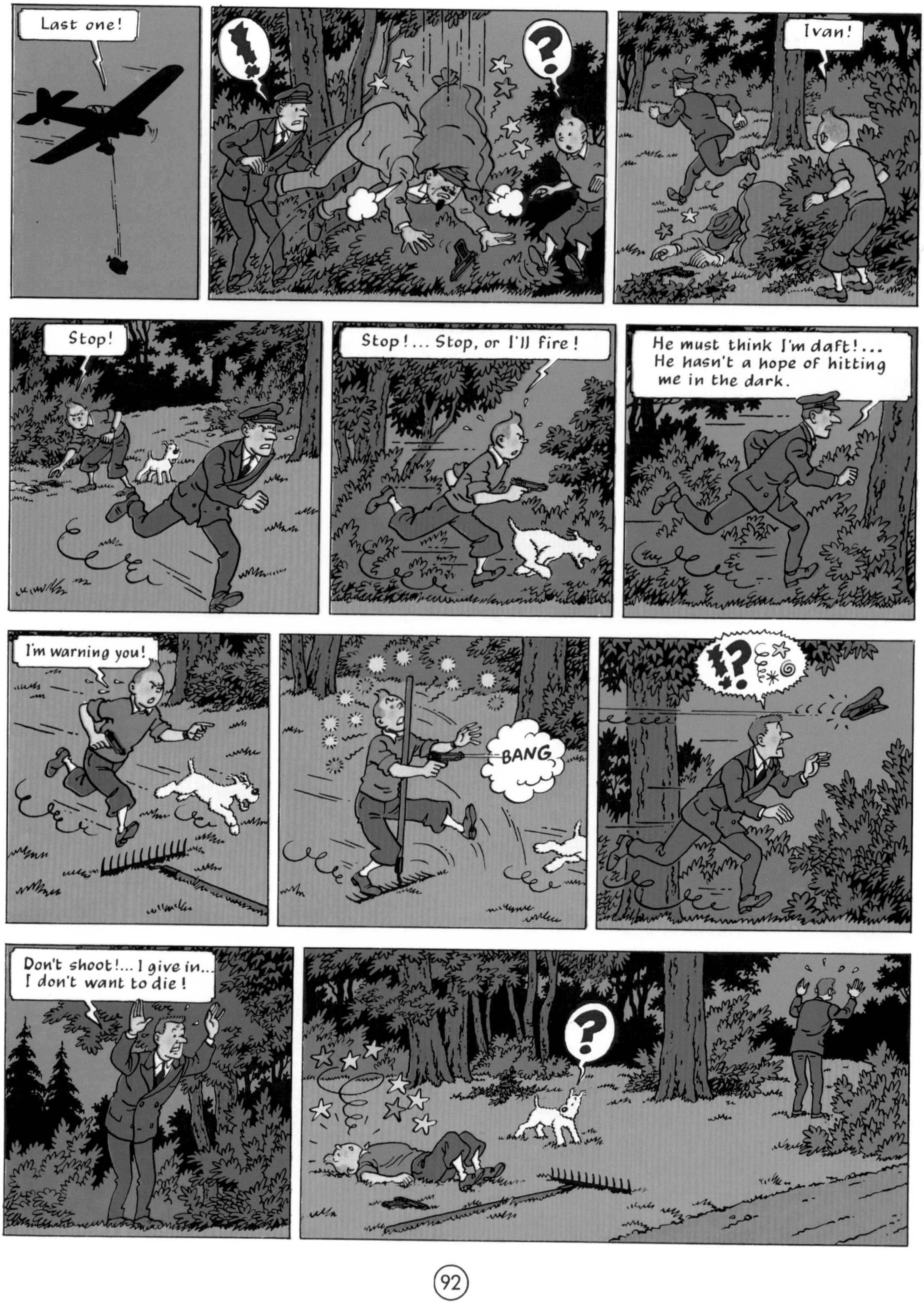
Last one!
?
Ivan!
Stop!
Stop!... Stop, or I'll fire!
He must think I'm daft!... He hasn't a hope of hitting me in the dark.
I'm warning you!
BANG
!?
Don't shoot!... I give in... I don't want to die!
?

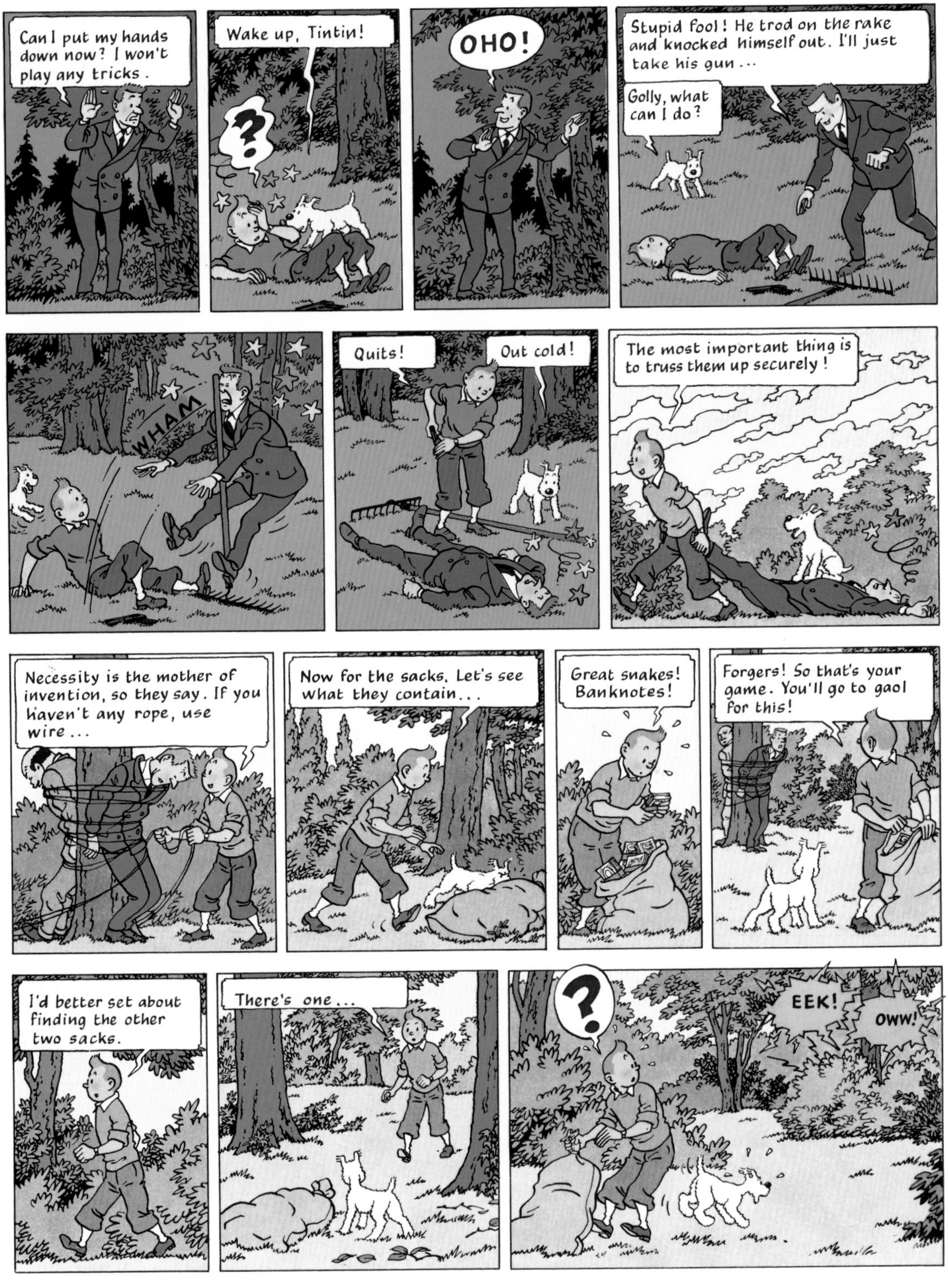

Can I put my hands down now? I won't play any tricks.
Wake up, Tintin!
?
OHO!
Stupid fool! He trod on the rake and knocked himself out. I'll just take his gun...
Golly, what can I do?
WHAM
Quits!
Out cold!
The most important thing is to truss them up securely!
Necessity is the mother of invention, so they say. If you haven't any rope, use wire...
Now for the sacks. Let's see what they contain...
Great snakes! Banknotes!
Forgers! So that's your game. You'll go to gaol for this!
I'd better set about finding the other two sacks.
There's one...
?
EEK!
OWW!

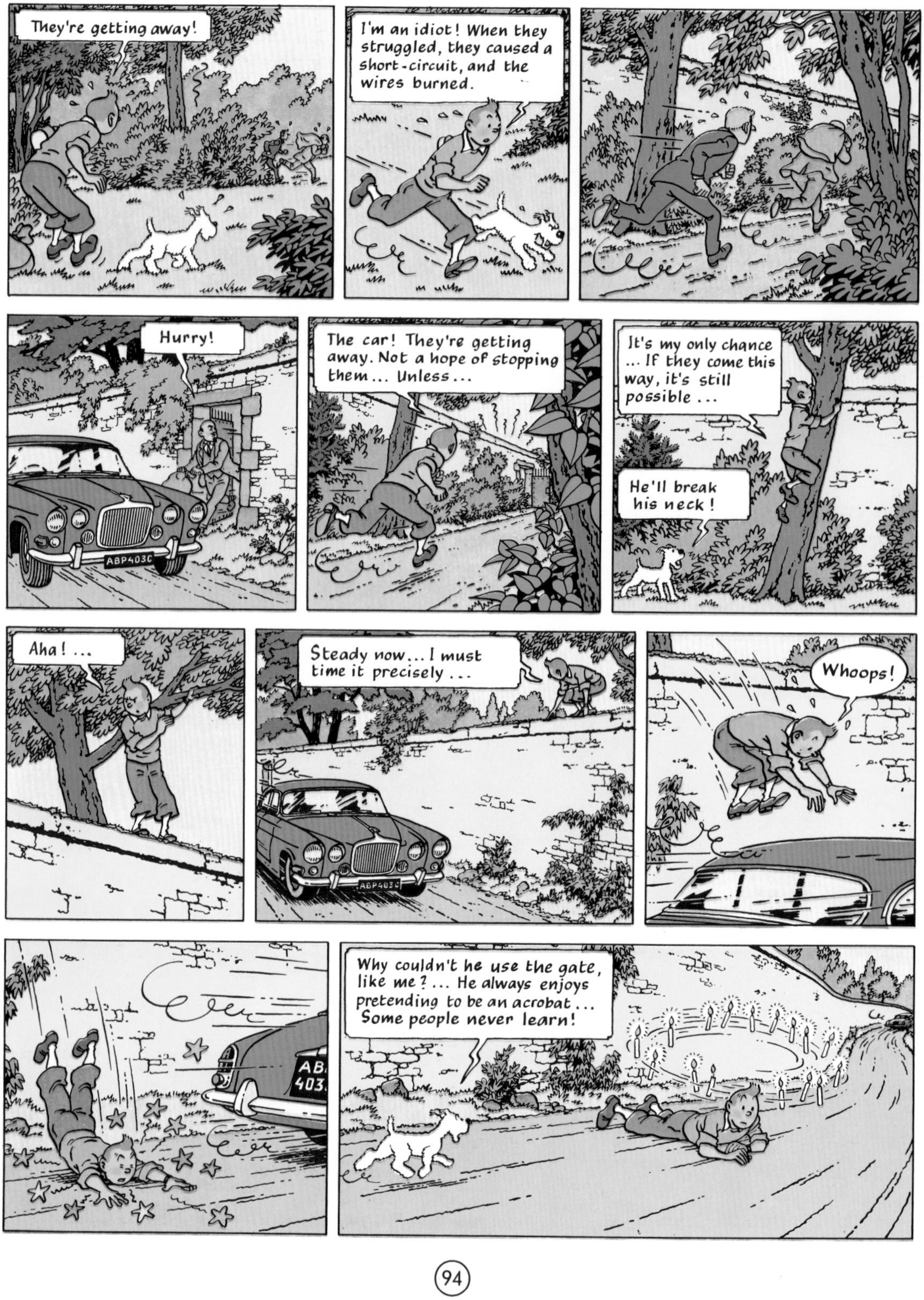
They're getting away!
I'm an idiot! When they struggled, they caused a short-circuit, and the wires burned.
Hurry!
ABP403C
The car! They're getting away. Not a hope of stopping them ... Unless ...
It's my only chance ... If they come this way, it's still possible ...
He'll break his neck!
Aha! ...
Steady now ... I must time it precisely ...
ABP403C
Whoops!
Why couldn't he use the gate, like me? ... He always enjoys pretending to be an acrobat ... Some people never learn!

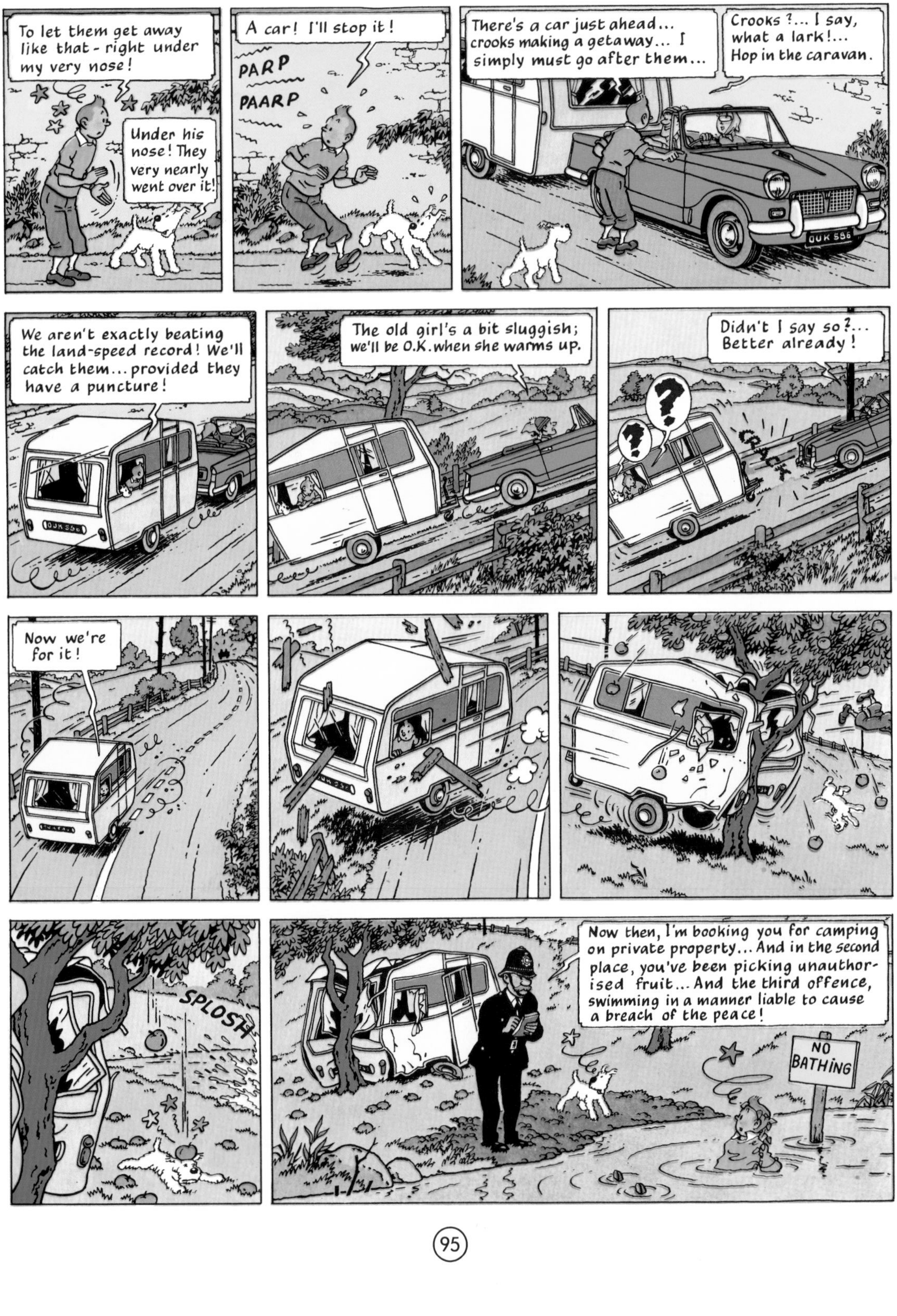

To let them get away like that - right under my very nose!
Under his nose! They very nearly went over it!
A car! I'll stop it!
PARP
PAARP
There's a car just ahead... crooks making a getaway... I simply must go after them...
Crooks?... I say, what a lark!... Hop in the caravan.
We aren't exactly beating the land-speed record! We'll catch them... provided they have a puncture!
The old girl's a bit sluggish; we'll be O.K. when she warms up.
Didn't I say so?... Better already!
CRACK
Now we're for it!
SPLOSH
Now then, I'm booking you for camping on private property... And in the second place, you've been picking unauthorised fruit... And the third offence, swimming in a manner liable to cause a breach of the peace!
NO BATHING

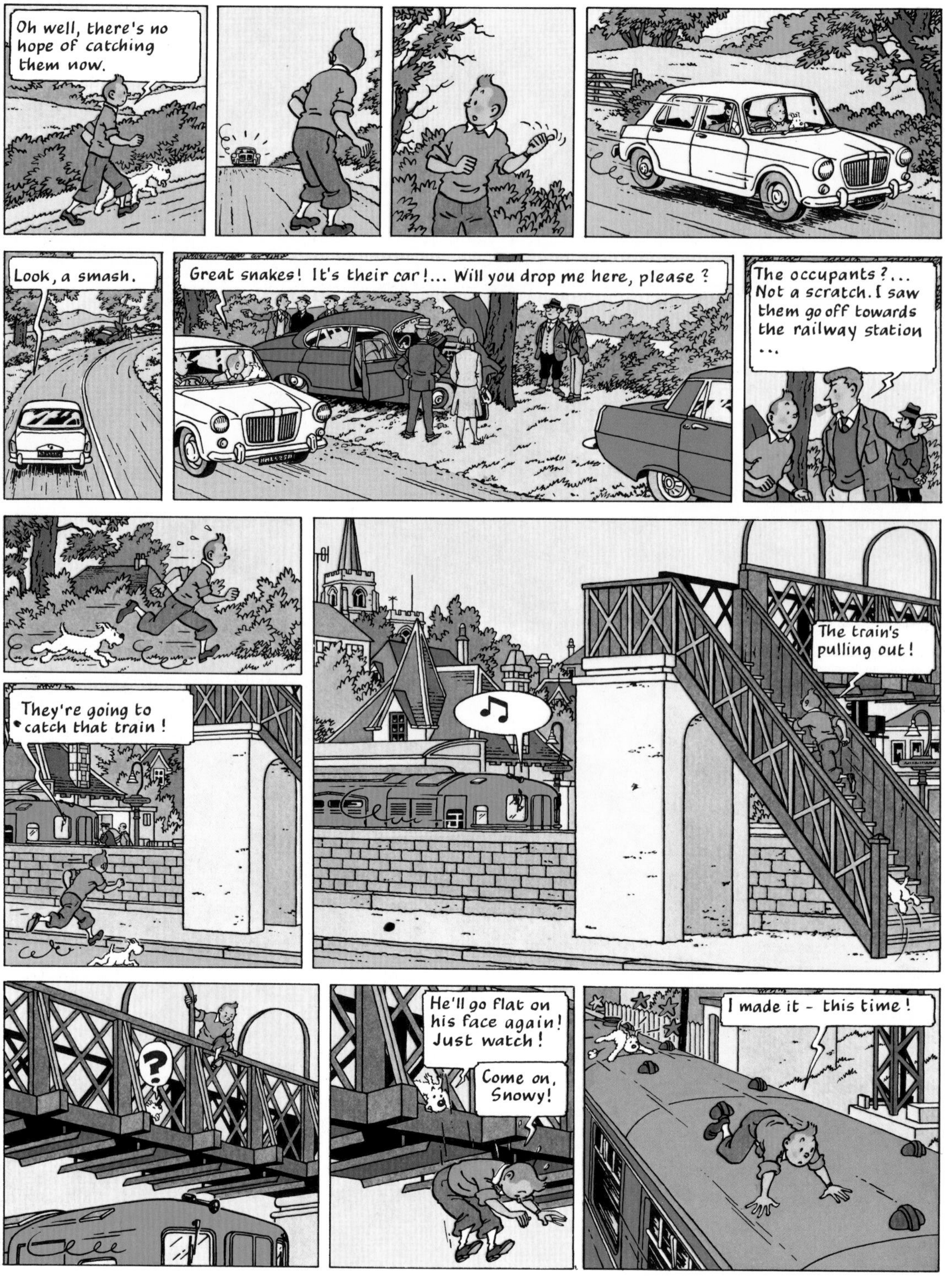

Oh well, there's no hope of catching them now.
Look, a smash.
Great snakes! It's their car!... Will you drop me here, please?
The occupants?... Not a scratch. I saw them go off towards the railway station...
The train's pulling out!
They're going to catch that train!
He'll go flat on his face again! Just watch!
Come on, Snowy!
I made it - this time!

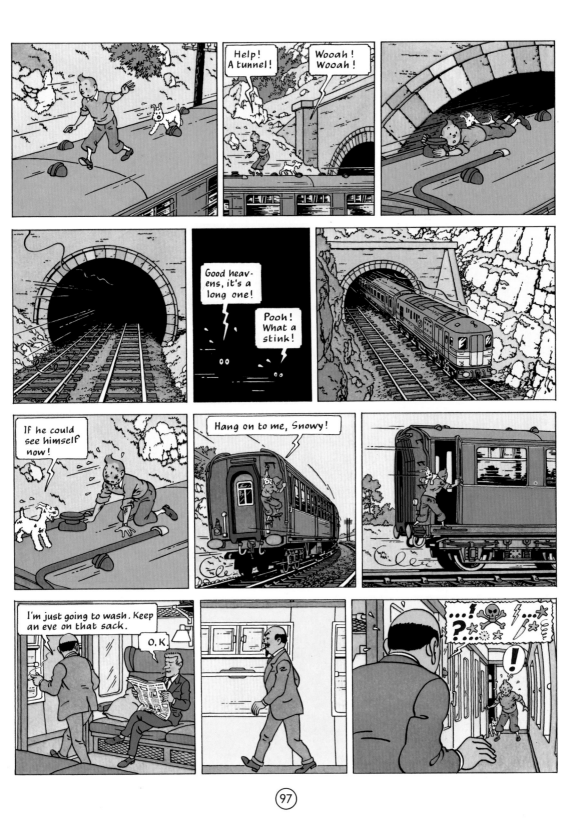

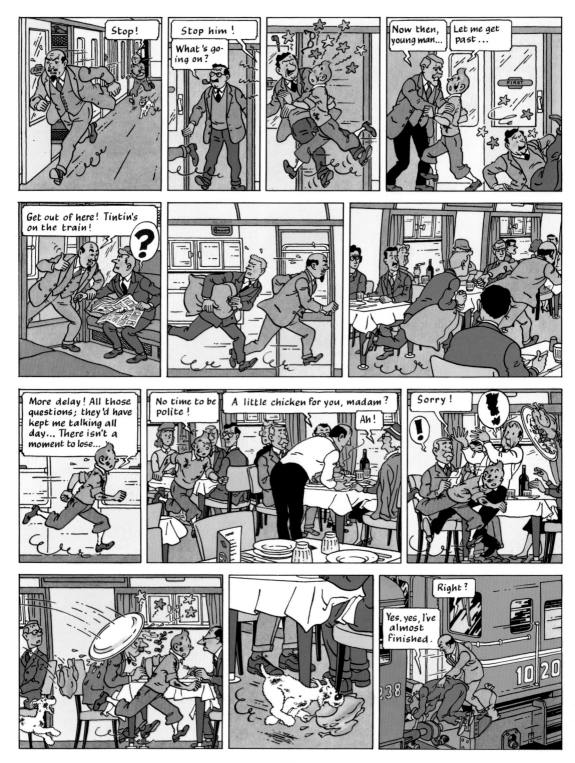

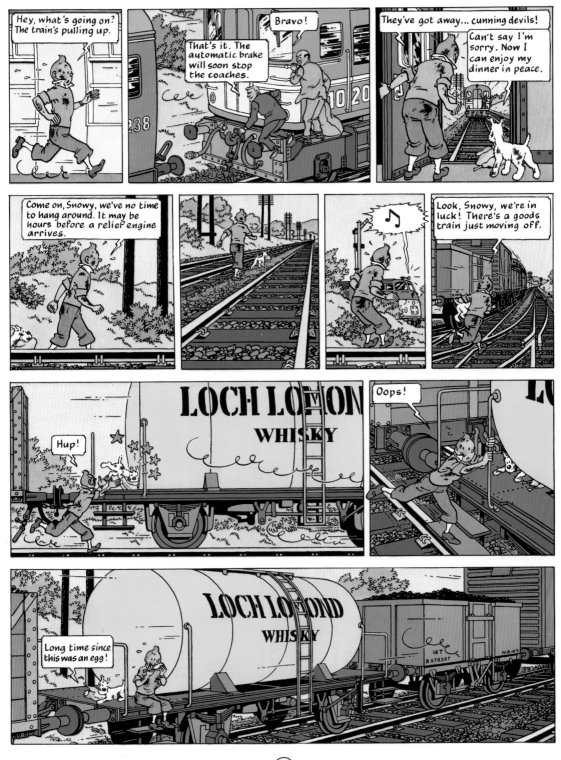

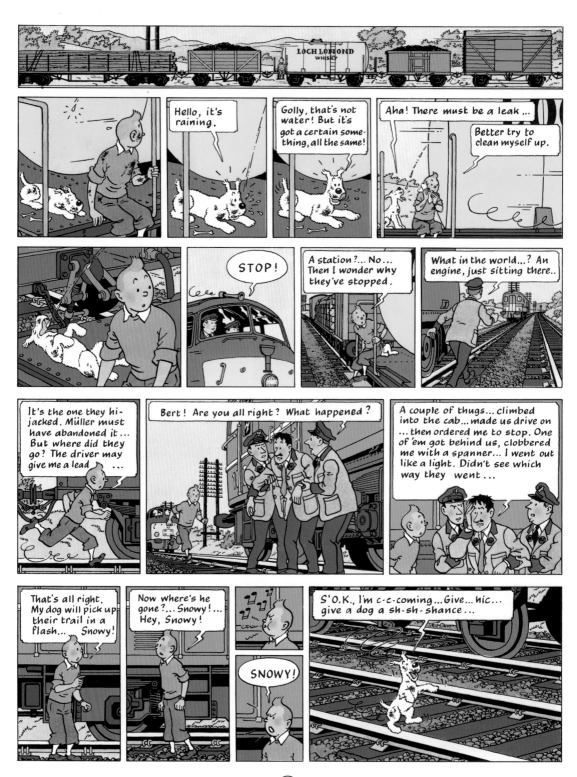

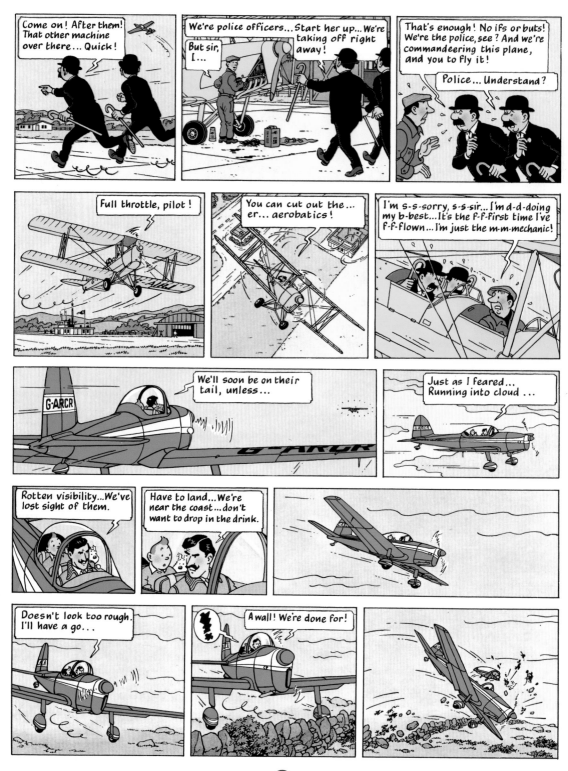

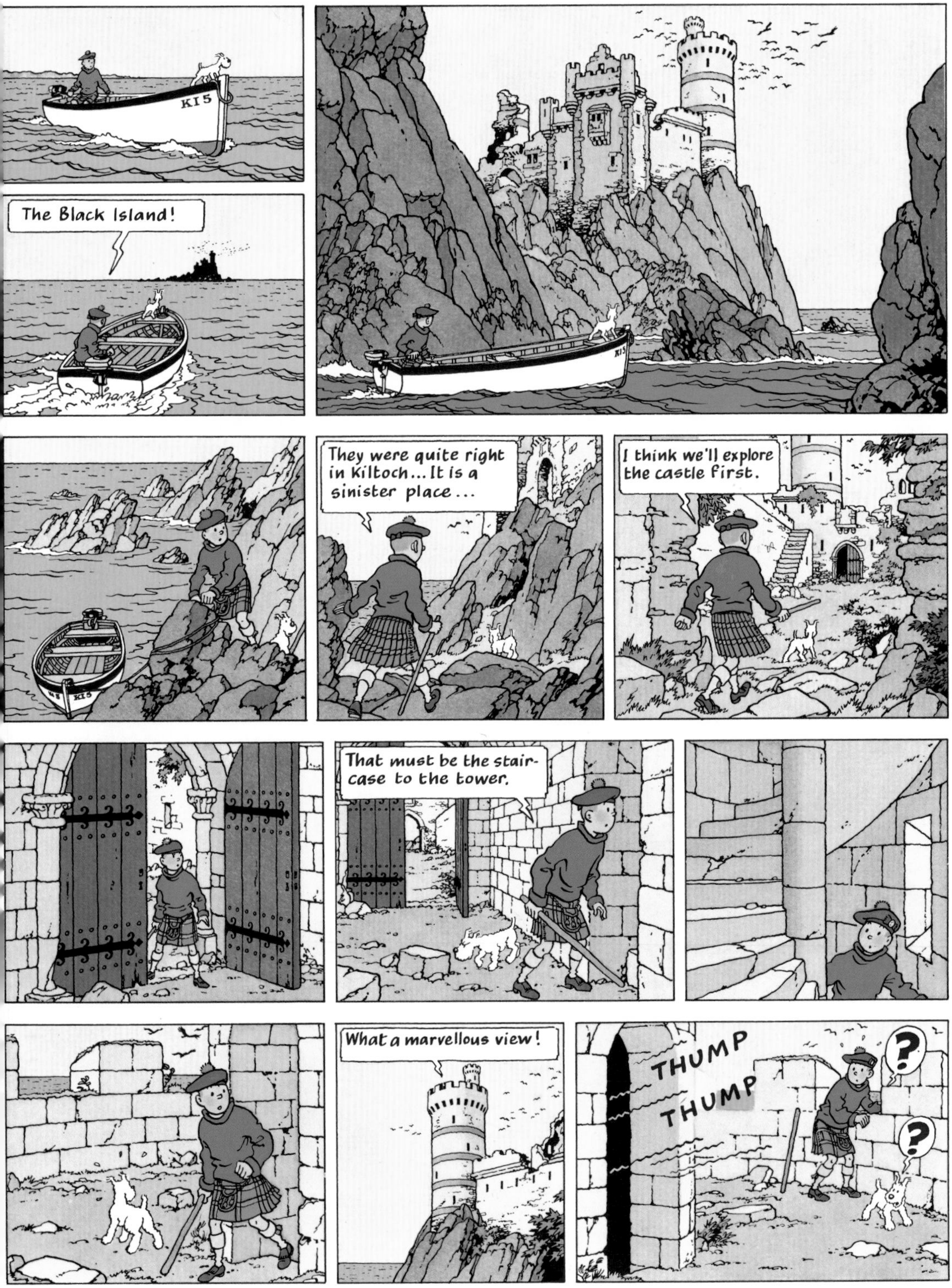
KI 5
The Black Island!
They were quite right in Kiltoch... It is a sinister place...
I think we'll explore the castle first.
That must be the staircase to the tower.
What a marvellous view!
THUMP
THUMP
?
?

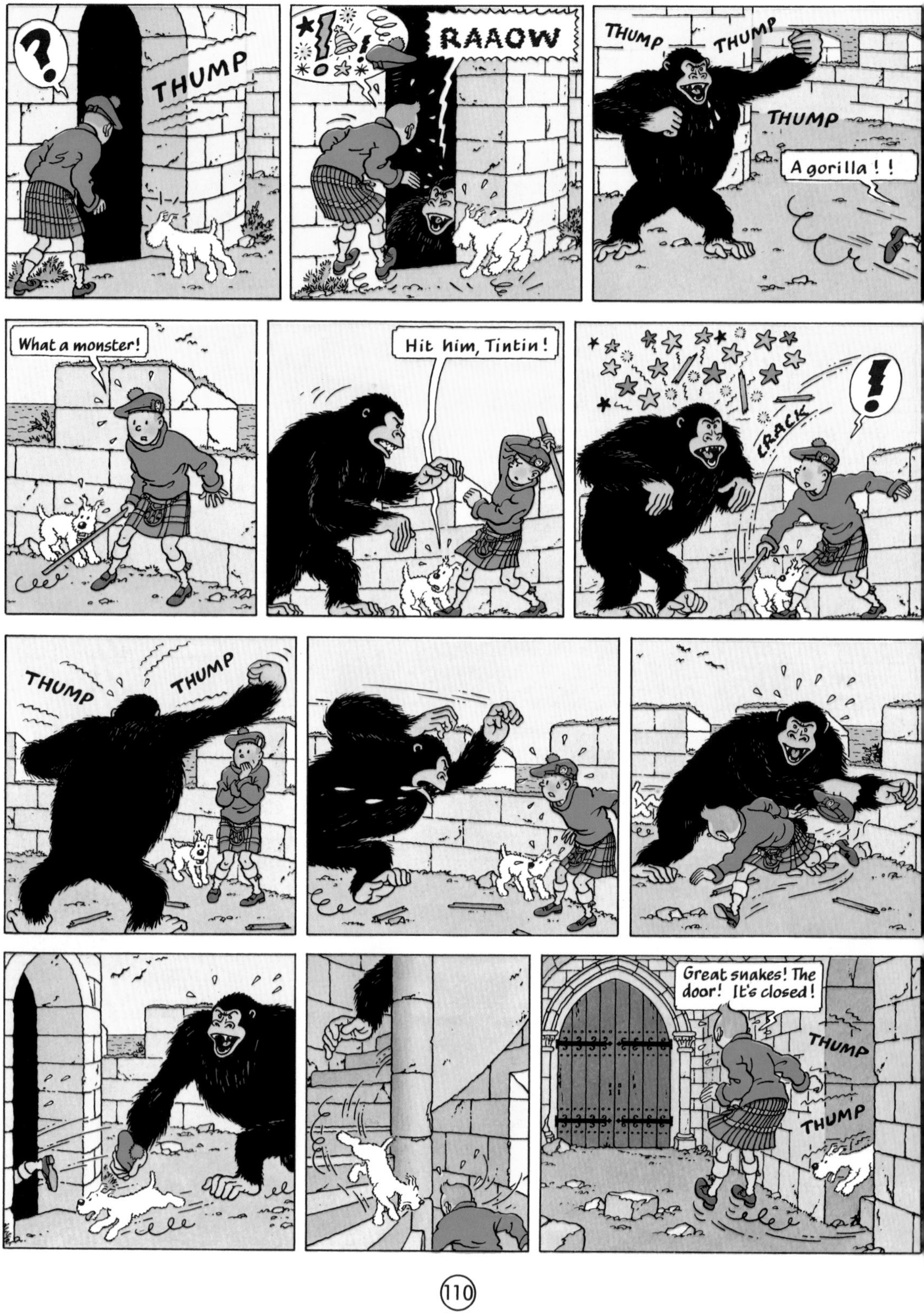
?
THUMP
RAAOW
THUMP
THUMP
THUMP
A gorilla ! !
What a monster!
Hit him, Tintin !
CRACK
!
THUMP
THUMP
Great snakes! The door! It's closed!
THUMP
THUMP

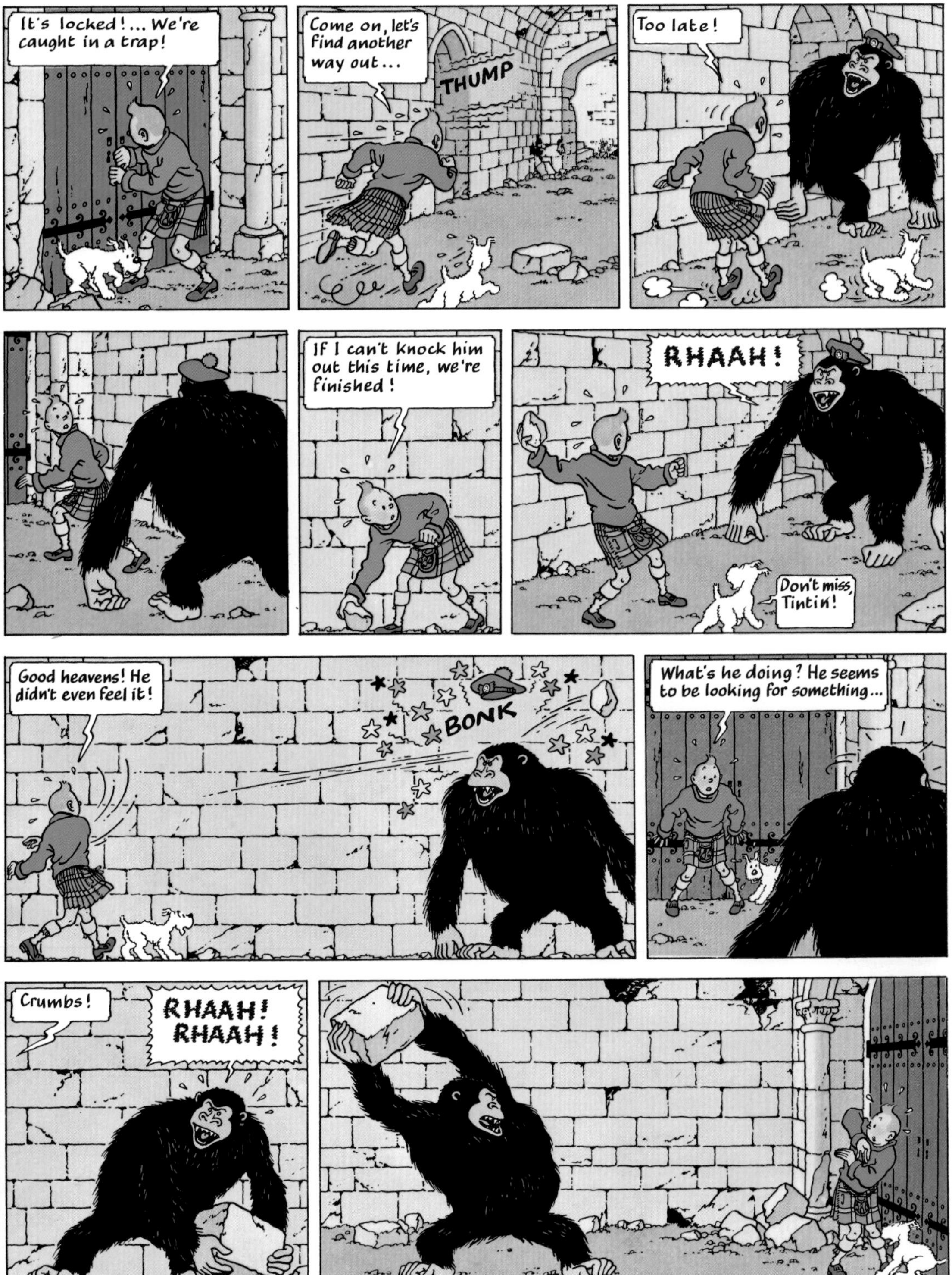
It's locked! ... We're caught in a trap!
Come on, let's find another way out ...
THUMP
Too late!
If I can't knock him out this time, we're finished!
RHAAH!
Don't miss, Tintin!
Good heavens! He didn't even feel it!
BONK
What's he doing? He seems to be looking for something ...
Crumbs!
RHAAH! RHAAH!

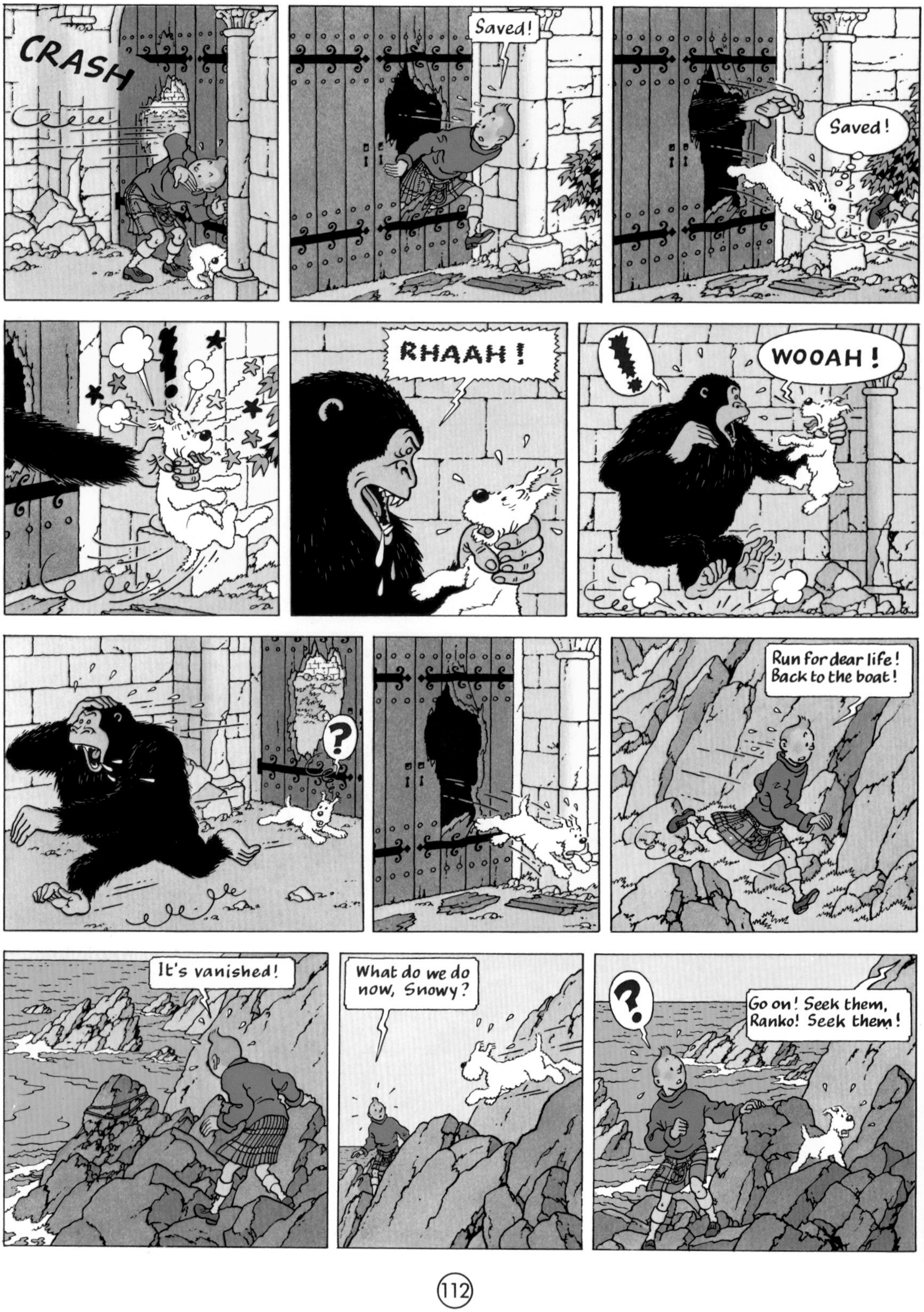
CRASH
Saved!
Saved!
RHAAH!
WOOAH!
Run for dear life! Back to the boat!
It's vanished!
What do we do now, Snowy?
Go on! Seek them, Ranko! Seek them!

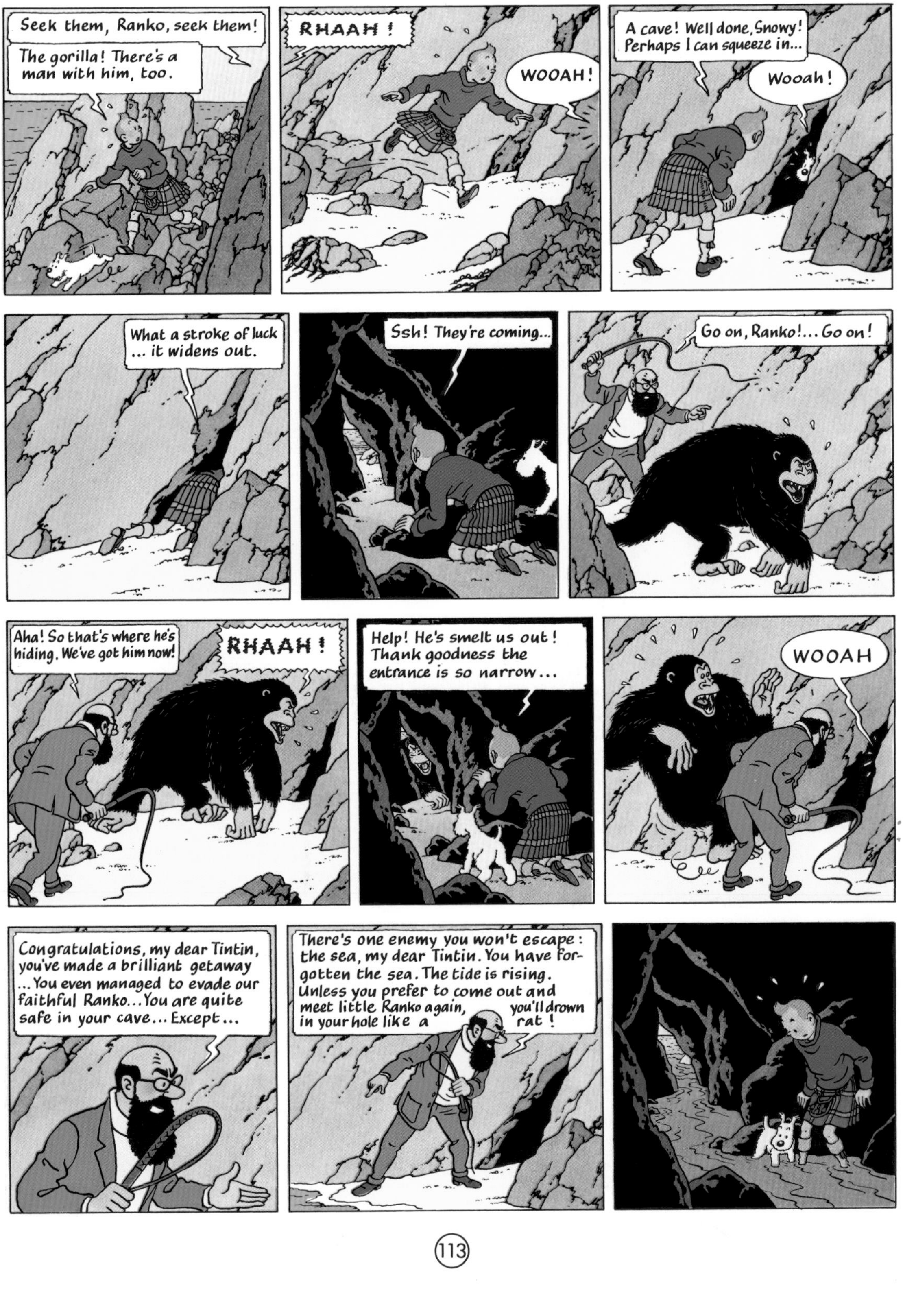

Seek them, Ranko, seek them!
The gorilla! There's a man with him, too.
RHAAH!
WOOAH!
A cave! Well done, Snowy! Perhaps I can squeeze in...
Wooah!
What a stroke of luck ... it widens out.
Ssh! They're coming...
Go on, Ranko!... Go on!
Aha! So that's where he's hiding. We've got him now!
RHAAH!
Help! He's smelt us out! Thank goodness the entrance is so narrow...
WOOAH
Congratulations, my dear Tintin, you've made a brilliant getaway ...You even managed to evade our faithful Ranko...You are quite safe in your cave... Except...
There's one enemy you won't escape: the sea, my dear Tintin. You have forgotten the sea. The tide is rising. Unless you prefer to come out and meet little Ranko again, you'll drown in your hole like a rat!

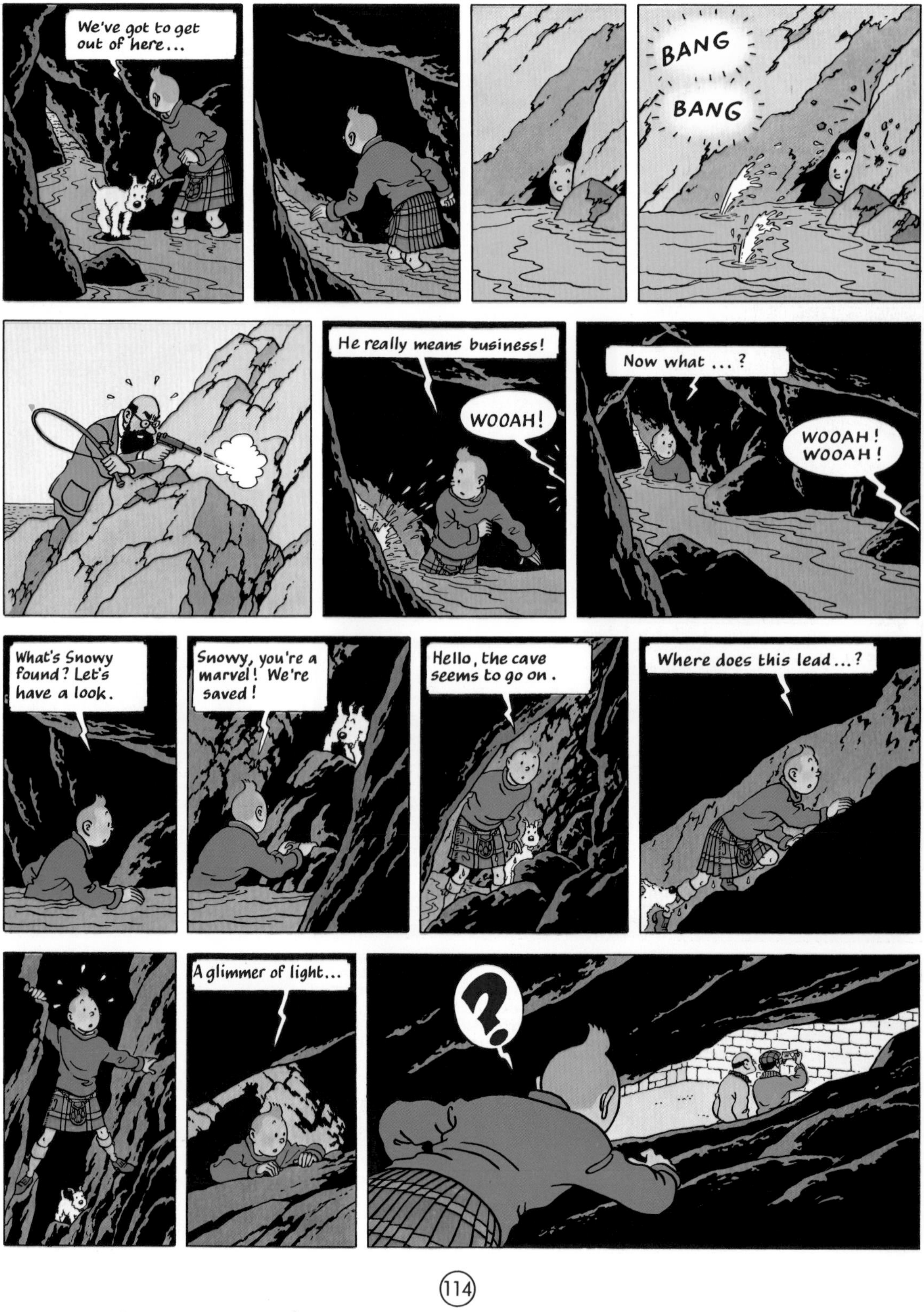

We've got to get out of here...
BANG
BANG
He really means business!
WOOAH!
Now what ...?
WOOAH! WOOAH!
What's Snowy found? Let's have a look.
Snowy, you're a marvel! We're saved!
Hello, the cave seems to go on.
Where does this lead...?
A glimmer of light...
?

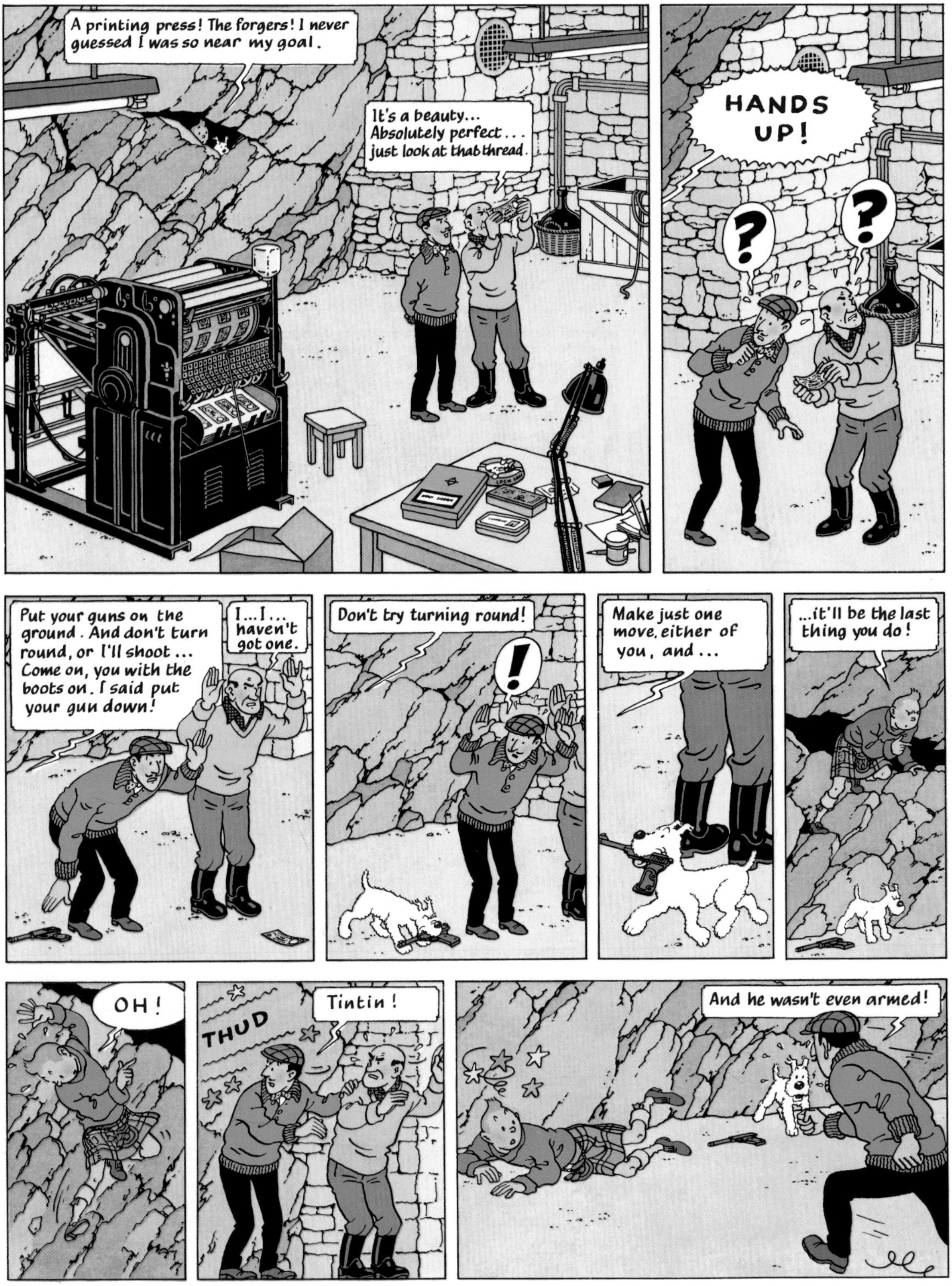
A printing press! The forgers! I never guessed I was so near my goal.
It's a beauty... Absolutely perfect... just look at thab thread.
HANDS UP!
?
?
Put your guns on the ground. And don't turn round, or I'll shoot... Come on, you with the boots on. I said put your gun down!
I...I... haven't got one.
Don't try turning round!
!
Make just one move, either of you, and...
...it'll be the last thing you do!
OH!
THUD
Tintin!
And he wasn't even armed!

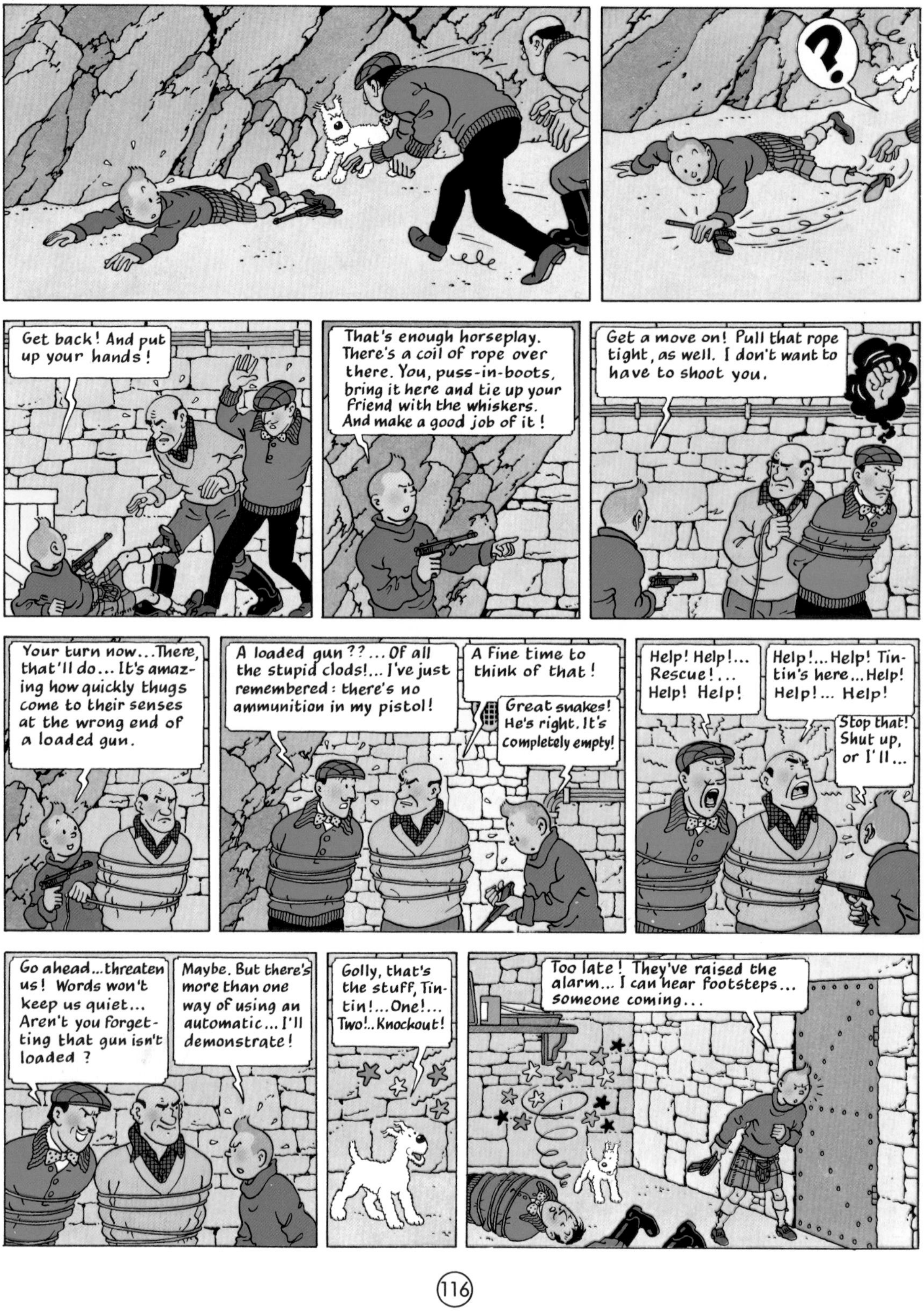
?
Get back! And put up your hands!
That's enough horseplay. There's a coil of rope over there. You, puss-in-boots, bring it here and tie up your friend with the whiskers. And make a good job of it!
Get a move on! Pull that rope tight, as well. I don't want to have to shoot you.
Your turn now... There, that'll do... It's amazing how quickly thugs come to their senses at the wrong end of a loaded gun.
A loaded gun??... Of all the stupid clods!... I've just remembered: there's no ammunition in my pistol!
A fine time to think of that!
Great snakes! He's right. It's completely empty!
Help! Help!... Rescue!... Help! Help!
Help!... Help! Tintin's here... Help! Help!... Help!
Stop that! Shut up, or I'll...
Go ahead... threaten us! Words won't keep us quiet... Aren't you forgetting that gun isn't loaded?
Maybe. But there's more than one way of using an automatic... I'll demonstrate!
Golly, that's the stuff, Tintin!... One!... Two!.. Knockout!
Too late! They've raised the alarm... I can hear footsteps... someone coming...

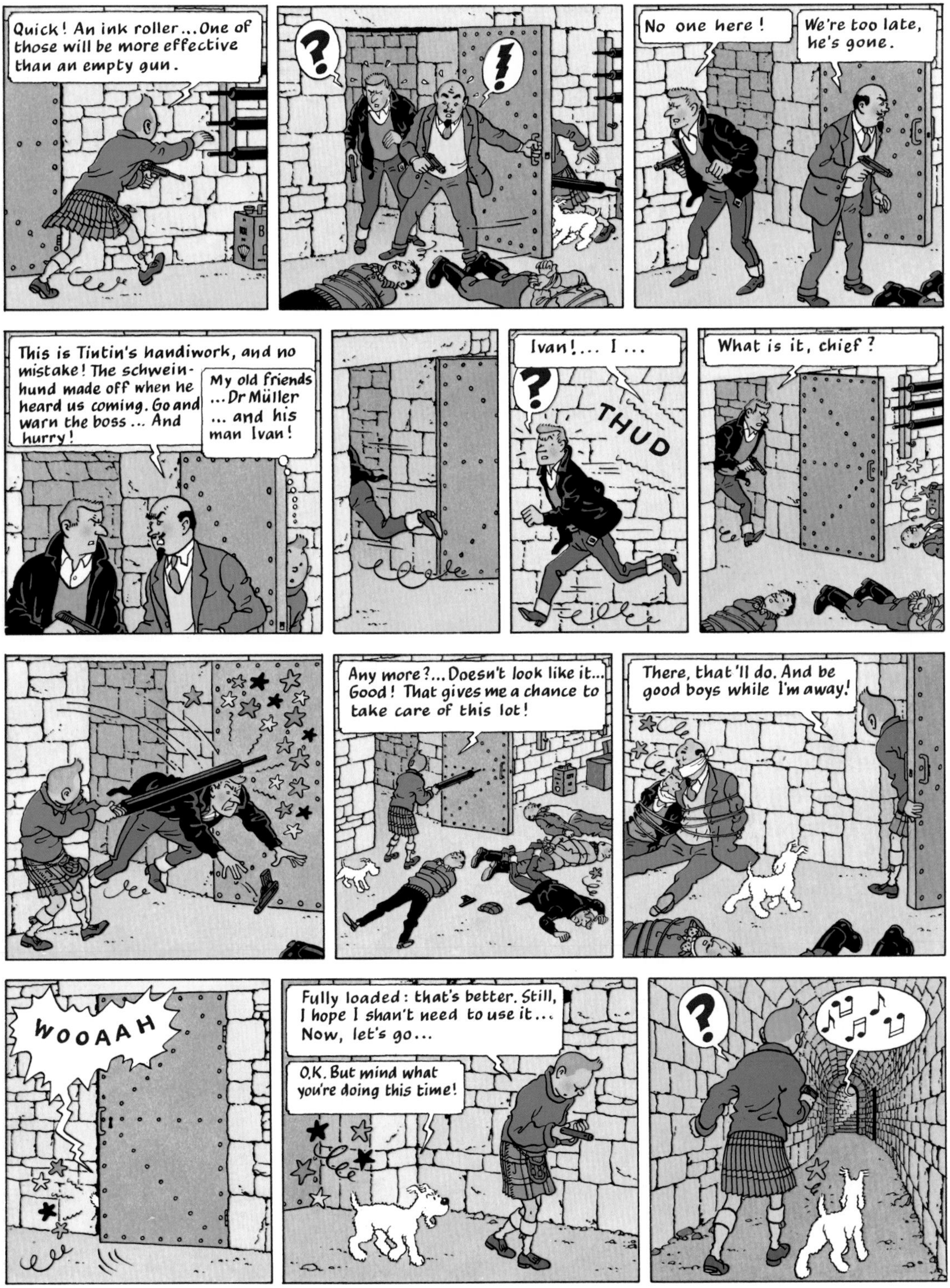

Quick! An ink roller...One of those will be more effective than an empty gun.
?
!
No one here!
We're too late, he's gone.
This is Tintin's handiwork, and no mistake! The schweinhund made off when he heard us coming. Go and warn the boss... And hurry!
My old friends ...Dr Müller ... and his man Ivan!
Ivan!... I...
?
THUD
What is it, chief?
Any more?... Doesn't look like it... Good! That gives me a chance to take care of this lot!
There, that'll do. And be good boys while I'm away!
WOOAAH
Fully loaded: that's better. Still, I hope I shan't need to use it... Now, let's go...
O.K. But mind what you're doing this time!
?

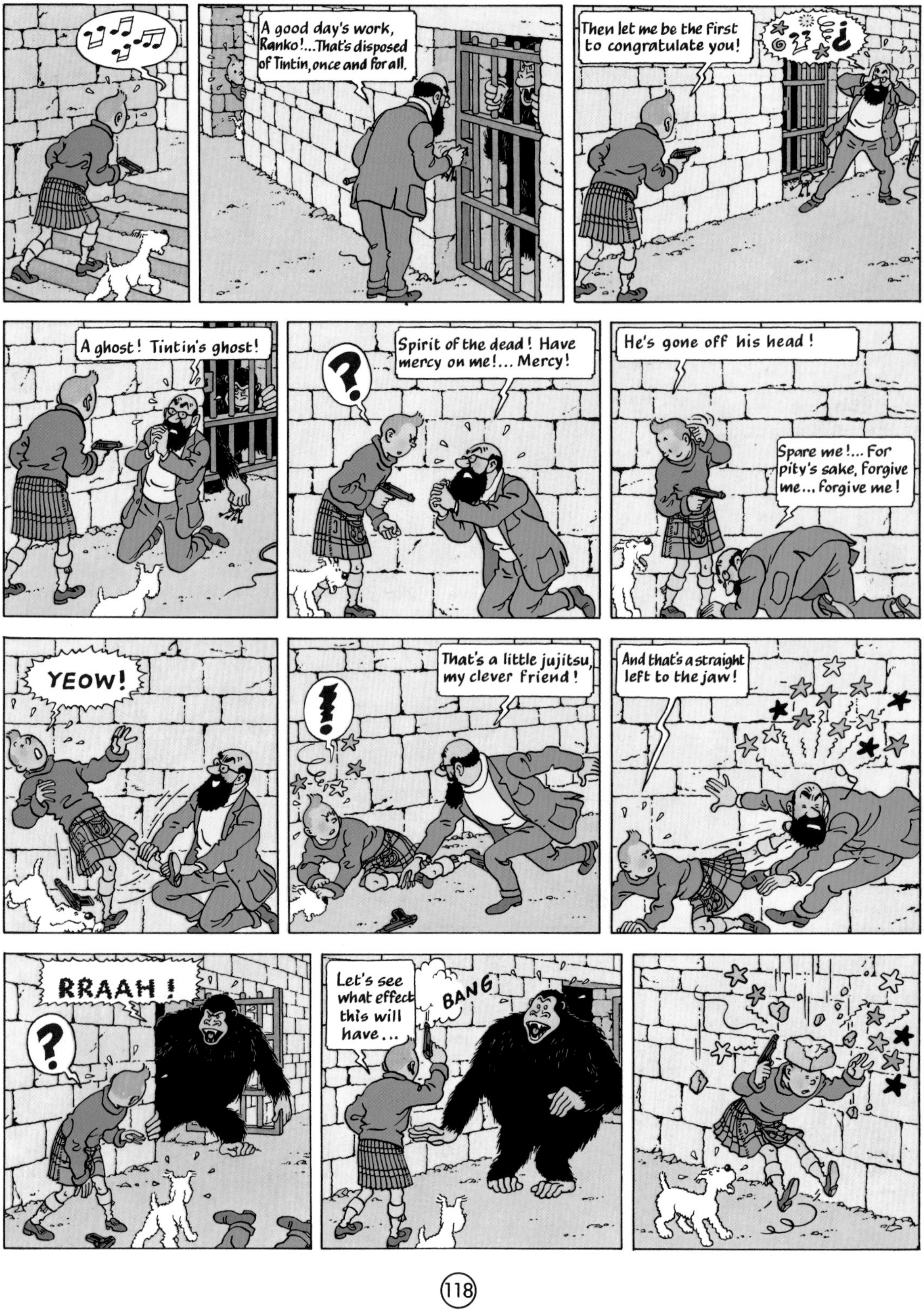
A good day's work, Ranko!... That's disposed of Tintin, once and for all.
Then let me be the first to congratulate you!
A ghost! Tintin's ghost!
Spirit of the dead! Have mercy on me!... Mercy!
He's gone off his head!
Spare me!... For pity's sake, forgive me... forgive me!
YEOW!
That's a little jujitsu, my clever friend!
And that's a straight left to the jaw!
RRAAH!
Let's see what effect this will have...
BANG

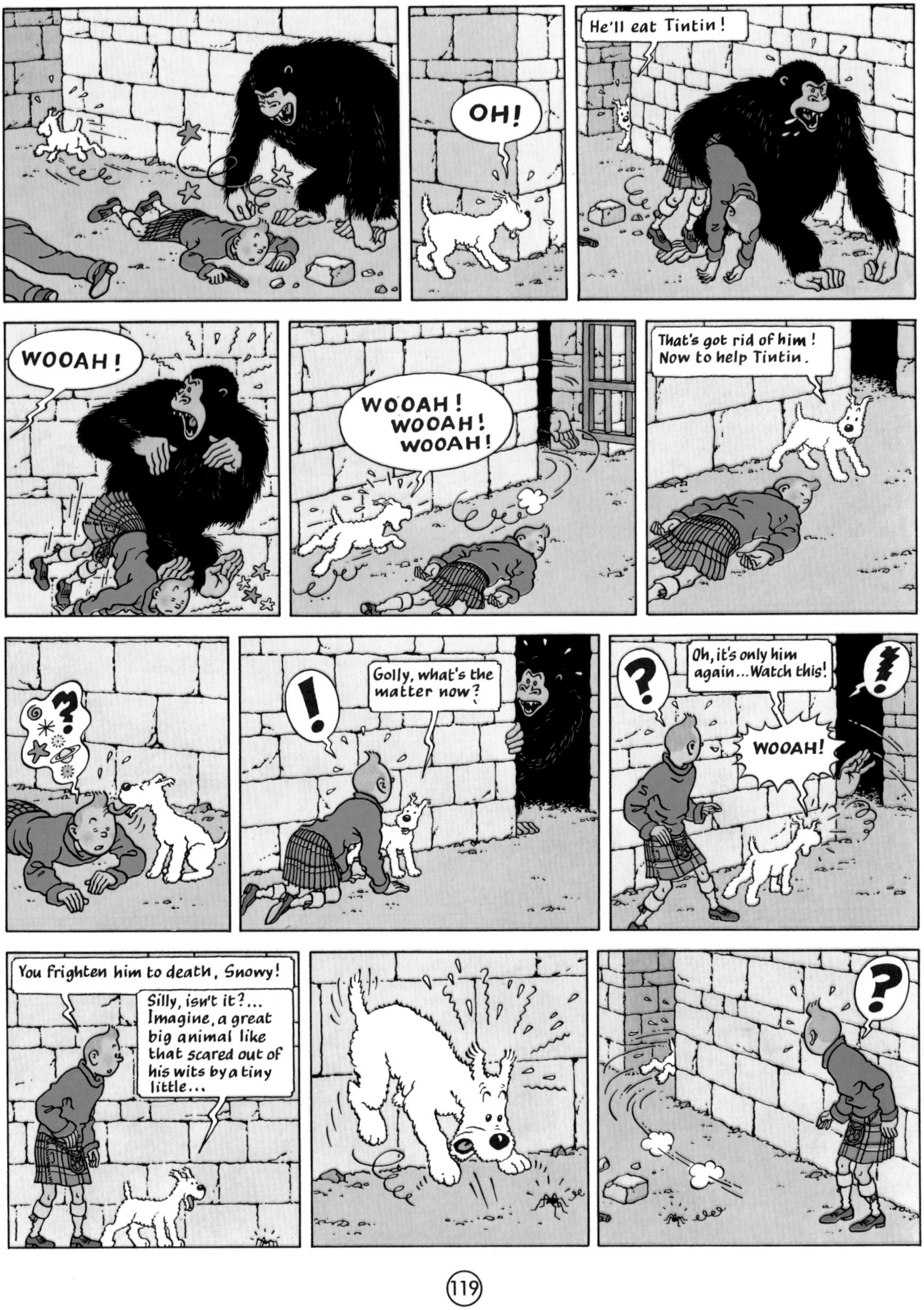
OH!
He'll eat Tintin!
WOOAH!
WOOAH! WOOAH! WOOAH!
That's got rid of him! Now to help Tintin.
Golly, what's the matter now?
Oh, it's only him again... Watch this!
WOOAH!
You frighten him to death, Snowy!
Silly, isn't it?... Imagine, a great big animal like that scared out of his wits by a tiny little...

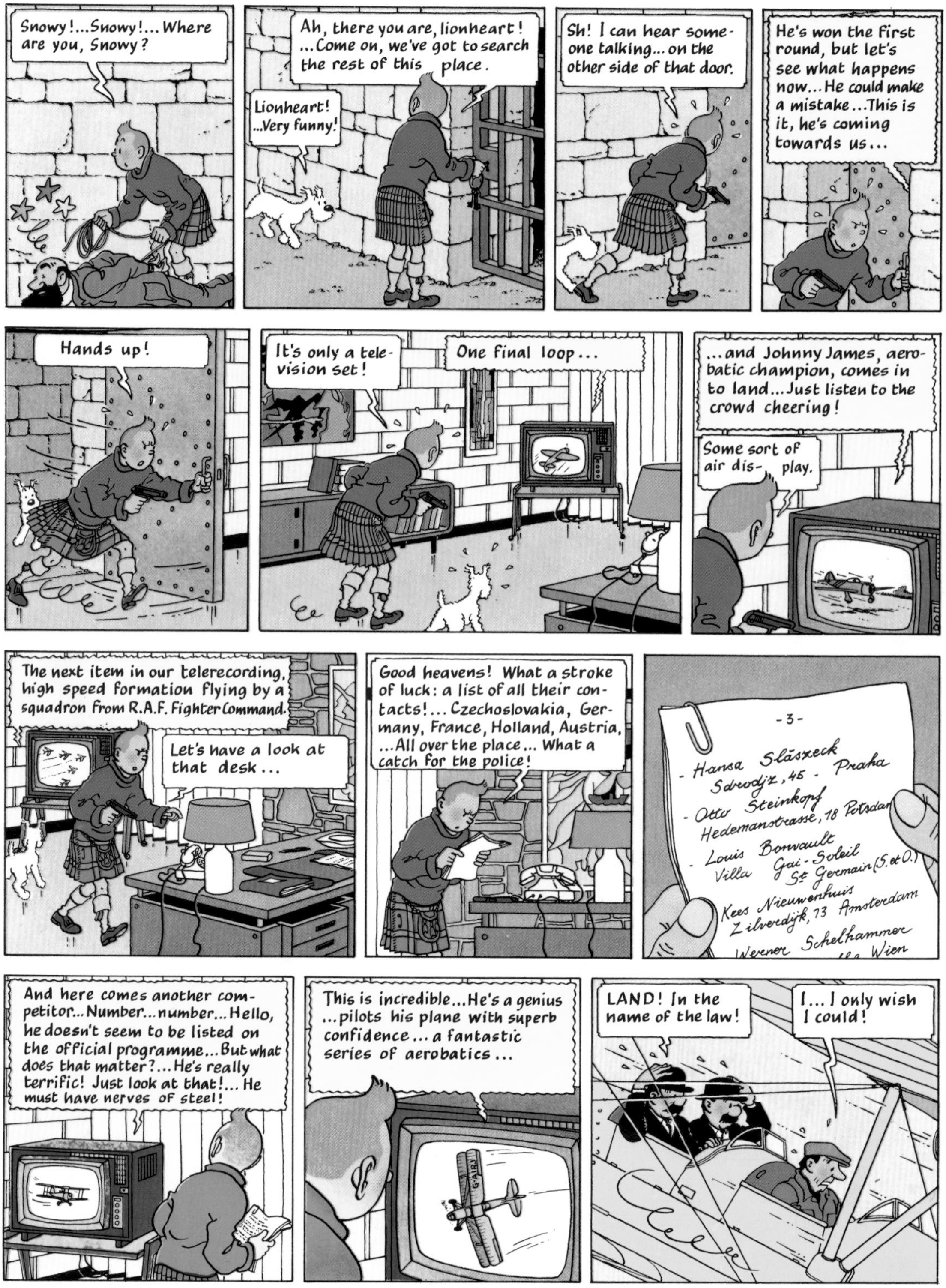
Snowy!...Snowy!... Where are you, Snowy?
Ah, there you are, lionheart! ...Come on, we've got to search the rest of this place.
Lionheart! ...Very funny!
Sh! I can hear some-one talking... on the other side of that door.
He's won the first round, but let's see what happens now... He could make a mistake... This is it, he's coming towards us...
Hands up!
It's only a tele-vision set!
One final loop...
...and Johnny James, aero-batic champion, comes in to land... Just listen to the crowd cheering!
Some sort of air dis- play.
The next item in our telerecording, high speed formation flying by a squadron from R.A.F. Fighter Command.
Let's have a look at that desk...
Good heavens! What a stroke of luck: a list of all their con-tacts!... Czechoslovakia, Ger-many, France, Holland, Austria, ...All over the place... What a catch for the police!
-3-
Hansa Släszeck
Sdrodjz, 45 - Praha
Otto Steinkopf
Hedemanstrasse, 18 Potsdam
Louis Bonvault
Villa Gai-Soleil
St Germain (S. et O.)
Kees Nieuwenhuis
Zilverdijk, 73 Amsterdam
Werner Schelhammer
Wien
And here comes another com-petitor... Number... number... Hello, he doesn't seem to be listed on the official programme... But what does that matter?... He's really terrific! Just look at that!... He must have nerves of steel!
This is incredible... He's a genius ...pilots his plane with superb confidence... a fantastic series of aerobatics...
LAND! In the name of the law!
I... I only wish I could!

HERGÉ

THE ADVENTURES OF TINTIN

KING OTTOKAR'S SCEPTRE

eih bennek *eih blavek*

KING OTTOKAR'S SCEPTRE

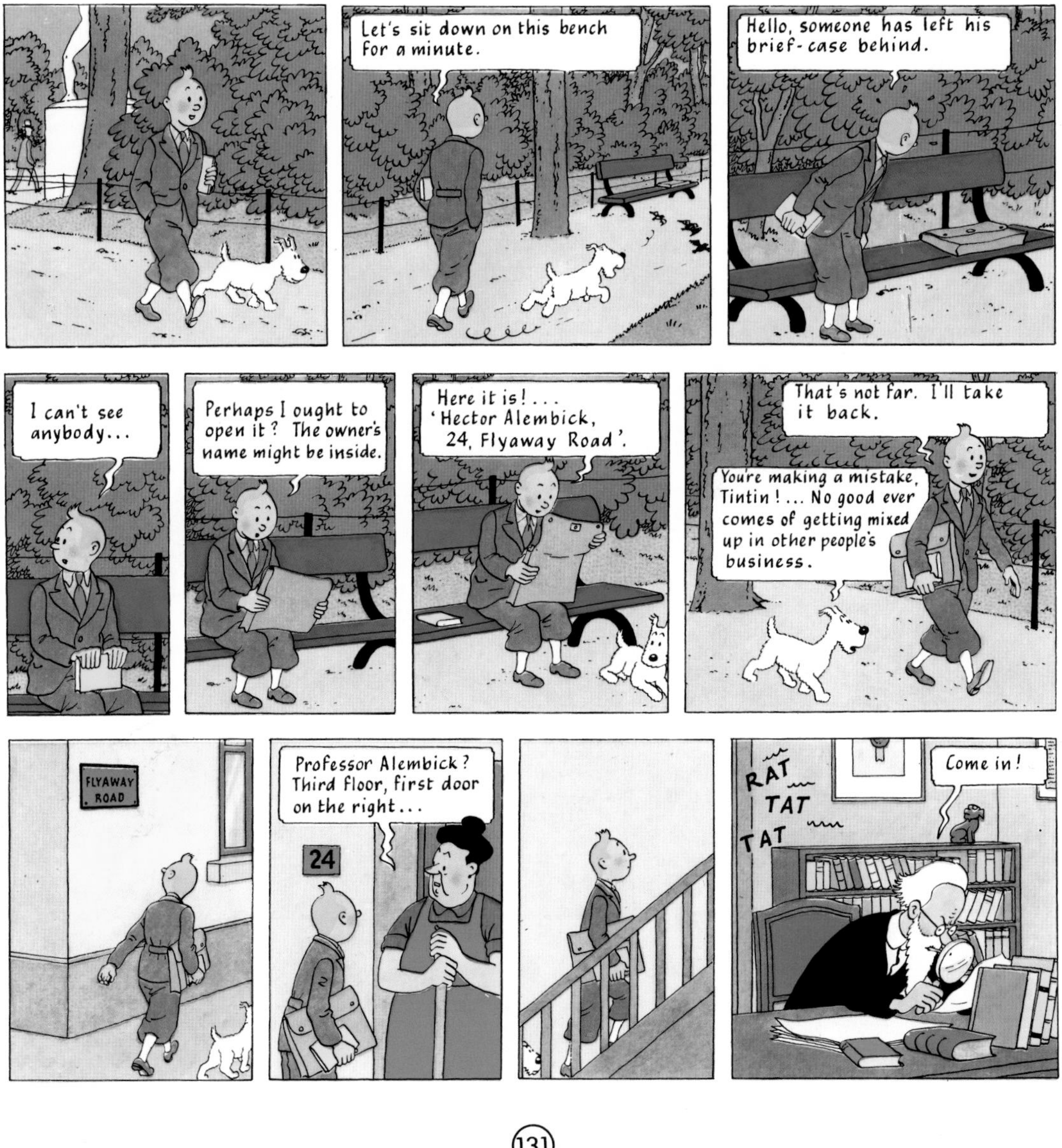

Let's sit down on this bench for a minute.
Hello, someone has left his brief-case behind.
I can't see anybody...
Perhaps I ought to open it? The owner's name might be inside.
Here it is!... 'Hector Alembick, 24, Flyaway Road'.
That's not far. I'll take it back.
You're making a mistake, Tintin!... No good ever comes of getting mixed up in other people's business.
FLYAWAY ROAD
Professor Alembick? Third floor, first door on the right...
24
RAT TAT TAT
Come in!

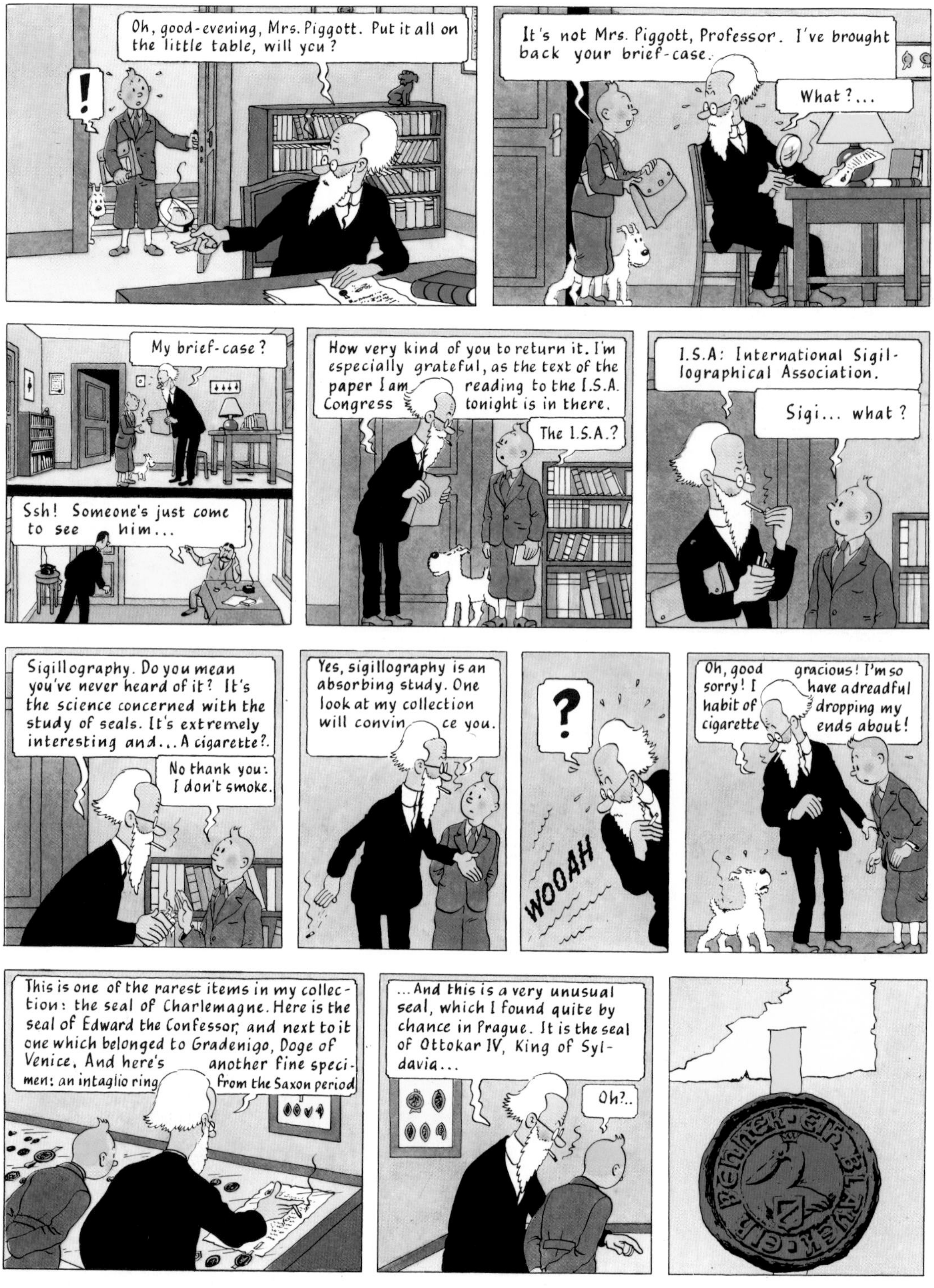
Oh, good-evening, Mrs. Piggott. Put it all on the little table, will you?
!
It's not Mrs. Piggott, Professor. I've brought back your brief-case.
What?...
My brief-case?
Ssh! Someone's just come to see him...
How very kind of you to return it. I'm especially grateful, as the text of the paper I am reading to the I.S.A. Congress tonight is in there.
The I.S.A.?
I.S.A: International Sigillographical Association.
Sigi... what?
Sigillography. Do you mean you've never heard of it? It's the science concerned with the study of seals. It's extremely interesting and... A cigarette?.
No thank you: I don't smoke.
Yes, sigillography is an absorbing study. One look at my collection will convince you.
?
WOOAH
Oh, good gracious! I'm so sorry! I have a dreadful habit of dropping my cigarette ends about!
This is one of the rarest items in my collection: the seal of Charlemagne. Here is the seal of Edward the Confessor, and next to it one which belonged to Gradenigo, Doge of Venice. And here's another fine specimen: an intaglio ring from the Saxon period
...And this is a very unusual seal, which I found quite by chance in Prague. It is the seal of Ottokar IV, King of Syldavia...
Oh?..

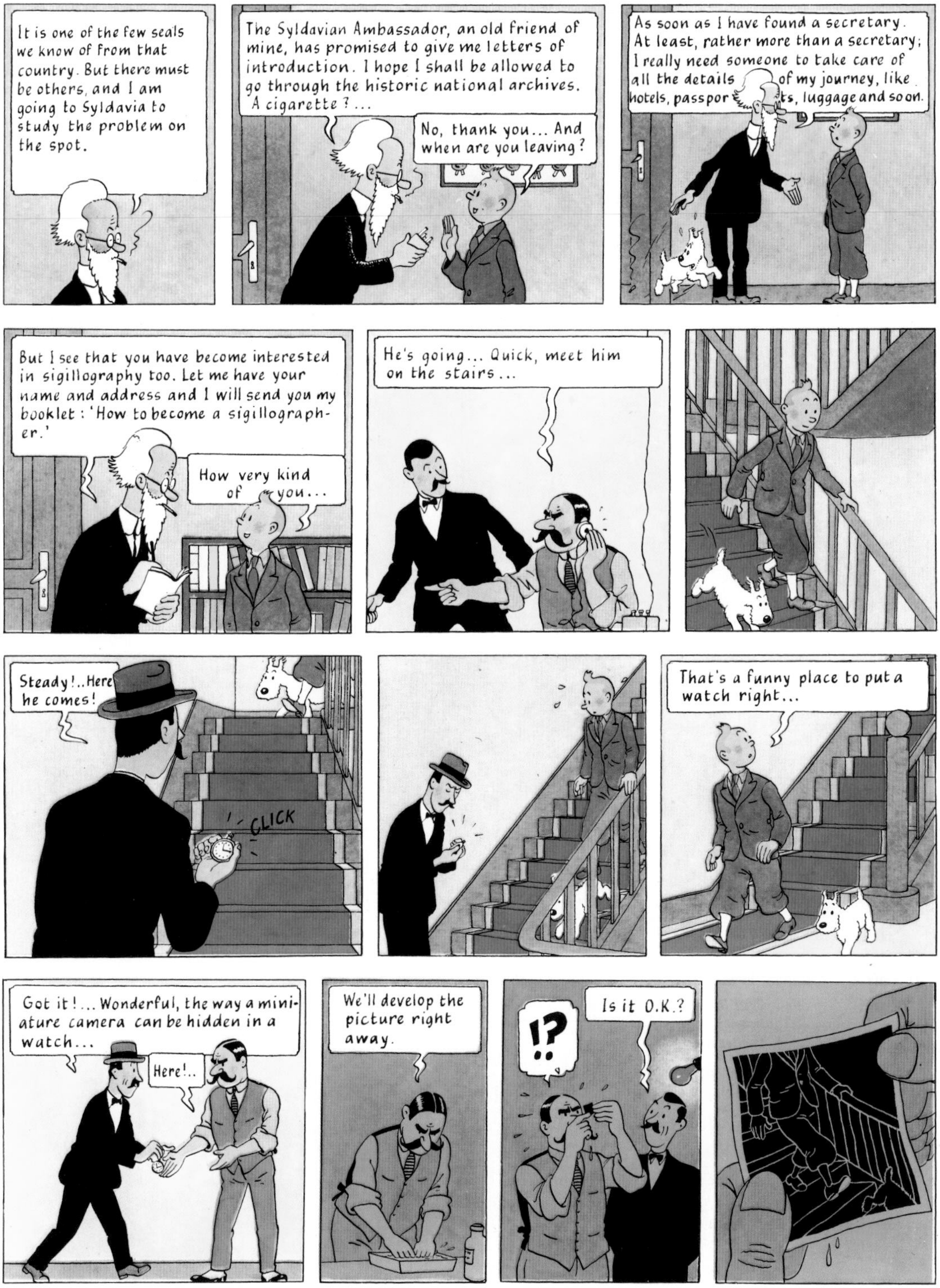
It is one of the few seals we know of from that country. But there must be others, and I am going to Syldavia to study the problem on the spot.
The Syldavian Ambassador, an old friend of mine, has promised to give me letters of introduction. I hope I shall be allowed to go through the historic national archives. A cigarette?...
No, thank you... And when are you leaving?
As soon as I have found a secretary. At least, rather more than a secretary; I really need someone to take care of all the details of my journey, like hotels, passpor ts, luggage and so on.
But I see that you have become interested in sigillography too. Let me have your name and address and I will send you my booklet: 'How to become a sigillographer.'
How very kind of you...
He's going... Quick, meet him on the stairs...
Steady!.. Here he comes!
CLICK
That's a funny place to put a watch right...
Got it!... Wonderful, the way a miniature camera can be hidden in a watch...
Here!..
We'll develop the picture right away.
!?
Is it O.K.?

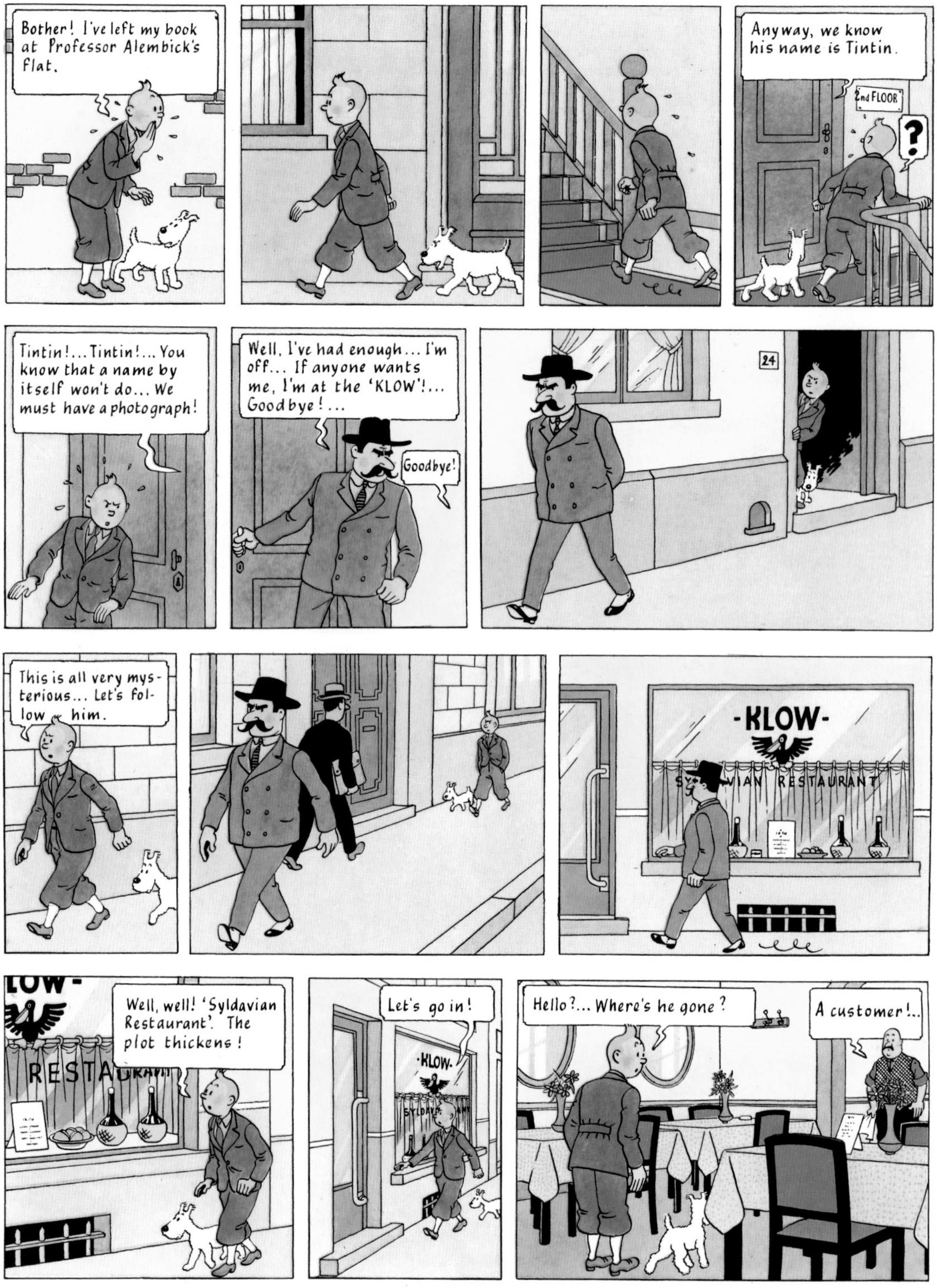
Bother! I've left my book at Professor Alembick's flat.
Anyway, we know his name is Tintin.
2nd FLOOR
?
Tintin!... Tintin!... You know that a name by itself won't do... We must have a photograph!
Well, I've had enough... I'm off... If anyone wants me, I'm at the 'KLOW'!... Goodbye!...
Goodbye!
24
This is all very mysterious... Let's follow him.
-KLOW-
SYLDAVIAN RESTAURANT
Well, well! 'Syldavian Restaurant'. The plot thickens!
Let's go in!
-KLOW-
Hello?... Where's he gone?
A customer!..

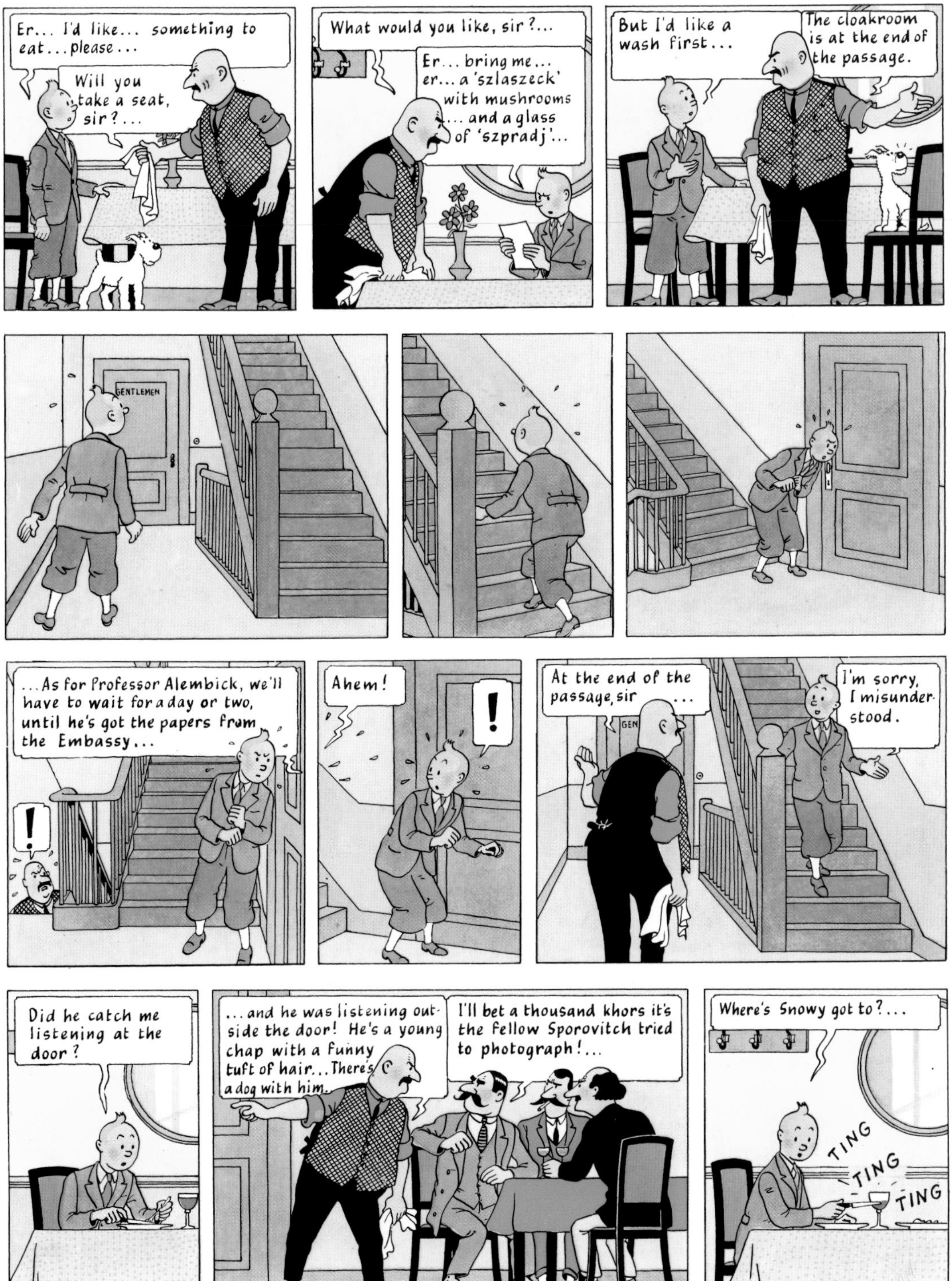
Er... I'd like... something to eat... please...
Will you take a seat, sir?...
What would you like, sir?...
Er... bring me... er... a 'szlaszeck' with mushrooms ... and a glass of 'szpradj'...
But I'd like a wash first...
The cloakroom is at the end of the passage.
GENTLEMEN
...As for Professor Alembick, we'll have to wait for a day or two, until he's got the papers from the Embassy...
!
Ahem!
!
At the end of the passage, sir ...
GEN
I'm sorry, I misunderstood.
Did he catch me listening at the door?
...and he was listening outside the door! He's a young chap with a funny tuft of hair... There's a dog with him.
I'll bet a thousand khors it's the fellow Sporovitch tried to photograph!...
Where's Snowy got to?...
TING
TING
TING

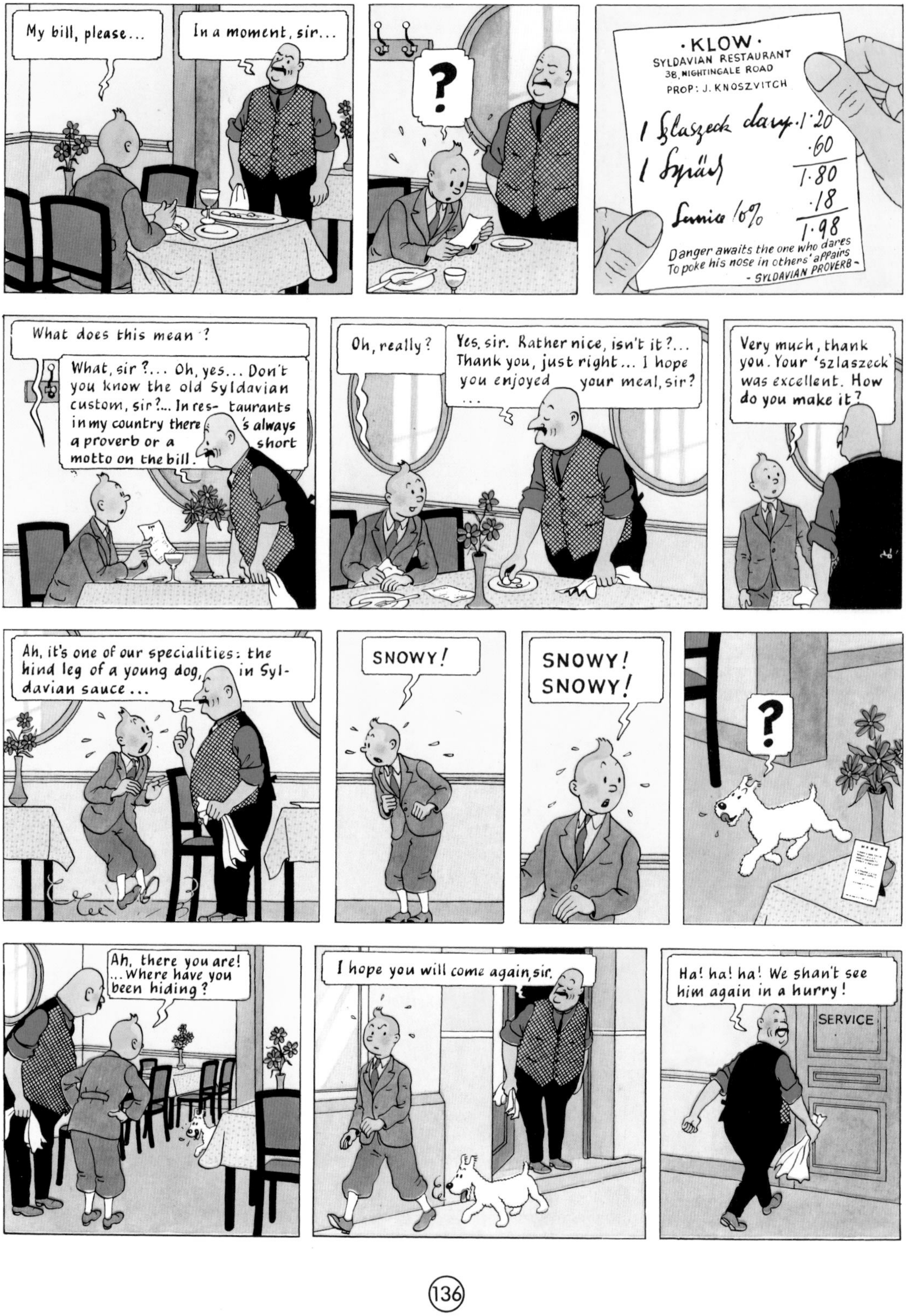

My bill, please...
In a moment, sir...
?
·KLOW·
SYLDAVIAN RESTAURANT
38, NIGHTINGALE ROAD
PROP: J. KNOSZVITCH
1·20
·60
1·80
·18
1·98
Danger awaits the one who dares
To poke his nose in others' affairs
- SYLDAVIAN PROVERB -
What does this mean ?
What, sir ?... Oh, yes... Don't you know the old Syldavian custom, sir ?... In restaurants in my country there's always a proverb or a short motto on the bill.
Oh, really ?
Yes, sir. Rather nice, isn't it ?... Thank you, just right... I hope you enjoyed your meal, sir? ...
Very much, thank you. Your 'szlaszeck' was excellent. How do you make it ?
Ah, it's one of our specialities: the hind leg of a young dog, in Syldavian sauce...
SNOWY!
SNOWY! SNOWY!
?
Ah, there you are! ...Where have you been hiding ?
I hope you will come again, sir.
Ha! ha! ha! We shan't see him again in a hurry!
SERVICE

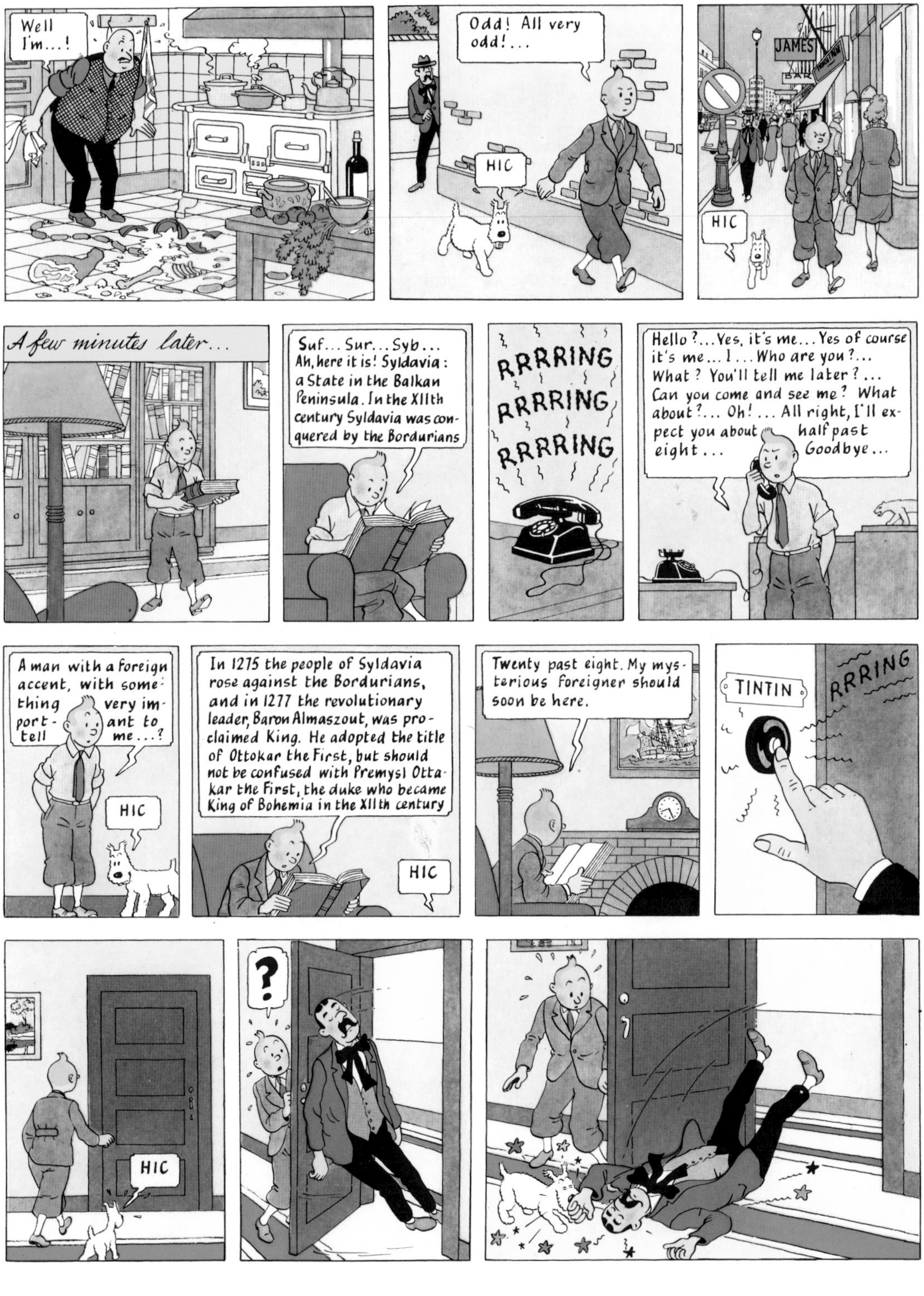
Well I'm...!
Odd! All very odd!...
HIC
JAMES
BAR
HIC
A few minutes later...
Suf... Sur... Syb... Ah, here it is! Syldavia: a State in the Balkan Peninsula. In the XIIth century Syldavia was conquered by the Bordurians
RRRRING RRRRING RRRRING
Hello?... Yes, it's me... Yes of course it's me... I... Who are you?... What? You'll tell me later?... Can you come and see me? What about?... Oh!... All right, I'll expect you about half past eight... Goodbye...
A man with a foreign accent, with something very important to tell me...?
HIC
In 1275 the people of Syldavia rose against the Bordurians, and in 1277 the revolutionary leader, Baron Almaszout, was proclaimed King. He adopted the title of Ottokar the First, but should not be confused with Premysl Ottakar the First, the duke who became King of Bohemia in the XIIth century
HIC
Twenty past eight. My mysterious foreigner should soon be here.
TINTIN
RRRING
HIC
?

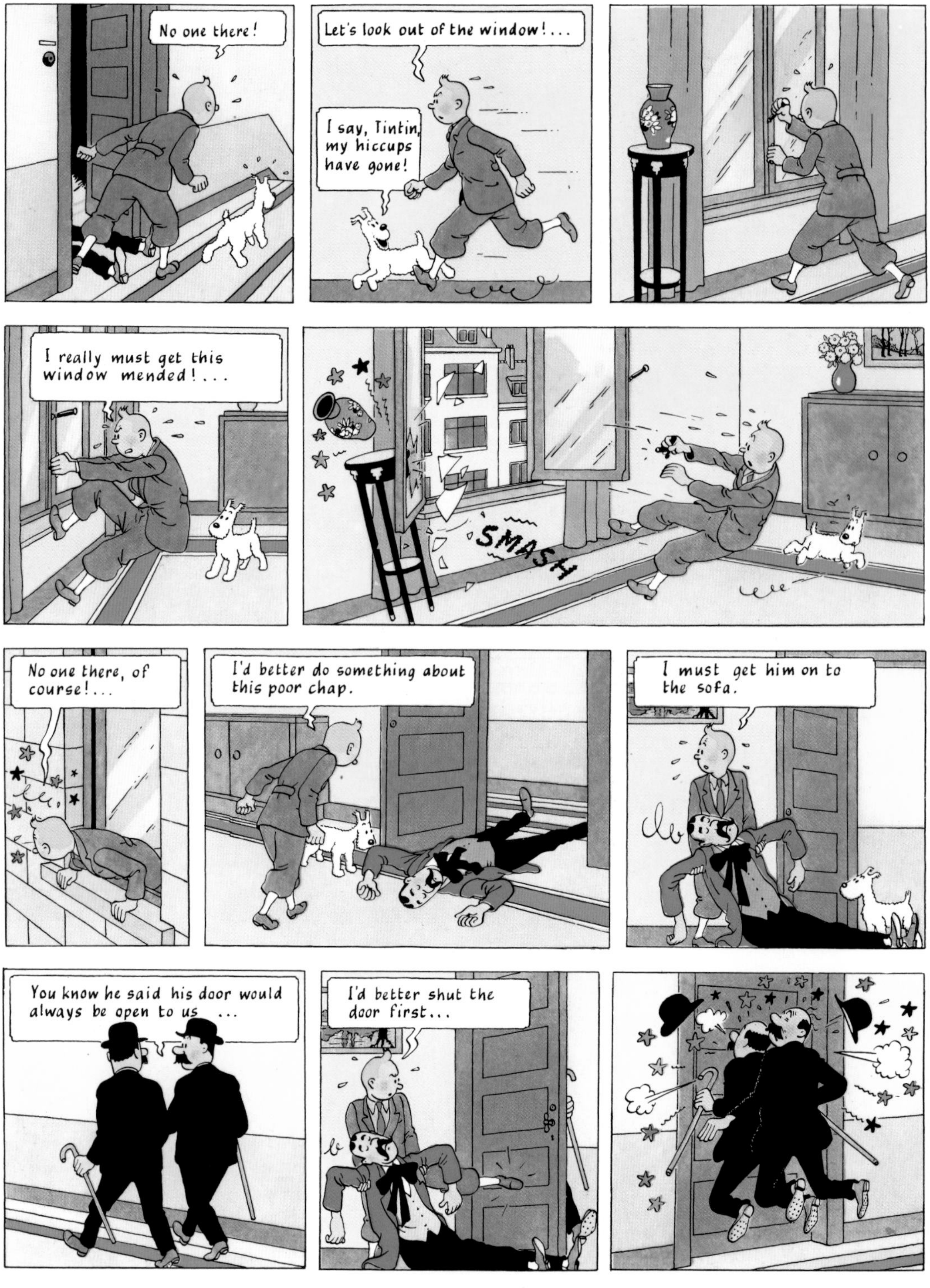

No one there!
Let's look out of the window!...
I say, Tintin, my hiccups have gone!
I really must get this window mended!...
SMASH
No one there, of course!...
I'd better do something about this poor chap.
I must get him on to the sofa.
You know he said his door would always be open to us ...
I'd better shut the door first...

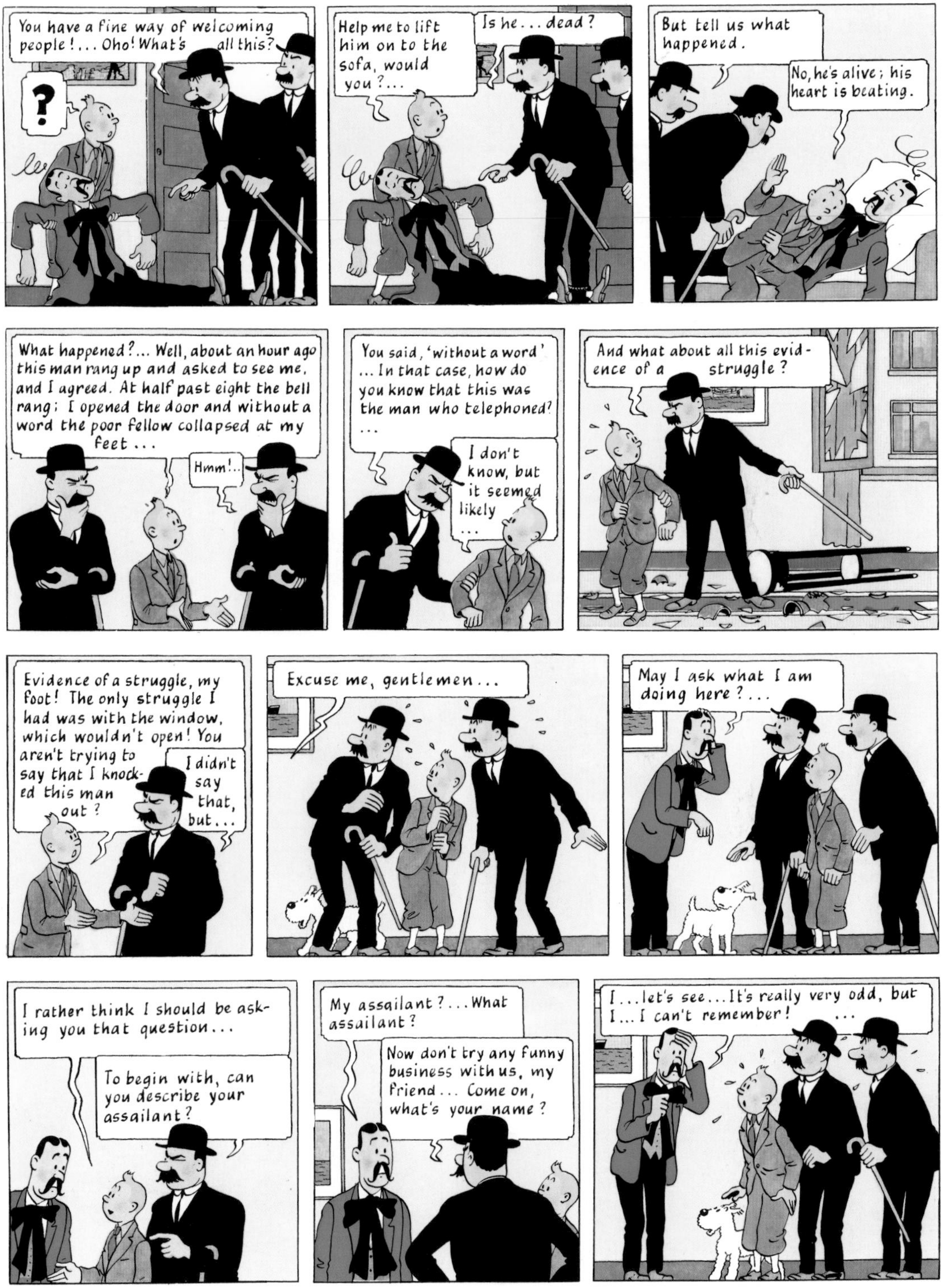
You have a fine way of welcoming people!... Oho! What's all this?
?
Help me to lift him on to the sofa, would you?...
Is he... dead?
But tell us what happened.
No, he's alive; his heart is beating.
What happened?... Well, about an hour ago this man rang up and asked to see me, and I agreed. At half past eight the bell rang; I opened the door and without a word the poor fellow collapsed at my feet...
Hmm!..
You said, 'without a word' ... In that case, how do you know that this was the man who telephoned? ...
I don't know, but it seemed likely ...
And what about all this evidence of a struggle?
Evidence of a struggle, my foot! The only struggle I had was with the window, which wouldn't open! You aren't trying to say that I knocked this man out?
I didn't say that, but...
Excuse me, gentlemen...
May I ask what I am doing here?...
I rather think I should be asking you that question...
To begin with, can you describe your assailant?
My assailant?... What assailant?
Now don't try any funny business with us, my friend... Come on, what's your name?
I... let's see... It's really very odd, but I... I can't remember! ...

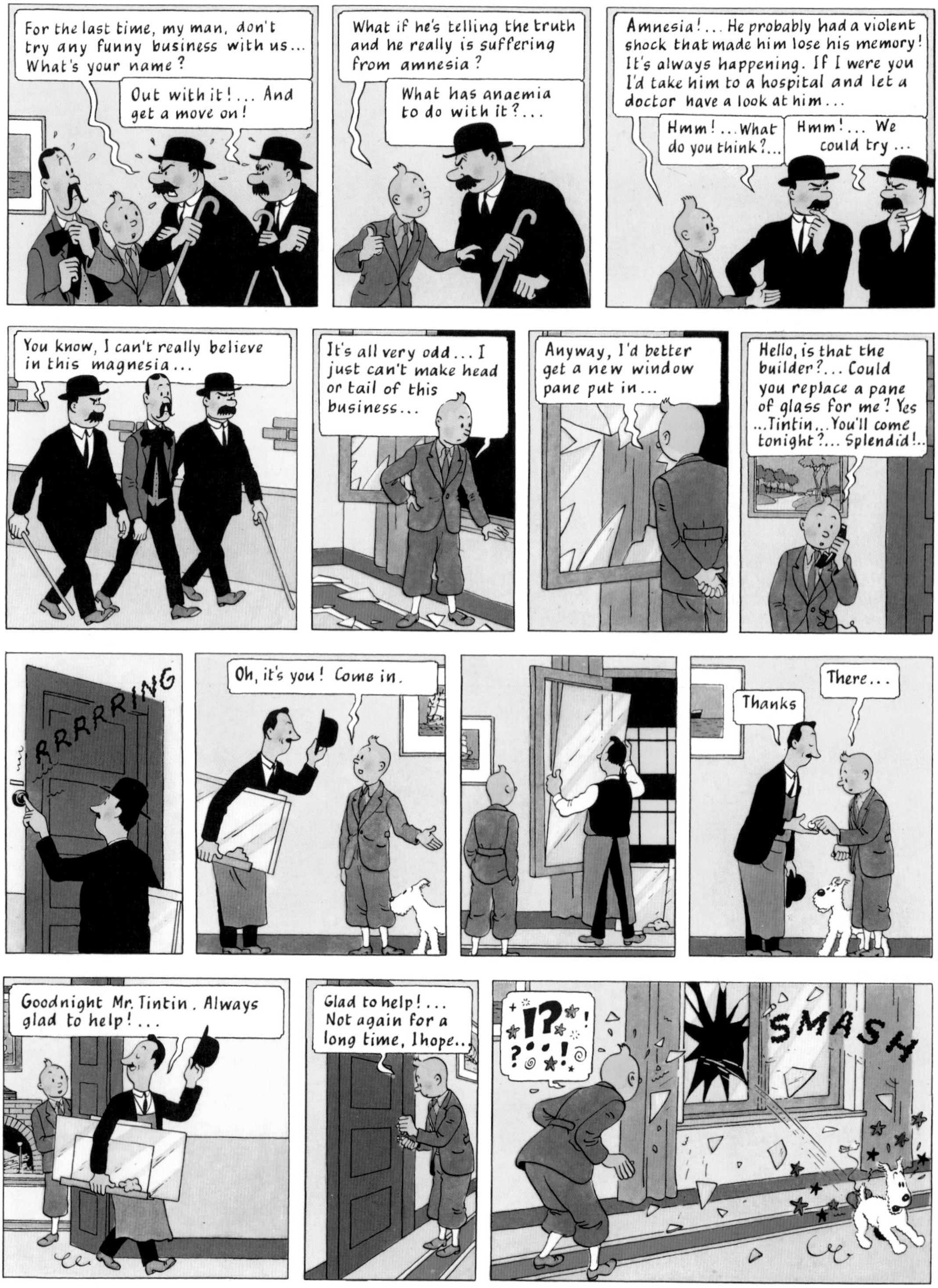
For the last time, my man, don't try any funny business with us... What's your name?
Out with it!... And get a move on!
What if he's telling the truth and he really is suffering from amnesia?
What has anaemia to do with it?...
Amnesia!... He probably had a violent shock that made him lose his memory! It's always happening. If I were you I'd take him to a hospital and let a doctor have a look at him...
Hmm!... What do you think?...
Hmm!... We could try...
You know, I can't really believe in this magnesia...
It's all very odd... I just can't make head or tail of this business...
Anyway, I'd better get a new window pane put in...
Hello, is that the builder?... Could you replace a pane of glass for me? Yes ...Tintin... You'll come tonight?... Splendid!..
RRRRRRING
Oh, it's you! Come in.
Thanks
There...
Goodnight Mr. Tintin. Always glad to help!...
Glad to help!... Not again for a long time, I hope...
!?
SMASH

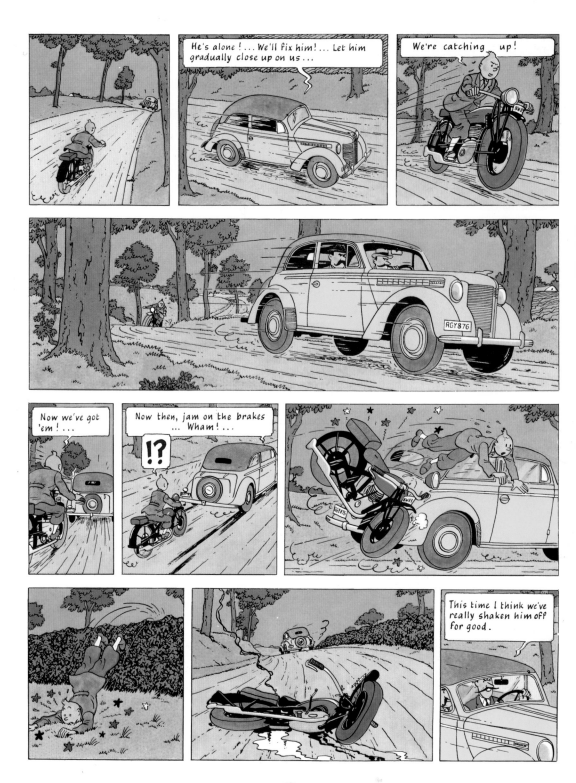

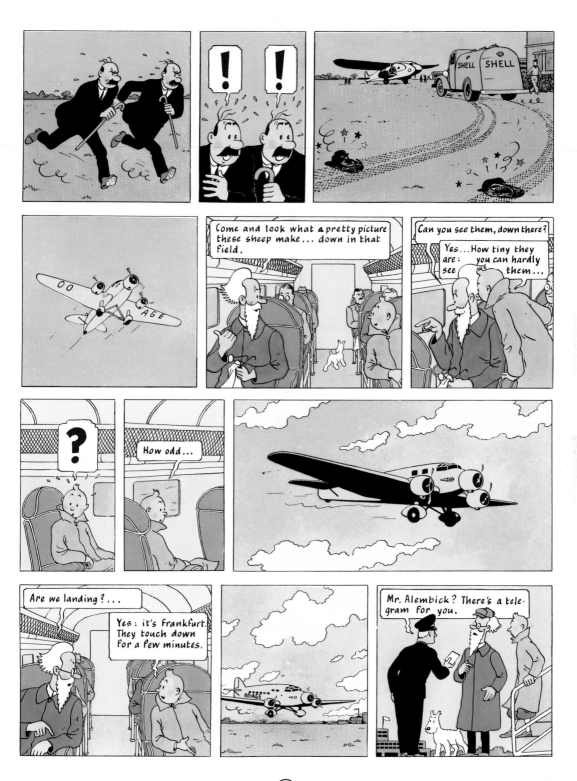

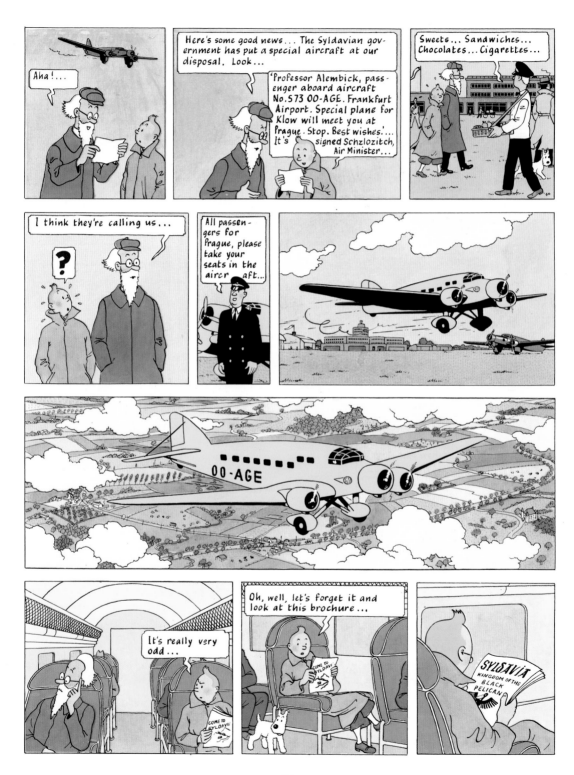

SYLDAVIA
THE KINGDOM OF THE BLACK PELICAN

MONG the many enchanting places which deservedly attract foreign visitors with a love for picturesque ceremony and colourful folklore, there is one small country which, although relatively unknown, surpasses many others in interest. Isolated until modern times because of its inaccessible position, this country is now served by a regular air-line network, which brings it within the reach of all who love unspoiled beauty, the proverbial hospitality of a peasant people, and the charm of medieval customs which still survive despite the march of progress.

This is Syldavia.

Syldavia is a small country in Eastern Europe, comprising two great valleys: those of the river Vladir, and its tributary, the Moltus. The rivers meet at Klow, the capital (122,000 inhabitants). These valleys are flanked by wide plateaux covered with forests, and are surrounded by high, snow-capped mountains. In the fertile Syldavian plains are corn-lands and cattle pastures. The subsoil is rich in minerals of all kinds.

Numerous thermal and sulphur springs gush from the earth, the chief centres being at Klow (cardiac diseases) and Kragoniedin (rheumatic complaints).

The total population is estimated to be 642,000 inhabitants.

Syldavia exports wheat, mineral-water from Klow, firewood, horses and violinists.

HISTORY OF SYLDAVIA

Until the VIth century, Syldavia was inhabited by nomadic tribes of unknown origin.

Overrun by the Slavs in the VIth century, the country was conquered in the Xth century by the Turks, who drove the Slavs into the mountains and occupied the plains.

In 1127, Hveghi, leader of a Slav tribe, swooped down from the mountains at the head of a band of partisans and fell upon isolated Turkish villages, putting all who resisted him to the sword. Thus he rapidly became master of a large part of Syldavian territory.

A great battle took place in the valley of the Moltus near Zileheroum, the Turkish capital of Syldavia, between the Turkish army and Hveghi's irregulars.

Enfeebled by long inactivity and badly led by incompetent officers, the Turkish army put up little resistance and fled in disorder.

Having vanquished the Turks, Hveghi was elected king, and given the name Muskar, that is, The Brave (Muskh: 'brave' and Kar: 'king').

The capital, Zileheroum, was renamed Klow, that is, Freetown, (Kloho: 'to free', and Ow: 'town').

Guard at the Royal Treasure House, Klow

A typical fisherman from Dbrnouk
(south coast of Syldavia)

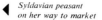 Syldavian peasant
on her way to market

A view of Niedzdrow,
in the Vladir valley ▶

(149)

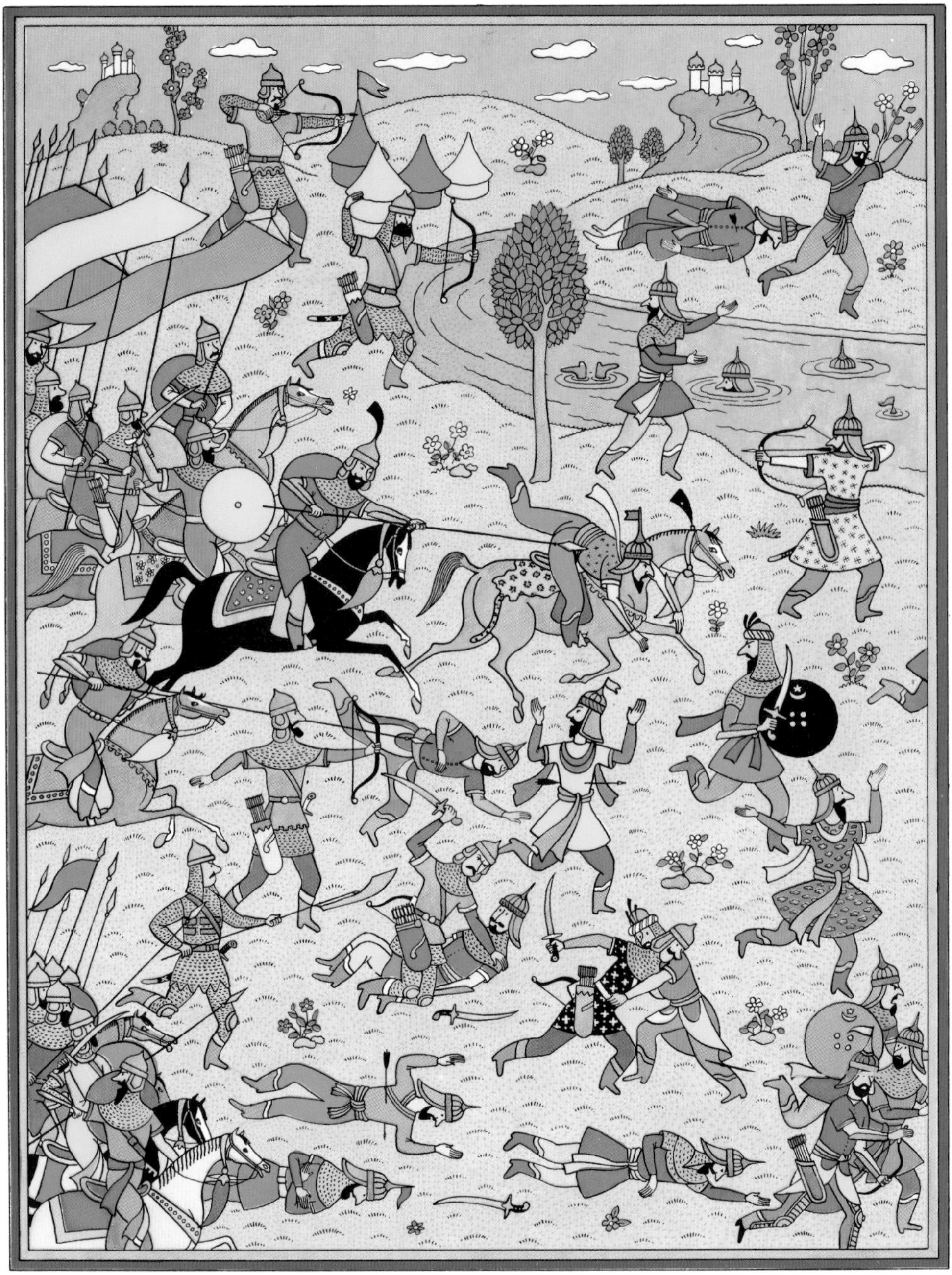

THE BATTLE OF ZILEHEROUM
After a XVth century miniature

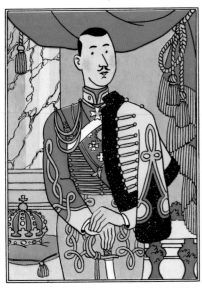

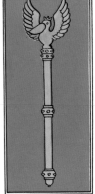

H.M. King Muskar XII, the present ruler of Syldavia in the uniform of Colonel of the Guards

Muskar was a wise king who lived at peace with his neighbours, and the country prospered. He died in 1168, mourned by all his subjects.

His eldest son succeeded to the throne with the title of Muskar II.

Unlike his father, Muskar II lacked authority and was unable to keep order in his kingdom. A period of anarchy replaced one of peaceful prosperity.

In the neighbouring state of Borduria the people observed Syldavia's decline, and their king profited by this opportunity to invade the country. Borduria annexed Syldavia in 1195.

For almost a century Syldavia groaned under the foreign yoke.

In 1275 Baron Almaszout repeated the exploits of Hveghi by coming down from the hills and routing the Bordurians in less than six months.

He was proclaimed King in 1277, taking the name of Ottokar. He was, however, much less powerful than Muskar.

The barons who had helped him in the campaign against the Bordurians forced him to grant them a charter, based on the English Magna Carta signed by King John (Lackland). This marked the beginning of the feudal system in Syldavia.

Ottokar I of Syldavia should not be confused with the Ottakars (Premysls) who were Dukes, and later Kings, of Bohemia.

This period was noteworthy for the rise in power of the nobles, who fortified their castles and maintained bands of armed mercenaries, strong enough to oppose the King's forces.

But the true founder of the kingdom of Syldavia was Ottokar IV, who ascended the throne in 1370.

From the time of his accession he initiated widespread reforms. He raised a powerful army and subdued the arrogant nobles, confiscating their wealth.

He fostered the advancement of the arts, of letters, commerce and agriculture.

He united the whole nation and gave it that security, both at home and abroad, so necessary for the renewal of prosperity.

It was he who pronounced those famous words: '*Eih bennek, eih blavek*', which have become the motto of Syldavia.

The origin of this saying is as follows:

One day Baron Staszrvich, son of one of the dispossessed nobles whose lands had been forfeited to the crown, came before the sovereign and recklessly claimed the throne of Syldavia.

The King listened in silence, but when the presumptuous baron's speech ended with a demand that he deliver up his sceptre, the King rose and cried fiercely: 'Come and get it!'

Mad with rage, the young baron drew his sword, and before the retainers could intervene, fell upon the King.

The King stepped swiftly aside, and as his adversary passed him, carried forward by the impetus of his charge, Ottokar struck him a blow on the head with the sceptre, laying him low and at the same time crying in Syldavian: '*Eih bennek, eih blavek!*', which can be said to mean: 'If you gather thistles, expect prickles'. And turning to his astonished court he said: '*Honi soit qui mal y pense!*'

Then, gazing intently at his sceptre, he addressed it in the following words: 'O Sceptre, thou hast saved my life. Be henceforward the true symbol of Syldavian Kingship. Woe to the king who loses thee, for I declare that such a man shall be unworthy to rule thereafter.'

And from that time, every year on St. Vladimir's Day each successor of Ottokar IV has made a great ceremonial tour of his capital.

He bears in his hand the historic sceptre, without which he would lose the right to rule; as he passes, the people sing the famous anthem:

Syldavians unite!
Praise our King's might:
The Sceptre his right!

Right: The sceptre of Ottokar IV

Below: An illuminated page from 'The Memorable Deeds of Ottokar IV', a XIVth century manuscript

eih bennek
eih blävek
Pir Ottokar
dus pollez
ez könikstz
dan fronn eszt pho
mã Czeillã czäi=
dã ön eltcãr alpũ
kzommetz pakkeh:
o lapzãda könikstz
itd o alpũ klöppz=
Staszrvitchz erom
szũbel ő. Dãzsbick
tällta őpp o carrő.

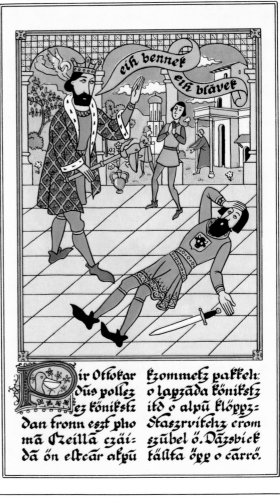

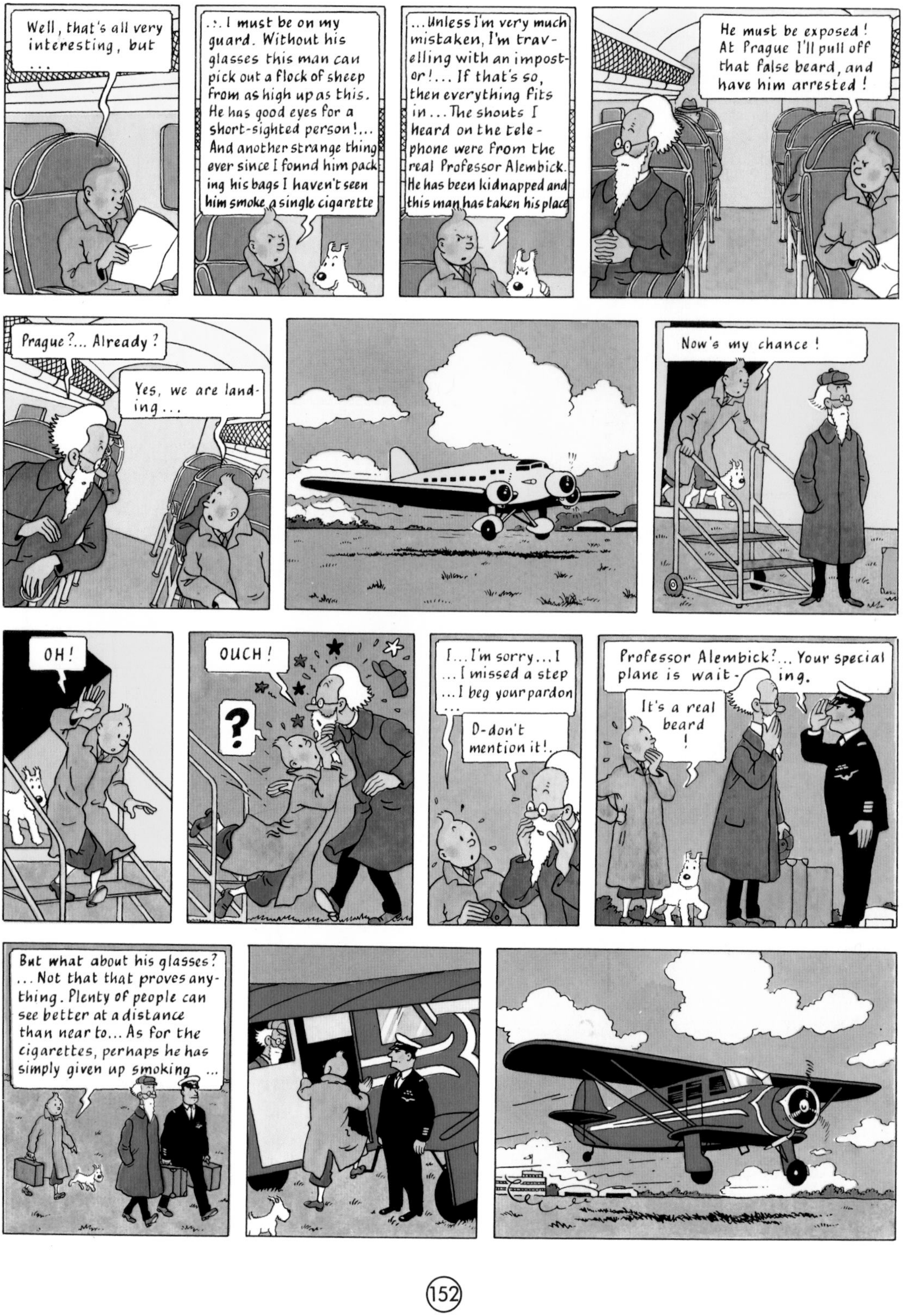
Well, that's all very interesting, but ...
... I must be on my guard. Without his glasses this man can pick out a flock of sheep from as high up as this. He has good eyes for a short-sighted person!... And another strange thing ever since I found him packing his bags I haven't seen him smoke a single cigarette
...Unless I'm very much mistaken, I'm travelling with an impostor!... If that's so, then everything fits in... The shouts I heard on the telephone were from the real Professor Alembick. He has been kidnapped and this man has taken his place
He must be exposed! At Prague I'll pull off that false beard, and have him arrested!
Prague?... Already?
Yes, we are landing...
Now's my chance!
OH!
OUCH!
?
I... I'm sorry... I ... I missed a step ... I beg your pardon ...
D-don't mention it!...
Professor Alembick?... Your special plane is waiting.
It's a real beard!
But what about his glasses? ... Not that that proves anything. Plenty of people can see better at a distance than near to... As for the cigarettes, perhaps he has simply given up smoking ...

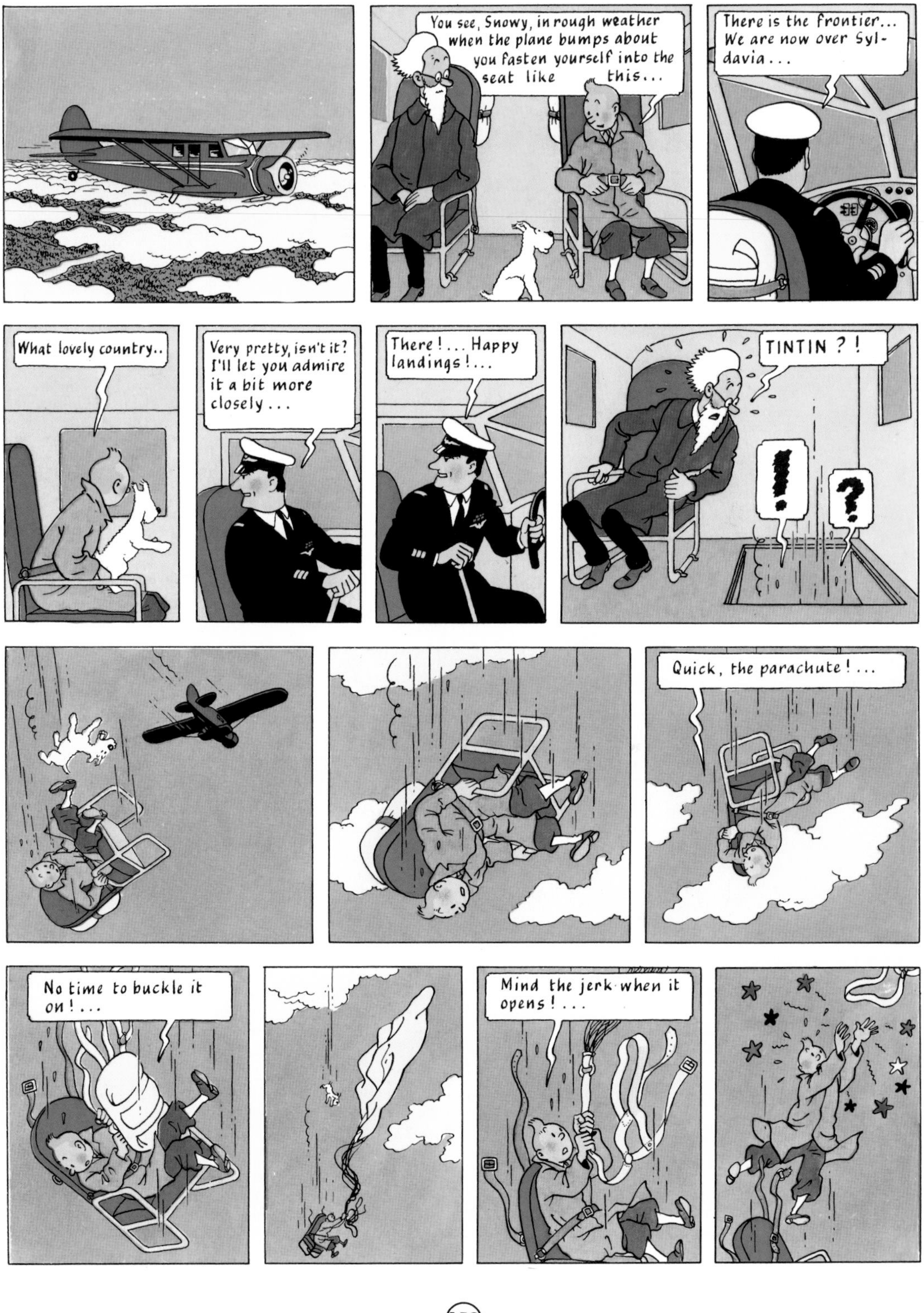
You see, Snowy, in rough weather when the plane bumps about you fasten yourself into the seat like this...
There is the frontier... We are now over Syldavia...
What lovely country..
Very pretty, isn't it? I'll let you admire it a bit more closely...
There!... Happy landings!...
TINTIN ?!
!
?
Quick, the parachute!...
No time to buckle it on!...
Mind the jerk when it opens!...

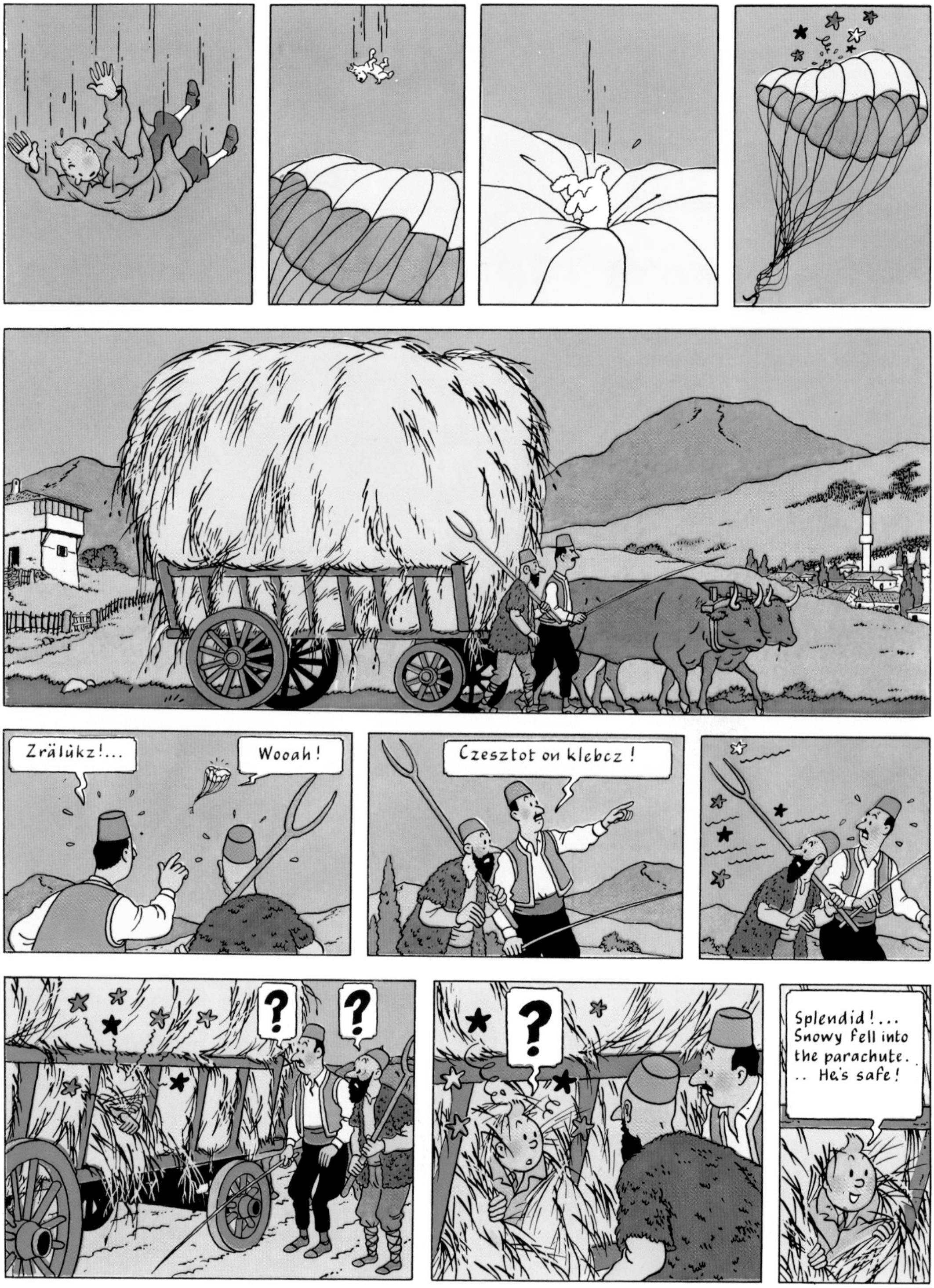
Zrälùkz!...
Wooah!
Czesztot on klebcz!
?
?
?
Splendid!... Snowy fell into the parachute. .. He's safe!

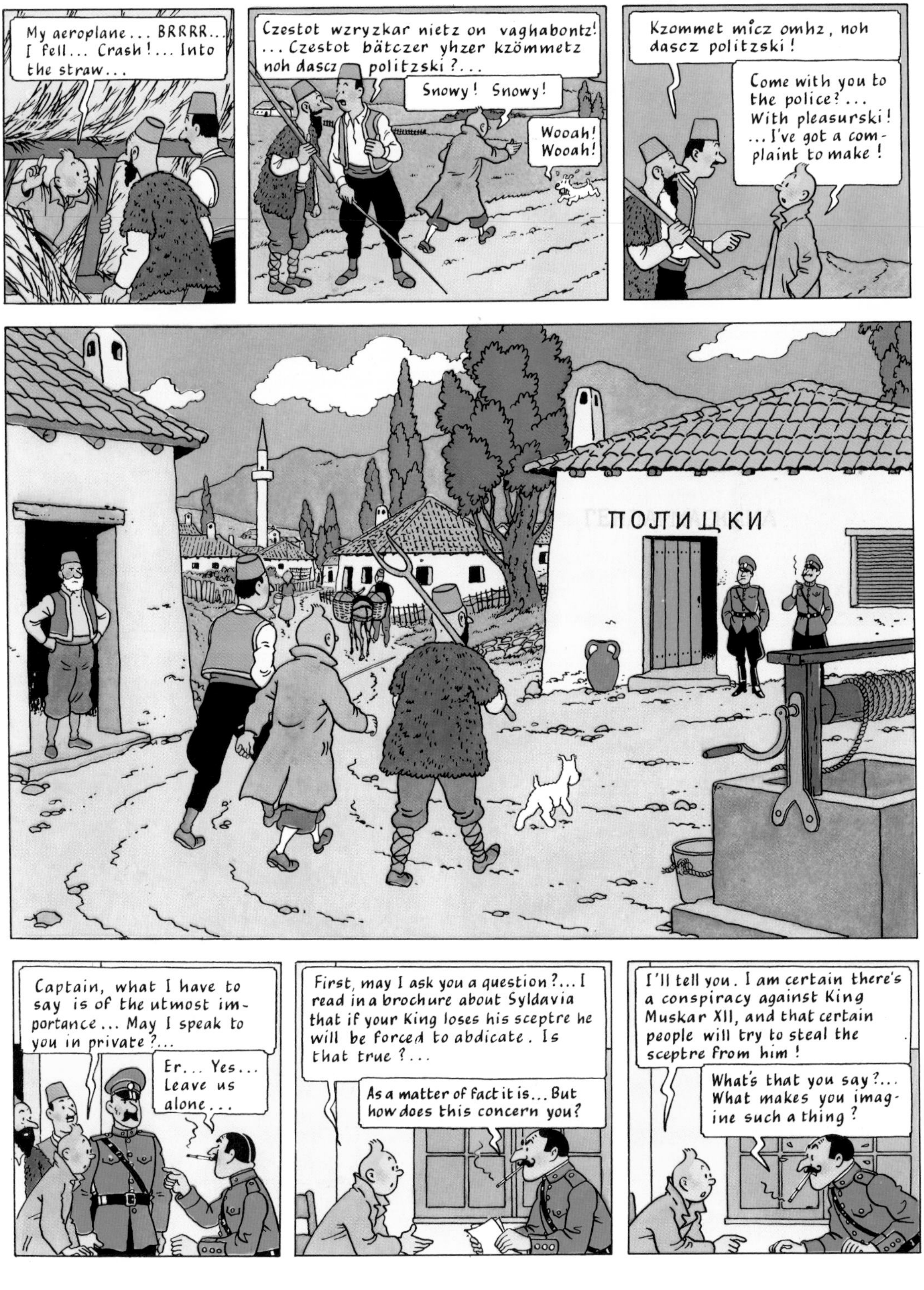
My aeroplane... BRRRR... I fell... Crash!... Into the straw...
Czestot wzryzkar nietz on vaghabontz! ... Czestot bätczer yhzer kzömmetz noh dascz politzski?...
Snowy! Snowy!
Wooah! Wooah!
Kzommet micz omhz, noh dascz politzski!
Come with you to the police?... With pleasurski! ... I've got a complaint to make!
ПОЛИЦКИ
Captain, what I have to say is of the utmost importance... May I speak to you in private?...
Er... Yes... Leave us alone...
First, may I ask you a question?... I read in a brochure about Syldavia that if your King loses his sceptre he will be forced to abdicate. Is that true?...
As a matter of fact it is... But how does this concern you?
I'll tell you. I am certain there's a conspiracy against King Muskar XII, and that certain people will try to steal the sceptre from him!
What's that you say?... What makes you imagine such a thing?

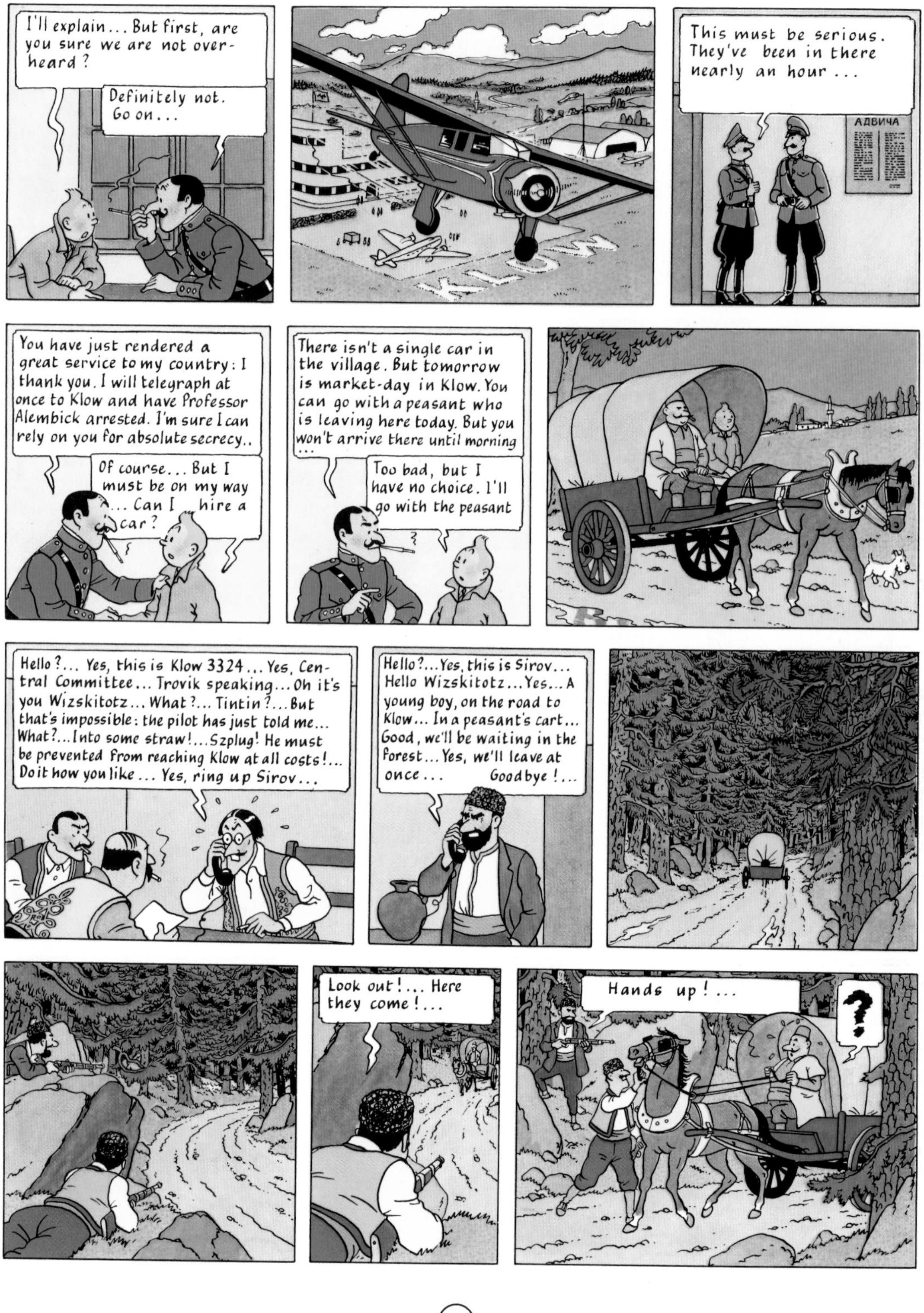
I'll explain... But first, are you sure we are not over-heard ?
Definitely not. Go on...
KLOW
This must be serious. They've been in there nearly an hour ...
АДВИЧА
You have just rendered a great service to my country: I thank you. I will telegraph at once to Klow and have Professor Alembick arrested. I'm sure I can rely on you for absolute secrecy..
Of course... But I must be on my way ... Can I hire a car?
There isn't a single car in the village. But tomorrow is market-day in Klow. You can go with a peasant who is leaving here today. But you won't arrive there until morning ...
Too bad, but I have no choice. I'll go with the peasant
Hello?... Yes, this is Klow 3324... Yes, Central Committee... Trovik speaking... Oh it's you Wizskitotz... What?... Tintin?... But that's impossible: the pilot has just told me... What?... Into some straw!... Szplug! He must be prevented from reaching Klow at all costs!... Do it how you like... Yes, ring up Sirov...
Hello?... Yes, this is Sirov... Hello Wizskitotz... Yes... A young boy, on the road to Klow... In a peasant's cart... Good, we'll be waiting in the forest... Yes, we'll leave at once... Goodbye !...
Look out!... Here they come!...
Hands up! ...
?

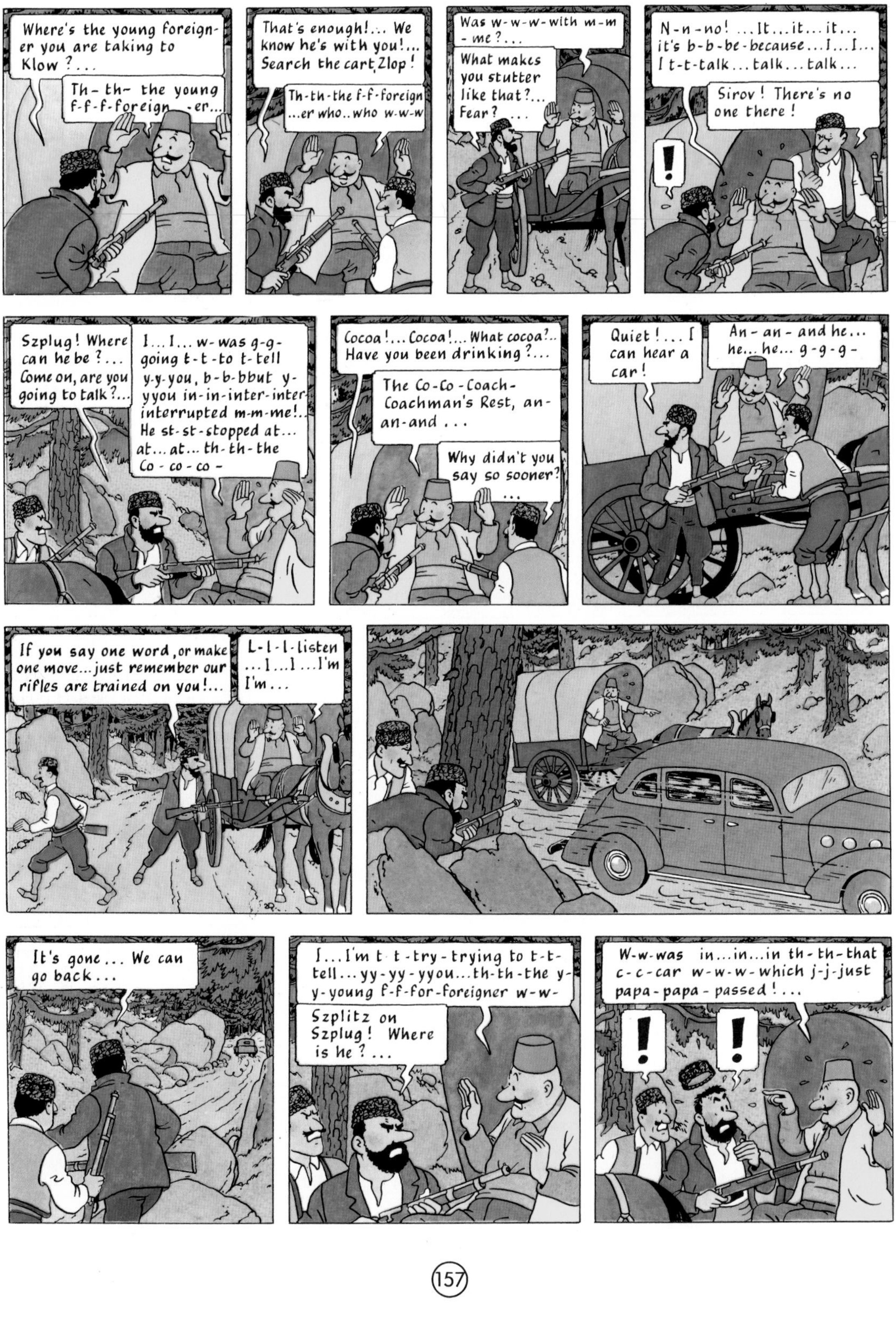

Where's the young foreigner you are taking to Klow ?...
Th- th- the young f-f-f-foreign -er...
That's enough!... We know he's with you!... Search the cart, Zlop!
Th-th-the f-f-foreign ...er who..who w-w-w
Was w-w-w-with m-m - me?...
What makes you stutter like that?... Fear? ...
N-n-no! ...It...it...it... it's b-b-be-because...I...I... I t-t-talk...talk...talk...
Sirov! There's no one there!
!
Szplug! Where can he be?... Come on, are you going to talk?...
I...I...w-was g-g-going t-t-to t-tell y-y-you, b-b-bbut y-yyou in-in-inter-inter interrupted m-m-me!.. He st-st-stopped at... at...at...th-th-the Co-co-co-
Cocoa!... Cocoa!... What cocoa?.. Have you been drinking?...
The Co-Co-Coach-Coachman's Rest, an-an-and ...
Why didn't you say so sooner? ...
Quiet!... I can hear a car!
An-an-and he... he... he... g-g-g-
If you say one word, or make one move... just remember our rifles are trained on you!...
L-l-l-listen ...I...I...I'm I'm...
It's gone... We can go back...
I...I'm t-t-try-trying to t-t-tell...yy-yy-yyou...th-th-the y-young f-f-for-foreigner w-w-
Szplitz on Szplug! Where is he?...
W-w-was in...in...in th-th-that c-c-car w-w-w-which j-j-just papa-papa-passed!...
!
!

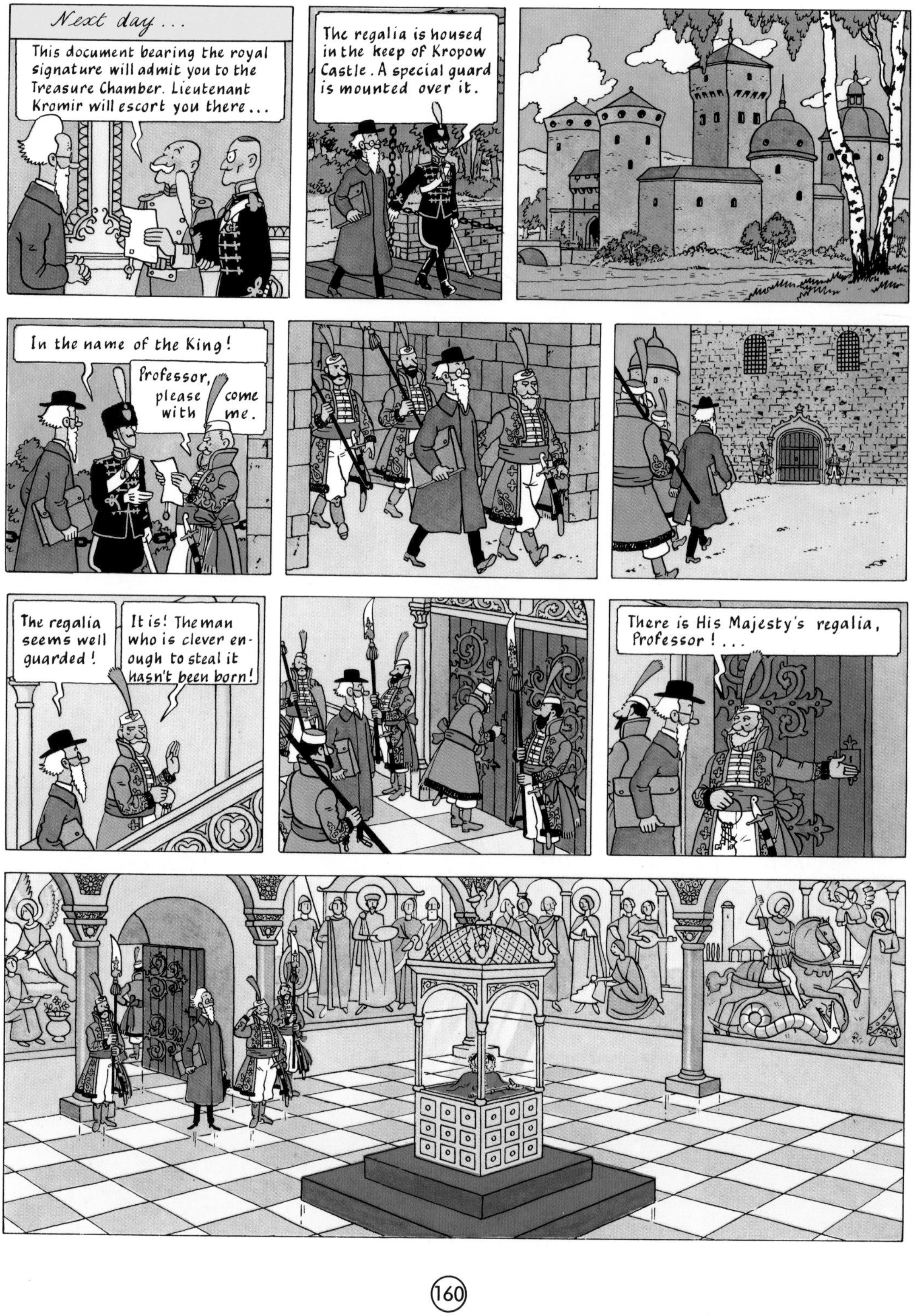

Next day ...
This document bearing the royal signature will admit you to the Treasure Chamber. Lieutenant Kromir will escort you there ...
The regalia is housed in the keep of Kropow Castle. A special guard is mounted over it.
In the name of the King!
Professor, please come with me.
The regalia seems well guarded!
It is! The man who is clever enough to steal it hasn't been born!
There is His Majesty's regalia, Professor! ...

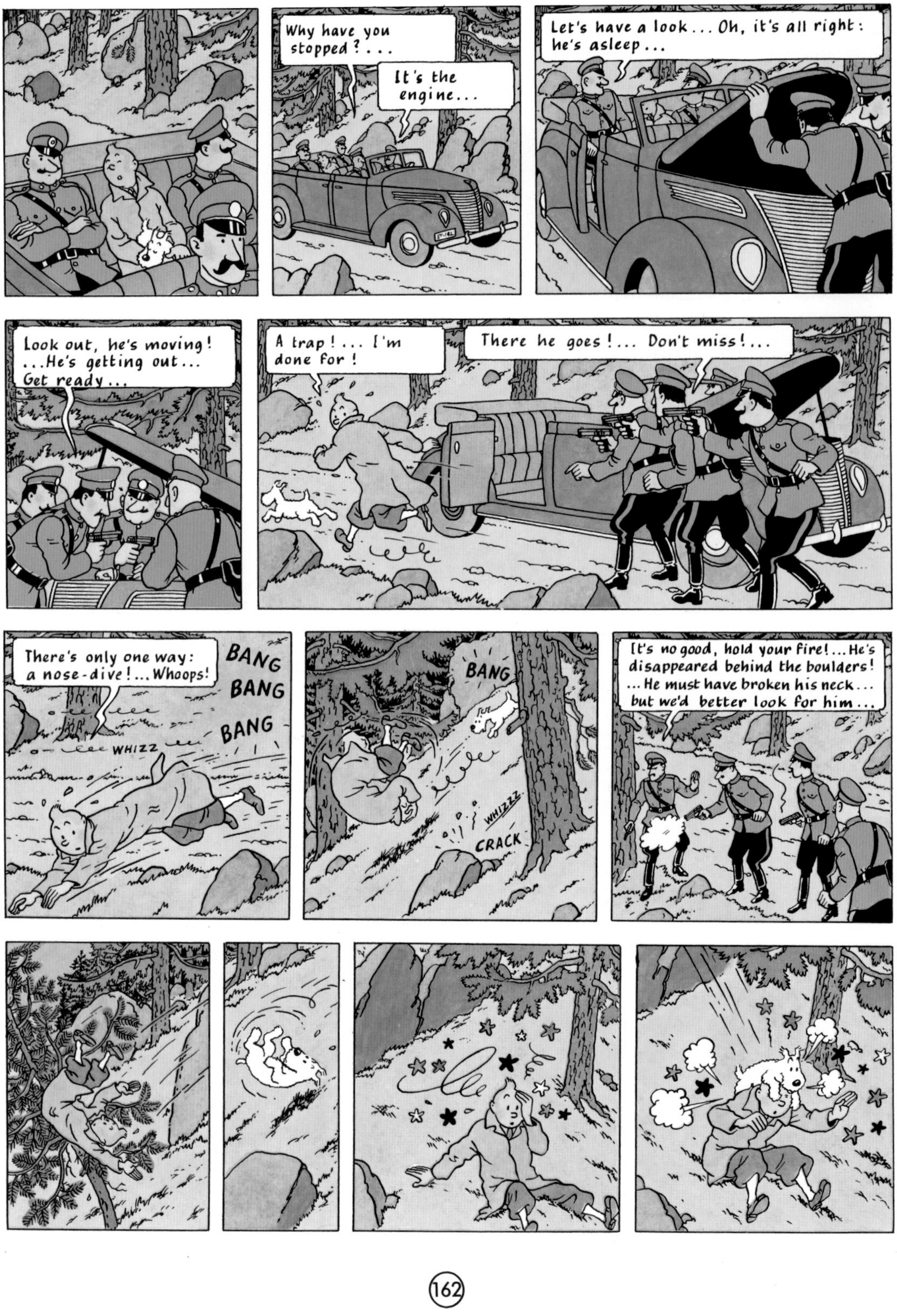
Why have you stopped?...
It's the engine...
Let's have a look... Oh, it's all right: he's asleep...
Look out, he's moving! ...He's getting out... Get ready...
A trap!... I'm done for!
There he goes!... Don't miss!...
There's only one way: a nose-dive!... Whoops!
BANG
BANG
BANG
WHIZZ
BANG
WHIZZZ
CRACK
It's no good, hold your fire!... He's disappeared behind the boulders! ... He must have broken his neck... but we'd better look for him...

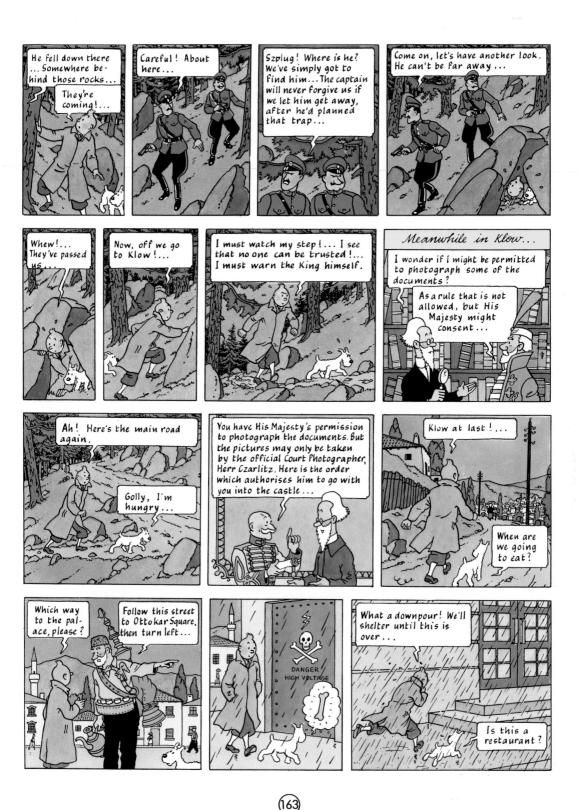

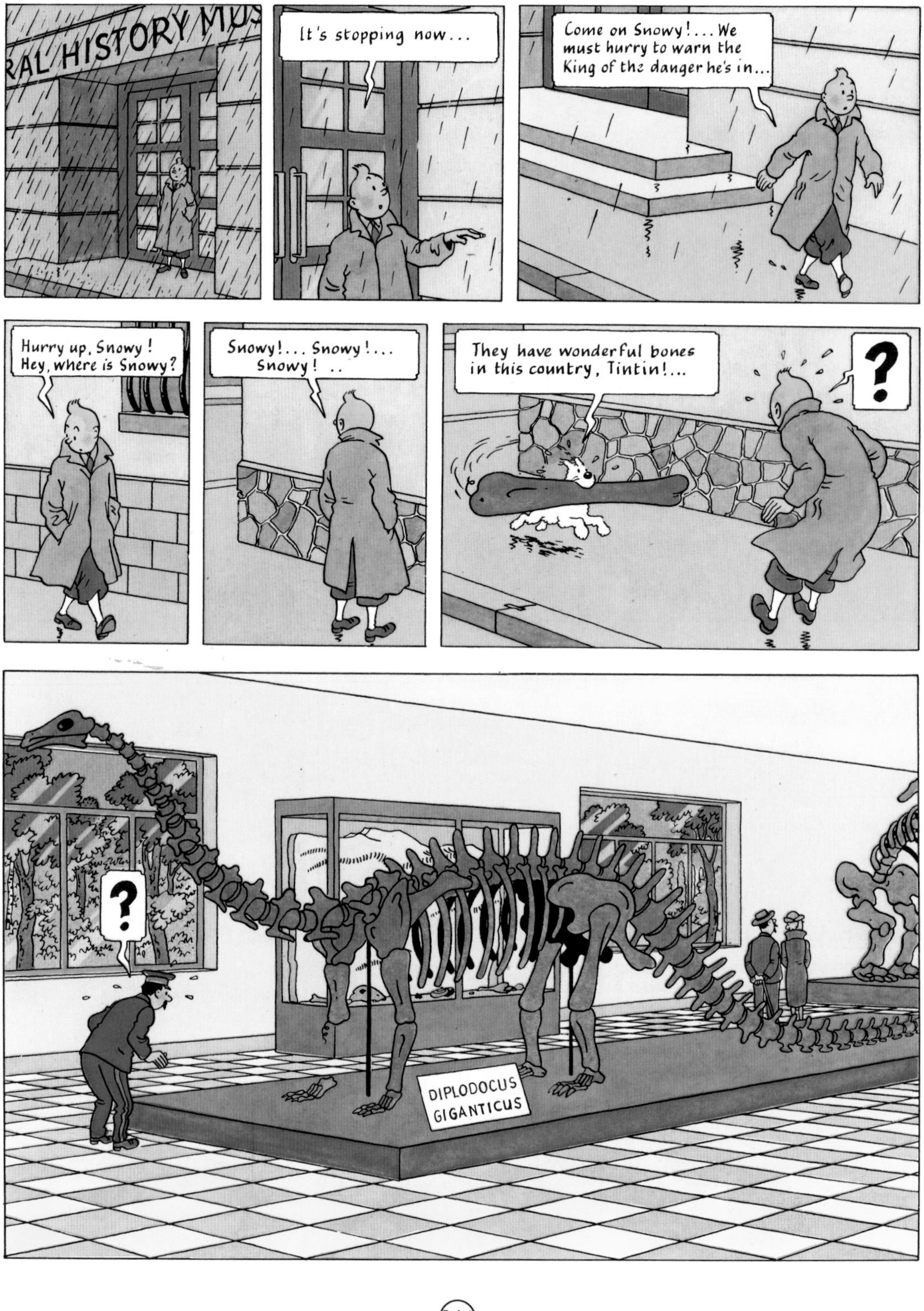
RAL HISTORY MUS
It's stopping now...
Come on Snowy!... We must hurry to warn the King of the danger he's in...
Hurry up, Snowy! Hey, where is Snowy?
Snowy!... Snowy!... Snowy! ..
They have wonderful bones in this country, Tintin!...
?
?
DIPLODOCUS GIGANTICUS

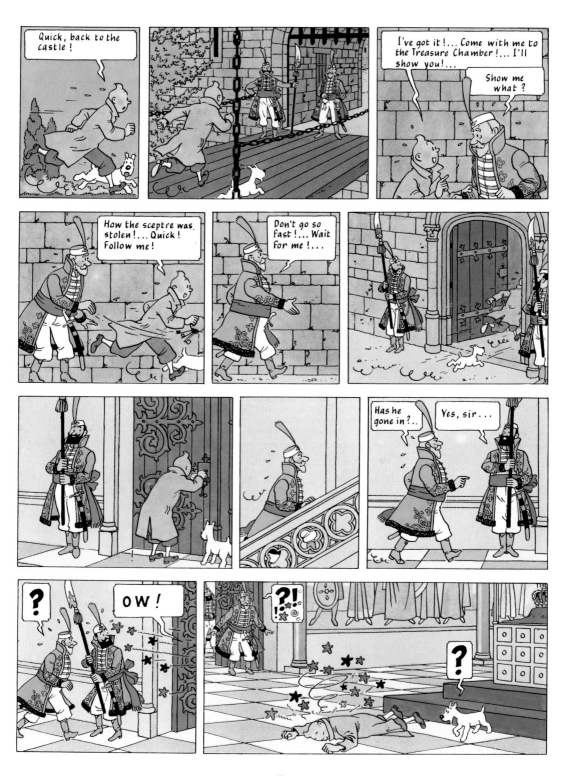

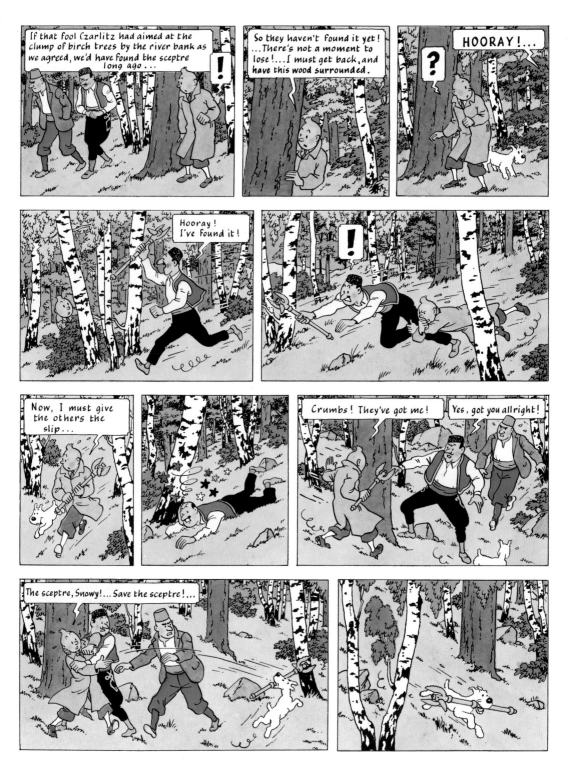

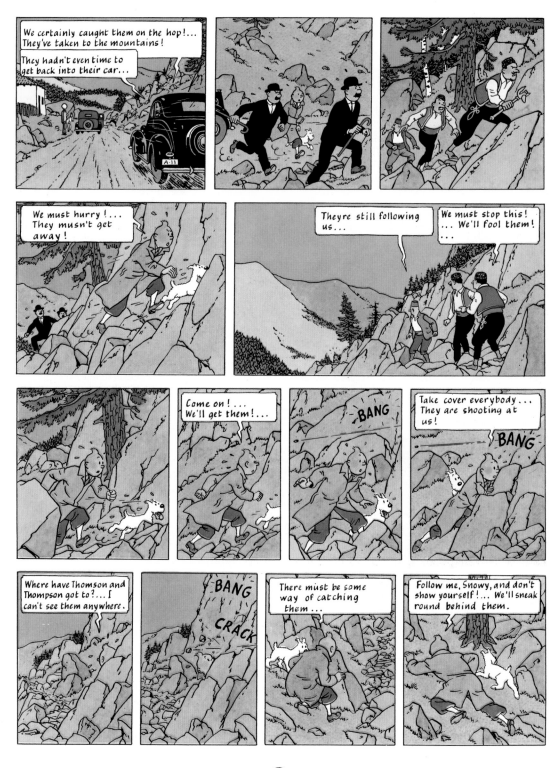

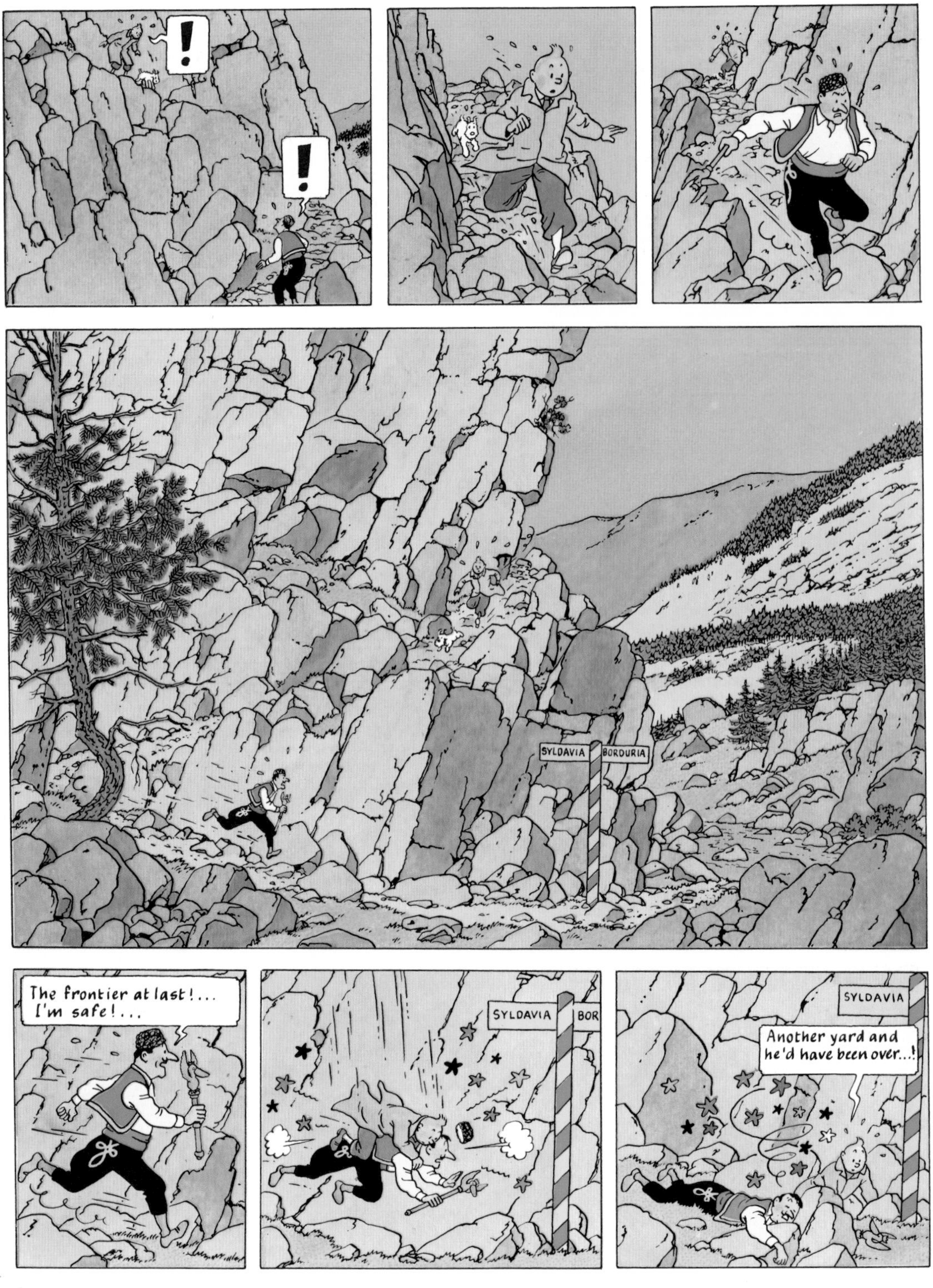
!
!
SYLDAVIA
BORDURIA
The frontier at last!... I'm safe!...
SYLDAVIA
BOR
SYLDAVIA
Another yard and he'd have been over...!

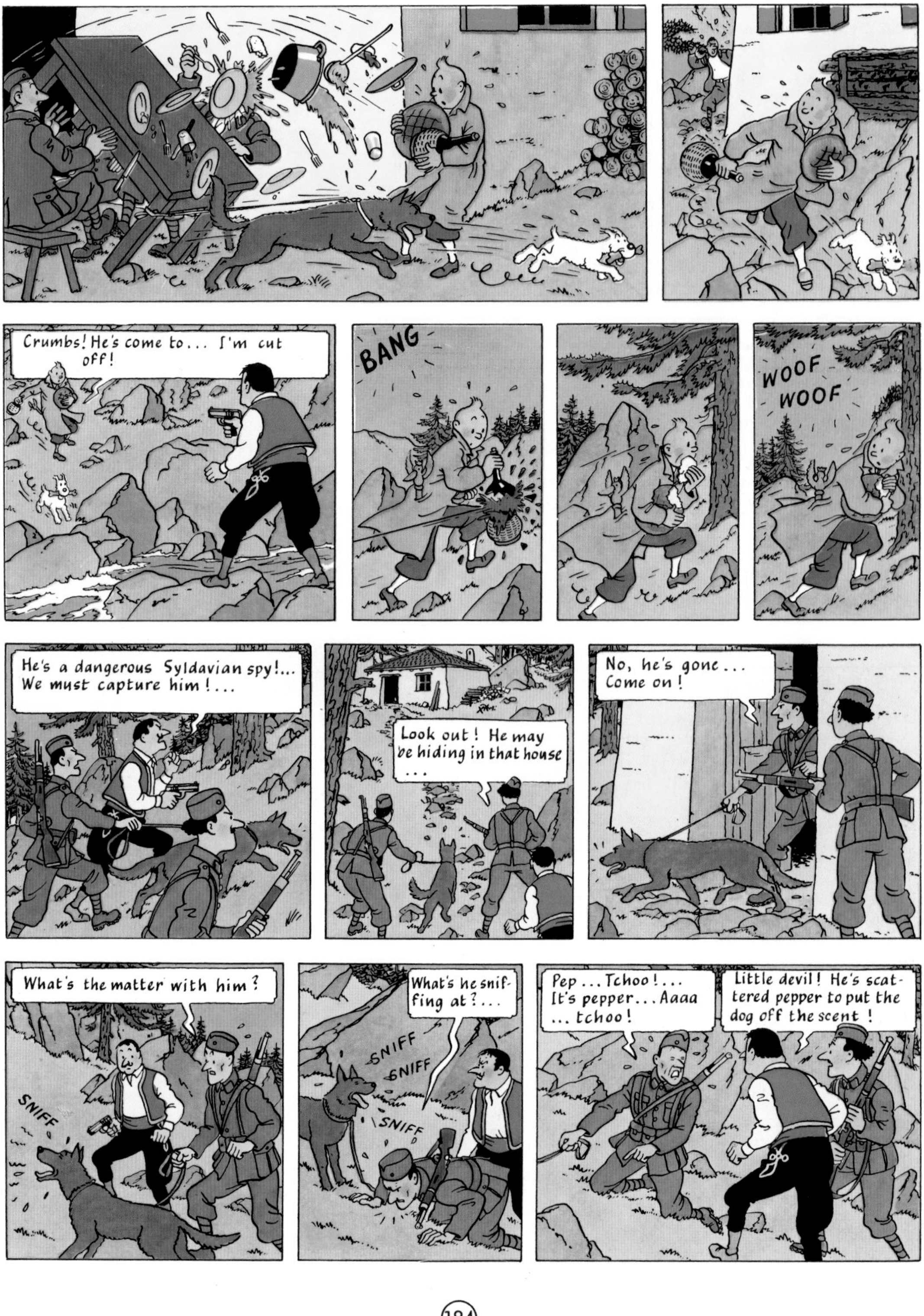
Crumbs! He's come to... I'm cut off!
BANG
WOOF
WOOF
He's a dangerous Syldavian spy!... We must capture him!...
Look out! He may be hiding in that house...
No, he's gone... Come on!
What's the matter with him?
SNIFF
What's he sniffing at?...
SNIFF
SNIFF
SNIFF
Pep... Tchoo!... It's pepper... Aaaa... tchoo!
Little devil! He's scattered pepper to put the dog off the scent!

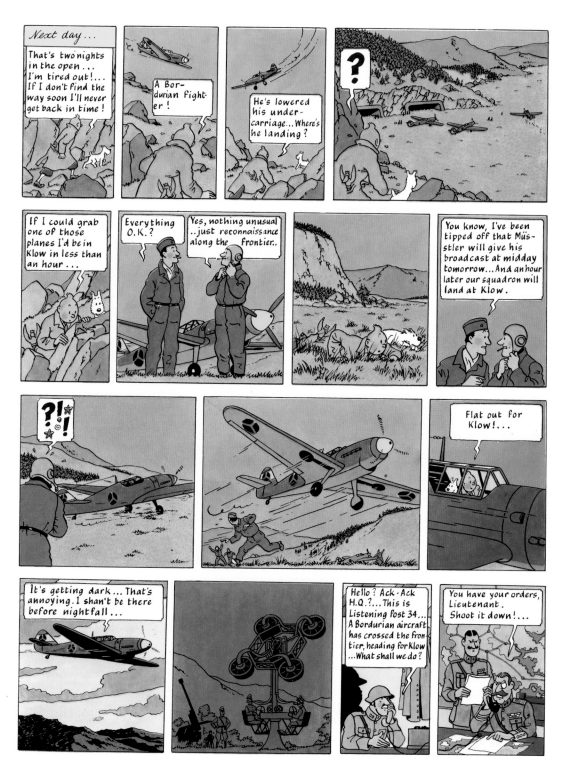

Next day...

That's two nights in the open... I'm tired out!... If I don't find the way soon I'll never get back in time!

A Bordurian fighter!

He's lowered his undercarriage...Where's he landing?

?

If I could grab one of those planes I'd be in Klow in less than an hour...

Everything O.K.?

Yes, nothing unusual ..just reconnaissance along the frontier..

You know, I've been tipped off that Müstler will give his broadcast at midday tomorrow...And an hour later our squadron will land at Klow.

?!!

Flat out for Klow!...

It's getting dark...That's annoying. I shan't be there before nightfall...

Hello? Ack-Ack H.Q.?...This is Listening Post 34... A Bordurian aircraft has crossed the frontier, heading for Klow ...What shall we do?

You have your orders, Lieutenant. Shoot it down!...

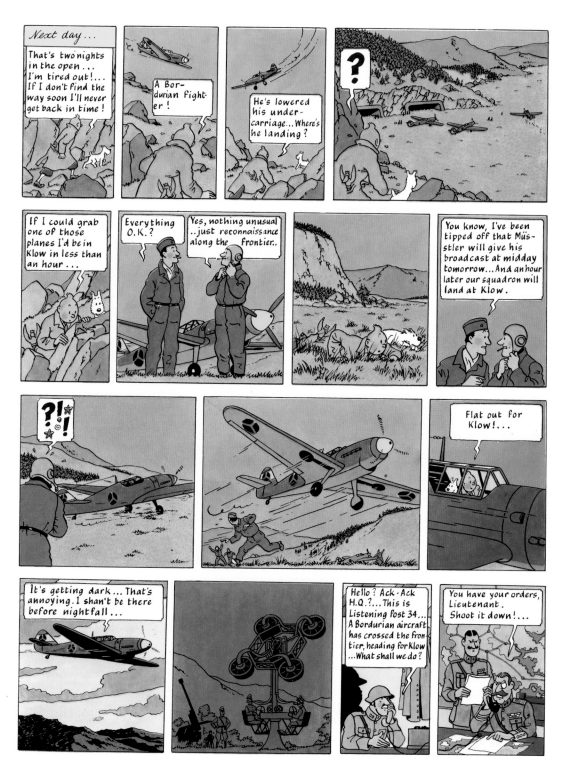

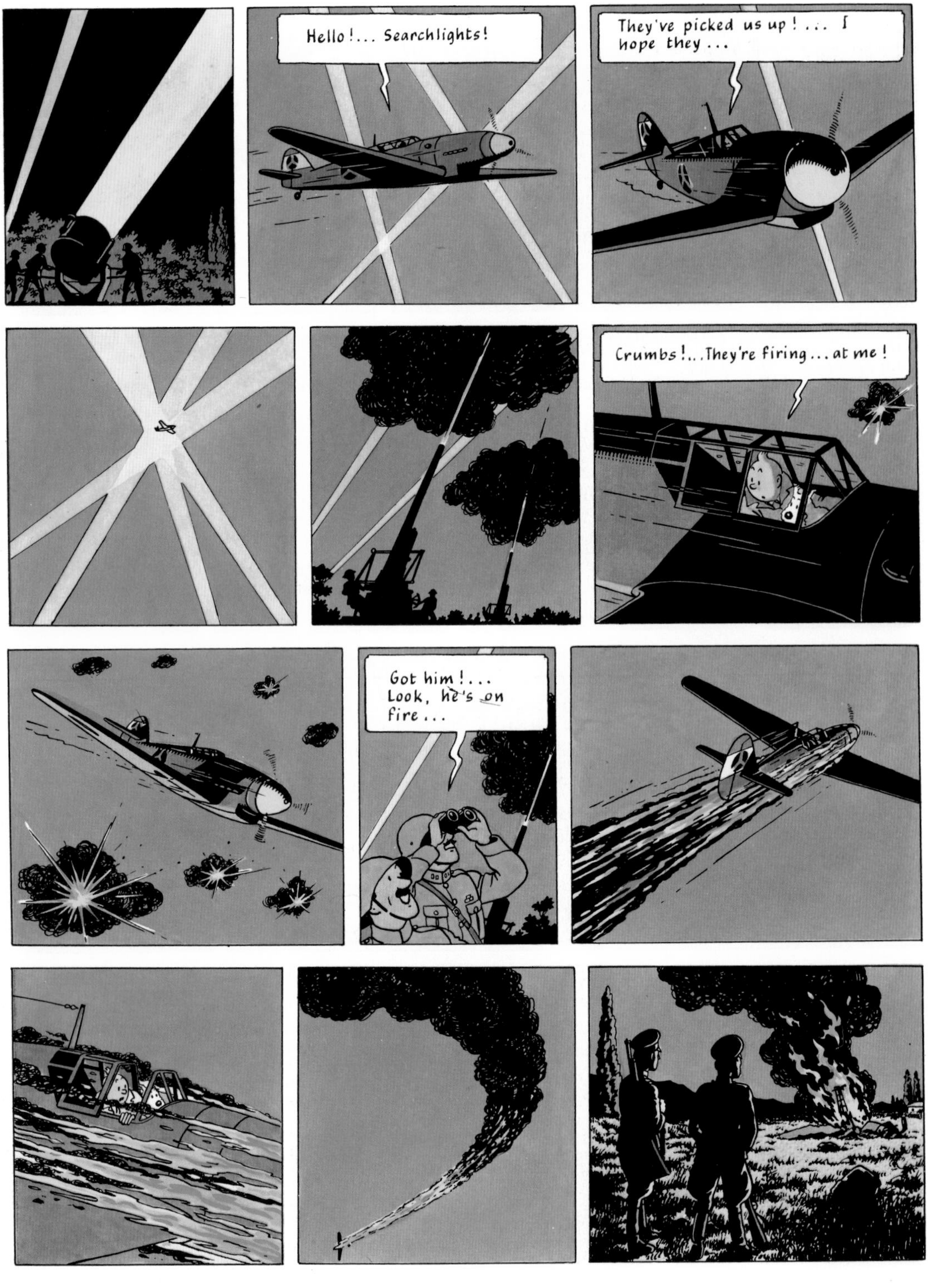
Hello!... Searchlights!
They've picked us up!... I hope they...
Crumbs!... They're firing... at me!
Got him!... Look, he's on fire...

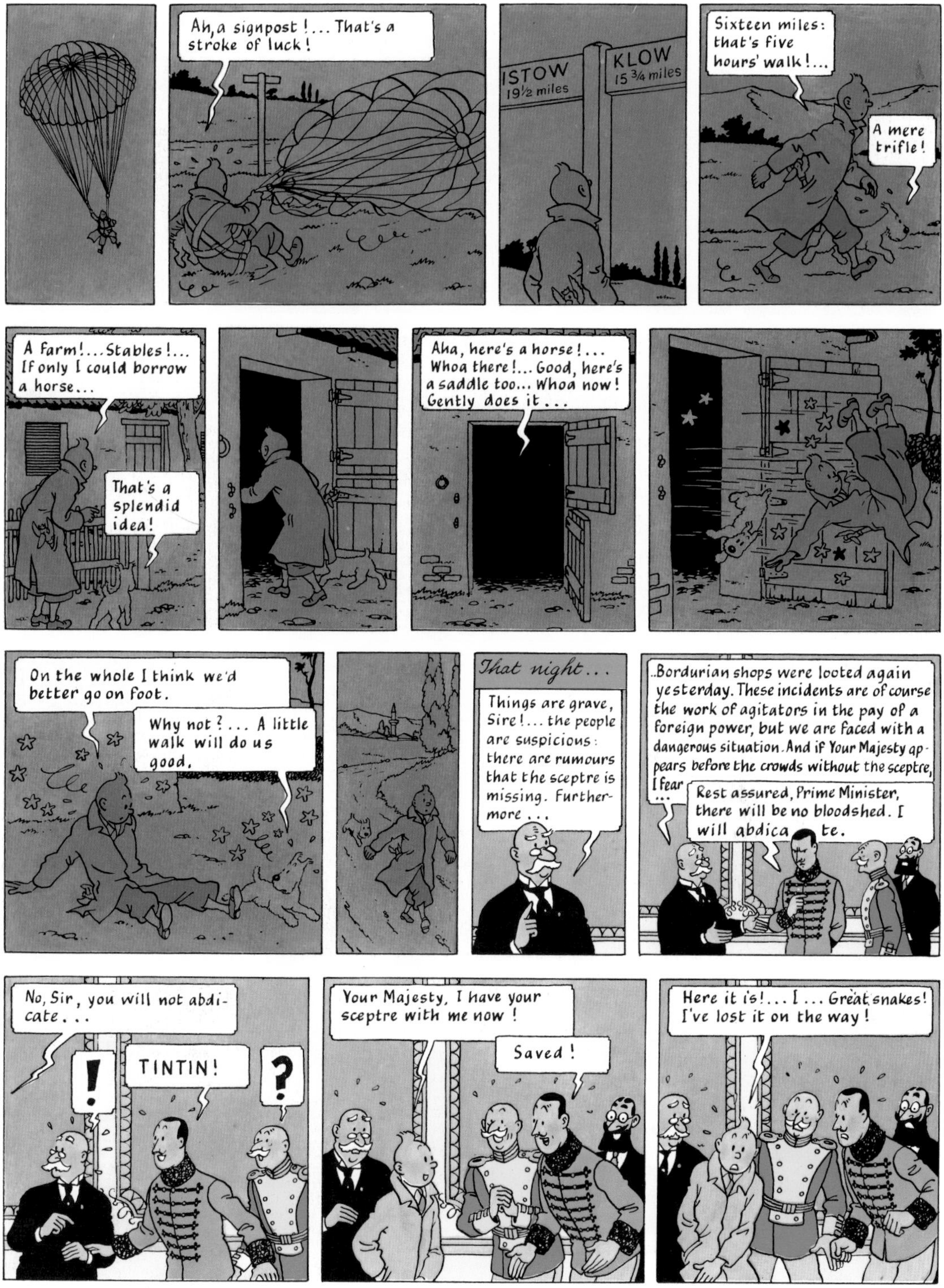
Ah, a signpost !... That's a stroke of luck !
ISTOW 19½ miles
KLOW 15 ¾ miles
Sixteen miles: that's five hours' walk !...
A mere trifle !
A farm !... Stables !... If only I could borrow a horse...
That's a splendid idea !
Aha, here's a horse !... Whoa there !... Good, here's a saddle too... Whoa now ! Gently does it...
On the whole I think we'd better go on foot.
Why not ?... A little walk will do us good.
That night...
Things are grave, Sire !... the people are suspicious: there are rumours that the sceptre is missing. Furthermore...
..Bordurian shops were looted again yesterday. These incidents are of course the work of agitators in the pay of a foreign power, but we are faced with a dangerous situation. And if Your Majesty appears before the crowds without the sceptre, I fear ...
Rest assured, Prime Minister, there will be no bloodshed. I will abdica te.
No, Sir, you will not abdicate...
!
TINTIN!
?
Your Majesty, I have your sceptre with me now !
Saved !
Here it is !... I ... Great snakes ! I've lost it on the way !

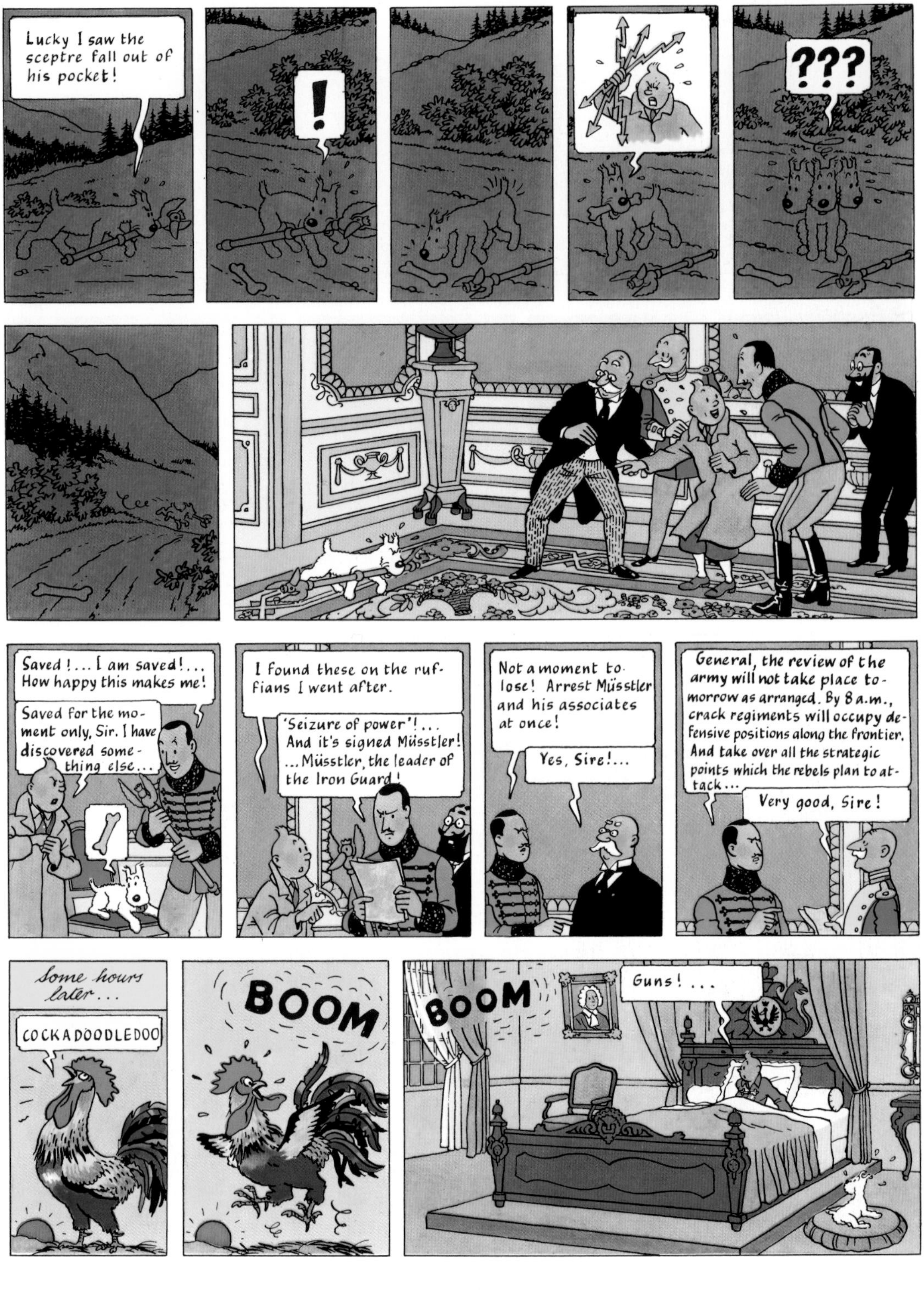

Lucky I saw the sceptre fall out of his pocket!
!
???
Saved!... I am saved!... How happy this makes me!
Saved for the moment only, Sir. I have discovered something else...
I found these on the ruffians I went after.
'Seizure of power'!... And it's signed Müsstler! ...Müsstler, the leader of the Iron Guard!
Not a moment to lose! Arrest Müsstler and his associates at once!
Yes, Sire!...
General, the review of the army will not take place tomorrow as arranged. By 8 a.m., crack regiments will occupy defensive positions along the frontier. And take over all the strategic points which the rebels plan to attack...
Very good, Sire!
Some hours later...
COCKADOODLEDOO
BOOM
BOOM
Guns!...

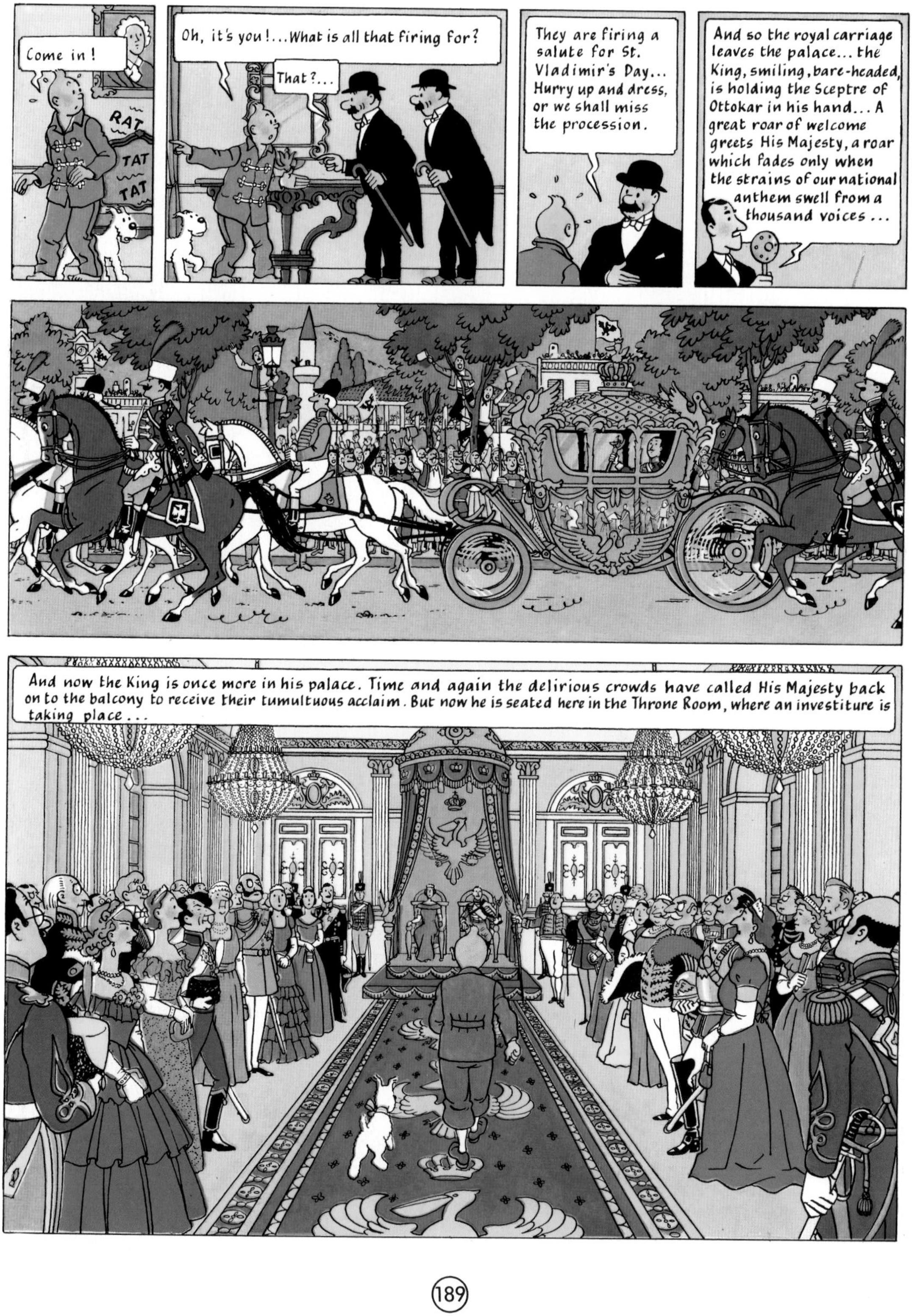
Come in!
RAT
TAT
TAT
Oh, it's you!... What is all that firing for?
That?...
They are firing a salute for St. Vladimir's Day... Hurry up and dress, or we shall miss the procession.
And so the royal carriage leaves the palace... the King, smiling, bare-headed, is holding the Sceptre of Ottokar in his hand... A great roar of welcome greets His Majesty, a roar which fades only when the strains of our national anthem swell from a thousand voices...
And now the King is once more in his palace. Time and again the delirious crowds have called His Majesty back on to the balcony to receive their tumultuous acclaim. But now he is seated here in the Throne Room, where an investiture is taking place...

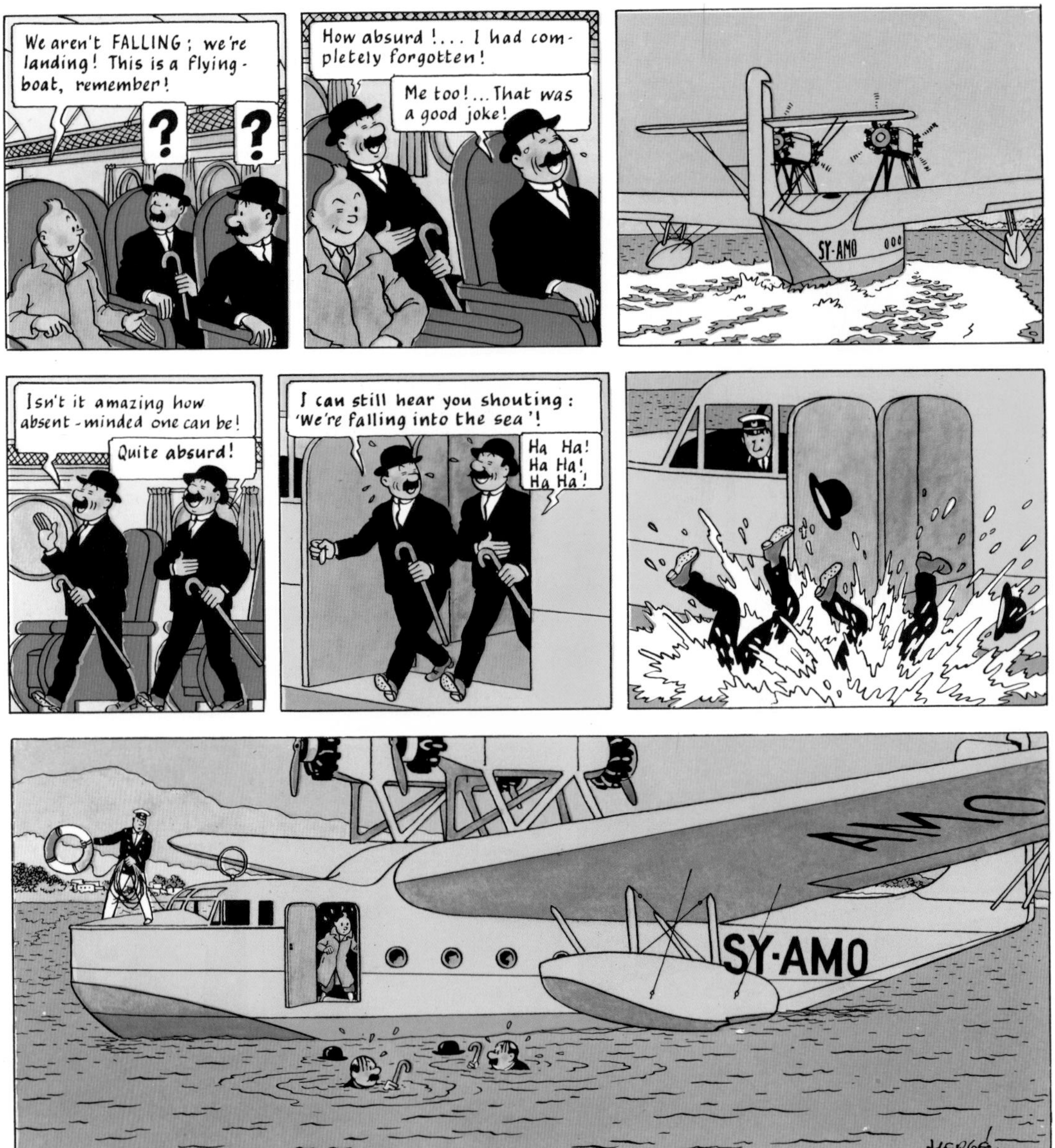
We aren't FALLING; we're landing! This is a flying-boat, remember!
?
?
How absurd!... I had completely forgotten!
Me too!... That was a good joke!
SY-AMO
Isn't it amazing how absent-minded one can be!
Quite absurd!
I can still hear you shouting: 'We're falling into the sea'!
Ha Ha! Ha Ha! Ha Ha!
AMO
SY-AMO
HERGÉ.

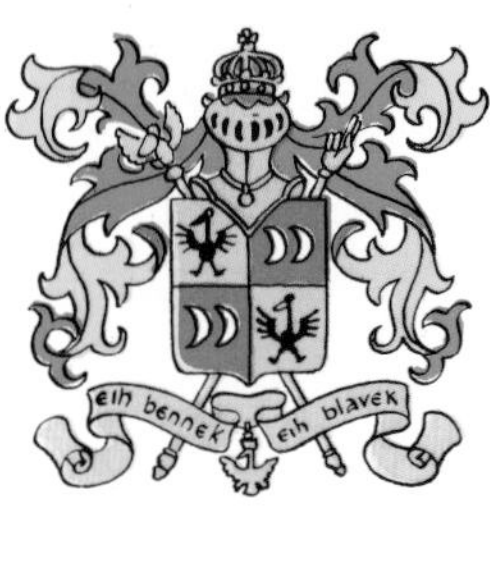
eih bennek
eih blavek

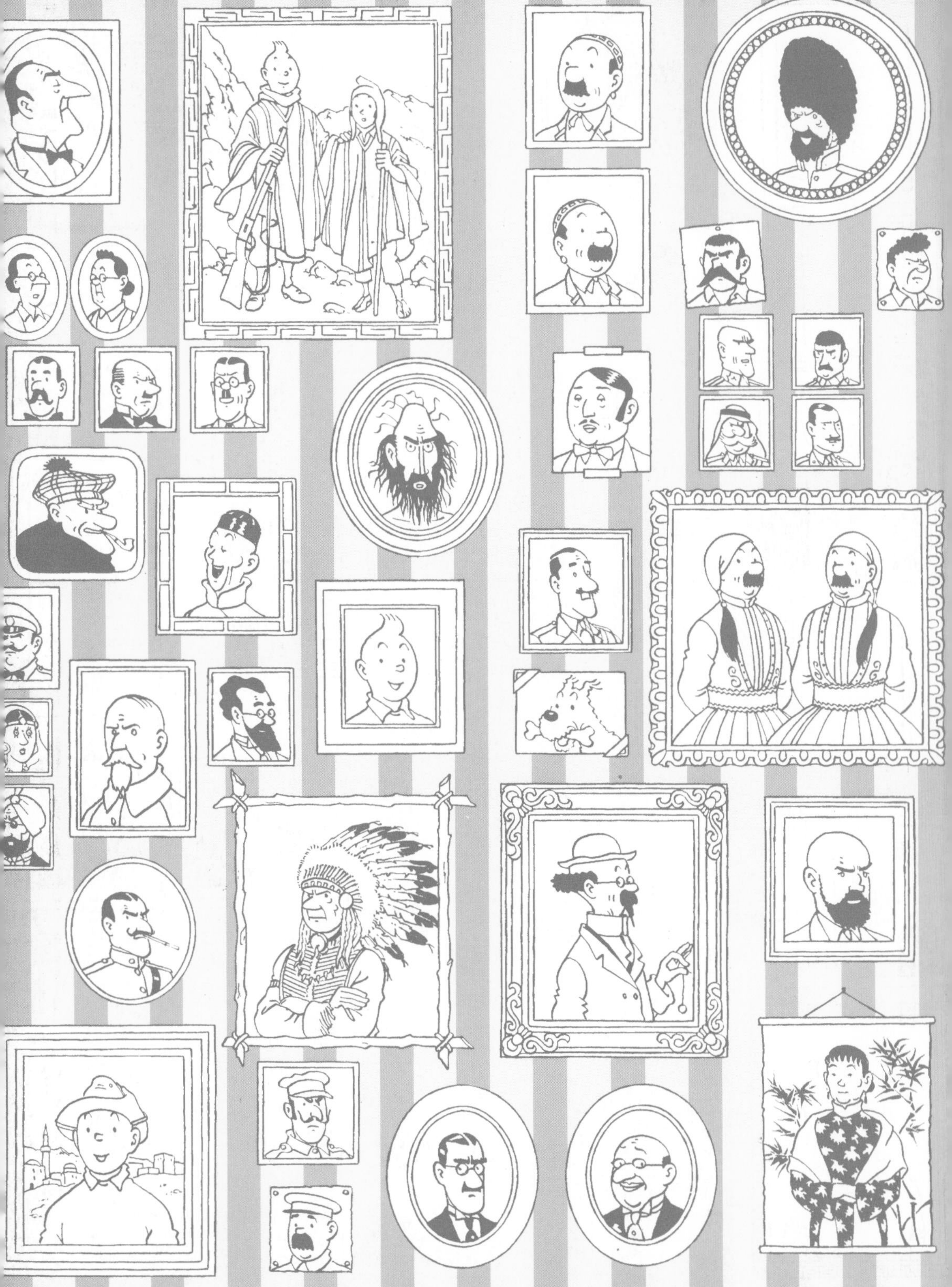